ALSO BY CRISTINA ALGER

The Darlings

This Was Not the Plan

Cristina Alger

Touchstone

New York   London   Toronto   Sydney   New Delhi

Touchstone
An Imprint of Simon & Schuster, Inc.
1230 Avenue of the Americas
New York, NY 10020

First Touchstone hardcover edition February 2016

TOUCHSTONE and colophon are registered trademarks of Simon & Schuster, Inc.

For information about special discounts for bulk purchases, please contact Simon & Schuster Special Sales at 1-866-506-1949 or business@simonandschuster.com.

The Simon & Schuster Speakers Bureau can bring authors to your live event. For more information or to book an event, contact the Simon & Schuster Speakers Bureau at 1-866-248-3049 or visit our website at www.simonspeakers.com.

Interior design by Akasha Archer

Manufactured in the United States of America

10   9   8   7   6   5   4   3   2   1

Library of Congress Cataloging-in-Publication Data
Alger, Cristina.
This was not the plan : a novel / Cristina Alger.—First Touchstone hardcover edition.
    pages cm
1. Widowers—Fiction. 2. Fatherhood—Fiction. 3. Domestic fiction. I. Title.
PS3601.L364T48 2015
813'.6—dc23
2014048887

ISBN 978-1-5011-0375-9
ISBN 978-1-5011-0377-3 (ebook)

For Jonathan

Mira's Birthday

Exactly four years ago today, Mira and I were sprinting through Times Square in hot pursuit of the Naked Cowboy. It was a Wednesday in June; I was supposed to be in a client meeting. Instead, I was participating in a citywide scavenger hunt that had taken me to four boroughs in just under five hours. There were six teams of two, and my wife and I were in the lead. The only thing that stood between us and victory was a man who wandered around the city wearing only a cowboy hat, a pair of tighty-whities, and a guitar.

When I asked Mira what she wanted to do on her birthday, "scavenger hunt" was not the answer I was expecting. But then, nothing about my wife was ever expected. She delighted in surprises, in spontaneity, in throwing caution to the wind. She was endlessly curious. Her insatiable appetite for the world was so infectious that it could inspire a square peg like me to play hooky on a Wednesday *just because*. Because why the hell not, Charlie? Carpe diem, Charlie. You only live once, Charlie! Mira, you see, she got me. She knew me better than I knew myself. Case in point: on that particular Wednesday, she knew that, instead of reviewing tax returns in a windowless conference room, the best thing for me to be doing was to chase a naked man down Eighth Avenue in the middle of rush hour traffic. And so we did. And so we won.

Mira knew how to make me live.

She would have been thirty-two today.

Her birthday is my least favorite day of the year, I've decided, though Halloween definitely gives it a run for its money. Mira loved Halloween. She used to find the most absurd costumes for us, the more embarrassing the better. Two months after we started going out, she made me go to a party dressed as an Almond Joy. She was a Mounds. On the back of my wrapper it read: I HAVE NUTS. On the back of hers: I DON'T.

The things you do for love.

You'd think I'd actually hate March thirteenth the most, but I don't, not really. That's the day that Chip McCleary, a pilot with an unfortunate tendency to drink on the job, accidentally flew my wife's plane into the Atlantic Ocean. There were no survivors.

With 270 casualties, the crash of Flight 1173 just missed making the list of top ten deadliest aviation disasters in history. It tied with the Lockerbie bombing at number eleven, a statistic that reporters cited with a tinge of disappointment, as though they were just one casualty shy of a truly spectacular story. Still, they loved to talk about it. For weeks, Flight 1173 was the only thing on every channel every hour of every day. There were pictures of the wreckage and of Chip and the flight crew and the passengers and of us, the passengers' families, and, when those were exhausted, pictures of the wreckage and pilot and the crew and the passengers and the passengers' families of other aviation disasters (Lockerbie was a favorite). There were interviews with everyone from the air traffic controller on duty that day to conspiracy theorists who were convinced that Chip had ties to Al Qaeda to senators with strong opinions on post-9/11 aviation security. Chip's estranged wife, a former flight attendant named Jazz with frosted hair and a megawatt smile, loved being on air so much that she managed to parlay her two minutes of fame into a gig as a local weather girl. The story was dissected for so long and from so many angles that, by summer, all that was left was an occasional spot featuring a fourth cousin of some other pilot who suffered from alcoholism. I didn't watch much of it. None of it resonated. Drunk pilots and senators had nothing to do with me or with Mira or the life we shared together. The crash of Flight 1173 was a public tragedy. The loss of Mira was a private one.

This past March thirteenth marked the second anniversary of the crash. As with the first anniversary, photos of the wreckage were suddenly on every channel. CNN ran the names of the victims on a ticker tape at the bottom of the screen, like stock symbols or breaking celebrity news on E!. I got phone calls from friends and old colleagues and distant cousins, and a whole pile of mail from a group that called themselves the Families of 1173, informing me of a class action lawsuit against the airline and inviting me to a candlelight vigil at JFK Airport. My buddy Moose showed up at my apartment unannounced, armed with a lifetime supply of booze and a half-eaten box of Junior Mints. I appreciated all of it—the booze especially—but in truth I felt surprisingly numb all day. It was just a gray Tuesday in March, more melancholy, perhaps, than the Tuesday before it, but not markedly so. Not nearly as bleak as Mira's birthday.

• • •

An urgent e-mail from Fred, my boss, pops up in my in-box.

How's it going? it says.

Okay, I guess. Tougher than I would have thought. Thank you for ask-ing, I type, before realizing he's referring to the Harrison Brothers' memorandum I'm supposed to be reviewing, not Mira's birthday. I delete my e-mail.

Good, almost done, I reply. *Will send ASAP.*

Great. Tx. Need by close of business today.

Understood.

Sighing, I flip to the end of the memorandum. One hundred and fifty pages down, fourteen to go. I'm one paragraph in when I hear a rap on my office door.

I spin my chair around. In the doorway stands Todd Ellison, my least favorite person at Hardwick, Mays & Kellerman. As usual, Todd has missed the memo that he is not, in fact, a partner, and is wearing a custom-made suit, an Hermès tie, and a pair of shoes that likely cost more than my first car. Todd's father, Todd Ellison Sr., runs a giant hedge fund, TCE Capital Partners, which happens to be our firm's biggest client. Last year TCE was responsible for forty percent of our corporate business. Suffice it to say, the part-ners handle Todd Jr. with kid gloves. In the ten years he's been at the firm, I'm not sure he's ever actually practiced any law. While the rest of us are billing ninety-hour weeks, Todd is given cushy assignments, like organizing our firm's holiday party and acting as head camp counselor for the summer associates.

"Hey, Todd." I give him a curt nod and look back at my com-puter screen, hoping he'll buzz off and bother someone else.

"Hey, Charlie," he says, missing my cue. When he saunters through my door, I notice a gaggle of nerdy-looking kids behind him. "Just taking the newbies for a tour. Thought maybe you could tell these guys a little bit about your practice."

The summer associates cram into my office and glance around, taking in the panoramic view of Central Park, the sleek Barcelona chairs, the wall bearing my diplomas, the shelves of client binders with the names of nearly every major bank and hedge fund on the Street. They look suitably impressed.

"Well," I say, scratching my head, "I joined the firm almost ten years ago, same class as Todd. I'm a senior associate in the Litigation group. I work primarily with Fred Kellerman, whom you may have met during recruiting. Fred runs Litigation here at Hardwick. He's also the Kellerman in Hardwick, Mays & Kellerman."

Eager nodding from the summer associates. They know Fred. Fred's a legend. They teach classes about Fred in law school. He's probably the reason that half of these kids wanted to work at Hardwick in the first place. Fred's the reason I wanted to work at Hardwick in the first place, and he's the reason I stay working at Hardwick, despite the hellacious hours, unending stress, and morally bankrupt clients.

Long before I arrived at Hardwick, I considered Fred a role model. As an economics major at SUNY Albany, I made a point to read the *Wall Street Journal* every day, taking note of all the banks and hedge funds and law firms that regularly appeared in its pages. One morning I came across a short but exuberant profile of Fred, who had just recently built a library at his alma mater, SUNY Purchase. In the article he said: "Any time I see a strong résumé from a SUNY graduate pass my desk, I take notice. A lot of law firms, my own included, hire almost exclusively from the

Ivy League. I want to change that. Pedigrees don't mean crap to me. I value three things: hard work, integrity, and loyalty. Those aren't just the characteristics that make for a successful lawyer; they make for a successful person." *Now here,* I thought, *is my kind of guy. The kind of guy I want to work for. The kind of guy I want to become.*

When I showed up at Hardwick, Fred took a shine to me right away. He singled me out from a class of newly minted associates and made a point of mentoring me. It was a relief; most of the other partners turned their noses up at my cheap suits, the way I occasionally still dragged out the "aw" in "coffee." Not Fred. Like me, Fred was raised by a single mom in a small blue-collar town on Long Island. Like me, he had a chip on his shoulder because of it. Unlike me, however, Fred wore his background like a badge of honor. *Embrace the chip, Charlie,* he told me once. *Love the chip. It's your edge. The chip is what keeps you hungry.*

In the past decade, Fred and I have amassed scores of victories and only one notable defeat. We're a good team, arguably one of the best in town. I'm willing to put up with his famously short temper and penchant for middle-of-the-night phone calls, so long as he takes the time to counsel me and champion my career internally. It hasn't always been easy. Sometimes working for Fred feels like trying to run a marathon in the middle of a hurricane. But in just a few months' time senior management will decide who makes partner and who does not. Knowing I have Fred in my corner gets me through my toughest days at Hardwick.

"Why don't you tell them what's exciting about today?"

It takes me a second to realize that Todd, too, is talking about Harrison Brothers, not Mira's birthday.

No one here gives a shit about Mira's birthday, I remind myself. Now, the Harrison Brothers dismissal, that's big news.

"Why don't you tell them about the Harrison case?" Todd prompts.

"Right, yeah. Okay. So today a court dismissed a class-action lawsuit against our client, Harrison Brothers. Harrison Brothers, as you probably know, was accused of predatory lending practices during the subprime mortgage crisis in 2008."

More eager nodding.

"And how long have you been working on that case, Charlie?" Todd persists. It occurs to me that Todd has been told to entertain the summers for an hour or so and, having no real work experience himself, he has no idea what to talk about.

"Well, Todd, I've been working on this case for four years. I've billed 1,900 hours this year already, ninety percent of which is to this case. I've been in the office for the past seventy-two hours. It's possible that my son has forgotten what I look like. This is a fairly common occupational hazard for lawyers."

Nervous laughter from the crowd. I make eye contact with Todd, who's shooting me an aggressive "shut the fuck up" stare.

"But the point is," I conclude quickly, "it's all been worthwhile. The suit was dismissed. Our clients are thrilled. There are very few firms where you can work on cases this complex and this important. Hardwick represents the biggest banks and hedge funds in the world. And there are very few firms where you get to work side by side with lawyers like Fred Kellerman."

A couple of the guys in the front row practically have to wipe tears from their eyes. I've hooked them, I know. They all come to Hardwick, Mays & Kellerman with big dreams, the same dreams I had when I graduated from law school. I recognize the far-off look on their faces. Right this second, they're envisioning themselves offering counsel to Fortune 500 CEOs. They're imagining what it feels like to stride into a courthouse with a client who will be on the cover of tomorrow's *Wall Street Journal*. They're picturing themselves sitting at my desk, in my chair, just six months away from making partner at the most prestigious law firm in New York.

What they do not yet know is that this summer we will wine them and dine them. We will allow them to rub shoulders with the likes of Steve Mays and Welles Peabody and Fred Kellerman, who will pretend to take an interest in them and may even invite them to lunch to discuss these big dreams of theirs. We will staff them on only the most exciting cases while expecting them to do no real work and add no real value. We will take them to baseball games and Broadway plays, and at the end of the summer we will all get drunk together on a cruise around New York Harbor. They will gratefully, hungrily accept our offer of full-time employment at Hardwick, Mays & Kellerman. And then, when they return one year later as full-fledged members of the Bar, we will promptly crush their souls.

"Well, hey, thanks, Charlie," Todd says. "Anyone have any questions for Charlie?"

A few of the kids throw up their hands, like fourth graders dying to be called on.

"Uh, yeah, sure—you there," I say, pointing to one. "What's your name?"

"My name is Candice Cho. You said you've been here for nearly ten years. So when will you be up for partner?"

"Hi, Candice. I know at some firms, partner track is eight years long. Here at Hardwick, it's more like ten. I'll keep you posted. I'm up for it this year." I hold up crossed fingers.

A shy-looking guy at the back raises his hand. He bears such a striking resemblance to Rob, my childhood best friend, that it throws me for a moment. It's not just his face, it's how he carries himself that feels familiar. The way he stuffs his hands casually in his pockets, the awkward knotting of his tie, and his shoes, which are too beaten-up and casual to be worn with a suit. He looks at me with a cool, even stare. I realize I've got twenty eyes on me, waiting.

"Ah, sure, you there," I say, pointing to him. He pushes his hair out of his eyes before he speaks.

"Does it, like, ever bother you?"

The group turns to gawk at him.

I let out an awkward chuckle. "Sorry, I didn't get your name."

"Sam."

"Does what bother me, Sam?"

He's staring at me with eyes so blue they're practically translucent. He can see through my bullshit already, and I haven't even begun to answer his question.

"Does it ever bother you to represent people who you know are guilty? Harrison Brothers ruined millions of lives. They destroyed our economy. And yet their CEO got paid $25 million last year, and now they've gotten off from this class action suit scot-free. So I'm just wondering how you sleep at night."

Amazed guffaws go up from the crowd. They stare at me, agog, wondering how I will respond to such blasphemy.

Over the years I've gotten pretty good at pat responses to this kind of question. One has to when one is in my line of work. I usually fall back on that old law school rhetoric about everyone deserving a good defense and the obligation of every attorney to zealously advocate for their client no matter what, that sort of thing. It's all crap, of course, but once I throw in a couple of self-deprecating jokes, folks start to laugh and then they start to nod, and soon we can all move on to a different, more engaging topic than how it is that I can sleep at night, given that I'm Satan's attorney.

This kid, however, is one cool customer.

"Well, that's definitely one perspective. But I think we can all agree that it's a little more complicated than that," I say lamely. "And Harrison Brothers did agree to pay $300 million to the SEC, so they haven't exactly gotten off scot-free."

"Three hundred million dollars is less than they make in a day."

"That—I'm not sure that's accurate. In any case, it's the number the SEC agreed to."

Todd clears his throat loudly. "So does anyone else have a question for Charlie?" he says, trying to get the conversation back on the rails. Sam opens his mouth as though he has more to say, but stops himself.

Two more hands shoot up in the crowd, but my phone rings, my own home number blinking on its screen.

"Sorry," I say, "I have to take this call. Important client. But listen, feel free to stop by my office anytime. Welcome to the firm!"

As the associates begin to file out of my office, I throw on my headset.

"Could you hold for one second?" I say in my serious business voice. "Just wrapping up a meeting here."

"Uh, sure, Mr. Goldwyn. I can hold," my twin sister, Zadie, replies in her best imitation of my serious business voice.

I wave at Todd.

"Thanks, SUNY," he says loudly. "See ya later."

"Just close the door on your way out, Todd."

"Did that guy just call you 'SUNY'? As in 'State University of New York'?" Zadie asks, disgusted. Zadie, who has never managed to hold down a job for more than six months, is incapable of masking her contempt for mine. She thinks I'm some kind of corporate sellout, which, of course, is true. For the first year or so after I graduated from law school, she'd carp at me constantly for not taking a job at the DA's office or the public defender's office or Amnesty International—somewhere, anywhere, I might be able to contribute to society. By now she's more or less accepted the fact that I'm at Hardwick to stay, but still can't resist taking the occasional jab at my colleagues. To be fair, Todd is low-hanging fruit.

"Yup. I'm not sure Todd's actually ever met anyone from a state school before. I'm quite the novelty around here. It's like being Amish. Or an albino."

"Wow. What an asshole. He must have gone to Harvard." I can hear her rolling her eyes through the phone.

"Princeton, actually. Harvard Law School."

"He's not a partner, is he?"

"Nope. But he's up for it, just like me. In fact, it's possible he'll get it over me. His dad is a big hedge fund honcho."

"Ugh. I know I say this basically every day, but I really don't understand how you can work at that place."

"Well, I try to stay humble, Zadie, but white-collar defense really is God's work."

"I'm going to pretend you didn't just say that. So, speaking of, did the case—"

"Yes!" I say. "Dismissed! It's finally over."

"Fantastic! Does that mean you're coming home soon, then? I put a name tag on Caleb, just in case."

"*Har har.* Yeah, just finishing up one document and I'm out of here."

"Okay, terrific. Will you be home for dinner?"

"Yeah, I should be," I say, checking my watch. "How's Caleb been today? Has he asked about . . . you know?" "You know" is our shorthand for "Mira."

"No. He seems all right. I don't think he knows it's her birthday."

"Okay, good. Still, I want to have dinner with him tonight."

"I think that would be nice. Listen, Charlie . . ." Zadie trails off, hesitant.

"What's up?"

"Buck wants to come into the city tonight and take me out to dinner. We won't go out until after you're home, of course. No rush. That cool with you?"

I sigh internally. Buck is my sister's latest loser boyfriend. Usually they don't last long enough for me to worry, but Buck has stuck around for the better part of a year. Buck's not a bad guy, really. In fact, I'd potentially sort of like him if he weren't dating my sister. I'd just prefer to see her with a guy who's employed for once. Buck says he's in landscaping, which I'm pretty sure is a euphemism for growing and distributing massive quantities of weed.

Admittedly, Buck is an improvement over Casey, the previous loser boyfriend. At thirty-five, Casey was still living with his parents and working part-time at Uncle Funky's Boards, a skate shop on Charles Street. Zadie liked to describe Casey as "passionate," which Mira and I quickly realized meant erratic and prone to uncontrolled bouts of rage. One night Zadie turned up in our lobby with a split lip and a half-baked story about slipping on wet kitchen tile. By then Casey had taken up semipermanent residence in her tiny Brooklyn apartment, and she was afraid to return. I suggested killing him; Mira suggested that Zadie move in with us for as long as she needed. As usual, Mira prevailed.

A month later Mira was dead and Zadie was still living in the spare room behind our kitchen. We never discussed her staying; she just stayed. We never discussed her quitting her job so that she could watch Caleb while I was at work; she just did. At the time, Zadie was just about as lost as I was. She still hadn't recovered from our mother's death a year before. She had spent months as Mom's caretaker. She lived in Mom's house; she prepared her meals and gave her sponge baths and took her for walks around the block. She'd even enrolled in a caregiving class at the local college. After Mom passed, Zadie moved to Brooklyn and took a job as an in-home health aide for an elderly woman named Mrs. Zimmerman, but her heart wasn't really in it. Mrs. Zimmerman rarely spoke, she said, just watched television all day and asked Zadie to feed her cat. Zadie wanted to do more than change litter boxes and television channels. She was looking for someone to care for, someone else to love. And then there we were, Caleb and I, needing care and love more than ever.

It's been twenty-eight months. I think we both know this arrangement will at some point come to an end. Zadie will want to move on with her life. In theory, I want that for her, too. But frankly I can't imagine getting through a day without her. And Caleb—well, right now Caleb can't handle any more changes. His world's been rocked enough.

"Of course. No worries. You guys go have fun."

"You're sure? I know this isn't the easiest day for you."

"I'm fine, I promise."

"One last thing." Zadie clears her throat, something she does right before she tells me something I don't want to hear. "Dad called," she says. "Just to check in on you."

"Ah."

"I'm not suggesting you call him back. I just thought you'd want to know."

"Thank you," I say, trying not to sound stiff.

"Anyway," she says, speeding past the awkward tension that always arises whenever she mentions our father, "I'm making roast chicken tonight. Caleb's favorite. Sound good?"

"Sounds great."

In the background I hear a loud crash, followed by Norman's plaintive howl. "Oh, fuck! Caleb's playing dress-up with the dog again. Gotta run. See you soon."

"I'll be home by six," I say, but Zadie's already hung up. "Home by six." It's been a really long time since I've uttered those three little words. They feel good, I think. They feel right. I've really got to say them more often.

I rush through the Harrison Brothers memorandum, giving it less of a close read than it probably deserves. After correcting a few typos, I fire off a quick one-liner to Fred with the memorandum attached. Given that it's 164 pages long, I figure I've bought myself enough time for a leisurely dinner at least. With any luck, Fred won't get back to me until tomorrow.

My office door closes behind me with a satisfying thunk.

"Heading home, Charlie?" My assistant, Lorraine, looks up from her cubicle. She looks hopeful, if vaguely perplexed, by the sight of me leaving while it's still light out.

"You bet, Lorraine. Case closed. Going home to see the kid."

She flashes me a thumbs-up. "Nice!" she says. "You deserve it. What's it been this time? Three straight days in the office?"

"Uh, seventy-five hours. Not that anyone's counting."

She wrinkles her nose. "You lawyers sure know how to live."

"Livin' the dream, Lorraine. Livin' the dream."

The elevator door pings open.

"Go," she urges. "Go now before someone catches you."

"Thanks. If anyone calls—"

She waves me off. "If anyone calls, I'm telling them you're in a very important meeting with a very important client."

• • •

I'm about to step into the elevator when I feel a stiff hand on my shoulder. I spin around and find myself face-to-face with Welles Peabody, the head of the firm's Mergers and Acquisitions department. Welles is an old-school lawyer, the type who wears bow ties and seersucker suits without irony. He staffs his deals only with Ivy Leaguers who, like him, play a mean game of squash and mix a killer martini. Being that I'm just a lowly public university grad, Welles has almost never given me the time of day. I'm sure he squawked a little when Fred decided to hire me. Lately, though, Welles seems to be warming up to me. I get the occasional nod from him in the hallway, and just last month he stopped to congratulate me on the acquittal of Marcel Albin, the CEO of a multibillion-dollar hedge fund who had been accused of insider trading. Given that Welles chairs the partnership committee, he is at the top of my list of people I really need to start sucking up to.

"Hello, Charlie," he says with a stern nod. "Heading somewhere?"

I feel my heart sink into my stomach. "Uh, well, sir, I was, you know, heading home." I always get strangely tongue-tied around Welles.

Welles frowns. "Home? So early?" He checks his watch, just to be sure he's understanding the situation correctly.

"Yes, well, I've actually been here for seventy-five hours, and I haven't exactly slept or showered, so I was thinking—"

Welles begins to nod, like *Yes, yes, now I see.* "Oh, Charlie," he says. "You really don't need to worry about changing for the cocktail party. I know the Lowell Club usually requires a tie, but everyone knows you've been slaving away on the Harrison Brothers suit, so we're willing to cut you a little slack. And listen, if anyone at the door gives you a hard time, well, just tell them you know the club president." He throws me a little jab to the ribs with his elbow.

"Cocktail party?" I say weakly. I watch as the elevator doors slide closed in front of me. Suddenly it all comes flooding back. I've gotten at least six reminder e-mails about tonight's all-firm summer associate welcome party at the Lowell Club. It's the kind of event that no one, under any circumstance, is allowed to miss. Every partner is there, and every potential partner is definitely there, hoping for a chance to schmooze with the higher-ups. Last year, my friend Moose actually drove from Boston just to attend the party for an hour.

"Yes," Welles says, looking impatient, "the summer associate welcome party. You didn't forget, did you?"

"No, sir, of course not. I've been looking forward to it. I just didn't realize it was getting so late. I was hoping to, as you said, dash home and freshen up a bit."

Welles claps me on the back with an iron hand. "Nonsense, Charlie. Come as you are. In fact, if you're headed that way now, I'll walk with you. It will give us a chance to catch up."

I pause and look Welles directly in the eye. There is, I realize, no way to get out of this without lying my ass off.

"Terrific, sir," I hear myself say. "I'd like really that."

"You know, Charlie, everyone's impressed by the effort you've put in on this Harrison case. But, son, I've been at this business for a very long time and I'm going to let you in on a little secret." He gestures for me to come closer. "There are things in life that are more important than work. Sometimes, Charlie, you need to socialize. You need to relax, let your hair down a bit. You understand what I'm saying?"

"I think so, sir," I say, and suppress a sigh.

"Tonight, for example. I know there are probably e-mails you want to return, phone calls you have to make, documents you want to review. And I get that, son, really, I do. But tonight, it's more important for you to come to the club and share a few 'brewskis' "—here, Welles actually employs air quotations—"with the folks on the partnership committee. Let us get to know you. You deserve it, Charlie. Consider it a much-needed break."

The elevator doors ping open again, and Welles ushers me inside. As he drones on about the importance of socialization, I close my eyes and silently apologize to Caleb, my hilarious, eccentric, motherless five-year-old, who is, once again, about to be stood up for dinner.

The Speech

For those of you who have never been to the Lowell Club, let me set the scene for you. It's a snobby, stuffy, exclusive establishment on the corner on Park Avenue and Fifty-Second Street, of which Welles Peabody is, fittingly, the president. The Lowell Club counts among its membership three ex-presidents, fourteen senators, two Supreme Court justices, and countless blue-blooded scions of the wealthiest and most powerful families in New England. It has no female members, no Jewish members, no members of color. There is a strict jacket-and-tie policy for men, and I'm almost certain that never in the club's history has anyone ever asked for, or been served, a brewski. And yet, somehow, every year, all the attorneys of Hardwick, Mays & Kellerman gather together in its grand oak-paneled drawing room and attempt to make our summer associates—whatever gender, religion, or race they may be—feel like family.

The coatroom attendant gives me a withering stare as I hand him my laptop bag. If I wasn't standing next to Welles, it's possible he would ignore me altogether. My hand shoots self-consciously to my collar; for the second time today I kick myself for wearing a cheap button-down and chinos from Men's Wearhouse instead of one of my Brooks Brothers suits. Usually I'm a decent dresser.

After ten years at the firm, I've amassed a reasonably nice wardrobe. I'm no George Clooney, but I look well enough in a suit. At six foot two, with broad shoulders and a paunch that's easy enough to hide beneath a jacket, I'm assumed to be athletic even though I haven't had time to go to the gym since law school. I've got a nice head of hair, too. Black and thick, with just a few streaks of silver running through it. Zadie calls it "Clark Kent" hair. You'd have to be drunk to confuse me with Christopher Reeve, but it's what I've got, so I own it.

When I walk past the mirrored door of the coatroom, however, I stop and do a double take. The face looking back at me is drawn and exhausted. I hardly recognize myself. After three nights of sleeping in my office, my hair looks like a hedgehog that just crawled out of an electrical socket. I'm sporting a three-day-old beard and my glasses are sitting slightly askew on my nose. No wonder the coat-check guy didn't want to help me. He was probably wondering when the doctors in white coats were going to show up, cuff me, and drag me back to the asylum.

The party is in full swing when Welles and I walk in. The chatter of 120 attorneys and eleven summer associates bounces off the high vaulted ceilings of the Lowell Club drawing room. There's a bar at either end of the space, which everyone seems to be making good use of, and a handful of harried-looking waiters pass trays of minuscule hors d'oeuvres. As with everything at Hardwick, Mays & Kellerman, the room appears to be neatly divided by rank. The partners cluster together at the front of the room. The senior associates hang out nearby, hoping to be noticed by the partners. The mid-level associates gather in the center of the room, hoping to be noticed by the senior associates. Then come the junior associates and, finally, at the very back, the summer associates, who huddle around the bar and hope to be noticed by no one.

Welles makes a beeline for Steve Mays and Fred Kellerman, who are standing, martinis in hand, at the front of the room like generals leading their troops into battle. On any other day I might have followed him. Walked right over, clapped Fred on the back, congratulated him on our milestone victory. Shaken hands with Steve, made sure he knew my name. And then, after a sufficiently brown-nosey amount of time, I would've excused myself to the bathroom, slipped down to the lobby, and made a dash for home.

It's not any other day, though. It's Mira's birthday, I'm late for dinner, and I'm not in the mood to suck up. So, the second Welles is one step ahead of me, I hang a sharp left and disappear into the crowd. Foolish, maybe. Cowardly, absolutely. But right now my mood is black and I'm nearing clinical levels of sleep deprivation, and so instead of risking embarrassment in front of the entire partnership committee, I figure it's better to cut and run.

As soon as I am lost in the sea of suits, I whip out my Black-Berry and send Zadie a frantic and mildly incoherent text indicating that I've been hijacked by a senior partner and will be home as soon as possible. When she doesn't instantaneously respond with her customary "No worries," I feel my heart sink a little. I'm sure she told Caleb to expect me for dinner.

"WELL, LOOK WHAT THE CAT DRAGGED IN," Jamie "Moose" McClennan announces loudly when he sees me, at-tracting the attention of everyone within a twenty-foot radius. When Moose speaks, he's hard to ignore. He has a booming voice and a laugh like the Jolly Green Giant's. He's also six foot four, at least 250 pounds, and has recently grown himself a full, curly red beard that makes him look like the bastard love child of a Viking and a lumberjack. In fact, Moose *is* a bastard love child, but of socialite heiress Cassandra Moore, of the Kennebunkport Moores, and Hank McClennan, a local lobster fisherman with whom Cassandra once had a summer fling. Basically, this explains everything you need to know about Moose. He's a study in contradictions. He's wearing a suit tonight, which is a rarity, but he has artfully paired it with a loud plaid tie and hiking boots. If the guy hadn't graduated number one in his class at Yale Law School and served as a Supreme Court clerk, there's no way the Hardwick hiring committee would've let him through the door. But he did and he was, and so they've convinced themselves that Moose is simply a brilliant academic with a few charming eccentricities.

"Holy hell, man. You look like you crawled out of a Dumpster. I'm surprised they let you into this joint."

"Says the guy in the hiking boots."

Moose lets out a roaring chuckle. "Whatever, man. This is style, right here."

"It's definitely some kind of style."

"A little flair never hurt no one. Anyway, you never know what kind of honeys might turn up. Us bachelors need to look our best." He strikes a pose, drawing stares from the summer associate crowd.

I roll my eyes. Moose is fully aware of my disinterest in dating. As for him, he gets embarrassingly inarticulate around attractive women. Mira tried twice to set him up. The first girl had to take Moose to the ER after he choked on a peanut. The second girl refused to give Mira a lot of detail, except to say that she didn't find paintball to be the best venue to get to know someone. He means well, but there's definitely a chip missing when it comes to Moose and dating. I chalk it up to the fact that he was homeschooled.

"You look like you need a drink, dude. Seriously." Moose ushers me over towards the bar. "Whatever you want. I'm buyin'."

"Awfully generous of you, sir." I look at the bar, pondering my order. "Grey Goose and tonic, please," I tell the bartender. "Actually you know what? Just make that Grey Goose straight, on the rocks. Thanks."

"Go big or go home!" Moose shouts. "I heard you guys got your case thrown out. That's huge, man."

"Thanks," I say. I feel my shoulders relax a little. It's just beginning to sink in that the case that has dominated me for the last four years is actually over. In a day or so Marcia, the Litigation department staffer, will waddle her way down the hall to my office and inquire about my "capacity." This is code for *I hear your case was dismissed, so you obviously have the room to take on another soul-crushing eighty-hour-a-week assignment.* But until that happens, I'm a free man.

"You gonna celebrate tonight?"

"Well, I was on my way out to see Caleb when Peabody kidnapped me."

"Oh, brutal, man. Can you sneak out?"

"I have to." I scan the room, looking for the best escape route. "I haven't seen my boy in days."

"That's disturbing. Seriously, Chuck, you need to go home. No one expects you to be here. And if they do, they're assholes. How many hours did you clock on that thing?"

"You don't want to know. Let's just say I could stop working tomorrow and I would've already billed my full two thousand hours for the year."

Moose's eyes widen. "It's June, dude. That's messed up. You need to slow your roll. You've been working like a madman this year."

"Last two years, really." Moose bites his lip and looks away. *Whoops.* I didn't mean to make him uncomfortable. I might as well have said what we're both thinking: *I've been working like a madman ever since Mira died.* "Anyway," I add quickly. "That's what it takes, right? No rest for the weary."

"I don't know. You're an animal. They should just make you a partner right now."

I shrug. Moose is my best friend and the least competitive guy I know, but it still feels weird to talk about a partnership with him. He and I are both up for it this year. Though we're in different departments—he's in International Arbitration while I'm in Litigation—everyone knows there's a finite number of partnership spots available each year. Maribel Kingsley, a psychotic workaholic in Bankruptcy who happens to be the only woman eligible this year, is an obvious first draft pick. Martin Hamlisch in Intellectual Property was passed over last year, but word on the street is that he's definitely going to make it this time around. There're perennial favorites Ken Tanaka and Hunter Pierce in Mergers and Acquisitions, who together successfully pulled off the largest pharma deal in firm history. And then, of course, there's my litigation department nemesis, Todd Ellison. I'm not sure which bugs me more, the fact that Todd assumes he's a shoo-in because he went to Princeton and his dad does big business with the firm, or the fact that he might be right.

Moose and I are both solid workhorses. Moose has Steve Mays in his corner, and Fred treats me like his own son. No one would be shocked if we made partner; in fact, most of the firm expects that both of us will. But when it comes right down to it, there's nothing truly distinctive about either of us. Given the state of the world these days, with most law firms in a hiring freeze, there's no real reason for Hardwick to elect more partners than it needs to. Neither of us is going anywhere. Why pay us more than they have to? It's a question that keeps me up well into the night.

The truth is, while I'm sure he would very much like to make partner, Moose does not *need* to make partner. Moose is the only child of the sole heir to the Moore Paper Company. He's got no kids, no mortgage, and bizarrely monastic tastes in food and clothing. Moose's mom is on the Forbes Billionaires list, but the guy still wears a plastic Swatch he got for his fourteenth birthday. I, on the other hand, have unpaid law school loans and a hefty mortgage. More importantly, I have dependents: a son who has only one parent to support him; a sister to whom paying work is some kind of anathema; a rescue dog named Norman with an inordinately expensive bladder condition. Some days it feels as though I'll be in the red for the rest of my working life. I realize that my personal financial situation is not, in and of itself, a reason for me to make partner. And I know that I'm well-off in the grand scheme of things—financially speaking, anyway. But I've been busting my balls for years, during which time I've skipped countless family dinners and several weddings, and once came dangerously close to missing my own son's birthday party. Making partner wouldn't necessarily justify the eighty-hour weeks, but it sure would go a long way in easing their sting.

Before Moose and I can delve into a partnership discussion, Todd Ellison weasels his way between us.

"Blocking the bar, friends," he says.

He thrusts his empty glass at the bartender. "Fill it up, please. Less tonic this time."

"Sorry about that." Todd turns back to us, as though we were all in the middle of a conversation. "Charlie, thanks for chatting with the summers this afternoon."

"Sure, Todd. Anything for you," I say, swigging my drink.

"Oh, great. Well, in that case, we're looking for another speaker on our panel about work-life balance at the firm. No big thing. You speak for fifteen minutes, then open up to Q & A. I'm sure

Fred would really appreciate it if you stepped up and represented the Litigation department."

"Gosh, thanks, Todd, for telling me what Fred would appreciate."

Moose stifles a laugh by coughing loudly. "Listen, Todd, not sure Charlie's your boy for that. Can't you ask one of the more junior associates? Or maybe you could do it. You seem to have the work-life balance thing nailed."

"I'm organizing the panel, not sitting on it," Todd says, bristling. Pushback is clearly not something he's accustomed to. He fixes his glare on me. "Listen, Charlie, if you think you're too senior to sit on one of our summer associate panels, then don't worry about it. I'm happy to tell Fred that you weren't interested in helping out."

"Todd, do you know how many hours I've billed this year? I'm not sure I'm in a good position to opine on work-life balance right now."

Todd shrugs. "Everyone here works long hours, Charlie. Fred works long hours. I work long hours. But you don't hear either of us complaining."

Something in me snaps.

"Seriously, Todd? You want my thoughts on work-life balance at Hardwick? It doesn't exist. Period. End stop. You might as well hold a seminar on flying unicorns and the fucking tooth fairy."

Admittedly, this comes out a tad more aggressive than I intended. I'm practically yelling, and people are beginning to stare. Even Moose looks a little startled. But I'm fired up and it feels good. I throw back the rest of my drink and signal the bartender for another.

Todd raises his palms defensively. "No worries. I'll find someone else for the panel."

"Tell Fred I'll do the panel," I say, lowering my voice.

Todd nods. "Okay, man," he says with the slow, calming cadence of a hostage negotiator. "I'll tell Fred."

"When is it?"

"Uh, tomorrow at ten a.m. If you can't do it, seriously, no worries at all. Happy to find someone else."

"I told you I'll do it. So I'll do it, Todd. Okay?"

"Cool, man, cool." Todd pulls out his BlackBerry. "Wow, gotta
take this call. See you, Charlie."

And with that, Todd Ellison Jr. flees for his life.

"You doing okay there, buddy?" Moose says, once Todd is out
of sight.

"Yeah, I'm fine," I say, and polish off my drink. "It's Mira's
birthday."

Moose's eyes widen slightly. "Oh, brother. I'm sorry. I
should've remembered."

"It's okay. It's not a big deal. I'm just in a shitty mood, that's all.
And I really hate that guy."

"Who doesn't?" Moose says, and nods agreeably, though I can
see he's a little shaken by my momentary freak-out. Truth be told,
I'm a little shaken, too. I've never had much of a temper. I can't
remember the last time I bit someone's head off like that. And if
anyone had asked me yesterday, I probably would've told them
that I loved my job and that my hours were tough but manageable
and that, yes, I'd be happy to speak on a panel about work-life balance. Perhaps Todd just caught me at a low moment. Or perhaps
Todd just rubs me the wrong way and eventually I was bound to
ignite. Either way, he seems to have tapped into some dormant
reservoir of anger.

Another drink seems like just the thing. I signal the bartender
once again, who gives me a weary look before filling up my empty
glass.

"Maybe you should slow down there, Tiger," Moose says, and chuckles nervously. "I mean, if you want to get blackout drunk, I totally support that, but not sure this is the best venue."

"I think this is the perfect venue," I say, and grit my teeth. "The drinks are free. I think I'm owed a few drinks on the firm's tab right now. Don't you?"

Moose hesitates. "How about this: we do a lap now, say our good-byes, and then I'll take you to any bar you want and get you sauced. Sound cool?"

I know he's right. For a guy my size, I'm pretty much a total lightweight. I'm about half a drink away from slurring my words. Maybe less. From across the room I see Fred chatting away with a few other senior partners. He catches my eye and raises his glass. I raise mine back and say a silent prayer that he doesn't feel inspired to come over and chat.

"Yeah, cool," I say, relenting. "But let me finish this drink. And you have to help me work on what to say to these summers about work-life balance. Clearly it's not a subject I'm well versed in."

Moose shrugs. "I don't know. Why don't you just tell them the truth? This is a hard job. A brutal job. Sometimes I wish someone had been honest with me when I started working here."

"Huh. Honesty. I like it."

"Never a bad policy."

"You're a good man, Moose."

"I'll be a better man once I get you out of here. You're starting to become a liability. Come on. Let's split."

We're almost out the door when Welles clinks a fork against his glass.

"I just want to thank everyone for coming out tonight," he announces, as the murmur of the crowd dies down. "Most especially Fred Kellerman and Charlie Goldwyn, who today had a class-action suit against Harrison Brothers dismissed in court. Where are you, Fred and Charlie? Come up here and join me."

Suddenly the room is buzzing, and heads are turning back and forth, and everything seems as though it's spinning like a giant Tilt-A-Whirl at a state fair. I feel Moose's hand on my back, guiding me into the crowd.

"You gotta go up there, buddy," he whispers to me, propelling me forward. "He's asking for you."

As I make my way up to the front through a sea of clapping colleagues, it occurs to me that I'm absolutely, 100 percent wasted. It takes every ounce of concentration to place one foot in front of the other in a straight progression, but still I feel as though I'm zigzagging like a sailboat tacking against a hard wind.

By the time I reach Welles and Fred, I've broken into an obvious sweat. I have to wipe down my brow before shaking Welles's hand, and he gives me a strange look before turning back to the crowd.

"The class action lawsuit against Harrison is a terrific example of the complex, challenging work we do here at Hardwick. I thought perhaps Charlie and Fred might take a few minutes now to tell you about the highlights of the case." He looks back and forth between us, and Fred is nodding his head encouragingly at me, and all of a sudden my drink is in one hand and a microphone is in the other.

The room grows quiet. The lights are so bright that I have trouble focusing my eyes. After a moment of consideration, I pull open the top button of my shirt. Todd, who is standing at the front of the crowd, holds his phone up like he's taking my picture. With the other hand he gives me a thumbs-up, so I flash one back at him, causing a few people to titter awkwardly.

Sensing a mounting tension, I tap the microphone, which lets off a sharp electronic squeal.

"Hey," I say quickly, "sorry about that. So, hi, everybody. For those of you who don't know me, my name is Charlie Goldwyn and I work in Litigation."

I scan the room, looking for a familiar face. My eyes settle on Sam, the summer associate from this morning. He is leaning against a wall, hands still in his pockets like a kid at a middle school dance. When he sees me looking at him, he gives me a small chin nod like he's just daring me to say something.

Suddenly I realize with complete clarity what it is I want to say to him.

"So today someone asked me how I sleep at night. Given that, you know, I represent schmucky clients like Harrison Brothers."

Nervous laughter rises from the crowd. Heads swivel and whisper. I look over at the partners and notice a few of them shifting uncomfortably. A few begin tapping frantically at their Black-Berries, perhaps googling the potential causes of action that might arise from an attorney referring to his own client as "schmucky." For a split second, Fred and I lock eyes. The pained expression on his face is enough to give me pause, so I look away before I lose my nerve. Sam, at least, is grinning from ear to ear. This is somehow the encouragement I need to plow ahead.

"To be honest with you, I was a little thrown by his question, so I didn't give him much of an answer. But now I've had several drinks and a few hours to think about it, and here's what I have to say.

"The truth is, when I first started working at the firm, I did have trouble sleeping at night. I used to lie awake thinking to myself, 'How did I get here?' When I was a kid, I wanted to be a firefighter. You know, someone who saves the world. What kid doesn't dream of that? I mean, no five-year-old says he wants to be a shill for the financial services industry when they grow up. Am I right?"

Crickets.

"Anyway, I went to law school thinking I could make a difference in the world. Become a prosecutor, maybe, or a public defender. But student loans piled up and the next thing I knew, I'm taking a job in Big Law. I told myself it would just be for a couple of years and then I'd jump ship. But that was ten years ago, and I'm still here. Despite all the stress and the nonstop pressure to bill more hours, I'm still fucking here."

Out of the corner of my eye, I see Moose shaking his big head at me—*No, no, no, for God's sake, man, stop*—but I ignore him. Instead, I stare at Sam and keep on rolling.

"My advice to the summer associates? Honestly, if you want to get ahead here, you're going to have to forget about having a family. Do you have a significant other? Dump 'em. Even if you're able to convince them to stick around once you start working hundred-hour weeks, your relationship is going to turn into one long apology for all the birthday dinners and date nights and weekend getaways you're inevitably going to have to cancel at the last minute. And who wants that? You're better off on your own, friends. Single? Great. Stay that way. It's going to make it a lot easier for you to volunteer for all those extra hours at the office. Don't spin your wheels going on dates with some girl you met on Match.com or whatever. Trust me, that's not an effective use of your time.

"Now, for those of you looking to be inspired by your work, there's the door. Let's get real. We're not doing God's work here. We're not saving lives. We're making fucking money, people, that's what we're doing. I don't know about everyone else, but I accepted the fact that my clients are guilty a long time ago. I mean, really, really, really guilty. Bad, bad people. But you just can't let that get to you.

"If you're going to work here, you gotta see this like a game. All that matters is how you play the game. Are you winning or are you losing? I, for one, like winning. Winning's *fun*. Hardwick, Mays & Kellerman is like the fucking Yankees. We always win. And the U.S. Attorney's Office, well, let's be honest, it's kinda like the farm team for the fucking Orioles. They always lose. I'm not sure how well I'd sleep if I lost case after case, day after day, year after year. I mean, that's gotta be pretty depressing, right? How do I go home every night and tell my kid that I just lost again? I may not be able to drop him off at school in the mornings. I may never get to have dinner with him at night, or hang out on weekends, or watch his own baseball games when he gets old enough to play. But at least, as long as I'm at Hardwick, I can tell him that his dad's a winner. My son is five. When I was five, I never saw my dad. But I was proud to be his son, and you want to know why? Because he was a big-shot lawyer at a firm in the city. His picture was in the paper. Sure, he wasn't around much. Actually, he wasn't around at all. But I still thought he was a superhero. I wanted to be just like him. And all I can say is, I hope my son feels the same way about me."

All of a sudden, loud clapping emanates from the floor. At first it's just Fred, but soon he's joined by the rest of the firm. Moose lets out a holler or two. My head is starting to spin, so it takes me a minute to realize that I am, in effect, being cut off.

Fred strides up next to me and offers me a handshake as though he's accepting an Oscar. As we lock hands, he manages to maneuver the mic away from me. Then he turns to the crowd, which, by the way, is just about going wild.

"Thank you, Charlie," he says, beaming, "for that exhilarating and colorful speech." He lets out a relaxed chuckle, as though this were all scripted, and everyone follows suit. "I couldn't agree with you more. We *are* a winning team here at Hardwick. Even when we take on the most challenging, most complex cases or deals, we rise to the occasion. We really 'go to bat' for our clients, so to speak." He gives me a playful wink. "Nothing illustrates that more clearly than today's dismissal of the class action against Harrison Brothers. We really batted a thousand on that case, and I couldn't be prouder."

He begins to clap at his own speech, and the crowd dissolves into giddy, enthusiastic cheering. I'm clapping, too, because, hey, you really have to hand it to the guy. He knows how to work a crowd.

Suddenly I feel Moose's thick arm descend around my shoulders.

"Interesting speech, champ," he says in a low voice. "Let's hope it doesn't end up on YouTube."

"Why not?" I say, swaying slightly. I fight the urge to rest my head on his arm. "I thought it was pretty damn good myself. And *honest*. Just like you said."

"It was great. Very inspiring. Now let's get the hell out of here before anyone hands you the mic again."

Army of Animals

It's past midnight when I finally stumble into the lobby of my building. Hector, the night doorman, is listening to Yankees game highlights on an old-school radio. He looks up when I walk in, mildly surprised to see anyone at this hour. We live in a condo building on Seventy-Fourth Street and Second Avenue that is almost exclusively inhabited by young families or octogenarians—not exactly a stay-out-late kind of crowd. Newly wed or nearly dead, as Moose once said. Sometimes I wonder which camp I fall into.

"Traveling for work again, Mr. Goldwyn?" Hector asks. Maybe I'm crazy, but he sounds a touch judgmental. Between the smell of booze on my breath and the wild-eyed look on my face, I probably look as though I'm returning from a bender in Vegas. "Been a few days since I've seen you."

"Something like that, Hector. Good to be home."

"Must be hard to be away from your son."

"It's the worst."

Hector nods solemnly. Unable to make small talk with yet another person, I turn and stare at the elevator doors. The lobby falls silent except for the static hum of Hector's radio. I'm so tired that it takes some effort to remain standing. I briefly consider sitting cross-legged on the floor, but mercifully the elevator doors ping open, and I step inside.

"Good night, Hector," I call over my shoulder.

"Good night, Mr. Goldwyn."

The apartment is dark and quiet when I enter. I tiptoe past the kitchen, which still holds the faint scent of roasted chicken. My heart aches a little when I see Caleb and Zadie asleep together on the couch. He's wearing his favorite *Dora the Explorer* pajamas and the rainbow-striped socks he insists on wearing to bed every night. His fuzzy blond head rests on her thigh; her hand lies gently on his shoulder. His pink fleece blanket—his "buddy," he calls it— has fallen to the floor. The television screen is lit but blank, the movie they watched long since over. I wonder, my heart heavy, how long he waited up for me.

I shed my shoes in the front hall so as not to wake them. When I go over and lift Caleb off the couch, his head lolls onto my shoulder.

"Mmmm-buh," he mumbles, his eyes twitching as though he's mid-dream.

Zadie sits up and looks around, disoriented. "You're home," she whispers, her voice still heavy with sleep. "What time is it?"

"Late," I whisper back. "I'm going to bring him to bed."

She nods silently, her eyes flickering at half-mast.

I carry Caleb down the hall. His room always smells the same, like fresh-baked bread and Play-Doh. An elephant-shaped humidifier whispers away in the corner. A fire engine wails past outside. My arms tense around him, but he doesn't stir.

I have to step over the army of stuffed animals ringing his bed. Several of Zadie's old My Little Ponies are the first line of defense. In the shadows, I can make out Roger the Dinosaur and Mr. Meatball the Bulldog, and Sylvester the Squirrel, all propped up against the dust ruffle. Elmo and Grover stand guard at the foot while Steve the Gorilla looms near the headboard. Their beady eyes glint back at me in the darkness, open and alert, ready to chase the monsters away.

"More, Daddy, more," Caleb always says whenever I line up the animals for him. "Aunt Zadie puts *all* the animals out. You have to do it right. They protect me while I sleep."

Indeed, Zadie has put out all the animals. There must be thirty tonight, more than usual. This is a bad sign. The number of animals is directly proportional to the shittiness of Caleb's day.

Caleb's had more than his fair share of shitty days. There've been days so shitty that "shitty" doesn't begin to suffice as an adjective: Mira's memorial service; our first Thanksgiving without her; Mother's Day. There've been countless run-of-the-mill shitty days: a kid on the playground makes fun of the way he's dressed; some well-meaning but underinformed grown-up asks him where his mommy is. There are days that start off well but devolve into unexpected shittiness: Caleb finds a photo of Mira he hadn't seen before; he watches a television commercial in which a mom hugs a boy about his age. There are days that are just plain old shitty, for reasons neither he nor I can fully understand or articulate.

And then, there are what I call disaster days. After Mira died, Caleb became obsessed with natural disasters. First, it was hurricanes. Hurricanes Danielle and Earl swept the eastern seaboard the summer after Mira's plane went down. In an epic fail fathering moment, I let Caleb sit on my lap while I watched some of the CNN coverage about the storms. He didn't sleep through the night for weeks after that. He still occasionally has a nightmare about the ocean "rising up and eating him."

After the hurricanes, it was volcanic eruptions. How big is

Mount St. Helens? Is it active? When did it last erupt? How far, exactly, is Washington State from New York City? Caleb's preschool teacher called me in to discuss his seemingly boundless curiosity about Pompeii. Lately we're on to earthquakes. Last week, Caleb made me take down the framed photo over his bed for fear it would fall on him should an earthquake hit in the middle of the night. He keeps telling me we have to bolt all the furniture to the walls, too, just in case. He found a checklist, God knows where, of items we absolutely need for our earthquake kit—we have six of the twenty-three—and has put a collection box in the kitchen to "raise money" for said kit. If anyone in the Los Angeles area is interested, Caleb is willing to consult for a fee.

It doesn't take a genius or a psychiatrist to figure out what this disaster obsession is all about. I do, however, wonder why Caleb's focus seems to be on disasters of the natural variety. There was nothing natural about the way Mira died, after all. Maybe he's just working his way through some disaster handbook, with hurricanes, volcanoes, and earthquakes appearing before plane crashes and terrorist attacks. Or maybe the idea that a human being could be responsible for widespread death and destruction is simply more than he can handle at this point. Hell, it's more than *I* can handle. If Mira had been killed by lightning instead of Chip McCleary, would I be any less sad? No, but it's possible I'd be less angry. Not to mention less guilty, because, after all, it was my fault that she was on that flight in the first place.

Caleb rolls onto his side when his head hits the pillow, his body curling into itself like a shrimp. As I pull away, his body convulses and he lets out an anguished cry.

"I've got you, buddy, everything's okay," I say. I lie down next to him and stare up at the glow-in-the-dark stars affixed to the ceiling. I can smell the alcohol on my breath as I begin to drift off into sleep.

After a while Caleb stirs, rousing me from my state of semiconsciousness. I lean over and kiss him on the back of his head. "I love you, bud," I whisper. He doesn't respond. I stay for a minute longer, listening to his labored breathing before I slip out of the room and close the door silently behind me.

"I'm sorry about dinner."

Zadie, who's fluffing the pillows on the couch, doesn't stop what she's doing.

"It was just one thing after another. I felt like a character in Super Mario Bros., just endlessly running through level after level of weird partner-created booby traps."

"Wow," she says, nodding thoughtfully. "So, how much did you have to drink tonight, exactly?"

"Some. Too much. But seriously, I'm sorry. I know you had plans tonight."

"It's fine, Charlie. Really, it was no big deal." She looks tired, maybe a little disappointed, but not angry. I almost wish Zadie would get angry with me sometimes. I certainly deserve it.

"You're not mad?"

She sighs. "No, I'm not mad. I know how demanding your job can be."

"Was Buck pissed?"

"Buck will survive."

"I sent you some texts. Did you get them? I was worried when I didn't hear back."

"Oh, no." She shakes her head. "Caleb dropped my phone in the toilet. Sorry, didn't mean to worry you." She laughs sheepishly. "Anyway, I've got to be honest: it was probably a good thing you were out there making money, because this afternoon set you back, at least a couple grand. Caleb spilled juice on Mrs. Goodrich in the elevator, so I offered to pay for her dry cleaning. Then he broke the lamp in the living room, somehow returned home from the park with only one shoe, and just for fun, he threw my new iPhone in the toilet. Oh, and he's refusing to wear pants now, so I caved and bought him a pair of turquoise Jeggings. Don't look at me like that. At least they're pants. You should see the outfit he was *trying* to get me to buy him. To cap things off, Norman ate a plastic kiwi from Caleb's play kitchen, so we spent two hours at the veterinary hospital—which, by the way, I think you're single-handedly keeping in business."

"Superb. Remind me to get you upgraded to a platinum Amex."

"The receipts are in the kitchen."

I sigh and sink into an armchair. Suddenly I feel excruciatingly tired. My head throbs from the beginnings of a hangover. I lean my head back on the cushion and wonder if I have the energy to make it down the hall to my bedroom.

"You all right?" Zadie says, frowning down at me. "You look kinda green."

"Yeah. I'm fine. You should go to bed. Sorry I kept you up."

"No worries." She pauses, biting her lip. "Hey, Charlie?"

"Yup?"

"So I was thinking, now that your big case is over, maybe you could take a little time off?"

"What would I do with time off?"

"Take Caleb on a vacation. Some fresh air would do you both good. Fresh air and sleep."

"Zadie, I'm up for partner this year. I really can't afford to slow down."

"Yeah." Another pause. "Honestly, I'm worried about you, Charlie. Ever since, *you know*, the hours you're working . . . well, it just can't be healthy. It's been years of this. They can't expect you to keep up at this clip."

"No one's expecting me to do anything." I'm slurring my words, I realize, but I'm too tired to care. "I like being busy. It keeps me sane."

Zadie nods. I can tell she's not buying what I'm selling, but she knows better than to argue.

"I haven't been around enough for Caleb. I have to be better about that. But I'm doing this for him. You know I am. I want him to have all the things we didn't have growing up. The kid lost his *mom*. I can't ever make up for that. But a better life—well, that I can give him."

"I know," Zadie says. She stares at some indeterminate spot on the carpet. "You're doing a great job, Charlie. I just thought—"

"I know. A vacation."

"Maybe just, like, a long weekend or something."

"I'll think about it."

"Okay." She gives me a brisk nod. "I'm going to hit the hay. Get some rest. You look wrecked."

"Mmm-hmm," I murmur as my eyelids begin to shut.

"We love you, Charlie." It's the last thing I hear before I fall into the deepest, longest sleep I've had in months.

Pizzazz

I roll over and reach for Mira. Instead of her slim waist or soft, round breasts, my hand hits a hot body covered in thick bristle-brush hair. I open my eyes to find Norman, his head on the edge of my pillow, staring directly at me. I realize I'm scrunched up in the corner of my bed, while Norman's seventy-pound body stretches out like a slinky across the rest of it. He appears to have recovered nicely from yesterday's kiwi incident. He lets out a gleeful yowl when he sees that I am awake and presses his cold snout against my ribs, nudging me to get up.

"Hey, buddy," I croak. "Give me a sec, okay?" I look around, trying to get my bearings. I'm still wearing yesterday's clothes. I have a vague recollection of falling asleep in the armchair in the living room; how I found my way to bed is a mystery. In fact, I don't remember much about last night at all. I close my eyes and dig my thumbs into my temples. My head feels like it's been crushed in a giant nutcracker. Norman doesn't care. He barks sharply, then rolls over, spread-eagled, waiting for his tummy rub.

When Mira and I moved in together, she decided that we needed a dog. I wanted to spring for a purebred Labrador or golden retriever. I spent hours scouring the Web for the top breeders in the tri-state area. I filled Mira's e-mail box with nausea-inducing photos from their websites, of puppies wriggling around in wicker baskets or frolicking joyfully in flowering meadows. Mira politely ignored my e-mails and demurred every time I suggested taking a weekend trip to visit one of the breeders. Little did I know that, for the past several months, she had been quietly volunteering at a shelter downtown. She walked the dogs around the block, groomed them, took them to the vet. One day she came home with Norman, and the rest, as they say, is history.

Norman's not going to win any beauty contests anytime soon, and I can't get him to recognize his own name, much less sit or fetch. He's also got irritable bowel syndrome, a weak stomach, a highly flawed urinary tract, and several skin disorders that cause him to shed, scab, and scale with alarming regularity. I'm on a first-name basis with all the receptionists at the animal hospital down the street. Norman's kind of like the secondhand Subaru I drove in college. Supercheap sticker price but, in the end, more costly than a Lamborghini and a lot less attractive. Even on his best day of grooming, Norman's hair is fixed in a perpetual Mohawk and he smells vaguely of old cabbage. But he's what I got, and I wouldn't trade him for anything.

Norman's eyes perk up when he hears the *pat-pat-pat* of small feet down the hall.

"Hi." Caleb appears in the doorway. He slouches against the doorjamb and crosses his arms. He is unhappy with me, evidently, and he wants me to know it.

"Hey, buddy. I've missed you. Can I have a hug?" I say, and open my arms.

Caleb cocks his head to one side, considering. "Will you take me to camp today?"

I hesitate, but only for a split second. "I would love to take you to camp today."

Caleb holds out a fistful of Mardi Gras beads: a peace offering. He's wearing several strands of them around his neck, too, as well as Hello Kitty Band-Aids on every finger. Hanging from the collar of his T-shirt is a pair of cat's-eye sunglasses. If there's one thing you can say about Caleb, the kid knows how to accessorize.

"What's this?" I say, reaching for the necklaces.

"Pizzazz," Caleb says matter-of-factly. He hops up onto the bed, his feet dangling over the edge.

"Hey, thanks." I loop a few strands around my neck. "How does this look?"

Caleb studies me with a critical eye. "Good." He hands me another strand. "But you need more pink."

"Who doesn't? So, buddy, is that what you're wearing to camp today?" I say this as casually as possible. Zadie and I have discussed ad nauseam Caleb's recent interest in dressing in girls' clothing, and what, if anything, should be done about it. Zadie, ever the free spirit, is a big believer in letting kids be their own person. If Caleb wants to wear a tutu to the park, that's cool with her, as long as he's warm enough. I'm more hesitant about letting Caleb out the door in anything too pink, too sparkly, or, well, too girly. It's not that I don't want him to be his own person; I just don't want him to be the kind of person who gets the shit kicked out of him at the playground.

"Yah," Caleb says breathlessly, smoothing out his multicolored skirt. I can't help but notice the sparkly purple nail polish that's been expertly applied (by Zadie? Did she take him to get an actual manicure in an actual salon?) to his small fingernails. "Isn't it pretty? Aunt Zadie got it for me. We went to Old Nay-bee."

"It *is* pretty, buddy. I just think, you know, maybe it's hard to go on the swings and stuff in a skirt."

Caleb cocks his head, considering this. "Fiona does it," he finally says.

"Okay. Fair enough. But, Caleb, do any of the other boys you know do it?"

Caleb's face falls, and I know instantly that I've made a mistake. "Dora," he whispers, more to himself than to me.

"What's that?" I say, leaning in. I put my hand on his back and I can feel him stiffen against my touch.

"He wants you to call him Dora," Zadie announces from the doorway. "Like *Dora the Explorer*." She gives me her "Don't ask" face and holds out a mug of coffee. "Thought you could use this." To Caleb she says, "Hey, bud! You ready to go to camp?"

"Actually, I thought maybe I'd take him," I say, reaching for the coffee. "In fact, I thought maybe I'd take the day off so we can hang."

Caleb's face lights up like a little Mardi Gras float.

Zadie smiles. "That would be nice."

"I need to get Fiona ready. She's always late for everything." Caleb rolls his eyes, presumably about Fiona's incompetence. Sighing, he heaves himself off the bed and disappears down the hall.

"Fiona?" I ask.

"The latest imaginary friend."

"What happened to Mr. Beep?"

"Who knows?"

"Is that seriously what he's wearing today?"

"Please don't start, Charlie. It's been a tough week."

"I just—"

Zadie shakes her head as though thoroughly disappointed in me. "Charlie, I really think it's just a phase he's going through. I promise you, I don't want him to get teased any more than you do, but he's still so young. I don't think the other kids even notice at this point. And a lot of them are obsessed with *Dora the Explorer*. Even the boys. Trust me, the other moms and I talk. It has nothing whatsoever to do with sexuality."

"Zadie," I say, frowning, "if Caleb's gay, that's one hundred percent okay with me. You know that, right?"

She hesitates for one second longer than I'd like her to. "Yeah," she says, looking unconvinced. "Of course. I know."

"I'm serious about this. I want Caleb to be his own person, I really do. I just don't want him to get hurt. Boys can be tough on one another."

"Listen, I get it. But Caleb marches to his own drum. And as far as I'm concerned, that's something we should encourage."

"I know. I just—"

"He's fragile, Charlie. If you could just see how happy it makes him when I let him get something like that—"

I'm about to respond when my BlackBerry begins to vibrate on the nightstand. I notice that I have more than one missed call. In fact, I have fourteen. That's pretty unusual, even when I'm in the middle of a big case.

"You should take that."

"No, it's okay. I'm taking today off." I let the phone go to voicemail, but almost immediately it starts to ring again.

"Just take the call, Charlie," Zadie sighs.

I glance at the screen and see it's my assistant. "Hey, Lorraine," I say, answering. "What's up?"

"Where are you? Are you okay?" Lorraine says, the alarm in her voice apparent.

"I'm fine. Why? I was just going to work from home today. Is everything—"

"Charlie," she says, her voice low, as though she's cupping her hand around the receiver. "What the hell were you thinking last night?"

This stumps me. "What was I thinking about what?"

"That speech. I mean, wow. *Wow*."

I scratch my head. "Yeah, I know. I was slurring my words for sure. But Welles just sprung it on me! And it's not like I'm the first person in history to have one drink too many at an office party."

Out of the corner of my eye, I see Zadie slip out into the hall. She closes the door behind her, giving me some privacy.

"Yeah, well, the slurring was one thing," Lorraine says. "But now it's online and . . ." She trails off. "Look, Fred and Welles both stopped by earlier looking for you. I think you'd better get your ass down here ASAP."

I frown into the phone. "What do you mean, 'it's online'?"

There is a long, deafening pause on the other end of the phone. "Have you checked your e-mail yet? Someone videotaped your speech and it ended up on YouTube. And it's, like, going viral, basically. I'm checking now . . . yeah, it's up to, like, seventy thousand views already. Welles is freaking out. Some of the stuff you said about your clients, well, I'm pretty sure they could sue you for it."

A sour feeling fills my stomach. "I think there must be some kind of mistake," I say feebly. "I'm sure I can clear things up. I'll be there as soon as I can."

"Good," Lorraine says, "because someone from Page Six just called for comment."

The YouTube

Welles sits across the conference table from me, silent. Every few minutes he shakes his head, as if he is trying, and failing, to come up with adequate words to address such a monstrous breach of etiquette. Beside him, Fred fidgets nervously and refuses to make eye contact. Next to Fred sits Steve Mays, who has absorbed himself wholly in his BlackBerry, and next to Steve is Lauren Hatchfelder, the delightfully slutty and self-important head of Human Resources. Lauren, who has perfected the art of sexifying business attire, has stepped up her game today and is wearing a tight pantsuit and a new pair of thick, black-framed glasses that make her look like a librarian in a skin flick. Of the five of us, Lauren is the only one who looks absolutely thrilled to be here. It's probably not every day that a Human Resources issue gets elevated to senior management.

When the clock hits eight thirty a.m., Lauren springs to life. She bounces from her chair and, bending over in a way that makes it impossible not to look down her shirt, slides a small sheaf of paper across the table to me. "Here you go, Charlie," she says, and offers me a pouting smile, the kind you give a significant other right before saying something like, *Look, it's not you, it's me.*

But it *is* me. That much is clear. Fred, who less than twenty-four hours ago was treating me like the son he never had, now can't bear to look at me. No one is looking at me. Not knowing what else to do, I stare down at the printouts in front of me. I don't need to read beyond the headlines; I know how much trouble I'm in. But I do anyway, because it appears that that is what is expected, and it saves me from looking helplessly across a table at a bunch of people who are trying their damnedest to pretend I no longer exist.

After what feels like an eternal silence, Welles clears his throat. I look up: eight eyes are now fixed on me. I manage a weak smile that is not returned.

"So, Mr. Goldwyn," Welles says, sounding exhausted already. "I don't think I need to explain to you why we're all here this morning."

Mr. Goldwyn. Yesterday I was Charlie. This can't be good. I offer my most concerned nod.

"Your speech last night was inappropriate, to say the least. I think I speak for all of us here when I say that I found your characterizations of our clients here at Hardwick offensive, defamatory, and just plain wrong."

"Sir, if I may—"

He silences me with a flick of the hand. "Now, it would be one thing if you had chosen to given this speech in the privacy of your own home. It's another when it's at a firm gathering. And it's *quite another* when it ends up on 'the YouTube' "—he uses air quotes here, as though he's not entirely certain what YouTube is—"where, I understand, it has"—air quotes again—" 'gone viral.' "

"Well, see, that's the thing, sir," I say quickly, before realizing I haven't actually been asked a question or been given permission to speak. "If I may say a few words?"

"Please," Welles says. He makes a grand sweeping gesture. "By all means, tell us what's on your mind, Mr. Goldwyn."

"I'm just wondering how this *did* end up on YouTube. Why would someone put this online if not to damage the firm's reputation?"

Suddenly, with bone-chilling clarity, I know the answer to my own question.

Todd.

That little weasel. I don't remember much from the previous evening, but I do remember him holding up his phone. At the time I thought he was snapping a picture, but now I realize he was sealing my fate.

Welles is talking, but I've stopped listening.

"I'm sorry," I say, cutting him off. "But it was Todd Ellison. He filmed me last night. I'm sure of it. He's the one who leaked the video. He's the one who put the firm's reputation in jeopardy."

From the look that Welles gives Fred, it's clear that they at least suspected as much.

"Don't you see?" I snap. "He's trying to eliminate his competition. We're the only two associates in Litigation up for partner this year and, let's be honest, everyone knows I'm better qualified. Me screwing up is the best thing that could possibly happen to Todd right now. I have to hand it to him, though: he's smarter than I thought. Filming me while I made an ass of myself was pretty clever. But leaking it, well, that's a stroke of evil genius."

Welles shifts uncomfortably in his chair. He knows I'm right, but of course he'll never admit it. Like any good lawyer, he's already thinking ahead to a potential lawsuit.

"We don't know how this video became public. What Mr. El-lison did or did not do is not relevant to this discussion," he says curtly. "The fact is, this video made its way onto some legal blog, and from there it was picked up by the mainstream press. It is, as we speak, gaining traction. Whether you like it or not, Mr. Gold-wyn, you are rapidly becoming some kind of anticorporate poster child. The voice of a disaffected generation. Not unlike that fellow at Goldman Sachs who penned that very angry op-ed in the *New York Times*."

"That's totally different!" I explode. "That guy wrote a fucking op-ed! I made a fool of myself at an office party. I was drunk, that's all. Haven't you ever said something you didn't mean when you were drunk?"

Welles pretends not to have heard this question. "As you might imagine," he continues, as if reading from a script, "this is a pub-licity nightmare for the firm. It shows a terrible lack of judgment on your part, one that will be very difficult to explain to clients. Clients hire us, Mr. Goldwyn, for our clarity of thought, our pro-fessionalism, and our discretion. You have demonstrated none of the three."

I feel the mood shift in the room. Lauren's closed her eyes as though I'm a puppy about to be put down and she can't bear to watch. Fred is tugging on his eyebrow, something he does during particularly stressful client meetings. All of a sudden it hits me like a ton of bricks: I'm not being reprimanded. I'm being fired.

The anger I felt one minute earlier rushes out of me like air from a balloon. "It will blow over. I'll take some time off. Unpaid, of course. Tell them I'm still in mourning. It will all blow over."

"I'm afraid it's not that simple, Charlie," Steve Mays pipes up. He doesn't look angry, just sad. Somehow this is worse. "This job is very stressful. We all know that, and we can appreciate that you went through a particularly challenging personal time with the loss of your wife. But clients . . . well, I'm not sure they will be so forgiving. Let's put aside the fact that you expressed some very strong opinions about the finance community generally. How can you ask a client to trust a lawyer who not only doesn't respect him, but who can crack so easily under stress?"

He's got a point. I slump back in my chair, close my eyes. This whole thing is a fucking nightmare. Some small part of me still clings to the hope that at any moment I will wake up and it will all be over.

"This can't be happening." I shake my head. "I've given up everything for this firm. My whole life is this firm. I have nothing else."

"We are fully prepared to offer you a very generous severance package, and we will assist you in finding another job," Welles says. "Lauren here will go over the details of the offer, as well as specifics regarding health insurance, your 401(k) . . ."

"You can't seriously be firing me." I'm muttering to myself, since no one else appears to be listening. Has the air conditioner malfunctioned? It's a hundred thousand degrees in here all of a sudden. I look at Fred. How can he sit there so calmly while Welles tears me apart? I strip off my blazer and tug at my tie, which is knotted far too tightly around my neck.

"The firm will, of course, be issuing some sort of press release addressing the situation. The last thing we need is for one of your former clients to sue us, though of course that is certainly a possibility. We've already engaged a public relations firm which specializes in crisis management—"

"Is it hot in here?" I look to Lauren. "I'm having trouble breathing."

"Charlie?" she says. Her face twists with concern. "Are you okay?"

"We'd like you to speak with the head of the PR team as soon as possible. He may want you to apologize publicly to any clients you may have offended."

"Not okay," I manage. My right hand shoots to my left bicep, which is throbbing with an unusually unpleasant burning sensation. The track lighting on the ceiling is getting brighter and brighter; I feel like I'm looking directly into the sun. What is going on in here? I have to get out. I stand up and spin around, looking for the nearest exit.

Welles pauses and peers at me over the top of his glasses. "Mr. Goldwyn? Are you listening to me?"

"No," I squeak. "I'm not listening. I have to get out of here. I'm having a heart attack."

And with that, I collapse onto the cold, hard conference room floor. The last things I see before I black out are Lauren Hatchfelder's pendulous breasts swinging towards my face as she lunges at me, yelling something about calling the paramedics.

Family History

"How are you feeling, Mr. Goldwyn?"

My eyes flicker open. A strikingly handsome man in a white jacket smiles at me from my bedside. "I'm Dr. Fabulan. Would it be all right if I ask you a few questions?"

I blink at the man. What did he say his name was? Dr. Fabio? Dr. Fabulous? He doesn't look like a real doctor. He looks like an actor playing a doctor on a telenovela. His teeth are suspiciously white, a shade that can't possibly exist in nature.

"Do you know what day it is, Mr. Goldwyn?"

"Excuse me?"

"Do you know what day it is?" he says more slowly, enunciating his syllables in a way that is simultaneously condescending and terrifying. *Dooo yooo know what day eet ease?*

"Friday?" I guess, still wondering if this is some incredibly realistic dream in which I play a patient on a show being broadcast on Telemundo.

Dr. Fabio writes something down on his clipboard.

"And can you tell me your address?"

"Two fifteen East Seventy-Fourth Street. Listen, I think the guy in the ambulance asked me all of this before. Does a heart attack cause temporary amnesia or something?"

Dr. Fabio looks up from his clipboard. "Mr. Goldwyn, you didn't have a heart attack. I believe what you had was a panic attack." *Pan-eek attack.*

"Excuse me?"

Before he can answer, the door opens, and Zadie comes flying through.

"Charlie! I'm so sorry it took me so long to get here! I had to find someone to watch Caleb. What happened? Are you okay?"

I stare at the cardiac monitor beside my bed. A little green heart flashes on the screen, signaling that I am, in fact, alive.

"It's nothing," I say, thinking how hard it is to appear casual while wearing a paper dress. "I thought I was having a heart attack. And then I sort of passed out—"

"Oh my God." Zadie's face is wrought with worry.

"But everything's fine—"

"Charlie, a heart attack? Everything is *not* fine."

Dr. Fabio clears his throat.

"Oh, I'm sorry." Zadie looks up as though she's just noticing Dr. Fabio for the first time. It might be my imagination, but I swear she gives him a reflexive once-over. "I didn't see you there. How rude of me. I'm Zadie," she says with a flurry of giddy laughter.

"It's nice to meet you, Mrs. Goldwyn," Fabio says.

"Oh, no, no," we both say in unison.

"I'm his—"

"She's my—"

He looks at us, amused.

"Sister," we both conclude.

"Ah. Well. Please take a seat, Mrs. . . . ?" He trails off.

"Miss," Zadie says, batting her eyelashes. "Miss Goldwyn. But please call me Zadie."

"All right, Zadie."

I cough, reminding them of my existence.

"As I was saying," Dr. Fabio says quickly, "while what Mr. Goldwyn experienced—chest pain, shortness of breath, heart palpitations, vertigo—may have felt very much like a heart attack, it was, in fact, nothing more than a panic attack."

"No"—I shake my head—"it was a heart attack. I'm sure of it."

"I know it may have felt that way to you, Mr. Goldwyn," Dr. Fabio says, "but neither your EKG nor your blood work showed any signs of a heart attack."

"Your tests are wrong, then. Run them again."

"This is a good thing, I assure you," Dr. Fabio says, appealing to Zadie, who he's already correctly identified as the more reasonable adult in this situation. "Your heart is healthy as can be."

"It's a good thing, Charlie," Zadie says, bobbing her head in agreement. "It's such a relief. A heart attack—my God."

"If my heart's so healthy, then why did it completely malfunction for no reason?" I argue. "I mean, I *passed out.* That's not just in my head. I didn't just make that up."

"No, no, Mr. Goldwyn, you're misunderstanding me. I don't mean to downplay the significance of what you experienced. The symptoms of a panic attack, particularly an acute one such as yours, are real and terrifying. They are also similar to those experienced during a heart attack, so it's quite common for patients to confuse the two."

"It's just good there's no damage to your heart, Charlie. But you've got to take better care of yourself, okay? Less stress, okay? Caleb needs you. I need you."

"Have you been under stress lately, Mr. Goldwyn?"

He's got me there. "Yes," I concede. "I guess. A little bit."

"His wife was on Flight 1173," Zadie offers.

"I'm so sorry, Mr. Goldwyn."

I nod, willing him to move on.

"And our mom died a year before that. She had stomach cancer."

I shoot Zadie a look.

"I'm just giving him the whole picture, Charlie."

"I'm very sorry, Mr. Goldwyn," Dr. Fabio says in a grave voice that I imagine he reserves for the most depressing of patients. "That's a lot of stress for one family to bear."

"We live together," Zadie blurts out. "I mean, I live with Charlie and his son in their apartment. I help take care of Caleb. It's worked out well so far. No complaints. But I know it's probably a lot for Charlie. I mean, what thirty-five-year-old wants to come home to his sister every night, right?" She lets out a nervous chuckle.

I close my eyes and lean back against the pillow.

"Anyway, my point is, he's got a lot on his plate. It's been a tough few years."

Dr. Fabio smiles sympathetically at Zadie, who in turn picks at her cuticle and stares at the floor.

"Your son's name is Caleb?" he says to me, after a second.

"Yes. He's five."

"He's your only?"

"My one and only, yes."

"That can't be easy, being a single father."

"It's been a blast."

Dr. Fabio recoils a little. Apparently, this is not the time for sarcasm.

"What do you do for a living, Mr. Goldwyn?" he asks, his words crisp.

"I'm a lawyer."

"White-collar defense. At a big firm. His job is also very stressful," Zadie adds knowingly.

"On a scale of one to ten, how would you quantify your recent stress level?"

I pause. *A fourteen?* I think.

"An eight?"

"Would you say that is higher than normal?"

"Maybe a little."

"He's been really stressed lately," Zadie pipes up. "And this isn't the first time he's had a panic attack."

Dr. Fabio perks up. "What do you mean? Can you describe for me what happened before?" He eyes me suspiciously, as though I'm a defense witness who's been withholding vital information.

"This hasn't happened before. Zadie, what are you talking about?"

She widens her eyes at me, sister code for: *You know exactly what I'm talking about.*

"I'm talking about the time I set you up on that date with my friend Andrea." She looks up at Dr. Fabio. "He hyperventilated in the middle of a restaurant."

"That's really not how I remember it."

"I think she's still in therapy."

"I wasn't ready to date. I *told* you that."

"Are you on any medication, Mr. Goldwyn?" Dr. Fabio asks. "Do you take anything to sleep, or for anxiety, depression, anything like that?"

"No. I mean, I take Tylenol PM sometimes to sleep," I say, thinking of the three pills that I habitually swallow every night. "I know that's not good for me, but it's only occasional."

"Do you smoke?"

"No."

"Use drugs?"

"Never."

"Do you drink alcohol?"

"Yes, of course. I mean, most people do, don't they?"

"How often would you say you drink? Once or twice a week?"

"A bit more than that."

"Every day?"

"About."

"How many drinks would you say?"

"I don't know." I sigh impatiently. "I'm not, like, a boozehound or anything. I go to a lot of client dinners. And office parties. Everyone drinks at those parties, right?"

"Have you ever met with a psychiatrist or a counselor of any kind?"

"No. Why, do I seem unbalanced or something?"

"Not even after your wife's passing?"

"No. I work. I don't have time to lie around on a couch and talk about my feelings."

Dr. Fabio doesn't respond. He keeps scribbling and scribbling like some kind of profiler for the FBI. I sit up and crane my neck, but it's fruitless: the clipboard is too far away, and anyway, I can't read upside down.

"Any family history of depression or anxiety?"

"No. My mother was one of the happiest people I've ever met. She genuinely loved life."

"She was a little depressed at the end," Zadie says quietly. "I mean, who wouldn't be?"

I clear my throat. Zadie's words hang uncomfortably in the air, a reminder that it was her, not me, who cared for our mother in her final days.

"Anyone else you can think of? Your father? Aunts? Uncles? Cousins?"

"No."

"Actually . . ." Zadie bites her lip.

"What?"

"Well, Dad has panic attacks." She refuses to look at me as she says this. Instead, she stares at her hands, like she's just testified against me on the stand. "Or he used to, anyway. He took something for it. Xanax, I think."

"How do you even know that?" I say, annoyed.

"I don't know. Mom must've told me." Her voice quavers.

"Dad's issues have nothing to do with me."

"He's asking questions, Charlie," Zadie sighs. "I'm just trying to be honest. Depression and anxiety can be genetic, you know."

"I'm not depressed!" I practically shout. "I just had a bad fucking day!"

"Okay," Dr. Fabio intervenes. "Mr. Goldwyn, could you tell me what you were doing at the onset of this attack? Where you were, who you were with, how you were feeling? Please be as specific as you can."

"I was, uh, in a meeting at the office. With, um, three partners and the head of Human Resources."

"And how were you feeling at this meeting?"

"Pretty stressed, I guess. It was a stressful meeting."

"Can you be more specific? Walk me through what happened."

"Well, the meeting ended, and I stood up and felt a pain shooting up my arm. Like I had acid in my veins. And suddenly the room felt very hot and I couldn't breathe. I was sweating, but no one else seemed to notice. And the pain in my arm kept getting worse and worse. It was like an elephant on my chest, just crushing me. My heart was beating so hard, I thought it was going to explode. And then . . ." I trail off, remembering Lauren's breasts swinging towards me like twin wrecking balls.

"And then?" Dr. Fabio prompts. "What's the last thing you remember?"

"That's it. That's all I remember."

Dr. Fabio turns back to his clipboard, writing. Finally, he rips a piece of paper off it and hands it to me. "Mr. Goldwyn, this is the name of a colleague of mine. Dr. Harris is a clinical psychiatrist as well as a grief therapist. She's very good. I'm going to recommend that you go see her, the sooner the better."

Zadie nods enthusiastically. "I think that's a *great* idea," she declares. She snatches the paper out of the doctor's hands and slips it into her purse as though I can't be trusted with it.

"In the meantime, it's essential that you relax. Rest as much as you can. Is it possible for you to take a small break from work? Perhaps a few days?"

"No problem there," I say, though neither Zadie nor Dr. Fabio picks up on the sarcasm in my voice. They exchange satisfied glances.

"Terrific," Dr. Fabio says. "And please do call Dr. Harris as soon as you are able. She isn't taking new patients right now, but I'll put in a call to make sure she'll see you. She's a close, personal friend of mine."

I'll bet she is, I think as he offers me a wink.

"Well, he's great," Zadie says once the doctor is gone.

"That guy? He looks like he should be wearing a pirate shirt on the cover of a romance novel."

Zadie makes a face. "Why do you always get so weird about therapy?"

"What? When have I ever gotten weird about therapy?"

"Um, every single time someone brings it up. Remember that woman who kept bringing over casseroles to check up on you? Catherine Klatsky or something? She mentioned that she had a great therapist, and it was like game over for you. You pushed her out the door and didn't stop making fun of her for weeks."

"Who's Catherine Klatsky? Oh, right, Crazy Eyes Klatsky. The one with the seventeen cats and the, you know . . ." I cross my eyes for effect.

"Yes," Zadie says, annoyed. "So fine, she's just the slightest bit cross-eyed. She's still very pretty."

"Are you serious?"

Zadie closes her eyes and lets out an exasperated sigh. "Catherine Klatsky is beside the point, Charlie."

"You think? I don't even know what we're talking about."

"I'm just trying to understand why you're so resistant to the idea of therapy. You don't have to just power through everything. You have to allow yourself to grieve."

"Maybe this is how I grieve. Maybe focusing on work is what makes me feel better. Not everyone grieves in the same way, you know."

"I'm not really sure pretending it didn't happen is a sustainable strategy. Grief is like that, Charlie. You can't just ignore it. It manages to seep out in other ways. Look at today, for example. Look where you are right now."

"What, this?" I say, pointing to my hospital gown. "This has absolutely nothing to do with Mira."

Zadie raises one skeptical eyebrow. "You know what I think?" she says.

"What do you think, Zadie?"

"I think you are still blaming yourself for Mira's death. That's what I think. And it's eating you alive."

"Well, she should have never gotten on that plane. So, yes, I do blame myself for that."

Zadie winces and looks away.

"But this has nothing to do with that." I pause, take a deep breath. "I got fired today."

"I'm sorry?"

"I. GOT. FIRED. TO. DAY."

Zadie's mouth actually falls open.

"Holy crap, Charlie," she says. "Are you serious?"

"Thanks for those kind and inspiring words of support."

Suddenly her arms are around me, squeezing me so hard it hurts. Without warning, I start to cry.

Not manly tears, either.

A full-blown, snot-filled sobfest.

As I blubber on, Zadie strokes my head the way our mom used to do when I was a kid. Unlike Zadie and Mom, who were both passionate and emotional and highly in touch with their feelings, I never cried about anything. So when I did, they both knew it was a very big deal.

It's only when I calm down enough to listen to what Zadie is saying that my crying momentarily turns into laughter.

"Holy shit, Charlie," she says. "I think that might be the best goddamn news I've heard all week."

The Other Charlie Goldwyn

I was just a few months into my tenure at Hardwick when the other Charlie Goldwyn joined the firm.

I was a lowly first year associate. He was fifty-six and already a partner. He had been a rainmaker at his previous firm, Graves & LaSalle. Hardwick had reputedly wooed him away with a multi-million-dollar bonus and the promise of a corner office.

"He wants your e-mail address," Fred told me, in a voice that left no room for negotiation. "It's going to be a huge pain in the ass for you. But it's what he wants, so it's what we're going to do. What's your middle name?"

"I don't have one."

"That's too bad." Fred shook his head, like I had really let him down on this one. "I was going to say you should just start going by it."

"You want me to *change my name*?"

"Just, you know, professionally. But at the very least you'll need to give up your e-mail address."

"So if he's Charlie Goldwyn at Hardwick dot com, what will that make me?"

Fred shrugged. "How the fuck should I know?" he said, exasperated. "Ask someone in Tech."

The logistics of having two Charlie Goldwyns at one firm turned out to be nightmarishly complicated. The switchboard was forever mixing up our calls. The front desk regularly sent clients to the wrong office. At least sixty percent of my e-mails ended up in the other Charlie's in-box. Internally, people started referring to me as "Associate Charlie Goldwyn," or, more irritatingly, "Chuck." One morning I arrived at my office to find that a new nameplate had been affixed to the door. Instead of "Charlie Goldwyn," it now read "Charlie Goldwyn, Ass." I took a photo and texted it to Moose. Then I called Lauren Hatchfelder and told her that everyone had a line and mine had officially been crossed.

Lauren was, of course, mortified, and the sign was taken down within the hour. Still, my friends couldn't resist knocking on my door and inquiring whether or not Charlie Goldwyn, Ass., was available. By noon the joke had gotten old.

"Fuck off, Moose! I'm working!" I shouted, after the third knock in an hour.

There was a long pause. Finally a soft female voice said, "Hello? May I come in?"

A woman in jean shorts and flip-flops poked her head into my office. She had wild white-blond hair and wore a tank top that kept sliding off her shoulder. In one hand she carried a purple thermos. She offered me a nervous smile. When she waved, I noticed a tattoo of a bird on the inside of her wrist.

"Hi," she said, "I'm Mira."

"I'm so sorry, please come in. I thought you were someone else."

"You thought I was a moose?" she said, looking bemused.

"Moose is a friend," I said, feeling my face flush with embarrassment. "It's just a nickname. He's big. And from Maine."

She nodded and glanced around my office. "Should I sit?"

"Yes, please." We smiled at one another from across my desk. I opened my mouth but couldn't think of anything to say. She was exquisitely beautiful. There was something almost otherworldly about her. Her eyes were different: one was bright blue, the other, green. Her skin was pale and clear, the color of milk. She stared at me, unflinching. Nervous, I began shuffling the papers in front of me into piles.

"So, is he coming back soon?" she asked after a few seconds. I could feel her watching me with those incredible eyes.

"Who? Moose?"

"No. Charlie."

"I'm Charlie."

"What?" She frowned. "I'm looking for Charlie Goldwyn. We're supposed to have lunch"—she checked her watch—"right now."

"I'm Charlie," I said again, and then: "Oh."

"What?"

"You must be looking for the other Charlie Goldwyn. There are two of us here. The front desk keeps sending guests to the wrong office. You mean Charlie Goldwyn the partner, right?"

"I think he's a partner," she said. "Tall guy, silver hair? He's my godfather."

"Hold on," I said, dialing the other Charlie's extension. "I'll get you to the right place."

"What now?" he barked as a greeting. By then he was used to me calling about annoying name-related mix-ups. He always acted as though this whole thing was my fault, like it was rude for an associate to dare to have the same name as a partner.

"Well, sir, your goddaughter is in my office. Should I send her up to you?"

"Oh, Jesus H. Christ. Is it noon already? I'm stuck on a call on

the other line. I completely forgot about lunch. Could you entertain her for twenty minutes or so? And then I'll be down to get
her. You don't mind, do you?"

I glanced across the desk. Mira smiled at me, revealing a dimple
in her left cheek.

"Not at all," I said.

"Thanks, Charlie," Charlie said. His usual gruffness had dis-
sipated now that I was doing him a favor. "Ask her if she doesn't
mind waiting."

I cupped my hand over the receiver. "He's stuck on a call," I
whispered to Mira. "He asked if you wouldn't mind waiting here
until he's ready."

"Of course not," she replied. "As long as I'm not in your way,
that is."

"We're fine," I said to Charlie. "Take your time."

I hung up the phone. "So," I said.

"So." She smiled back.

"Is that a bird tattoo?"

She held up her wrist. "It is."

"So, what's it, like, mean?"

"You know . . ." she leaned in to the desk, one eyebrow raised,
"that's kind of a personal question."

"Oh, is it? I'm sorry. I didn't mean—"

"Yeah, in some circles, asking a stranger about her tattoo, well.
It could get you killed."

"I'm so sorry. I had no idea."

She giggled. "I'm just joking."

"Oh, thank God," I said, feeling both relieved and embarrassed.

"I just like birds. They're so *free*. This"—she ran a thumb over her tattoo—"I guess it reminds me to be myself. That probably sounds stupid, right?"

"Not at all. Now, if it was supposed to remind you to be some-one else, that would be stupid."

Mira let out a surprised laugh, like she hadn't expected me to be funny.

She was about to say something when my phone began to ring.

"I'm sorry," I said, trying to ignore it. "You were saying?"

"No, please go ahead. Take the call."

"It's okay. It'll go to voicemail in a sec."

The phone fell silent. Just as I was opening my mouth, it began to ring again. Mira set down her thermos on the edge of my desk and pulled a beat-up paperback from her bag. "I've got a book," she said, holding it up. "And my tea. Please, I'll feel terrible if you let me interrupt your work."

"Oh, no. I'm not busy at all," I said, though this was, of course, an enormous lie. As if on cue, the phone began to ring a third time. I leapt up to silence it and knocked Mira's thermos over in the process.

"Fuck, fuck, fuck!" I shouted. I snatched up a stack of deposi-tions and flapped them wildly in the air. It was too late: the top pages of each were sopping wet.

"Oh, jeez—here." Mira hopped to her feet and tried to mop up the spill with a scarf that was tied around the strap of her bag. "I'm so sorry!"

"No!" I shouted at her. "No—I mean, I didn't mean to yell—sorry, I just don't want you to ruin your scarf. I'm sorry about your tea."

"What about your desk? It's everywhere!"

"My desk is fine!"

"Okay!" She widened her eyes at me. "Just stop yelling!"

We both burst into laughter.

"I'm sorry," I said, shaking my head. "I'm a little stressed-out today."

"I can see that," she said, and dropped to her knees, searching for the thermos cap under my desk. "You want to talk about it?"

"No, just one of those days at work, you know?"

She stood up, holding up the cap. From her blank smile I could tell she didn't. "My work place is pretty zen," she said almost apologetically. "I teach yoga and meditation."

"I love yoga," I said, another lie. Unable to stop myself, I added: "I've been thinking I should try meditation, too."

"Really," she said, her eyes skimming my soft waistline. "Well, I teach at a little studio in the West Village. You should stop by sometime. We have a wonderful seminar coming up, an introduction to meditation. Actually, here"—she pulled a brochure out of her bag and handed it to me—"here's some information on it. You can sign up online."

"That would be terrific," I said, giving it a quick once-over. My eyes bugged out slightly. "Wow, seven hours?"

She laughed. "Usually the seminars are two days long. But this is just a quick introduction. Don't look scared. If it's too much for you, you can always do a private session instead. Those are just ninety minutes."

"Do you teach privates?"

She laughed again. "Not usually. But maybe I can make an exception."

Just as I was about to say something witty and charming, Moose barged through my office door, a cigarette dangling from his lips.

"Chuck, what a fucking day. I'm going for a smoke. You wanna come?" His eyes fell to Mira. "Oh, sorry. I didn't realize you had company."

"This is Moose," I explained to Mira. "Moose, Mira is the other Charlie's goddaughter. She ended up in my office by accident."

"Got it. Yeah, poor Chuck here. Your godfather stole his name. This morning he ended up with a sign on his door that said—"

"Moose, don't you have somewhere to be?"

Moose's eyes widened. "Oh, right, yeah, sure. Nice to meet you."

"Wait!" Mira said. "What did the sign say? You can't leave me hanging like that."

Moose grinned. "So your godfather is a partner, right? And this idiot here is just a lowly associate. So they've started slapping 'Associate' on everything he does, just to keep the two of them straight. So this morning he shows up and"—Moose started to chuckle—"there's a sign on his door that says, 'Charlie Goldwyn, Ass.' They must've run out of space or something. Priceless."

Mira burst out laughing. "No wonder you're on edge today," she said, turning to me.

I shrugged, too mortified to respond.

"I have a picture," Moose said, digging his phone out of his pocket.

"Oh, show me!" Mira squealed delightedly.

"Here. I already made it the wallpaper on my desktop. It just cracks me up every time."

"*Moose.*" They both looked up at me, like kids busted mid-prank.

"Oh, right," he said. He made a show of checking his watch. "Yup, definitely have somewhere to be. It was nice to meet you."

"Likewise," Mira said.

"So, Chuck, no smoke, I take it?"

"No." I glared at him. "I don't smoke, remember?"

"Right, right." He winked. "My mistake. Okay, well, catch you later."

A week later I lay on a hard floor in a pool of my own sweat, wondering if I would ever feel my legs again. My smoker's lungs heaved from exertion. Moose lay beside me panting, his body encased in a neon yellow Lycra getup that made him look like a gigantic banana.

"I think she sees us," he hissed, rolling over onto his side. "She's looking this way."

"She'd have to be blind not to. You look like a human highlighter."

"It's a cycling suit. So cars can see me at night."

"Cars could see you from outer space in that thing."

"You're just jealous that you don't have the body to pull this off."

"Lie back and close your eyes." Mira's soft voice carried over the tinkling of new age music. "It's time for Shavasana, or Corpse Pose."

"Corpse Pose is right," I muttered to Moose. "I can't feel my legs. It's possible I'm dying."

"Shh." The woman in front of me turned around and glared. "Some of us are trying to get something out of this class."

"Trust me, we're trying to get something out of this class, too," Moose whispered back at her. "My buddy's not leaving without the teacher's phone number."

Mira dimmed the lights and lit a candle. The music stopped; it was so quiet you could hear a pin drop. Seconds passed, then minutes. The longer we lay still, the faster my mind raced. The wooden floor was remarkably hard. I couldn't quite get comfortable. I wriggled. Shifted. Shimmied. No one else was moving. Moose was even snoring lightly. How could he be so relaxed? I couldn't remember the last time I had taken a Saturday morning off. Fred was probably storming around the office, wondering where the fuck I was. I felt an irrepressible need to check my BlackBerry.

Suddenly a lavender-scented pillow descended onto my eyelids. I flinched involuntarily, feeling helpless. "Relax," Mira whispered. "I don't bite." Her face was just a few inches from mine; I could hear her breathing. Her thumbs dug into the knots in my shoulders, miraculously releasing a week's worth of tension.

"Calm your body, calm your mind," Mira announced, loud enough so that the rest of the class could hear her. Her fingers massaged their way up my neck and over my scalp. I felt a rush of pleasure when she began to rub my ears. In fact, I had to bite down hard on my lip to suppress a moan. Afraid of becoming physically aroused, I began to mentally run through my to-do list until at last the rubbing stopped.

"Namaste," Mira whispered. She pulled off the eye pillow and then slipped away into the darkness.

A fifteen-second ear rub, and I was infatuated. Also, I was hooked on the class. Ninety minutes of sweaty, spasm-inducing hell now felt strangely worthwhile.

"That was fucking awesome," I said to Moose as we rolled up our mats. "Holy crap. I feel like I'm on drugs."

Moose threw me a skeptical look. "You need to get out more, bro," he said.

"You didn't think that was incredible?"

He shrugged. "I like Zumba. Have you done Zumba? The girls are gorgeous. And there's never any guys at Zumba, for some reason. The girls, they fawn over me, dude. It's the best-kept secret in New York."

"There are no guys in Zumba for a reason, Moose. Anyway, at Zumba you don't get a head massage at the end."

"What?" Moose stared at me, perplexed. "What head massage?"

"Oh," I said, stifling a smile. "Never mind."

Moose nudged me. "Look. Here she comes."

I turned to see Mira walking towards us, a yoga mat tucked beneath her arm. Beside her stood a tall, buff guy with a ponytail. Like Mira, he radiated health and well-being. He looked like the kind of guy who spoke earnestly about his spirit animal. A guy who, when not practicing yoga, volunteered at soup kitchens and designed his own turquoise jewelry. The kind of guy a woman like Mira should date instead of a coffee-guzzling, stress-addicted smoker who ate Tums like jellybeans and hadn't properly exercised since the Clinton administration.

Ponytail Guy leaned in close to her and said something that made her throw her head back with laughter. I sucked in my gut and wiped the sweat from my brow.

She spotted us and waved. Ponytail Guy gave her an unnervingly long hug. When it was over, she skipped towards us, smiling.

"Hi!" she said. "Thanks for coming. I love seeing new faces in my class."

"It was a great class," I said. "I'm Charlie, by the way. And this is Moose. From Hardwick, Mays & Kellerman?"

"I remember. The Other Charlie Goldwyn. And how could I forget a name like Moose?"

"Well, my real name is Jamie," Moose said, turning red. "But you can call me Moose. Everyone else does."

"Okay, Jamie," Mira said with a kind smile. "You guys enjoy the class?"

"Terrific."

"Amazing."

"Can't wait for the next one."

"That's great! I'm so happy to hear. I was thinking maybe I should have done more chanting at the end. But, you know, Mercury's in retrograde right now, so that just changes everything. I was really just trying to stay in tune with the class's aura."

"Absolutely," I said, as earnestly as possible. "I think you, uh, read the aura just right."

"Exactly the right amount of chanting."

Mira's face broke into a wide, wicked smile. "I'm just fucking with you," she said. "Anyone up for a burger? Corner Bistro's not too far from here. I'm starving."

And that's when I knew I was in love.

The Run In

Of the eleven phone calls, seventeen text messages, and 215 e-mails I receive while in the hospital, I look at only one. It is from Moose, and the subject line reads: DUDE, YOU ARE TREND-ING.

The body of the e-mail contains a link, which, after some hesitation, I click. I regret it the minute I do. There I am, ignobly sandwiched between some celebrity's baby and a Brazilian stripper who claims to have slept with a senator. It's a terrible photo of me, a profile shot gleaned from the Hardwick website in which I'm sporting a hideous salmon-colored tie and an unusually aggressive cowlick. Beneath my smiling face is the nauseating headline: "ALL MY CLIENTS ARE GUILTY"—WALL STREET LAWYER'S LAMENT GOES VIRAL.

I skim the article just enough to learn that the video originally appeared on abovethelaw.com, a gossipy news site devoted to the legal community. Given that Todd's on-again, off-again fling, Marissa, works for the site, it doesn't take a genius to figure out how it got leaked. From there it was picked up by several blogs, then Page Six, and eventually an actual journalist at the *Wall Street Journal* by the name of Antonia Yates, who has made a career of exposing financiers for the unethical, morally bankrupt criminals that they are. She's left me three voicemails, none of which I intend to return.

After some heavy cajoling, Dr. Fabio released me with a script for Xanax and a strong reminder that I ought to see Dr. Harris, the grief therapist, as soon as possible. My guess is that I'm going to need something stronger than Xanax, but it's a start. Zadie and I leave the hospital and head directly to Duane Reade. I'm reading the label on an herbal mood stabilizer when I hear:

"Ohmygod—*Charlie*?"

I freeze in place. It's been years since I've heard that gravelly, slightly menacing voice, but it still makes my blood run cold. Slowly, I place the mood stabilizer back on the shelf and turn around.

"Hi, Alison," I say, doing my best to smile. *Of all the Duane Reades in the world,* I think.

"Ohmygod, Charlie, this is *crazy*," Alison announces. With velociraptor-like speed, she pounces on me. For a woman who weighs a hundred pounds soaking wet, she's got a freakishly strong grip.

"I was literally just thinking about you," she breathes into my ear. "I mean, are you okay? You're, like, all over the press."

I manage to wriggle out of Alison's embrace just as Zadie rounds the corner.

"Charlie, the Xanax will be ready in fifteen min—Oh, hi." Zadie gives me the exact same mortified look that she gave me in eleventh grade when she walked in on me with my hand up Faith Patterson's shirt.

"Hi," Alison says, her face hardening. She sticks out her hand so fast that for a moment I think she's going to knife one of us. "You must be . . ." She trails off, waiting for Zadie to fill in the blank.

"Zadie. Charlie's sister."

Alison brightens substantially. "Oh! That's great. I'm Charlie's ex. You know, the one that got away." She flashes a saccharine smile.

"It's nice to meet you," Zadie says sweetly. I can see the gears in her head turning as she gives Alison the once-over. Alison's typical daytime uniform of head-to-toe Lululemon spandex highlights her emaciated body. Her skin glows from a recent spray tan, and from one arm hangs an alligator skin purse and a cluster of shopping bags from Bergdorf Goodman. There's a reason I never bothered to introduce Alison to Zadie when we were together. Alison's a lot of things, but substantive isn't one of them.

"Sorry, I look like such a mess," Alison giggles, knowing, of course, that she doesn't. She runs a hand through her perfectly smooth, highlighted hair. "Jerry and I are leaving for the Hamptons tonight and I've been like a total crazy person getting everything together."

She widens her eyes in sudden surprise. "Ohmygod, Charlie, did I not tell you?" she says, as though we're in regular communication.

"Tell me what?"

She extends her left hand. On her ring finger glitters the golf ball–size diamond she always wanted. "Jerry and I got engaged!"

Who's Jerry? I want to say, but resist the urge.

"Congratulations," Zadie says, saving me. "That's wonderful news."

"We're getting married at his place in East Hampton in August. It's a little quick, I know, but Jerry's like a hundred years old so we have to get moving!" She laughs shrilly. "No, no, don't tell him I said that. He's like, not even fifty, but I like to tease him. You know what? We should totally get together out east!" She puts her

hand on my forearm. "Charlie, you would *love* Jerry! He's a lawyer, too. Or, like, he used to be before he realized that all the money's in finance. He works in private equity now. Have you found
a new job? You should totally talk to him! He *loves* mentoring
people. You go out to the Hamptons in the summer, right? What
am I saying—everyone goes out to the Hamptons in the summer."

Before I can respond, Alison's Swarovski crystal-encrusted
phone begins to buzz. "Sorry, you guys, this is my driver. I've been
wandering around here for, like, an hour. It's one of those days
where I can't find anything, you know? He must be, like, '*Hello,
Earth to Alison, where are you?*'"

She leans in for a double air kiss. "It was so good to see you,
Charlie. Keep me posted. I'll be thinking about you."

She gives Zadie a condescending smile. "It was nice to meet
you, Sadie," she says, and flounces off to meet her chauffeur.

"Wow. She really does look like a mess. She obviously doesn't
spend nearly enough time focused on her appearance." Zadie can
barely control her smile.

"Please, let's just not talk about it."

"Why haven't I met her before? Mom would have *loved* that
girl. She's just like all those adorable cheerleaders you liked in high
school."

I groan. Mom, who always had an opinion on everything, was
particularly vocal when it came to my taste in women. While Zadie
could drag home every punk wannabe drummer in town without
comment, I was openly mocked for dating uptight, prissy girls
like Lindsey Calhoun and Faith Patterson. If I brought a girl over,
Mom and Zadie were always perfectly friendly to her face. But the
moment she was out the door, they would gleefully commence
analyzing and imitating the way the girl tossed her hair, chewed
her gum, picked at her food, overused the word "like." I think the

reason it irked me so much was because, somewhere deep down inside, I knew they were right.

Predictably, Mom and Zadie both loved Mira and told me so the first time they met her. But then, everyone always loved Mira. With her warmth and kindness and wit, her boundless creativity and breathtaking generosity of spirit, Mira was nothing if not easy to love.

Three days before Mom passed away, I drove out to her house to see her. Mira and Caleb, both suffering from strep throat, stayed behind. It was a Tuesday afternoon, and there was hardly any traffic on the Long Island Expressway. Though I had allotted an hour for the drive, it took me only thirty-five minutes. I winced when I noticed that: it took less time to drive there than it did to take a cab down to SoHo. Why hadn't I come more often?

The moment Zadie opened the door, I knew it would be the last time I saw Mom. All the lights in the house were off. Zadie's eyes were dull with pain. She led me wordlessly up the stairs to Mom's bedroom. Each step creaked beneath my weight, as though the house itself had grown old overnight. When I heard a voice behind the door, my heart leapt a little: Zadie had told me that Mom was getting too weak to speak. But when I pushed it open, I saw that it was Veronica, Mom's nurse, reading aloud to her. Mom's body was covered by a thick duvet. She was always cold now because she had lost so much weight. Her eyes were shut and her lips were parted, as though it took too much effort to close them.

Veronica stopped reading when she saw me. "Your son is here," she told Mom quietly, then patted her hand and left.

"Hi, Mom," I said, taking a seat in Veronica's chair. She didn't respond. I glanced up at Zadie, unsure of what to do. She nodded her chin towards Mom. "She can hear you," she said.

"Mom, I'm sorry I haven't been here more often. Work . . . well, it's not an excuse. Zadie's been keeping me up to date. And I know Mira's been out to visit, too. Mira really wanted to come today. She and Caleb have strep throat. The doctor said they shouldn't come because of your immune system and everything. But they're thinking of you."

Mom's eyes flickered open then. It startled me, because I thought she was asleep. When she spoke, her voice was raspy, as though she hadn't had a drink in a very long time. I leaned in to listen, my knees brushing up against the edge of the bed.

"I never liked any of the girls you brought home," she said. "They had no joie de vivre. You had such terrible taste in women." Her eyes shut again. I reached out and took her hand, willing her to wake up. I refused to accept "You had such terrible taste in women" as my mother's dying words.

After a second, her eyes reopened and she continued to speak as though she hadn't stopped. "And then you brought Mira home, and I thought, 'Well, she'll never agree to marry him, but at least maybe there's hope.'"

I laughed. Mom made a slight coughing sound, as though she was trying to laugh with me but couldn't quite manage it.

"I don't know how you pulled it off, but that girl's terrific. Caleb, too."

"Well, he's just like his mom," I said, tears beginning to well up in my eyes. "And his grandma."

Mom shook her head. "Charlie," she said, after clearing her throat, "he's just like *you*. Full of heart. Smart as hell. Don't let anyone break his spirit, you hear?"

"I won't, Mom, I promise," I said. I squeezed her hand, but she didn't respond. Her eyes had closed again and she was gone, lost between sleep and consciousness.

When we walk into the kitchen, Caleb hardly looks up from his Magna-Tiles, which he is industriously grouping into piles based on color on the floor. My son, I think fondly, may be the only person in the tri-state area who is not laughing at me behind my back.

"*Daddy's home!*" Our neighbor and occasional babysitter Monica hurls herself in my direction when we enter the kitchen. Monica is a thirty-six-year-old single nursery school teacher with a biological clock so loud I can practically hear it ticking from across the hall. When she is not busy connecting with potential soul mates online, Monica is more than happy to watch Caleb, a perk of our building that ensures we will never move. Zadie likes Monica because she's basically always available and is trained in child CPR. I am mildly creeped out by her hugs, which in my opinion happen far too frequently and last for about six seconds longer than necessary, and the fact that she insists on bringing her cat, a fluffy Persian named Princess who Norman despises. I am, however, willing to overlook these issues in the name of readily available child care.

"Ugh, Charlie, I'm so glad you're okay," Monica says after releasing me from her vise grip. She holds my hands and looks me up and down the way my grandmother used to on her biannual visits from Florida. "When Zadie called, I was about to go to the gym, but I dropped everything and came right over. I was so worried about you."

"Thanks, Monica, I really appreciate it. I'm honestly fine. Bruised ego, maybe, but that's about it."

Monica glances back over her shoulder at Caleb, to make sure he isn't listening. "But how's your H-E-A-R-T?" she says in a low voice, her eyes wide. "Stress is no joke, Charlie. It's a silent K-I-L-L-E-R. That's why I won't date lawyers anymore, you know. Remember Tyler? He seemed great at first, but the guy was so stressed-out all the time. Clients used to call him at all hours of the night, and he popped Xanax like candy, and I think he had to take Lipitor, too, even though he was, like, thirty-two. It was just too much bad energy, you know?"

"What kind of candy is Xanax?" Caleb pipes up from the floor.

"Honestly, I'm totally fine," I assure her. "It was just a false alarm. Sorry to have scared you."

"You're the best, Monica," Zadie says, sounding tired. "Thank you so much for stepping in." She shoots me a look that means, *Pay her, please, so that she'll leave.*

"Oh, right." I pull my wallet out of my back pocket. "How much do I owe you?"

Monica shakes her head, looking horrified. "Oh my God, nothing! I couldn't possibly take your money right now. You and Caleb are like family. It was my pleasure, honestly."

I look to Zadie, not entirely sure what to do. She gives a small, imperceptible shake of her head.

"No, no," I say, "I can't allow that." I shove an overly large handful of cash in her direction. "Please take this."

Monica steps back as though I'm offering her crack cocaine. "Charlie, no way. I mean"—she lowers her voice as if Caleb can't hear her if she's whispering—"I can't possibly take money from someone who's just been F-I-R-E-D."

Before I can respond, Monica skips over to Caleb, crouches down beside him, and plants a kiss on the top of his head. She scoops up Princess with one hand, gracefully ignoring the cat's hostile hissing.

"Bye-bye, buddy," she says. "Thanks for hanging out with me today."

"Bye, Monica." He holds up a piece of paper covered in marker scrawl. "I made this. You can have it if you want."

"Oh, that's so sweet, buddy. You know what? Why don't you give it to your daddy? I think he could really use a gift right now." She straightens up. "Call me if you need *anything*," she says to me, letting the implication of this offer sink in. "Anything at all, okay? Princess and I are here for you, Charlie." She puts her hand over her heart. "You're in our prayers."

Once we hear the front door close, Zadie lets out a long sigh. "Well, one thing's for sure," she says. "The women of New York are rallying behind you."

"Swell," I say, before heading to the fridge to get myself a beer.

The Dud

Caleb has reflux. Mira and I learned this when, at three months old, he morphed from a peaceful newborn into Rosemary's baby, seemingly overnight. He screamed literally every second he was awake and occasionally even when he was asleep. Nothing soothed him. He hated pacifiers. Detested the swing. He screamed even louder in the stroller, and so we gave up on taking him for walks altogether for fear some passerby would call Child Protective Services on us. Most of all, he hated eating. Breast milk or formula, bottle or boob—Caleb didn't want any part of it. If anything, eating seemed to make things worse. Several times a day, Mira had to grit her teeth and attempt to feed our little hellion, an endeavor that typically ended with everyone covered in tears and breast milk.

Mira put on a brave face, but I could tell she took the whole thing personally. She changed her diet. She stopped eating soy and spices, then dairy and broccoli. She eliminated suspect foods one by one until there was nothing left but a monastic menu of chicken and rice. When that didn't work, she started buying products I didn't know existed: nipple shields and slow-flow bottles and special nursing pillows. She read books on breastfeeding and colic. She even hired a lactation consultant, an impossibly peppy woman named Bonnie who, for two hundred dollars, came to our apartment, felt Mira up, and proclaimed what I already knew: Mira had fabulous breasts, a healthy milk supply, and the problem couldn't possibly lie with her.

The problem, clearly, was Caleb. Short of buying earplugs and making the occasional joke about being "past our rescission period," I didn't know what more I could do.

"At what point," I said to Mira one night, after a several hour scream-a-thon, "do we just admit that we got a dud?"

I began to resign myself to the fact that I just might not be a baby person. Maybe Caleb and I would bond once he could toss around a football, I reasoned. It's not like we had a lot of common interests. He couldn't move. He didn't smile. It was just cry, sleep, poop, repeat. No one tells you this when you have a baby, but for the first three months they're about as dynamic as sea monkeys. Some nights I would stand over Caleb's crib, watching him sleep and waiting. I didn't know what I was waiting for exactly, but I had the distinct sense that I should be feeling something deeper for my own child than I currently was. It wasn't that I didn't love him; I did. But it was an academic sort of love, detached and distant. Sometimes when he cried, all I felt was irritation.

Mira was the opposite. She was a wellspring of love for Caleb. His pain was her pain, she said. When he was sad, she felt it in her gut. Even when he screamed like a banshee, her face radiated warmth and tenderness when she looked at him. She professed to miss him during the night, so she took to sleeping on the pull-out couch in his nursery. She carried him with her everywhere in a sling and gamely encouraged him to suckle her breast on the Lexington Avenue bus or while in line at Starbucks. He was a part of her, she said. The best part. She once told me she felt as though her heart had sprouted legs and was running around outside her body.

Their connection was obvious. The only time Caleb was ever at peace was in Mira's arms. If I picked him up when he was crying, it only made things worse. If I tried to soothe him in the middle of the night, his face would twist in rage. Eventually, Mira would shuffle into the nursery and take him from me and the crying would stop. I would return to our bedroom alone and the two of them would fall asleep in the rocker where she nursed him, their bodies braided together.

They looked alike, too. Fair-haired and blue-eyed, Caleb was every bit Mira's kid. In family photos I loomed behind them, a swarthy interloper casting a dark shadow over mother and son. In a video taken in the hospital, I hold him stiffly, as though he were an incendiary device that might ignite at any second. I thought fatherhood would come naturally to me. I was wrong. In the beginning, Caleb felt like an acquired taste. Not unlike cigars. Something I could see myself getting into down the road but that currently made me nauseous in large quantities.

As for his reflux, Mira refused to give up hope. In fact, the sicker Caleb seemed, the more she doted on him. "Something's wrong," she kept saying over and over. "It's not *him*. He's trying to tell us something. I just have to figure out what it is."

Our pediatrician, a lovable, slightly doddering, older gentleman by the name of Dr. Bone, wasn't hugely helpful. "It might be reflux," he said, stroking his white beard. "But he never vomits after eating?"

We looked at one another. "No," we said, mildly disappointed. "Never."

"Then it's probably colic."

"So, how do we treat colic?" Mira asked hopefully.

"You don't. You just have to ride it out."

"I'm taking him to a specialist," Mira said, once we were out of the doctor's door. "There has to be something we can do."

A specialist in what? Screaming babies? I thought, but kept my mouth shut. I had my doubts. I was sticking to the dud theory.

A week later Mira returned home from Weill Cornell Medical Center triumphantly waving a prescription for Zantac over her head. Her days of hitting re-dial had apparently paid off; somehow she had finagled an appointment with some famous pediatric gastroenterologist who made getting an eight o'clock reservation at Per Se look easy.

"He has reflux!" she crowed gleefully, as though Caleb had just been declared the world's most brilliant baby. "I'm so proud of him! You should have seen him, Charlie. He was so good during the exam. And the doctor said that with medication we can control his symptoms completely." I had my doubts but was willing to try anything. So what if my three-month-old took the same medication as my grandpa?

Sure enough, within days of starting on Zantac, Caleb's screaming and squirming abated. He began to eat a little. He even smiled. I had always loved the little monster, but I actually started to like him.

Once medicated, Caleb rebounded quickly. I, however, did not. I was thrilled that he was no longer crying all the time, but the experience left me feeling strangely hollow. Why hadn't I seen what Mira had seen: that Caleb was simply uncomfortable and needed help? Why had I been so quick to write him off as a difficult kid? I'd lie awake thinking about this, worrying about how and when my lack of paternal instinct would next fail me.

"Are you okay?" Mira asked me during a particularly pleasant afternoon walk in Central Park.

"He seems so happy." I stared down at Caleb, who was peacefully ensconced in his stroller. "He almost never cries anymore."

"Isn't that a good thing?"

"Of course. I just . . . I don't know. It's stupid."

"What's stupid?"

"I feel guilty. I sort of hated him when he was crying all the time."

Mira nodded. She understood, at least theoretically.

"It was tough," she said, "but we're through it now."

"But only because of you. You knew there was something wrong. I just thought he was high-strung. Fuck. I'm a horrible father, aren't I?"

"Charlie, you can't beat yourself up. Dr. Bone didn't even know what the problem was."

"Dr. Bone is a hundred and seventy-five years old."

Mira laughed. "Well, so maybe we need a different pediatrician. Look, we're new at this parenting thing. We're going to make mistakes."

"If it weren't for you, he'd still be screaming. If I was on my own with him, we'd never make it."

Mira sighed. "That's not true. But regardless, that's never going to happen."

"Promise?"

"I promise."

"You'll never leave me? I can't do this without you."

"Never, Charlie. We're in this thing together, you and me."

Persona Non Grata

I wake up thinking about revenge.

I want Todd fired. No, I want more than that. I want him publicly humiliated and then fired, just like I was. He more than deserves it. What he did was so unethical, so below the belt, that my heart starts racing again just thinking about it. Welles wants to lecture *me* on clarity of thought, professionalism, and discretion? The guy who spent ten years toiling away in a windowless conference room while Todd was teeing off on the fourth hole at the Maidstone Club? What I did was stupid, yes. But what Todd did was foolish, immature, profoundly damaging, and potentially illegal. Where is the justice?

In the sobering light of morning, my mandate seems clear. I cannot waste time wallowing in my misery. I don't need to sit in some psychiatrist's chair bemoaning the inequities of my situation. What I need is to get my job back, and fast. And the best and most effective way to do that is to get Fred, Welles, and Steve to see who the real enemy is here: Todd Ellison.

"Well, *hello*," Zadie says when I stride into the kitchen. She looks me up and down, assessing my newly shaven face, my suit and tie, my neatly gelled hair. "You look nice."

"Thanks."

"You going somewhere?"

"I'm going to the office."

"Huh," she says. She begins to crack eggs into a bowl. "You really think that's a good idea?"

"Yes, as a matter of fact, I do."

She shrugs, her shoulders tense. "Okay," she says simply, and begins to beat the eggs with a whisk.

"What do you suggest I do?" I say, annoyed. "Just slink away without a fight? Start collecting unemployment checks and watch *Wheel of Fortune* all day?"

Though her back is to me, I can feel her rolling her eyes.

"No need to get dramatic."

"This *is* dramatic, Zadie! I lost my job, for Chrissake!"

She turns and glares at me. "First of all," she says, pointing at me with the whisk, "Caleb is asleep, so please keep your voice down. He was up and down all night last night and he needs his rest. Second, yelling at me is not going to fix anything. None of this is my fault, and you know it."

"Fine," I say, gritting my teeth. "I'm sorry."

"I understand why you're upset, Charlie. Of course I do. But I really don't think storming your office is a good idea. For starters, it's a Saturday. Why don't you take the weekend off and just try to relax? Spend time with Caleb. Enjoy the fact that your BlackBerry won't be going off every forty-five seconds. And then, when you're in a better head space, you can come up with an actual plan."

I open my mouth to argue but I can't. As of right now, I have no plan other than to show up at Fred's office and demand he hears me out.

"Anyway, the doctor said very specifically that you need to rest.

He said it was *essential*. Why don't you come to the zoo with Caleb and me? It'll be fun. He'd love to spend some time with you."

I sigh. "What time are you going to the zoo?"

"It opens at ten."

I look at my watch. It is nearly eight a.m., right around the time that Fred typically shows up at the office, even on Saturdays. "Okay," I say, "I'm in."

"Really?" Zadie's face lights up. "That's awesome, Charlie."

"But I'm going to go to the office quickly first. I just want to talk to Fred. Otherwise I'll just be thinking about it all day."

Zadie turns back to the kitchen counter. "Okay," she says, her voice flat.

"I'll be back by ten, I promise. Eleven for sure. Okay? Don't leave without me."

"Whatever you say, Charlie," Zadie replies, in a tone that implies that she's already written me off as a no-show.

Because it's Saturday, the lobby of 392 Park Avenue is relatively empty. I lower my head and walk towards the turnstiles, hoping not to run into anyone I know. I swipe my ID card swiftly through the reader but nothing happens. A second time—still nothing. I'm beginning to draw stares. A small line accumulates behind me. It's not until my third try that I realize what's happened: they've already invalidated my ID.

Humiliated, I slink off towards the visitors' reception desk. Terrence, the friendliest of the building's security guards, sits behind it reading the paper. I let out a small sigh of relief when I see him. Unlike some of the other guards, Terrence never hassles anyone for forgetting or misplacing their ID. If anyone is going to let me upstairs without one, it's him.

"Hey, man," he says when he sees me. He stands up and offers me a fist bump. "How you feeling?"

I shrug, embarrassed by his candor. You'd think he'd at least pretend not to know what happened yesterday.

"I'm okay. Thanks for asking, Terrence."

"Juan said you got hauled outta here on a stretcher, man. That don't sound okay to me."

"It wasn't my finest hour."

"Well, I hope you got some rest." Terrence glances nervously at his computer. "You got a meeting or something?"

"Nah. I just wanted to pick up some things from my office." I feel my cheeks turn pink as I say this; I've never been much of a liar. But something tells me he's not going to let me upstairs to see Fred without Fred's explicit permission. "Could you swipe me in?"

Terrence lets out a sigh. "I wish I could, man. But you know they've gotten real strict about that, so . . ."

"I hear you," I say, and offer him a tight smile. "It's okay."

"I can call upstairs and see if someone will sign you in as a visitor."

For a moment I consider just walking away. Who would I call? Suzanne at the Hardwick front desk? She acts put out if you ask to borrow her pencil; there's no way she'd do me this kind of favor. I could call Moose, but he usually works from home on Saturdays. The thought of being turned away by Fred is too mortifying to contemplate.

I am persona non grata at my own firm. This is beginning to sink in. Not only have I been fired, but I've been stripped of small dignities: packing up my own office, for example, or sending a parting e-mail from my firm account. Yesterday, after I was carried out by paramedics, someone went to the trouble of disabling my

ID card. Like I was some kind of disgruntled worker who might just show up with an AK-47 and start shooting.

"I can call Lorraine," Terrence suggests. "She came in about an hour ago."

"Lorraine!" I exclaim, feeling a surge of hope. "Yes, call Lorraine. She'll sign me in."

"You got it, man," Terrence says, looking relieved. He turns away from me as he dials her extension. After some animated whispering, he hangs up the phone. "She's coming down," he says.

"She's coming down?" My eyebrows shoot up. "I'm not allowed upstairs?"

Terrence shrugs. "I don't know, man. All I know is, she's coming down."

The elevator doors part and Lorraine darts across the lobby. She glances right and then left as though she's deep into enemy territory.

"Charlie!" she exclaims, and throws her arms around me. "What are you doing here?"

"I came to see Fred. I have to talk to him, Lorraine. It can't wait."

Lorraine smiles sadly at me. "You can't go up there, Charlie. I wish I could help, but I don't want to get in trouble."

"I don't want to get you in trouble, either. But if I could just talk to him face to face, I know I can straighten this whole thing out."

Lorraine shakes her head. "Trust me, now's not the time. He's with Steve and Welles. They're meeting with some crisis management person about how to handle all the negative press. I was just in there. Everyone seemed really tense. Fred's doing that thing where he tugs at his eyebrow."

I wince, picturing the scene.

"Really, you should go before someone sees you. I think it'll just make things worse."

"Will you at least tell Fred I stopped by?"

"Charlie, I—"

"Or just tell him I called. Could you do that? He has to give me another chance, Lorraine. He just has to."

Lorraine pauses just a half second before saying, "Sure, Charlie. I'll do that."

"Thank you. I need all the help I can get right now."

Lorraine looks like she might start crying. "Charlie, we're all rooting for you upstairs. No one wants to see you go. You're one of the good ones. Everyone thinks so."

"Thanks, Lorraine. That means a lot."

"I truly believe this is going to straighten itself out," she says with a firm nod. "Just have faith. Don't give up."

"I won't."

We hug again. She squeezes me extra-hard before releasing me, and when she pulls back, I notice tears in her eyes.

"Hey, Lorraine?" I call out just as she's turning away. "Any idea what's going to happen to Todd?"

"To Todd?" she asks, perplexed.

"Well, yeah. Since he was the one who leaked the video of me online."

Her eyes widen. "Really? You're sure?"

"Pretty sure. Yes. One hundred percent sure."

"Can you prove it?"

"I—" I pause. Rage wells up inside me. Todd hasn't been so much as slapped on the wrist, and here I am, standing in the lobby with a defunct ID card in my hand. "I'm sure I could find proof. It was definitely him," I say, feeling desperate.

"You gotta do that, Charlie," Lorraine says excitedly. "If Fred and Welles and Steve have someone else to blame for this mess, maybe they'll let you off the hook."

"You're right. That's what I need to do. I need to prove my case."

"And in the meantime I'll tell Fred to call you."

"Thanks, Lorraine. You're the best."

"You're not alone, Charlie. We're all behind you."

Lorraine throws me a final wave and disappears back into the elevator. For a minute I stand in the lobby wishing there was something more I could do. Then the other elevator doors open and out walks Martin Hamlisch. When our eyes connect, his face turns white as a sheet. Before I can say anything, he offers me a short, embarrassed nod and then turns his attention to his Black-Berry. Our shoulders nearly touch as he walks straight past me without so much as a word.

Pinnipeds

Zadie and Caleb are standing on the sidewalk in front of our building, hailing a cab. I spot him from down the block; he's wearing his hot pink Dora backpack and leggings to match. Sunglasses are pushed up on his head. He's gesticulating enthusiastically as he talks. Zadie throws her head back and laughs as a cab pulls up alongside them.

"Hey!" I call out. "Wait up, you guys!"

Caleb spins around, his sunglasses falling down onto his nose. When he sees me jogging towards them, his face lights up.

"He's here!" he shouts to Zadie, so loudly that I can hear him from fifty yards away. "See, I told you he'd come!"

Zadie looks both pleased to see me and annoyed at me for impeding their progress.

"You getting in or what?" the cabby snaps from the front seat. "Meter's running."

"If the meter's running, you've got nothing to worry about," Zadie replies. To me she says, "Hurry up, Charlie. We don't have all day."

"Yeah, they feed the sea lions at eleven thirty," Caleb announces. "But there's always a crowd around the tank so you have to get there ahead of time if you want to get a good spot."

"Well, we obviously can't miss that," I say, slamming the cab door closed behind us. "Central Park Zoo, please, sir. We're in a bit of a rush."

Once inside the zoo, Caleb jets ahead of us, securing his position at the edge of the sea lion tank. I notice a gaggle of older boys—eight or nine years old, I'd guess—standing off to the side. One nods his head at Caleb's outfit, and the rest burst out laughing. Caleb either doesn't notice that he's being made fun of or he doesn't care; his eyes stay laser focused on the sea lions.

"Do you see that?" I nudge Zadie. I can feel my heart thumping angrily inside my chest. "They're laughing at him."

Zadie shades her eyes. She looks at Caleb, then at the boys, then back at Caleb.

"He doesn't see them," she says, her voice quiet. "It's okay."

"Yeah, but *I* see them. I should go say something."

Zadie puts her hand on my forearm. "No, Charlie," she says, holding me back. "Don't. It'll just make it worse."

"Caleb needs to know I've got his back."

"There are other ways of showing him that."

Caleb turns and waves at us. "Come on, you guys! They're about to start!"

Zadie smiles wide. "We're coming!" she calls back, then skips through the gathering crowd until she's by his side. Without warning, she grabs him beneath the arms and hoists him up as high as she can, so that he's eye level with the sea lions. He shrieks with delight when one swims by, spraying them both with water.

I hang back for a minute and watch them together. They chatter back and forth like old friends. It occurs to me that Zadie genuinely enjoys Caleb's company. She's not just listening to him for the sake of it; she's actually interested in hearing what he has to say.

"Whatcha guys talking about?" I ask as I slip in behind them.

"Pinnipeds!" Caleb shrieks.

"Naturally," I say, raising an eyebrow at Zadie. "I was just thinking about pinnipeds myself."

"Really?" Caleb frowns, scanning my face. "Were you really?"

"I was thinking that pinnipeds are absolutely delicious and that maybe I should order us some for dinner."

"No! You don't even know what they are!" Caleb dissolves into a fit of giggles.

"You got me. I don't know what a pinniped is."

"Sea lions are pinnipeds," Caleb says earnestly. "It means a fin-footed marine nanimal."

"Mammal," Zadie corrects.

"Nammal. It says so over there," Caleb says, pointing to a large sign affixed to the sea lion tank.

"I learn a new thing every day."

"I know about a lot of stuff," Caleb says with a shrug.

"I bet you do, bud," I say. I attempt to ruffle his hair but he pulls away, adjusting his sunglasses instead. "I gotta hang out with you more often."

"Yup," he replies with a nod. "Then you'd know more about pinnipeds."

"How was your meeting?" Zadie asks me. We're sitting at the dining room table, relaxing after putting Caleb to sleep. "What did Fred have to say for himself?"

"Nothing. At least, not to me. He was in a meeting, so we didn't get a chance to speak."

"Ah."

"I saw Lorraine, though. She said everyone was rooting for me, which was nice."

"I always liked Lorraine."

"She had a good idea, actually. She said what I need is proof. That way I can show Fred that it's Todd who's the problem, not me."

"What?" Zadie squints at me. "Proof? What are you talking about?"

"Proof that it was Todd who leaked the video of me to that website, Above the Law. I think I can get it, too. Remember Alison, the girl we ran into yesterday? She went to college with Marissa. Marissa is Todd's on-again, off-again girlfriend. And Marissa works at Above the Law. If I can just get Alison to get Marissa to tell me if it was Todd who told her about the video, I'll have proof positive that he orchestrated this whole thing to get me fired."

"I literally have no idea what you're talking about."

"Forget it."

"Okay," Zadie says, staring at me quizzically. "You're acting a little crazy. You know that, right? I don't think revenge is what you should be focusing on right now."

"I'm focused on getting my job back. Anyway, I just spent the whole afternoon at the zoo with you and Caleb."

"That was fun, wasn't it? Caleb was so happy you made it. And see? You learned all about pinnipeds."

"I was happy to get some time with him."

"Well, on that note . . ." Zadie pauses, biting her lip.

"What?"

"I was wondering if you wouldn't mind if I took a few days off. Buck and I were thinking of going out to the Hamptons. Ordinarily, I wouldn't ask for something like this, but since you aren't working right now . . ."

"It's only temporary."

"I know, Charlie. I'm literally just asking for a few days. A week at most. I also thought it would give you some time with Caleb."

Zadie stares at me expectantly. Her arms are crossed tightly against her chest. I can tell she thinks I'm going to say no. And I want to say no; of course I want to say no. How am I going to go about getting my job back if I've got to watch Caleb, too? Not to mention the fact that I've never spent more than an afternoon taking care of Caleb by myself. I'm not sure I'd know where to start.

But of course I can't possibly say no. Zadie's never taken a vacation. Hell, she's never even taken a sick day. She watches Caleb on nights and weekends when I'm at the office or on the road or simply too tired to put up with him. She's raising him herself, with far too little help from me. She deserves to take a few days away with her boyfriend.

"Of course," I say with a sigh.

"Really? You're sure?"

"Of course I'm sure."

"You guys will be okay? I can show you everything. How he likes his eggs in the morning and this special hummus that I make for him from scratch . . ."

"Whoa, there, sister. Let's not get crazy here. We can do takeout for a few days."

Zadie leans back in her chair. For the first time in weeks she looks visibly relieved. "I'm so glad this is okay with you. I know the timing is tough, but Buck said, 'When else is Charlie going to have the time to watch him?' So—"

I wave her off. "Don't say another word. Done deal."

"You're the best, Charlie."

"I try." I stand up and stretch. "It's late. I'm going to try to call Alison before I go to bed."

Zadie raises her eyebrows. "Ohmygod, really?" she says, in a nearly pitch-perfect impression of Alison.

I shoot her a look.

Zadie lets out a giggle. "You *totally* should call Jerry, Charlie. He loves to mentor young people. Maybe you guys can get together *out east.*"

"I'm leaving now."

"Tell Alison 'Sadie' says hello!"

Alison, unsurprisingly, picks up on the first ring.

"Charlie," she coos. "Ohmygod, I was just thinking about you."

"It was nice seeing you yesterday, Alison."

"Loved it. Love you. And Sadie is so adorable."

"She sends her best. Listen, I hope this isn't too presumptuous of me, but I was hoping you might be willing to do me a favor."

"Charlie, for you? Anything."

It takes me a while to explain to Alison what I need her to do.

"So basically you want me to get Marissa to rat out her boyfriend?" she says, annoyed. Clearly, this is not the favor she was anticipating.

"Well, I don't know if Todd is Marissa's boyfriend. I mean, he definitely sees other people . . ."

"So you want me to tell Marissa that her boyfriend is a cheater and then get her to rat him out?"

"Not *rat out* per se. Just, you know, be honest. What he did was really horrible, Alison. I lost my job. I may never be able to work again because of what he did to me."

Alison sighs. "I feel terrible that you got fired. Obviously. You don't deserve that, Charlie. And if Todd is behind it, then he's an even bigger asshole than I thought he was. I just don't want to put Marissa in an uncomfortable position. She's, like, a friend. We were in the same *sorority*. That's supposed to mean something."

I take a deep breath and force myself to count to three. When

we were together, Alison never showed anything resembling loyalty to a female friend; in fact, I was convinced that she maintained
her female friendships solely in order to have people to compare
herself favorably to. It's hard to believe that she genuinely cares
about Marissa's feelings, a girl she once described as "so nice that
sometimes I think she might have had a lobotomy."

"Like, what if she and Todd get married? I would definitely not
be invited to their wedding," Alison continues. I can tell that she's
getting herself worked up, and if I don't try a different tactic, I'll be
on the phone with her until sunrise.

"You know what? You're right. Don't call Marissa. I don't want
to make you uncomfortable. I'll find some other way to prove my
case." I pause for a dramatic effect before adding, "Thank you for
listening, Alison. I really appreciate it."

"Wait, Charlie! Don't go."

"It's late. I've bothered you enough already."

"No!" Alison squeaks. "It's no bother. Look, I'll talk to Marissa.
I'll just explain the situation. Maybe if she hears that you, like, *lost
your job* because of that video, she'll feel guilty enough to come
clean. I mean, you're a father, after all. A single father. How could
anyone sleep at night knowing they caused you to lose your job?"

"Thank you, Alison. I can't tell you how much this means to
me."

"I can't promise anything, but I can try to help," Alison says,
and for the first time, maybe ever, I hear genuine sweetness in
her voice. "It's going to work out for you, Charlie. I just know it.
You're too good a guy for it not to."

As I hang up the phone, I feel a shiver of excitement. *I may be
down, Todd,* I think to myself, *but I'm sure as hell not out. Not quite yet.*

Out of Office

"You're going to be okay, right?" Zadie asks me for the eighteenth time this morning. She doesn't wait for a response. "I wrote down everything I can think of there," she says, pointing to a notebook on the kitchen counter. "Dosing for all his medications. Emergency phone numbers. And you can call me anytime, of course. I'll have my cell."

"We're going to be fine," I say as confidently as possible. "I am actually his father."

"I know you are, but—" Zadie bites her lip, like I've gotten her on a technicality.

"I'm happy you and Buck are getting away. It'll be nice for me to spend some time with Caleb. Otherwise I'll just mope around the house."

"Make sure he eats a good lunch. Dr. Frank is a little concerned about his weight."

"I'll make sure he has a good lunch."

"And not too much TV."

"Understood."

"And just be easy on him about the clothes. Let him wear what he wants."

"Zadie, please. Stop."

She raises her palms in the air. "Okay, okay," she says. "You're right. I'm micromanaging. Sorry."

"God, if Mom could see us now."

"I know." Zadie shakes her head and chuckles. "Cohabitating at thirty-five."

"Both unemployed."

"Eh." Zadie shrugs. "Mom wouldn't be surprised to see me unemployed."

"Both unmarried."

"Mom was thrilled that you convinced Mira to marry you somehow. She figured you'd be a bachelor forever."

"She loved Mira."

"Mira was one of us."

"It's true," I say, nodding. By "us" I know she means Mom and her, not Mom and her and me.

"Probably the only three women in the world who could put up with you."

"Probably."

We both laugh.

"At least you and I are getting along. That has to count for something."

"And raising the best kid in the world."

"I wish she could see Caleb."

"I know. God, Mom loved that kid. You know how she was. Always telling us to be true to ourselves and not give a shit what other people think. I think about her every time Caleb and I go shopping. She would have had so much fun with him, just picking out the craziest outfits together and shocking the hell out of all those stuck-up Upper East Side mommies at Caleb's school. She would have rolled into that place in a purple feather boa and leather pants and Caleb would be rocking out a princess dress and everyone would be staring at them and she would've been all, like, 'What? We've arrived, bitches.'"

"That sounds like Mom."

Zadie lets out a loud sniff. "I miss her so goddamn much, Charlie."

"I know, Z. Me too." I put a hand on her shoulder and give it a comforting squeeze.

"All right," I say after a second, clapping my hands together. There's only so much sentimentality I can handle at seven in the morning. "You packed? When's Buck picking you up?"

"I'm all set. He should be here soon. We wanted to beat the Hamptons weekend traffic."

"Fancy."

"You know me."

Caleb rounds the corner, dragging Zadie's rolling suitcase behind him. "Aunt Zadie, where are you going?"

"Going to the beach, bud. With Uncle Buck."

Caleb makes a face. "But who's going to take me to camp?"

"Your daddy is. Remember?"

Caleb narrows his eyes at us, as though there's more to this story; he just can't figure out what. "Daddy has to go to the office."

Zadie and I exchange a quick glance. "Not today," I say. "I'm going to hang out with you while Aunt Zadie is away."

"But he doesn't let me sleep in his bed," he appeals to Zadie, as though maybe he can get her to change her mind. "That's why I sleep in yours."

Zadie sighs. "Well, maybe he'll make an exception."

"Thanks for that," I mutter under my breath.

"When are you coming home?"

"I'm not sure yet, bud. Soon. I promise, you won't even miss me. You guys are going to have so much fun together."

The buzzer rings, announcing Buck's arrival. Zadie doesn't move.

"I think he's here," I say.

"Yup. Okay. I should go," Zadie says, sounding unconvinced. Caleb attaches himself to her leg like a barnacle. She buries her nose in his mop of hair and makes a snuffling sound.

"Zadie."

After a few seconds Zadie manages to detach herself from Caleb and steer him back in my direction. "I'll call you boys tonight," she says, sounding teary.

"Have fun," I remind her. I pick up her suitcase and usher her out the front door.

She gives me a ferocious hug. "Maybe you and Caleb can come out and visit us this weekend?"

"Maybe. Don't worry about us. Really. You haven't had a vacation in forever."

The elevator doors open.

"Go," I say, pushing her inside.

"I love you guys."

"*We* love *you*. Stop looking so worried! I've got everything totally under control." Never, I think, as the elevator doors slide closed behind her, has a statement been further from the truth.

It takes us exactly two hours to get out of the house. I can't tell you what happened during those two hours; all I can say is that it felt vaguely like a scene out of *Apocalypse Now*. I can, however, tell you what did *not* happen. Caleb categorically refused to eat breakfast until I allowed him to watch an episode of *The Backyardigans*. He screamed like the world was ending when I suggested the possibility that he might have to clothe himself before leaving the house. Have you ever tried to forcibly dress a writhing five-year-old? It's like trying to stuff an angry squirrel into a sock. Eventually we compromised on his *Dora the Explorer* pajama pants, a polo shirt, and fuchsia Crocs. I did not eat breakfast, check e-mail, or imbibe a single sip of the pot of coffee that Zadie thoughtfully brewed for me just before she left. I did not manage to call Fred, as I had planned to do every single morning until he gives me my job back, and I did not respond to the three text messages Alison has sent me, updating me on her attempts to contact Marissa. In short, it was a shit show.

Every time I'm doing something wrong, I run into our elderly neighbor, Mrs. Goodrich. Mrs. Goodrich is a grand old dame. You know just by looking at her that her name can be found in the Social Register. She's the sort of woman who doesn't leave the house without perfectly coiffed hair and a purse that matches her shoes. Occasionally, she slips a handwritten note under our door informing us that the noise level from our apartment is, once again, unacceptable or that our Amazon.com boxes are blocking the back entrance to her apartment. Other than that, we have almost no contact, except, of course, when I'm in the middle of doing something untoward. Mrs. Goodrich was there the day I got the stomach flu and vomited all over the elevator floor. She witnessed the only screaming fight Mira and I ever had. The argument was, of course, about my work schedule: Mira wanted to go to a wedding in Big Sur; I was in the middle of a case and couldn't imagine leaving the office for an evening, much less a full weekend. I was yelling something to that effect when Mrs. Goodrich rounded the corner of Seventy-Third Street and Lexington Avenue. The horrified, condemnatory expression on her face will be forever etched in my memory. Mrs. Goodrich was also present the night I stumbled home drunk from a friend's bachelor party wearing a feather boa and carrying a light saber. There's really nothing that sobers me up faster than a steely "Good morning, Mr. Goldwyn" from a woman who's a dead ringer for Barbara Bush.

So it is inevitable that Mrs. Goodrich is standing in the vestibule, waiting for the elevator, when Caleb and I emerge from our apartment. She is looking especially proper today in a cream-colored suit and hat. As our door clicks closed, she casts a reproachful eye over us, as though we are hobos who have elected to set up camp in her foyer.

"Good morning, Mrs. Goodrich," I say loudly, hoping Caleb will follow suit.

"Do-do-do-do-do-do-Dora!" Caleb shouts, a rough approximation of the *Dora the Explorer* theme song.

"Good morning," Mrs. Goodrich intones.

She takes a quick step back as Caleb makes a swipe for her purse.

"Caleb!" I bark. "Stop it! What are you doing?"

"I want to touch!" Caleb flops back beside me, frustrated.

"That's not polite, Caleb. So sorry," I say, with an awkward laugh. "We're training him to pick pockets. Gotta earn his keep somehow, you know."

Mrs. Goodrich does not know. She presses the elevator call button several times in rapid succession, keeping a close eye on Caleb the way one would a wild-eyed homeless person on a subway platform.

"And where is your sister this morning?" she asks me primly. "Not sick, I hope. I hear there's a nasty stomach bug going around."

"No, no," I say, smiling as pleasantly as I am able. "Nothing like that. She's out in the Hamptons. We're having a superfun Daddy Day today. Right, Caleb?"

"No." Caleb glares at me, still annoyed about the purse.

"Ha ha, well. We're trying our best anyway."

The elevator doors open, sparing Mrs. Goodrich from having to respond.

After some Tetris-like maneuvers with Caleb's scooter, the three of us manage to squeeze uncomfortably into the elevator. Caleb, I notice, is still eyeing Mrs. Goodrich's purse. Mrs. Goodrich notices, too, and tries to move as far away from him as possible. The tension between them is palpable.

Just before we reach the lobby, Mrs. Goodrich turns, looks me straight in the eye and says, "You know, Mr. Goldwyn, I have never been a fan of profanity."

"Mmm-hmm," I murmur, wondering if somehow a curse word unknowingly escaped my lips in the last four minutes. Deciding it's possible, I add, "I'm so sorry."

She shakes her head, rejecting my apology. "I must tell you, I did not approve of the language you used in that speech of yours."

I nod, dumbfounded. You know a video has gone viral when *Mrs. Goodrich* has seen it. I'm frankly surprised to hear she has an Internet connection.

"That being said," she continues, "you addressed the very important issue of balancing a career with family life. My husband, Frank, God rest his soul, was an investment banker with J.P. Morgan. He spent every waking second in his office. In fact, he died in his office. At the time he died, he was a wealthy man. But both of our sons moved to the West Coast right after college. He never called them. He hardly ever saw them. In fact, I imagine if you were to ask them, they would tell you that their father spent far too much time thinking about money and far too little thinking about them. These early years with children are precious, Mr. Goldwyn. Don't waste them."

"Daddy! Door's open!" Caleb screams.

"Thank you, Caleb," I say quickly, before turning back to Mrs. Goodrich.

"He's a special boy," she says, as we exit the elevator together. "Great spirit. And very, very smart."

"He is," I say, thinking about the pinnipeds. My heart swells with pride. "I hope to be more like him when I grow up."

Mrs. Goodrich nods. "You're a good father, Mr. Goldwyn. Your heart is in the right place. Enjoy this time with your son." And with that, Mrs. Goodrich sweeps out of the lobby doors.

Richard, the doorman on duty, offers me a quiet high-five. "Way to go, man," he says. "Mrs. Goodrich's a tough crowd."

"You're telling me," I say. I'm smiling as my feet hit the pavement outside. The sky is a cloudless, brilliant blue. Caleb finally seems calm, humming quietly to himself in a way that is adorable instead of irritating. *It's going to be okay,* I think. *It might even be a good day.*

My good mood dissipates when we arrive at Caleb's preschool, where he is enrolled in summer camp for June and July. If our apartment was *Apocalypse Now*, the drop-off scene is straight out of *Lord of the Flies*. Kids are everywhere. They push past me with the urgency of morning commuters on the 6 train. Their mothers and nannies, too, are frenetic. There's not nearly enough space for all of the strollers and scooters, and only the most aggressive manage to weasel their way into the lobby of the building. Instead of pushing, I decide to hang back until the crowds have thinned a bit. I am, I notice, the only father here.

Caleb cranes his neck around and looks at me. "I'm going to be late," he says, his voice tense. He points to the lobby. "I'm supposed to go in there."

"I know, buddy," I say. "But it's pretty crowded, so let's just hang out for a sec, okay?"

"You're not supposed to be late. Then you miss 'The Welcome Song.'"

I wonder how my laid-back hippie of a sister manages to navigate this crowd every morning without going into cardiac arrest. I can't see her pushing and shoving her way into the lobby like some of these crazy women. Still, I would bet dollars to donuts that, under Zadie's watch, Caleb has never once missed "The Welcome Song."

When we finally make it into the building, no one is behind the registration desk. Two nannies stand beside it, chattering away in Spanish. A clique of moms in yoga pants huddle together in the corner of the lobby, their shoulders pressed together in a way that doesn't exactly invite questions. All the kids have been whisked off, presumably to sing "The Welcome Song," by caretakers more adept than me. I look around for a friendly face, feeling suddenly like a freshman on the first day of high school.

"Caleb," I say, trying to sound casual. "Do you know where to go?"

He looks at me blankly, then shakes his head. It's only his second week of camp, I realize. He probably hasn't totally gotten the hang of things himself.

"Okay, no worries, buddy. I'll figure this out."

The Spanish nannies are leaving, laughing riotously as they go. I take a deep breath and head towards the Mommy Corner.

As if on cue, they all turn and stare at me. A couple of them look suspicious, as though it's possible I'm a pedophile here to prey on their children. Most, though, offer me sugary smiles. I see them assessing the situation: the pajamaed child, the unshaven father. I can practically hear them whispering to one another, "Oh, how *adorable*! What a good husband. Peter doesn't even know the kids are doing a summer camp; there's no way he'd take the time to drop them off himself."

"Hi." I wave awkwardly. Caleb's grip tightens around my other hand. "Could one of you help me? My son, Caleb, here is in the summer camp and we're a little late, and I'm not entirely sure where to go." I smile helplessly at the one who looks the least intimidating.

"Oh, sure," she says, stepping forward. Of all of the women, she's the only one who looks like an actual parent. She's got rings beneath her eyes, and her hair is tied back in a messy, unkempt bun. Like the others, she's wearing stretch pants and a sporty zip-up, but hers are old and overwashed, better suited for doing the dishes or lounging in front of the television than hitting the gym. The other mothers look like the grown-up version of the girls everyone hated in high school. They are thin, tan, and manicured. They all wear versions of the same thing: expensive-looking athletic wear paired with expensive-looking handbags and jewelry. It's a strange look, a kind of studied casualness that leaves men like me scratching their heads.

"Is he in Sports Kids, Gym Kids, or Gym Juniors? Or are you guys doing Me and My Special Grown-up?"

"Excuse me? Me and my what what?"

She smiles again, this time with marked condescension. "Are you staying with him for the class? Or does he do the program by himself?" She speaks slower now, as though English is clearly not my first language.

"Oh, no"—I shake my head—"I'm not staying. At least, I didn't think I was supposed to stay."

"Okay. So he's in one of the sports programs." She bends down and addresses Caleb directly. "Sweetie," she says, "do you remember what room you are in? The Blue Room, the Red Room, or the Green Room?"

"Pink," Caleb says defiantly. "My room's pink."

She frowns, puzzled. "No, sweetie, not at home. Here. There are only three rooms. Blue, Red, and Green."

"*I SAID PINK!*" Caleb shouts, loud enough to stop the other mothers cold in their tracks.

The mom stands up, her smile gone. She gives me a look that I can only interpret to mean: *You are raising a serial killer.*

"I'm sorry," I say. "His room at home isn't even pink."

The other mothers are getting antsy. Two are checking their iPhones. Another is inspecting herself in a small compact mirror. The last one is stretching her quads. My incompetence is the only thing keeping them from working out, and it's getting old fast.

"I would just check with the woman at the desk," the woman says, waving her hand in the direction of Reception. "She'll be able to tell you more."

One of the other mothers, a skinny brunette who looks vaguely familiar, steps forward and gives me a quizzical look. "Are you Charlie Goldwyn?"

For a moment I consider lying, but realize that's probably not the best example to set for Caleb.

"Uh, yep. That's me."

Her eyes flood with recognition. She smirks, but only for a second; she's too well-bred to openly laugh in my face. There's no denying it, though: she's seen the video. I can picture her at a dinner party with her fancy friends, everyone loose and chatty from too much wine, discussing the demise of some idiot named Charlie Goldwyn. "Our kids went to preschool together," I can hear her whispering candidly. "The son is a little odd. He dresses like a girl. Poor boy, being raised without a mother."

"My husband works at Harrison Brothers," she says. "Hunt Callahan?"

I remember Hunt, if only vaguely. I can picture his red, piggish face and shiny bald head and irritating penchant for pocket squares. This woman is an Amazon; Hunt is roughly the size of a hobbit. I wonder momentarily what any woman would see in Hunt before I remember that he's a Managing Director who probably rakes in a couple mil a year. He must look taller when standing on his wallet.

"Yes, Hunt, of course. Send him my regards."

"Mm-hmm," she says, but she's already turned away, sliding her sunglasses onto her nose. "Take care." She has no interest in sending Hunt my regards, I realize. She will mention me only as a funny side note tonight at home. I'm no longer Charlie Goldwyn, Attorney-at-Law. I'm Charlie Goldwyn, the Video Guy.

Caleb, understandably, has begun to cry.

I can't say I blame him. In fact, I'm pretty close to joining him. "Hey, buddy," I say, kneeling down. "Don't worry. We'll get you to the right class."

"I want Aunt Zadie," he whispers.

"I know, buddy," I say, ruffling his hair. "I know."

"I don't want to go to camp today. I want to go home."

I pause, bite my lip. It's hard to admit defeat before noon.

"You know what, buddy?" I say, straightening up. "How about we go to the park? It's a beautiful day. We shouldn't waste it inside."

I put my hand on Caleb's back and usher him towards the door. A few of the moms turn to gawk as we walk past; I do my best to ignore their judgmental stares.

"We can even stop for donut holes on the way there," I add, loud enough so that the moms can hear us. "The more frosting the better. I'm getting pretty hungry."

Caleb's mood brightens substantially. "Fiona likes donut holes. Not the kind with the jelly inside, though. The sugar kind."

"Great. I'm glad Fiona approves."

At least someone does, I think, as we head to the nearest Dunkin' Donuts.

We have the playground mostly to ourselves. Caleb throws himself gleefully into the sandbox, a sad-looking pit of grayish sand, which, I realize a moment too late, is potentially filled with hypodermic needles and dog urine. Two nannies sit on a bench close by, chatting as they sterilize plastic buckets and shovels with antiseptic wipes that they wisely carry in abundance. After reminding Caleb not to eat the sand, I find a quiet spot in the shade. I'm farther away than the nannies, but close enough, I reckon, for me to make a flying tackle if Caleb decides to make a break for it.

I'm drinking my coffee and enjoying the last donut hole when my BlackBerry begins to buzz. A slight shiver runs down my spine when Fred's number pops up on the screen.

I take a deep breath and answer his call.

"This is Charlie Goldwyn," I bark, the way I used to when I was in the middle of something important at work.

"Charlie? It's Fred."

"Hi, Fred," I say, trying not to sound desperately excited to have him on the phone.

"I'm sorry I'm just getting back to you now."

"No problem. I'm sure you've been busy."

"I have, yeah. But I know I owe you a call."

A call? I think furiously. *A call? You owe me a job, you asshole. I worked my tail off for you for ten years. And then I screw up once and you toss me out the door like yesterday's newspaper? You owe me more than a fucking call.*

The nannies are staring at me. I realize that I'm pacing back and forth, a nervous habit. I smile at them in an attempt to assure them that I'm not a lunatic. They return to sterilizing their buckets. I slip off behind an oak tree and lower my voice to a near whisper.

"I stopped by the office on Saturday. I was hoping we might meet in person."

Fred pauses. "Yeah, we can do that. But things are a little hectic on my end right now, so if you could wait a week or two—"

"I can't wait a week or two, Fred," I blurt out, unable to keep my cool any longer. "I need a job."

"I know, Charlie. I'm sorry," he says, and the sincerity in his voice disarms me. "Look, I hope you know that I don't approve of what happened to you at Hardwick. I fought Welles and Steve tooth and nail on that decision, but when it came down to it, we all had a vote and it was two against one. But I'm going to make sure you land on your feet. If you can just be patient and give me a little time to work things out, I promise you, I won't let you down. You just have to trust me."

I let out a long, jittery exhale. *That's the best answer he can give me,* I tell myself, *short of offering me my job back.*

"Thank you, Fred. I really appreciate that."

"I have a plan. I just need a week or so to work out some details. Can you hang in there for me?"

"Yes," I say, feeling my eyes fill with tears of relief. "Yes, I can do that."

"Good. You're a terrific attorney, Charlie. You're the best guy I have. We're going to move past this. You'll see."

"Thank you. I'm so grateful," I say, and let out an embarrassing sniff. I wipe my tears away with a quick brush of the hand. *Thank God for Fred,* I think. He's always had my back, from the minute I stepped foot into Hardwick. And he's got my back still, when I need his support the most.

"Nonsense. No need for gratitude. This is business," he replies, though I can hear emotion welling up in his voice, too. "So, how are you feeling? Lorraine tells me the doctor gave you a clean bill of health."

"Yes," I say, with an embarrassed laugh. "Just a little stressed out, as it turns out."

"Aren't we all," he says, and we laugh together. "I'm glad to hear you're doing okay. And Caleb? Are you getting to spend some time with him?"

"Yep, I'm with him now, actually."

"Oh, that's great. Well, I don't want to keep you. You go enjoy the day with your boy, okay?"

"Okay," I say, smiling. "Fred, thanks again. I just—"

"You don't need to thank me, Charlie. Just doing my job. I'll be in touch." And with that, Fred is gone.

And, I realize with utter horror, so is Caleb.

The Disappearance

The sandbox is empty.

The nannies that were sitting on the bench beside the sandbox just moments ago are gone. I scan the swings and the slides. I peer beneath the benches, behind the water fountain. I begin to call Caleb's name, over and over, louder and louder, panic rising in my throat. There is no response. There is only the rustle of wind in the trees and the far-off honking of the cars on Fifth Avenue. In the distance a baby begins to cry.

The gate to the playground, which bears a sign indicating that it should remain closed at all times, is open. When I see that, my heart drops into my stomach. It's scary enough to lose sight of a five-year-old boy in a fenced-in space; it's another thing altogether to lose him in Central Park. I take off, sprinting towards the gate. I'm just outside the playground when I realize I've left Caleb's scooter by the park bench. *Too late,* I think. Scooters can be replaced. Kids cannot.

I screech to a halt at the gate, unsure of which way to go. To the north is Cedar Hill, where I take Norman for his morning run; it's possible Caleb's headed there. To the south, though, is the boat pond, where Caleb likes to feed the ducks and watch the miniature sailboats glide by. I close my eyes and say a little prayer;

something tells me to pick ducks over puppies. I turn south. *Ducks over puppies,* I keep saying to myself, like a mantra, like a prayer. *Ducks over puppies. Please God, let him have picked ducks over puppies.*

A passing baby, who apparently thinks I'm involved in some kind of high-speed game of hide-and-seek, begins to laugh and clap her hands. "Bbbbbzeeee!" she shouts gleefully from her stroller. The mother frowns as I whiz past. She pulls her phone out and begins to dial. I momentarily envision being arrested for losing my child. I feel bile rising in my throat as my feet slap the pavement.

My head spins when I reach the boat pond; there are children everywhere. A little boy with fuzzy white-blond hair scoots by on a Razor. I reach out before realizing it's not Caleb; his mother glares at me and moves protectively between us. Across the water, two girls scream the *Dora the Explorer* song. There are dogs everywhere, running and sniffing and heading off down countless paths leading away from the pond.

It's hopeless, I think as I shout Caleb's name. *This is it. Now I've actually lost everything.*

The sunlight is almost unbearably bright. The voices around me are growing softer. I think I'm about to pass out, when suddenly the crowd parts and I see him. He's squatting at the edge of the boat pond just thirty feet away, his hand dangling dangerously close to the water.

"Caleb!" I shout. "*Caleb!*"

Caleb looks up from what he's doing. When he sees me, he smiles and waves, as though we're old acquaintances who just happen to be bumping into one another.

"Hi, Daddy!" he sings out, then turns back to the pond. He hasn't got a care in the world.

"Caleb!" I drop to my knees when I reach him, wrap my arms tight around his small torso. "Thank God, thank God you're okay." I rock him back and forth, the way I used to when he was a baby. "Please, don't ever do that again. Don't ever scare me like that again."

He pulls back, his fists pushing into my chest, and examines my face. He reaches up and touches my wet cheek. He looks perplexed. "Why are you crying, Daddy?"

"Because you scared me," I say, my voice hoarse. "You can't just run off like that. I need to be able to see you all the time, okay?"

Caleb's face crumples like a piece of old Kleenex. "I'm sorry," he says, staring at the ground. "Fiona wanted to see the duck babies. I told her to ask but you were on the phone."

I try to hug him again, but he's having none of it. He wriggles out of my arms, his small Croc'd feet kicking me in the shins. I'm still panting from the sprint, and I don't have the energy to fight him.

"Off, Daddy," he says, frowning. "Off."

"Okay, buddy." I raise my hands in surrender. "Off." I stand up, brush off my shins. I swipe my eyes discreetly with my sleeve. I realize I've cried more in the past five days than I have the past five years.

Get it together, Goldwyn, I tell myself, like a coach giving his team a half-time pep talk. *Stop crying. Man up, for Chrissake.*

"How about," I say, with a big phony smile, "we go buy some bread from that hot dog cart and we feed it to the baby ducks?"

"Yeah!" he says, punching my leg for emphasis. "That's *exactly* what I wanted."

"Cool, bud. Let's do it." I reach down and grab his hand. I hold it tight as we walk over to the hot dog cart. Even when we get there, I don't let go. I know I'll have to eventually. *Not right now. Not quite yet.* To my relief, Caleb doesn't seem to want to let go, either.

For lunch, I let Caleb eat a giant pretzel smeared in ketchup from the hot dog vendor. I momentarily consider whether or not ketchup can be considered a vegetable before remembering that tomatoes are actually a fruit. Still, I'm willing to consider it a nutritional victory; it's better, anyway, than what we ate for breakfast. Caleb picks at his pretzel the same way he did with his donut hole, carefully peeling off the crust first until only denuded bread innards remain. Mira used to do that with her bagels. I always thought there was something so sad and exposed about those decrusted bagels.

"You want?" she used to say, pushing her plate towards me while absently reading the *New York Times*.

"But the middle is the best part."

"And that's why I saved it for you." Then she would smile at me, revealing her ever-so-slightly-overlapping front teeth, and she would tuck a tuft of white-blond hair behind her ear, and I would fall in love with her just a little harder.

"You want it, Daddy?" Caleb says, holding out the pretzel inside.

I've been staring at his pretzel, I realize, remembering Mira.

"Oh," I reply. "No. You should have it."

"Okay," he says, and shrugs. "I'll save it for you just in case."

"You ready to head home?"

"We left my scooter in the playground." He skips off in that direction.

"It may not still be there, buddy," I say, jogging after him. Our chances of reclaiming that scooter, I think, hover somewhere around zero percent.

"It'll be there," Caleb replies, confident. There's something about his faith in humanity that both warms and breaks my heart.

"We can always buy a new one if it's not. Okay, bud?"

Caleb doesn't respond. He takes my hand and pulls me towards the playground gate.

"See?" he says when he opens it. "I told you."

Beside the bench, right where we left it, is Caleb's bright-purple scooter.

"Well, look at that," I say as Caleb reaches up and gives me a high five.

The Sads

I sleep poorly that night, plagued by dreams of losing Caleb. I awake skittish, jumping at everything from the sound of the alarm clock to the drill from the construction site next door. It's as though my paternal instinct has gone into overdrive, trying to compensate for yesterday's horrific mistake. Though Caleb begs me to let him ride his Razor to camp, I decline, buckling him firmly into his stroller instead. My nerves can't handle him dodging traffic on the two-inch aluminum scooter that Zadie affectionately refers to as "the Death Skate." No way. Not after yesterday.

While Caleb is at camp, I run to the grocery store, armed with the highly specific list of organic foods that Zadie has deemed acceptable for Caleb's consumption. It takes me twice as long as I anticipated, and I find only half of the items. I sprint back to our apartment, but the soy ice cream sandwiches have melted by the time I reach home.

I'm heading back towards the school when a heavy and unexpected downpour blankets Manhattan. Within minutes my clothes are stuck to my body and my feet are squishing uncomfortably inside my sneakers. Two mothers with umbrellas wrinkle their noses at me as I push past, my head swiveling left, then right, looking around for Caleb.

The scene is grim. Several caretakers, myself included, are late. Their unclaimed charges line the front hallway of Madison Avenue Preschool in various states of meltdown, like a toddler version of the *Boulevard of Broken Dreams*. Jeannine French, the program director, stands at the reception desk, her arms crossed and her face pinched into an expression that reads: *I really don't get paid enough for this.*

As usual, it's not hard to spot Caleb among his peers. Today he's wearing bright purple running shorts and a green tank top last seen on Richard Simmons in *Sweatin' to the Oldies*. Caleb's socks are pulled up almost to his knees, and the laces of his pink Converses are, as usual, untied. When I was Caleb's age, my clothes were a constant source of embarrassment for me. Money was always tight in our house, and so Zadie and I wore a lot of hand-me-downs from older kids in our neighborhood. Even in the best-fitting ones I felt conspicuous, like someone would be able to tell my sweater wasn't originally mine just by looking at it. I experienced an almost dizzying rush of envy every time I saw fathers and sons in coordinating polo shirts or bathing suits. It crushed me whenever I saw pictures of my own father in the newspaper in his sharp suits and ties. I swore to myself that my child would always have new clothes. Sometimes when I see Caleb I have to remind myself that he *is* actually wearing new clothes. Today he looks like someone dressed him straight from the half-off bin at the Salvation Army.

He's sitting alone on a bench beneath a giant quilted rainbow, his *Dora the Explorer* backpack on his lap. He looks sad. When he sees me, he waves with both arms like a shipwreck survivor about to be picked up by the coast guard.

"Hey, bud. How was camp today?" I ask, though from his mood I can already guess.

He shrugs, declining to answer.

"What did you guys do?"

Before Caleb can say anything, a stroller slams into the back of my calf. I look up, surprised, and find myself face to face with Hunt Callahan's wife.

"Oh, *hi*," she says, her voice dripping with disdain. "Could you maybe, like, move? You're sort of blocking the way." She raises her eyebrows; no easy feat, given her obviously deep commitment to Botox.

I glance around, verifying that there is, in fact, ample space to navigate a stroller around Caleb and me. There is. I refuse to budge.

"Well," I say, "we're almost ready to go here—"

"MOVE IT," her toddler commands from his stroller. He points at me with a single fat finger. I can't help but notice that he's dressed in chinos, a button-down shirt, and loafers. "MOVE IT OR LOSE IT."

"Excuse me?" I say, bending down towards him.

"We're in a rush," she says, more agitated this time. "You're really going to have to move."

I open my mouth to retort but realize Caleb is looking at me, gauging my response. I step back, holding Caleb's hand in my left hand, his stroller in my right. She pushes past so fast that her long, highlighted ponytail whips me in the face.

"Please," I mutter through gritted teeth. "Don't want you to miss your spin class."

She whirls around, her eyes blazing. "*What* did you just say?"

Whoops. Gulp. I hadn't actually intended for her to hear me.

"I said enjoy your spin class," I say as pleasantly as possible. I point to her SoulCycle bag for emphasis.

"Oh," she says. "Thanks." Then she turns on her heel and flounces off through the entry doors.

"That boy's mean," Caleb whispers when they're gone. "He said *Dora* is for babies."

"Well, he's wrong, buddy. *Dora* is for everyone."

"Yeah, I know," Caleb says, and squeezes my hand three times.

"Tough crowd around here, right?" I look up to see a bearded guy smiling at me. He's holding hands with a girl Caleb's age. Her cockeyed pigtails scream *my dad did my hair this morning*.

"I'm Tom," he says. "This is Delaney."

"Hey," I reply, with a cautious smile. "I'm Charlie. And Caleb."

"I know," Tom says, with a polite nod. "I've seen you. Not too many other dads around here at pickup."

"Yeah. Seems that way."

"So, is this, like, a temporary thing for you? Or are you now a 'SAD'?"

"Am I sad?" I repeat, frowning.

Tom smiles. "No. A 'SAD.' S-A-H-D. Stay-at-home dad. Some guys pronounce the *H*, you know—'SAHD'—like 'Saab' or something. I prefer 'SAD.' It's poetic, don't you think?"

"Poetic as in depressing?"

He laughs. "Yeah, or hilarious. Either way, potentially the worst acronym of all time."

"This is just temporary for me. Couple weeks, maybe."

Tom nods like he's heard that line before.

"I'm a lawyer, actually," I add quickly. "White-collar defense. Been at a firm in the city for ten years." Then I shut my mouth. I have no idea why I feel compelled to give this guy my résumé. Judging from his Birkenstocks and T-shirt, which reads *We Interrupt This Relationship to Bring You Football Season*, I'm not sure my professional credentials are going to carry much weight with him.

"Sweet," he says, and nods.

"So, what about you?"

"Yeah, this is my jam," he says, gesturing to the lobby filled with kids.

"Cool. That's very cool."

"Yeah, it is," he says with a genuine smile.

"Daddy, time for dance," Delaney says, pulling at his sleeve.

"Listen, man, I gotta run. I don't know if you'd be interested, but on Thursdays I always meet up with a bunch of guys and their kids. If it's nice we go to Sheep Meadow. We play kickball, Frisbee, whatever. Or we try to, anyway. If the weather's bad, we meet at someone's house. It's a cool group. Maybe you and El Capitán here can swing by sometime."

"Thanks. I'll think about it," I say, though I already know I won't. I have way too much going on to spend the afternoon throwing around a Frisbee with some dude who looks like he just got back from Burning Man.

"Great." He fishes around in his pocket, digs out a pen and a napkin that looks like it might contain used gum. He writes something on the napkin and thrusts it at me. "Here's my e-mail address. This would be a lot easier if I had a business card, huh?"

"Thanks," I say, stuffing the napkin in my pocket. "I'll see you around."

"Yeah, see you," he says, and ambles out the door like he's got all the time in the world.

"I met another dad at pickup today," I say casually to Zadie on the phone that night. "Some guy named Tom. He's a stay-at-home dad, apparently."

"Oh, yeah, Delaney's dad. She's a sweet girl. She was in Caleb's class last year. Caleb likes her."

"So, how many are there? Stay-at-home dads, I mean?"

"You mean, like, nationally?"

"No, I meant, like, that you've seen around."

"A few. There were some really successful moms in Caleb's class, you know. Tom's wife, Morgan, ran Sheppard Capital."

"Wow," I said, surprised. "I know that firm. They're really good. I always thought Morgan Sheppard was a guy."

I can hear Zadie rolling her eyes through the phone. "Of course you did."

"What does that mean?"

She doesn't immediately respond, but instead lets out a long, labored sigh. "You know she died giving birth to Delaney," she says. "Some kind of infection."

"Jesus. That's horrible."

"Yeah, it's just unthinkably sad. Tom's a terrific dad. He used to be an art teacher. He's so laid-back, always smiling. You should get to know him."

"He invited me to hang out with some dads' group he organized."

"You should go, Charlie. That sounds great. And it would be good for Caleb, too. He's shy, but once he gets comfortable, he might like being around other kids. I've been trying with the playdates, but it hasn't been easy."

"I don't know. I'm not sure I'd really, you know, *mesh* with Tom and his friends."

"Why? Because he's not some hard-charging corporate lawyer?"

"No, because he's just . . . he seems really chill. Doesn't he look like that dude from *The Hangover*?"

"Zach Galifianakis?" Zadie giggles a little, even though she's trying to be annoyed with me. "That's just because of the beard."

"And the beer belly. And the Birkenstocks."

"Charlie! You can be so judgmental sometimes. Seriously. Like with Buck. Why can't you just accept that not every guy is going to be as type A as you? Just because a guy is laid back doesn't mean he's some lazy, freeloading stoner."

"Buck *is* a stoner. We've established this."

"Okay, well, I don't think Tom is. And regardless, both are really nice, solid guys. It might do you some good to spend time with them."

We're heading for a fight, I realize, and a stupid one at that. "You're right," I concede. "I should get to know Tom."

"And Buck."

"And Buck."

"Good," she says, and inhales sharply. "Because I have some news."

"Oh, yeah?"

"Buck and I are engaged."

Though I can't honestly say it comes as a surprise, the nonchalance with which Zadie drops this news on me stuns me.

"Congrats," I say, sounding even less enthusiastic than I actually am.

"Gosh, thanks."

"I'm sorry, I'm just a little caught off guard by this."

"Come on, Charlie. You know I love him."

"It's not the engagement itself. It's just the timing I'm finding a little surprising."

"What timing? We've been together for a year."

"It's just not exactly an awesome time for *me* right now," I say, knowing full well how self-centered this sounds. "You moving out is going to be a big change for Caleb, and we haven't even told him about my job yet—"

"Please do not bring Caleb into this," Zadie snaps. "That is *not* fair to me. I live for that kid. You know that."

"I know you do. I just feel like the timing—"

"Yes, you said that already. The timing of my engagement is not working for you. Well, you know what, Charlie? Maybe I don't care. Maybe this is what works for *me*. Did you ever think about that?"

I bite my lip.

"Exactly," she says with a loud sniff.

"Listen, Zadie, I'm sorry. I'm not trying to be a prick. I'm happy for you."

"Yeah, you sound thrilled."

"So, do you have a date?" I ask, trying to change the subject.

"We were thinking July twenty-first."

"Jesus Christ, Zadie! That's in three weeks."

"So?"

"So, what's the rush?"

"The rush is that we are in love and we want to be together. Listen, you should be happy there's a wedding at all. Buck wanted to go to City Hall and just get it done."

"How romantic."

"Actually, I thought it was *very* romantic."

I roll my eyes.

"Don't roll your eyes," Zadie huffs.

"I didn't!"

"Could you just come out here to East Hampton, please?"

"What? East Hampton? Why?"

"I need your help planning. We want to get married out here."

"Zadie—"

"Just pack a big bag, come this weekend, and stay through the wedding. There's tons of room for everyone at this house."

I groan. "*This* weekend? Thanks for the heads-up."

"I'm sorry, I didn't realize you had such a full dance card."

I pause, unable to come up with a quick retort. Normally, I wouldn't be able to just toss a bag in a car and drive off for a spontaneous vacation. I'm way too much of a planner for that kind of thing. But right now I can't think of a good reason why not.

Maybe it's time to do things a little differently, I think to myself. *Maybe I need to loosen up.*

"Fine, fine," I scowl. "We'll come."

"Oh, hooray!" Zadie says, sounding both surprised and delighted.

"Do you have a venue in mind, at least?"

"Well, that was something I wanted to talk to you about."

"Oh, for crying out loud, Zadie. You need to find a freaking venue."

"We have a venue. It's just . . ." She trails off, and I realize that this is the part where she asks me for money. I cock the phone between my ear and my shoulder so I can rub my temples. "It's just a little complicated," she says.

"I bet it is. It would probably be less so if you gave yourself some lead time."

"Maybe. But how hard can it be? Buck and I are low-key people. We just need some flowers, some food, a band . . ."

"Famous last words."

"I have a dress."

"Well, that's something. Did he at least get you a ring?"

"Of course he got me a ring. And it's quite beautiful, thank you very much. It's an antique."

I bite my tongue. "So I don't get a vote on the date, huh?"

"No, you don't. Life's not fair."

"You really don't need to tell that to the thirty-five-year-old widower."

"Charlie, please. For once."

"You're right. I'm sorry. Look, I want you to be happy. Even if it means I have to pay for a big expensive Hamptons wedding. In three weeks."

"Who said anything about expensive?"

"Isn't that what 'complicated' means in bridespeak?"

"No," Zadie says, obviously offended. "'Complicated' means complicated. Anyway, *you're* not paying for the wedding. We have it all figured out."

"Buck's paying for something? Now I *am* rolling my eyes."

"And I'm hanging up."

"Fine. Congrats again."

"I really am happy, Charlie."

"I'm happy you're happy."

"I want you to be happy, too."

"Working on it."

"Well, work harder. Kiss Caleb for me, all right? I love you guys. Even when you're being a stubborn asshole, I still love you."

"I appreciate that," I say. After a second I add, "We both miss you, Zadie," but she's already hung up the phone.

Pickup

I'm on my knees, double-knotting Caleb's sneakers while he sits on the bench in the lobby of his preschool, when I get the sense that I'm being watched. I look up to see a woman hovering over me. She's wearing a low-cut blouse that's doing an inadequate job of covering up her ample breasts. She beams at me with such abject tenderness that I can only assume she's either intoxicated or a friend of Mira's who I can't quite remember.

"Hi, there," she purrs, her words slurring together with the slightest tinge of Southern drawl. "Charlie, right?"

"Yep." I pop to my feet as fast as I can so that she'll stop bending over me. She straightens up; the breasts mercifully recede into her blouse. I stare at her face, rack my brain for a name.

"I'm sorry," I say, unable to place her. "I can't seem to remember anyone's name today."

"Oh, we haven't met." She flips her hair over her shoulder and lets out a shrill laugh, as though this is the funniest thing she's ever heard. A manicured hand finds its way to my bicep. "I'm Coralie Davis. Arabella's mom."

"Right. Arabella's mom."

Caleb, drawn to Coralie's armload of glittering bangles, reaches for her.

"Well, hello there!" Coralie says, giving his hand a little squeeze.

"Pretty," Caleb says in response.

"What a sweetie you are!" Coralie shifts her focus back to me. "And what a good daddy *you* are." The way she says "good daddy" makes it sound vaguely dirty. Coralie moves in closer. I notice with moderate trepidation that she is not wearing a wedding ring.

"Oh, well. Thanks so much." I start to pull my arm away, but Coralie is having none of it. She tightens her grasp, the sharp points of her nails digging in through my worn *Star Wars* hoodie. Out of the corner of my eye, I see Caleb frowning at us disapprovingly.

"I mean, my ex-husband would never bother to pick up Arabella. Once he even sent his driver to pick her up and take her straight out to the Hamptons, all by herself. Can you imagine?"

"No," I say. "That sounds amazing. I'm jealous."

She looks at me, confused, until she realizes I've made a joke. "Oh!" She laughs, squeezes my bicep harder. "You're too much."

"Well, I don't know about that."

"It's just so refreshing to see a father make time for his family. It's so rare in Manhattan."

"Well, it's one of the perks of unemployment. It's either this or *SportsCenter*."

Coralie laughs again, nervously this time. She glances down at her watch—a diamond-encrusted Rolex—and her eyes widen in feigned surprise.

"Oh!" she says. "I better dash. Arabella hates it when we're late to ballet." She leans in and attempts an air-kiss. I flinch reflexively and end up whipsawing her in the face with my jawbone.

"It was nice to meet you, Charlie," she says, recovering gracefully. She smoothes back an errant strand of platinum hair. "Please let me know if you and Caleb ever want to come by for a playdate.

Arabella and I love company. In fact"—she reaches into her handbag and withdraws a card—"here's my number. Call me anytime."

Her fingers brush mine as I take the card. She flashes me a suggestive smile, one that I'm sure warmed the loins of many men a decade or so ago. Then she spins on her heel and disappears down the hall, her hips swaying like Jessica Rabbit's.

"I hate Arabella," Caleb announces once she's gone. "Don't make me play there."

"Don't worry, buddy," I say, wrapping my arm around him. "I won't."

"Her daddy has another family. They live in a duplo."

I think on that for a minute. "A duplex?" I ask.

Caleb shrugs. Duplo, duplex, it's all the same to him. "And she smells like cheese."

"That's not a nice thing to say, buddy," I say, suppressing a smile. "But I promise, you don't have to play with Arabella. Not on my watch."

Caleb doesn't respond. He stares glumly at his sneakers.

"Hey, is there anyone you *would* like to play with after camp?" I ask as cheerfully as possible. "I'm happy to organize a playdate for you."

"I want to play with Fiona."

"I meant someone—" I start to say "real" but stop myself when I see the look on Caleb's face. "Someone from camp."

"No," Caleb says, his face darkening. "No one."

"How about Delaney?" Tom's daughter, I realize, is the only one of Caleb's classmates whom I know by name. "She seems nice."

Caleb cocks his head to the side, considering this. "She's nice," he concedes.

"So maybe I'll call her daddy and we can all get together. I think that could be really fun."

"Okay," Caleb lets out a long sigh. He's been to this rodeo before. Then: "Can I have ice cream?"

"Sure, buddy. Let's get ice cream."

He smiles, his mood noticeably brightened by the prospect of sugar. "I want sprinkles, too. Rainbow ones."

"You got it."

"And you get the rainbow ones, too, okay."

"You're the boss," I say, helping him off the bench.

"Hey, man, wait up!" I turn and see Tom waving to us from across the school's lobby.

Caleb lights up. "Daddy, do you see?" he says, breathless. "It's Delaney and her daddy."

"Yeah, buddy, I see." Everyone else does, too. Tom and Delaney are hard to miss today in matching lavender jogging suits. The scary mommy crew exchange openly disdainful glances as Tom breezes past them. If he notices, it doesn't faze him. He and Delaney couldn't look happier.

"It's my birthday!" Delaney announces, beaming, when they pull up beside us.

"Happy birthday," I say. "How old are you today?"

She holds up five fingers. Each fingernail is painted either purple or pink.

"Wow, you're a big girl."

"Big enough to pick out our outfits today, right, Dee?" Tom beams at his daughter.

"Yeah," she says, delighted.

To me he says, "You wouldn't believe what you can find on sale at Bloomingdale's right now. Surprisingly, not too many plus-size women are in the market for purple tracksuits."

"It's a great color on you. Brings out your eyes."

"I think so. Slimming, too."

"Purple's my favorite color," Caleb says.

"Mine too." Tom nods enthusiastically. "Delaney doesn't like purple at all, though, right?"

"Yessssss I do!" Delaney laughs and twirls like a small, drunk ballerina.

"Hey, Purple Tornado! You're going to lose your lunch if you keep that up," Tom says. Delaney stops, sways in place, and then drops to the floor in a fit of dizzy laughter.

"Tornadoes are deadly. They kill sixty people a year," Caleb announces.

"Caleb." I give him a look.

"That's nothing. Avalanches kill more than one hundred and fifty people worldwide," Tom replies. "I got caught in one once, skiing in the Alps. Totally wild."

"No way," Caleb breathes, his eyes wide.

"Way."

"But you survived."

"I did."

"That's supercool." Caleb nods approvingly.

"Hey, thanks, man." Tom attempts to give Caleb a fist bump, which Caleb botches. "We'll work on that. Listen, you guys want to hit the park with us? We're meeting the Dads' Club at the Meadow."

"What do you think, bud? Wanna hang with Delaney and Tom?"

"Yeah!" Caleb throws an enthusiastic high kick in the direction of the door. I'm impressed by how quickly he's forgotten about the ice cream.

"So I saw you met Coralie," Tom says as we exit the building. He shoots me a wry smile. "She's kind of a one-woman welcoming committee. Especially for dads. She's like a heat-seeking missile. If there's a Y chromosome in the room, Coralie zeroes in."

"Uh, yeah, I got that vibe."

"She's a piece of work. Richer than Croesus. Been married four times, I think. Always to billionaires. Arabella's dad is Winston Davis."

"Wow. The oil guy?"

"Yep."

"Isn't he, like, a hundred and fifty?"

"Yep. He's married to a thirty-year-old now. She just had twins."

"Wow. Gotta respect that. I can barely keep up with one kid and I'm not even forty."

Tom laughs. "Something tells me good ol' Winston isn't doing the middle-of-the-night feeds."

"Yeah, probably not," I say, quietly wondering if I ever did any middle-of-the-night feeds myself. The unspoken rule between Mira and me was that I needed my sleep so that I could be productive at work. "So you guys don't have any help? No nanny or anything?"

"Nah." Tom shakes his head. "No nanny. Don't get me wrong, we have a ton of help. Both grandmas live nearby. Our neighbors have a kid Delaney's age, and they've been great about watching her if I'm jammed. And Morgan's old secretary—this very stern German woman who insists that I call her Mrs. Weinstein—babysits occasionally. Delaney loves her. I'm terrified of her. She stocks the freezer with, like, two weeks' worth of Wiener schnitzel every time she comes. It's weird. But if I've learned anything in the last few years, it's that you don't turn down good help." He smiles. I smile back, but it's forced. There's something devastating about his optimism.

"I was so sorry to hear about Morgan," I say, not quite looking at him.

"Thanks, man. I know you understand."

I nod, grateful that he brought up Mira so I don't have to. "Delaney seems to be doing great. She's always smiling."

"She's a great kid. I'm lucky."

"She's lucky to have you."

"Well, we've got each other. Just like you and Caleb."

"You really seem to have it together. I'm impressed."

Tom smiles then, and for the first time I see sadness in his eyes. "I didn't always. The first year was tough as all hell. Hang in there, man. It gets easier."

We walk for a while in silence. When we hit a red light, the conversation starts back up again. "So did you work before . . ." I trail off, realizing that there's no polite way to end that question.

"Before Morgan died?" Tom fills in easily for me. "Yeah, I did. I was a lower-school art teacher back in the day. Loved my job, loved the kids. Made next to nothing. So it didn't really make sense to me to spend my entire salary paying someone to play with my kid so that I could go play with someone else's kid. You know?"

"Lower school, huh? You must've been excited to become a dad."

"Honestly, I was scared shitless. Morgan and I had only been dating for six months when she got pregnant. We weren't even married. Her parents were furious."

"Wow."

"I loved teaching, but I didn't know how I'd be as a father. My dad wasn't around much when I was a kid. He was a pretty crappy dad, actually. Total workaholic. Law firm partner, always at the office. Made a nice living but wasn't really there for us, you know?"

"Yeah," I say, nodding. "I hear you."

"What about your dad?"

I bite my lip, considering how to answer. My father has never been a favorite topic of mine. In fact, if you were to take a poll of all my ex-girlfriends, they'd probably tell you that any discussion of him was strictly verboten. It took Mira nearly a year to work up the nerve to ask me about him, and this was long after she'd gotten to know my mom and Zadie. I usually deflect questions about my father in one of two ways: with humor or with good old-fashioned curtness. But I'm talking to a guy who's just opened up to me about losing his wife. Neither humor nor curtness feels particularly appropriate.

"He and my mom were never married," I say stiffly. "He was a partner at a law firm, too, actually. My mom was his secretary. He was married to someone else. They had an affair. Mom wound up pregnant with me and my twin sister."

"Dang." Tom lets out a whistle. "That's heavy. Did you get to see him growing up?"

"I've only met him twice." I omit the part when I used to take the train into the city from Long Island when I was in high school just so I could catch a glimpse of him walking home from work.

"Does he know that you're a lawyer?"

"I don't know. I don't really think about him," I say, although that's not true, either. I've kept close tabs on my father's career. I've always hoped he's done the same for me. Every time Fred and I appear in the press, I get a rush of excitement thinking that my father's out there, reading about my successes. *I made it without you, asshole. I did this without your help.*

And then: the video. I cringe at the thought of him watching it, shaking his head in disapproval and thanking his lucky stars he never publicly acknowledged me to be his son. In truth, it was the first thing that crossed my mind when I saw it myself. Not *What will my clients think?* Or *What will my boss think?* But *What will my father think?*

"Really?" Tom looks surprised. "It's a small city. You've never crossed paths?"

"We did once. At a black-tie thing, years back. My mentor at Hardwick was a guy named Fred Kellerman. He's a pretty big deal on Wall Street."

Tom nods, his face blank.

"Anyway, NYU Law had a dinner in Fred's honor. He invited me and a few other guys from the firm to sit at his table. So I'm sitting there and I look across the room, and there's my dad. And then I remembered: my dad went to NYU Law, too. He and Fred were classmates."

"Holy smokes. Did you say hello?"

"No. I just got up and left. It was snowing and there were no cabs. I walked all the way home in my tux."

"That's a crazy story, man. Did you tell your boss what happened?"

"Yeah. The next day he came by my office and was, like, 'What the hell happened to you last night? There were people there I wanted you to meet.' So I told him the truth. You know what he said?"

"What?"

"He said, 'Never liked that prick myself. He sued a client of mine once, a long time ago. Tried to take him for every last penny. Guy's a shark, always out for blood. You're probably better off without him in your life.'"

"Wow. That's amazing."

"Yeah," I say, "I guess it sort of is."

"So you didn't even hear from him after your wife passed

away?" Tom stops and frowns. "I'm sorry. That's probably a really personal question."

"It's okay." The truth is, my father did call. Several times, in fact. He still calls about once a month, despite the fact that I never pick up. Though Zadie has, on occasion, gently suggested that my boycott is childish, I just have no interest in speaking to him. At the end of the day, there's nothing he could possibly have to say that would improve my life in any way.

"No, he didn't. He never called," I say, just because it's easier.

"He really is a prick."

"Yeah."

"Hey, so there are the guys," Tom says, and points towards a cluster of kids and parents who have set up camp on Sheep Meadow.

"Tom!" A smiling brunette waves at us. "We're over here!"

"That's Elise." Tom nudges me with his shoulder. "She's a single mom. We grew up together. It's a long, sad story, but she's terrific. She's kind of an honorary member of the Dads' Club."

"Elise Gould?"

"Yeah," Tom says, surprised. "You know one another?"

"Uh, yeah. Sort of. She was in my law school class." I shade my eyes to get a better look, but I'm certain it's her. Elise was— and continues to be—one of the most beautiful women I've ever seen in real life. We struck up a fleeting friendship during our 1L year when we found ourselves seated next to one another in Civil Procedure. I got a B minus in the class, an unfortunate deviation from my straight-A average that I partially blamed on having to sit next to such a distractingly attractive woman. Like every other guy at school, I nursed a little crush on Elise for the better part of the year, the harmless kind that comes with the full understanding that a woman like Elise would never deign to date a mere mortal like me. Indeed, the last I'd heard, Elise had married a politician named J.P. or P.J. or J.M, some distant Kennedy cousin with presidential aspirations and freakishly good bone structure. I remember seeing their wedding announcement in the *Times* and, despite having been recently married myself, feeling the tiniest ping of jealousy.

It's hard to believe that the last time I saw her was ten years ago. Her dark hair has a touch of silver running through it, but otherwise she shows no sign of aging whatsoever. She stands up as we approach, unfolding a spectacular pair of tan mile-long legs. Reflexively, I suck in my gut.

"Hey, Elise, this is my friend Charlie," Tom says, giving her a hug.

"I think we went to law school together," I say awkwardly.

"Of course!" When she leans in to kiss me on the cheek, I get a whiff of her subtle but distinctive perfume. "How are you, Charlie?"

"I'm, uh, well, truthfully—" Blessedly, Elise interrupts my stammering. She smiles down at Caleb. "And who is this gorgeous boy?"

"This is my son, Caleb. Caleb, say hi to Mrs. . . . . uh . . ."

"Miss," Elise corrects me quickly, holding up her ringless left hand. "But you can call me Elise."

"Hi, 'Lise," Caleb says.

"This is my son, Lucas," Elise says, coaxing a boy out from behind her. "Lucas, say hi to Mommy's friends." Lucas mumbles something and retreats again behind Elise's calf.

"We just moved here from D.C.," Elise says, a touch apologetic. "It's been a big transition."

"Lucas is going to be in Delaney's and Caleb's kindergarten class in the fall," Tom announces.

"That's great!" I say enthusiastically. "It's a fantastic school."

"Oh, that's so nice to hear. We're so grateful to Tom. He helped us get in at the last minute. He's been amazing, introducing us to this group and everything. He's a godsend."

"It's nothing," Tom says, staring bashfully at his shoes. "Lucas is a great kid. Any school would be lucky to have him. Hey, Charlie, maybe you guys can arrange a playdate sometime. I'm sure Lucas would love another buddy in New York."

"That would be great," Elise says, nodding. "We're on Seventy-Fifth Street, between Second and Third. It's all boxes right now, but once we unpack, we'd love to have you over."

"We're neighbors, then. What building?"

"Two fourteen."

"Wow! How about that. We're two fifteen. I could, like, stare into your bedroom window." The words have already left my mouth before I realize how creepy they sound.

Elise chuckles. "You probably could. I don't even have shades up yet and it's killing me. I'm literally up at five every morning."

"Well, you guys are welcome over anytime. I mean, five might be a little early. But, you know, anytime after, say, six."

"Daddy, look!" Caleb tugs on my pant leg. He points to a cart with a striped umbrella, out of which a man is scooping Italian ice into paper cups. "Can I have some?"

"We were just heading that way," Elise says. "Caleb can come with us, if you don't mind."

I look at Caleb, expecting him to shake his head. Instead, he nods emphatically. "I want ice," he says.

"Me, too!" Delaney pipes up.

"Okay." I shrug, and dig into my pocket for some cash.

"I got this one," Elise says with a wink. "You can get the tab next time."

Tom and I watch as the kids race over to the cart, Elise trotting behind them.

"So Little Man's heavily into purple, I take it," Tom says, nodding at Caleb.

"Yeah. I don't know if it's purple so much as girls' clothing generally. We do pink. Accessories. Lately, we're liking sequins."

"Right on. Well, you should come over and raid Delaney's closet. It looks like Hello Kitty and the Care Bears threw up in there."

I laugh. "Be careful what you offer. We might run off with as many tutus as we can carry."

"We have enough to go around."

"Can I ask you something?"

"Sure."

"Do you think I should be worried?"

"About the disaster stuff?"

I frown. "No, about the tutus."

"Ahh, the tutus."

"My sister doesn't think it's a big deal. But as a guy . . . would you worry?"

Tom shrugs. "I don't know, man. Kids are funny. Remember Punky Brewster?"

"The girl with the pigtails?"

"Yeah. I got so into her when I was a kid that I started wearing two different shoes to school."

"That's hilarious."

"I thought it was rad. You know why I stopped?"

"Because you realized you looked ridiculous?"

"No, because some older kid told me I looked like a girl. And then he and his friends egged our house."

"That's what I'm afraid of."

"I don't know. It's no big thing. My point is, you gotta let kids be themselves. It meant a lot to me that my mom took me to the mall to buy two pairs of high-tops so that I could let my inner Punky Brewster shine. It would've hurt a lot more if she was the one who shamed me into stopping."

"That's sage advice."

"Maybe. You are talking to a guy in a purple Juicy Couture tracksuit."

"You and Caleb can go shopping together."

"Anytime. I dig that kid. I'm glad you guys came today, man."

"So am I. Thanks for inviting us."

"When I first approached you, I wasn't sure you'd be into this. I felt vaguely like a Jehovah's Witness."

"Trying to convert me to become a SAHD, huh?"

"Something like that. Or get you to embrace it, anyway."

"To be honest, when you first approached me, I hadn't really come to terms with . . . well, any of this," I say quietly. "I still haven't. I've worked so hard my whole life. In my high school yearbook I was voted 'Most Likely to Succeed.' I don't mean that in a self-congratulatory way. Actually, it makes me sound like an asshole. It's just been a big change for me, not working."

"Well, maybe this is a much-needed break for you, then."

"I guess. I've spent more time with Caleb in the last week than I probably have in his life so far. It's going to be hard to go back."

"Do you think you will?" Tom asks. "Go back to law firm life, I mean."

The question surprises me. "Yeah . . . I mean, for sure. What else would I do? I'm not qualified to do anything other than practice law. And I definitely can't afford not to work."

"There are a lot of things you can do with a law degree." Tom shrugs. "Talk to Elise. She says most of her law school friends don't even practice anymore. They become professors or writers. One of her friends started a fashion label—she's super-successful. Another one runs a dog-walking business."

"I could do that, maybe. Entry-level dog walker. I walk my dog, Norman, every morning."

"I'm just throwing things out there. There's a world of possibilities out there for a smart, educated guy like you. Maybe *The Real Housewives of New York City* would be interested in picking up a male cast member."

"Maybe we could start our own show. *Real Househusbands of New York City.*"

"Women would dig us, man. Can you imagine?"

"Yeah, and think of all the marketing potential. Househusband BabyBjörns. Househusband diaper bags."

"Househusband *calendars.*" Tom pats his gut. "I know it may not look this way, but there's a pretty serious six-pack under here."

We both laugh. "Ah, dude, that would be fun," I say with a sigh. "Wouldn't that be nice? To have, like, a fun job?"

"I had a fun job. I loved my job. It's totally none of my business, but why go back to a job you hate? You should do something you love. Or at least something you like. Everyone should, if you want my humble opinion."

"What about you? You think you'll ever go back to work?"

Tom smiles. "I don't know. I've been thinking about it. Don't get me wrong: I love hanging out with my girl here. Morgan did really well, financially speaking, so we're okay on that front. But in the fall Delaney will be in school for most of the day. I'd like to have something to do. Otherwise I'll turn into some freaky helicopter parent. And no one wants that."

"Maybe you should start a business. Like a support group for dads. Or a play space where dads can take their kids in pajamas and not feel judged."

Tom laughs. "I remember the first time I took Delaney to a music class at Little Maestros. When we walked into the classroom, everyone went silent. One mother even wrapped her arm around her daughter, like maybe I was a sexual predator. Suffice to say, we never went back."

"That's exactly how I felt the first time I dropped Caleb off at camp. I don't know which is worse, the looks of pity, disdain, or just outright concern."

"Totally. So maybe there is a market for a play space where shlubby dads and their grubby kids feel welcome. I'd dig it."

"Yeah. You could have classes, birthday parties, maybe even support groups. I think it could be good. Maybe really good. Honestly, you should do this. With your background—teacher, stay-at-home dad—you'd be the right guy to make it happen."

Tom chuckles. "Except I have no business experience to speak of. I don't even know how to use Excel."

"It's not hard. I can help. Setting up an LLC's a cinch."

Tom pauses, strokes his beard. "Man, I don't know. It's your idea. Maybe you should run with it."

"I have no actual skills outside of defending white-collar criminals. And an unfortunate tendency to humiliate myself online. Not exactly the makings of a small-business owner."

"Definitely the makings of a fine househusband, however. And househusbands don't have to bill by the hour."

"Yeah," I say, with a nervous laugh. "That would be a plus. I'll look into getting myself an agent."

Please God, I think as I turn away from Tom. *Please let me have my job back. I'll do anything. And I promise I'll never complain about the billable-hour system again.*

Sleeping Alone

It's midnight and I can't sleep. I know I should be happy for Zadie, but the truth is that her impending wedding has my head spinning, and not in a good way. All I can think is: First I get fired, and now this? While I know the two are unrelated— Zadie's engagement, in theory anyway, has nothing to do with me at all—I can't help but think that this is further proof that God is, in fact, out to get me. Even if Fred comes through and gets me my job back, there's still the issue of child care. Without Zadie around, who the hell is going to take care of Caleb?

Feeling lonely, I reach for my phone. I listen to a voicemail from my ex, Alison, informing me that Marissa has broken up with Todd and is happy to meet her for drinks next week. *Good,* I think. *One step closer to exacting my revenge.* There's a message from Lorraine, checking in. Another from my father, which I delete as usual. There are several texts from Moose. They range the gamut from hilarious: *"Dude, just got matched on eHarmony with JESSICA from tech support. Please call immediately to discuss the extreme awkwardness of this situation."* To nostalgic: *"Walked by Bagatelle yesterday and was thinking about how much fun we had at your bachelor party. Miss you, dude."* To just plain concerned: *"Chuck, am getting worried. Send a smoke signal, let me know you're okay."*

I halfheartedly draft a response before deleting the text chain altogether. I'm not quite ready to talk to anyone from Hardwick, even Moose. If there's one thing I don't need more of, it's pity.

Anyway, I don't really need to talk to Moose. I already know exactly how the conversation would go. He'll try to make me laugh, first with a couple of self-deprecating jokes about his love life or lack thereof. Then he'll casually rib me for not responding to his calls and texts and e-mails. Finally we'll get to the heart of it: the spectacle I caused at the firm's party, which, he will assure me, really wasn't as embarrassing as I thought it was and is all but forgotten by the other associates. By the end of the conversation, Moose will have almost convinced me that it was no big deal. And then, like a giant Labrador puppy, he will bound off in another direction, taking his goofiness and good humor along with him.

I consider calling Tom, but don't want to bother him after we already spent the whole afternoon together in the park. There's no way I'd call Coralie, the flirtatious mother from pickup; I'm lonely, but not quite that lonely. After a moment of hesitation, I pull up Elise's contact information and debate whether or not I should shoot her a "Welcome to the neighborhood" text. Would that be creepy or nice? She probably gets hit on all the time. *But I'm not hitting on her,* I remind myself. I'm an old friend who lives across the street and who happens to have a kid her age.

My finger slips and suddenly I've dialed her number. Horrified, I try to end the call, but it's too late.

"Hello?" I hear Elise say. "Hello?" Before I can get the phone to my ear, she says, "I can hear you breathing, you jerk," and hangs up.

I close my eyes and lean my head back against the wall. I feel like I'm thirteen again, repeatedly dialing Molly McInerney's phone number over and over and losing my nerve right when she answers. Suddenly my phone is buzzing in my hand: Elise is calling me back. At least, in 1990, Molly McInerney didn't have caller ID.

I flirt with the idea of sending her straight to voicemail before finally picking up on the fourth ring.

"Hi, Elise," I say, trying to sound cheerful and vaguely surprised. "So nice to see you today."

"Charlie?" she says, clearly confused. She probably was ready to give whoever picked up a piece of her mind. "Charlie Goldwyn, is that you?"

"Yes," I say with a little laugh. "Who else would it be?"

Long, deafening pause. "Oh. I'm sorry. I just got a call from this number so I called back."

"Really? How weird! Sorry, I must have pocket-dialed you or something."

"Oh!" Her voice floods with relief. "Oh, okay. No problem. I'm sorry. I picked up, but there was no one on the other line."

"Oh, sorry to scare you. You must've thought I was some crazy stalker or something."

"No, no," she says, though that is clearly the case. "I'm embarrassed to bother you so late. I just didn't know who was calling."

"No problem at all. Listen, now that you have my number, call me anytime. It would be great to get the kids together for a playdate."

"Yes, I'd love that. Any chance you guys are free the day after tomorrow?"

I pause a beat, pleasantly surprised.

"If not, no worries, of course," she adds quickly.

"Oh, no, we'd love to. Why don't you guys come over in the afternoon? Three or so?"

"That would be great. Thanks. I'd invite you to our house, but—"

"It would be our pleasure, really."

"Oh, that's great," she says happily. "I know Lucas will be so happy to see Caleb again."

"We're excited to see you both."

"Sorry again about calling so late."

"Please don't apologize. It's great to hear from you."

"You're too nice. All right, good night."

"Good night, Elise."

My hands are still shaking a little when I hang up. A smooth save, admittedly, but still a mortifying mistake to begin with. And poor Elise! Now she's going to bed thinking she's the asshole.

"Ugh," I mutter aloud. "What the hell is wrong with you?"

I hop out of bed and head to the kitchen.

I almost scream when I swing open the door.

There is Caleb, hands on hips, a superhero cape knotted around his neck. But for the cape, he is completely naked.

"Buddy!" I squeak, then slap my hand over my mouth. "What are you doing out here?"

"What are *you* doing?"

"I was getting a glass of water. You need to go back to bed."

"I want water, too."

"Okay, I'll bring you some water."

"And also there's a man in my closet. He spilled on my bed."

"I don't think that's the case, but I'll come make sure, okay? Where are your pajamas?"

Caleb's face scrunches up. "I don't know," he mutters, crossing his arms across his chest.

Suddenly I get the picture. "Bud, did you have an accident?"

"No."

"Okay. I'm going to get your water and some new sheets, just in case."

"Okay. Daddy?"

"Yeah, bud?"

"Don't tell anyone, promise?"

"I promise. Just between us guys."

Caleb nods. Even in the dark, I can see his eyes welling up with tears.

I crouch down and reach for him. After a second he opens his arms and wraps himself around me, his bare torso pressed on mine. He squeezes me so tight that I can feel his heart beating against mine.

"Wanna know a secret?" I whisper.

He pulls back a little. "Yeah," he says.

"I wet my bed until I was twelve."

"You did?" His eyes perk up, like this gives him hope.

"Yup. All the time. Lots of guys do."

"Okay." Caleb nods, considering this. Then: "Will you still check my closet?"

"I will. Listen, bud, it's pretty late. Maybe you want to just sleep in my bed tonight instead?"

Caleb hesitates, like maybe this is a trick. "Are you sure I'm allowed?"

"Totally. In fact, I'm having trouble sleeping myself, so you'd be doing me a favor. I don't really want to sleep alone tonight."

"Okay," he says. "Just for tonight."

"Just for tonight," I say, and drape my arm around his caped shoulders in the darkness.

The Survivalists

"What do you think?"

I'm wearing a purple polo shirt and cargo shorts, nearly identical to Caleb's. I strike a pose and make my best Blue Steel modeling face.

Caleb squints his eyes. "I like the shirt," he says.

"But?"

"The shorts have too many pockets."

I look down, then back up at him. He's sitting cross-legged on my bed, applying Dora Band-Aids to his fingers, like a football player taping up before a big game.

"Your shorts have that many pockets," I point out.

"Yeah. But I'm a kid."

I nod, turning back to the mirror. He's right, I realize. I look like an overgrown frat boy in these shorts. "Fair enough."

I dig around in my closet. After a minute's hesitation I hold up chinos in one hand, my nicest pair of jeans in the other. "Okay, Michael Kors. Which one?"

"The jeans," Caleb says without looking up from his Band-Aids.

"You sure?"

"Daddy." Caleb stops what he's doing and lets out a sigh. "It's just a playdate."

"Yeah, I know."

"You look nice. You should get sneakers like mine, though." Caleb points to his pink Converses. "They look cool with everything."

"Not sure they make those in my size, bud. At least, not in that color," I say with a forced smile. I'm considering suggesting that he might want to change shoes before the playdate, when Caleb hits me with:

"Why do you care so much about your clothes, anyway? Just wear what you want to wear."

"You're right, buddy."

"If someone doesn't like you because of what you're wearing, then they shouldn't be your friend." Caleb frowns and picks at the edge of his thumb. "That's what Aunt Zadie says."

"She's absolutely right," I say with a quick, embarrassed nod. "So, are you excited to see Lucas?"

"Yes."

"He seems really nice. I'm happy you guys are friends."

"I'm glad he's coming over to play," Caleb says with a thoughtful nod. Then: "You know what I think, Daddy?"

"What's that, bud?" I sit down beside him on the bed.

"I think that sometimes it's good to meet new people."

"I couldn't agree with you more."

"Look at you two!" Elise says when I open the door. "Twins!"

"Yeah, looks like Lucas got the memo." I point to Lucas's purple Spider-Man T-shirt. "We're a purple-only house, unfortunately."

She holds up her hands in surrender. "I can go home and change."

"We'll make a onetime exception."

"Phew." Elise wipes her brow. "We're new in town, you know. Still learning the rules."

"More than happy to show you around. Come on in. Make yourselves at home."

"Thanks," she says. She steps inside and smiles at me. I glance nervously away. Staring at a woman that beautiful feels wrong somehow, like looking directly into the sun.

"Great place," she says.

"Oh, thanks," I say, kicking myself for not straightening up more. With Zadie gone, the house feels like it's Scotch-taped together. Elise steps over my loafers and into our living room. A pair of Caleb's spaceship underpants hangs over the back of the couch like an accent blanket or throw pillow. How did I miss them?

"I'm making an emergency survival kit," Caleb announces, "in case of an earthquake or a hurricane. It has PowerBars and a flashlight and soap and toilet paper and Band-Aids and a poncho. I wanted to get a solar blanket, but Daddy said no."

Lucas offers him a polite, mildly confused smile.

"Caleb," I say gently, "why don't you show it to Lucas? It's pretty cool." I turn to Elise. "We actually set up a camping tent in his room this morning. Caleb wanted to make sure we knew how to use it, just in case. We Goldwyns like to be prepared for anything."

"That's very cool," Elise says, and actually looks impressed. "Doesn't that sound cool, Lucas?"

"Can I go see, Mama?"

"Of course, sweetheart." She smiles as the boys trot off down the hall.

"He's very attached to me lately," she says, her voice quiet. "Sometimes it's like he's afraid to leave my side."

"Totally understandable. A move is a big change."

"A move, a divorce. I feel terrible. I know it's so much for him to take in all at once. But we just couldn't stay in D.C. Things were just too complicated with my ex." She shoots me a guilty look. "I'm sorry. That is way too much information."

"Please. You're talking to the king of the overshare." I pause for a second, wondering if she's seen the video. "You should have seen the speech I gave at my firm's office party a few weeks ago," I add with a nonchalant chuckle.

She bursts out laughing. From the look in her eye, I can tell she's seen it. *Dammit,* I think. My heart sinks, but there's something about the way she's smiling at me that makes it feel okay.

"I loved that speech."

"You did?"

"Yeah." She nods emphatically. "You said everything that every working parent is thinking, basically all the time. It really resonated. And not just with me. The crowd went wild."

"I think they were just trying to cut me off."

"No, they were cheering because you were honest." She steps closer; my heart thumps a little harder. "Working at a big law firm is tough. I only lasted three years myself. I left on maternity leave and never went back. I actually enjoyed the work, but it was the hours I couldn't take. The idea of being away from Lucas all week was just too much for me to bear." She lets out a sigh. "Of course, here I am now with a five-year gap on my résumé, trying to find a job. And it's tough out there."

"I hear that."

"So, did you quit Hardwick completely? Or are you just taking some time off?"

"Neither. They fired me."

Her eyes widen. "Seriously?"

"Seriously."

"Because of the speech?"

I nod.

"Wow. I can't believe they would do that to you. What jerks."

"Well, some of them are, anyway," I say, thinking about Todd. I make a mental note to check in with Alison as soon as this play-date is over. "Fred Kellerman—he was my mentor at the firm—he's doing his best to convince the other partners to un-fire me. And I'm building a case against the guy who posted the video in the first place. He was just trying to steal my spot for partnership."

Elise raises her eyebrows. "So you'd want to go back to Hard-wick, then? Even after the way they've treated you?"

"Well, yeah, of course. I mean, I need to work. And I put in ten years at that firm. Ten hard years."

She nods, but says nothing.

"Anyway, Fred's terrific," I add quickly. "I really only work with him. And hopefully Todd, the asshole who posted the video, will get fired. So, you know . . . It could be worse."

Elise presses her lips together and nods. I can tell she has something else to say, but she holds back. After a second she tosses me a playful wink. "I bet you have loads of fans now, huh?"

"Fans?"

"Yeah, fans. Because of the video! Tom said the women in his book club were chattering on about how good-looking you are."

"He didn't tell me that," I say, my cheeks flushing.

"Well, you should look at the YouTube comments. There's a lot of female feedback on there."

"It's actually hard to imagine anything I'd like to do less than read the comment section on that video."

Elise chuckles. "I'm just saying. There's probably a line of women forming at your doorstep as we speak."

"Yes, because as we all know, women in this city really dig unemployed men."

"Mama!" Lucas calls out from Caleb's bedroom. "Come see Caleb's tent! It's the coolest!"

Elise nods her head towards the hallway. "I can't miss this! Let's go."

"Let's."

When she rounds the corner into Caleb's room, Elise's face lights up. Caleb has rolled himself up in a sleeping bag. Lucas is wearing Caleb's emergency survival kit (Zadie's backpack) and a pair of old hiking boots that I didn't know I still had.

"You two are having fun." Elise crouches low and peers into the tent. "Wow, Caleb, this is impressive."

"Daddy did it for me this morning. It's Buck's tent, but Daddy knows how to set it up really good."

"We did it together."

"Not really," Caleb says, and gives me his goofiest grin. "Mostly I just watched."

"If there's one thing law school taught me how to do, it's follow pages and pages of directions."

Elise grins. "Don't joke. That's an essential parenting skill. These kids come with so much gear! I'm useless with a screwdriver."

"I am good at gear. Gear is one thing I can do."

"Good at gear, super-organized. You guys are even in matching outfits! You make this single-parent thing look easy."

I start to protest, but stop myself. "Thanks," I say instead. "That's nice of you to say."

"He just needs shoes like mine," Caleb pipes up. "His are lame."

Elise laughs. "Caleb, yours are definitely cooler," she says. "I like the pop of color."

"Duly noted," I say with a sigh.

"Mama, can we get a tent?" Lucas asks. "Just like this one?"

"Sure we can." Elise turns around and mouths *Yikes* to me. "Lucas goes camping with his dad sometimes. I've actually never been, and I don't know the first thing about all the equipment. But I'm willing to learn."

"We can show you," I offer.

"Yeah, we can show you!" Caleb shouts. "We can go camping together."

"Yeah!"

"And where should we go camping?"

"Central Park!"

"Museum of Natural History!"

"Grand Central Station!"

"Space!"

The two of them dissolve into a fit of giggles.

"Space, huh." Elise chuckles. "You guys are getting pretty silly in here."

From inside, Lucas zips up the tent door, blocking our view. "We're camping!" comes his muffled voice. "No parents, please!"

Elise stands up and presses her hand to her lips, suppressing a chuckle.

"Charlie," she says to me, "have you seen the boys?"

"No, I haven't. Should we go look for them in the kitchen?"

The tent shakes with laughter.

"Yes, maybe they're in the kitchen. Let's look there."

We slip out of Caleb's bedroom and into the kitchen.

"I haven't seen Lucas this happy in a while," Elise says when we're out of earshot. "This is the best. You guys are so nice to have us over. It's so civilized over here. Living in boxes . . . well, it's been tough on both of us. It just doesn't feel like home yet, you know?"

I open my mouth to tell her that she needn't thank me, that this is the first playdate that Caleb's had in at least a year, that it's *me* who should be grateful to *her* for making today happen. I want to tell her that I haven't seen my son this happy in far too long, and that, while we're on the topic of happiness, I'm feeling strangely good myself ever since she came around. I open my mouth to say all those things, but she's staring at me with those crystalline eyes and her lips are parted just so, and as she runs a slender finger along the length of her clavicle bone I forget myself entirely.

"No prob," I say instead, and fix my gaze on my feet. "You want a drink or something? Water? Glass of wine?"

She smiles. "It's two in the afternoon."

"Right. So water, then?"

"Water would be great."

"Well, maybe a glass of wine another time." Before she can turn me down, I add, "So you want me to tell you everything you need to know about camping?"

"Yes, please. I can use all the help I can get."

"I know that feeling well."

"I don't know," she says, and cocks her head to one side. "You seem like you're doing just fine on your own. I mean, a tent in the bedroom? Lucas is in heaven."

"What can I say, we're outdoorsmen. Just living off the land, really."

"Survivalists?" Elise says with a laugh.

I smile. I couldn't think of a better term for us if I tried.

Hamptons Wedding

Mira and I had a Hamptons wedding. It was, believe it or not, her idea. I was surprised when she suggested it: Mira rarely did anything in a traditional way, and she was the furthest thing from stuffy. When I decided to propose to her, I assumed—well, feared is probably more accurate—that she would either want to do something wild and free-spirited and totally out of my comfort zone—get married on a beach in Bali, maybe, or on a mountaintop in Nepal—or that she wouldn't want to do anything at all, and we'd end up at City Hall on a Tuesday afternoon. A part of me worried that Mira would eschew the idea of marriage entirely. Her parents' marriage had been a disaster. They divorced when Mira was five. Her mother retreated to a commune in upstate New York where she raised chickens and grew wheatgrass; her father remarried three times, each time to a woman who was younger than her predecessor. By the time I met Jack, he had more or less settled down with a former Knicks City Dancer whose main interests appeared to be shopping, sunbathing, and plastic surgery. Her name was Francine, but Mira only ever referred to her as "Stitches."

Unlike most of the women I'd dated in my twenties, Mira never mentioned marriage. She never dropped hints about weddings or honeymoons or babies. She didn't comment on other women's engagement rings, nor did she dreamily recount stories of extravagant proposals in Paris. Most refreshingly, she refrained from asking probing questions about "our future together" or "where I saw things going." If anything, I could barely pin her down for a dinner reservation. It wasn't so much a commitment problem as it was a planning issue. Mira hated plans. Instead of a reservation at La Grenouille, Mira preferred to stumble into some random dim sum shop in Chinatown and take our chances. While I was an early user of Fandango, Mira thought it was fun to just show up at a movie theater on a Sunday afternoon and just see whatever happened to be playing next. Once, she called me at work and told me to meet her on the corner of Fifty-Seventh and Fifth at six p.m. sharp. I thought we were going to dinner. Instead, she showed up in a borrowed Volkswagen and we drove to Vermont. We spent the weekend in the first B and B we could find that had availability—no easy task given that there was some kind of maple syrup festival happening at the time. Mira would be the first to admit that the weekend was an utter disaster. The B and B was less of a hotel and more of a shrine to the owners' cats, who roamed the property with impunity. Framed portraits of them lined the stairwell, and everything from the linens to the toilet seat covers (yes, there were toilet seat covers) were feline-themed in some way. It rained so hard that we were forced to spend most of the weekend there, me muttering about my allergies and Mira gleefully snapping photos of our cat-shaped Jacuzzi and posting them on Facebook. It was a disaster, but it was a fun disaster. Mira made it fun. Mira could make anything fun. If there was one thing you could say about her, it was that she truly knew how to live in the moment.

I, however, do not. I never have. I was, am, and always will be a planner. I liked to think it was one of the reasons Mira and I worked well together. I planned moments. She lived in them.

It took me six weeks to organize my proposal. I was terrified Mira was going to say no, so I channeled all my nervous energy into logistics. Originally, the plan was to pop the question in Central Park with a picnic basket and a bottle of champagne. By the end, I had booked us the Presidential Suite of an outrageously expensive hotel in Cabo San Lucas, chartered a sailboat for a sunset cruise, and hired a mariachi band to greet us on the dock playing "Solamente una vez" ("You Belong to My Heart").

We never made it to Mexico. Somewhere over Texas, the pilot announced that we were experiencing technical difficulties and would have to make an emergency landing at the George Bush Intercontinental Airport in Houston. What appeared to be lightning flashed past the window as he spoke. Then the plane dropped three stories and passengers began to cry and scream. I was too pissed to cry; all I could think about was the nonrefundable deposits I'd laid down on the sailboat and the mariachi band. It wasn't until the flight attendant crossed herself and began to mutter the Lord's Prayer that it occurred to me that I might never see a band—mariachi or not—play ever again. I reached out and took Mira's hand.

"I don't particularly want to die at a Republican airport," she said through a tight smile. The plane lurched back and forth, causing another round of panicked screams.

"I don't want to die as your boyfriend," I said, and pulled the ring out of my pocket. Figuring we were well past seat belts anyway, I unclicked mine and dropped to one knee.

I still remember the look on her face. She always looked so beautiful when she was surprised. Her blue-green eyes got wide and her perfect mouth dropped into a little O and for a fleeting second I thought to myself: *This is it. This is all I need right here, and if she says yes, I'll die a happy man.*

"I never thought I'd ever say this to anyone, but *yes*," she said. "Yes, I would love to marry you, Charlie Goldwyn. Oh my God, *yes!*" She fumbled with the buckle of her seat belt. "Goddamn it!" she said. Her hands were shaking and I had to grab them and hold them steady to get the ring onto her finger. I worried that it was a little tight, but Mira said: "It's perfect."

"He's proposing!" one of the flight attendants shrieked. "Oh my God!" For a brief second everyone around us forgot they were dying. Then one guy started clapping, and soon everyone was applauding and shouting "Bravo!"

Mira's seat belt buckle finally snapped open and she fell into my arms. The plane lurched again and we tumbled into the aisle, her hair falling into my mouth and her knee slamming into my crotch.

"My balls," I croaked, curling up into the fetal position. "Oh, fuck, my balls."

"Christ, Charlie!" Mira's tears turned to laughter. She reached out and stroked my face. Through watery eyes, I noticed how beautiful the emerald-cut stone I had agonized over looked on her finger. It glittered beneath the plane's garish track lighting. "I'm so sorry about your balls!"

"I guess I'll never be a dad."

"You'll never be anything if you don't get back into your seat!" the flight attendant shouted. The plane lurched again, and suddenly the cabin was plunged into darkness.

"At least we can say we were engaged," Mira whispered to me as I helped her back into her seat. "At least we went out together."

"If I'm going to die, I want to do it next to you."

•   •   •

Later, at the La Quinta Inn next to the George Bush Intercontinental Airport, we had our first go at fiancé sex. Our nerves were still rattled from our recent brush with death, and the sex was explosively fast, almost violent. Mira bit and clawed at my flesh as though she couldn't get enough of me, and when she came, she screamed so loudly I wondered momentarily if security was going to show up at our door. Afterward we drank tiny bottles of tequila from the minibar and laughed about how ridiculous we were to have said such dramatic things on the plane.

"Did you really think we were going to die?" Mira said with a giggle. We couldn't stop laughing; suddenly the whole experience felt ridiculous and hilarious instead of terrifying. "You got so calm when the plane started lurching around. It was actually sort of freaky."

"I wasn't calm! All I could think about was how, despite two hundred man-hours of meticulous planning, I was going to end up proposing to you on a goddamn broken airplane."

"Did you see how they had to foam the runway for us? It looked like we were landing on a pile of shaving cream! When I saw that, I thought it was curtains for sure."

"I know. I kept thinking I was seeing lightning outside the window, but when I saw that—"

"You realized the wing of the plane was on fire?" We dissolved into hysterical laughter.

"I think this has to be the worst-executed proposal in the history of time," I said, shaking my head. "I tried, I really did."

"Charlie, it was perfect."

"Mira, it was about as unromantic as you could get!"

"I totally disagree. It was utterly, heart-stoppingly romantic.

What you said about not wanting to die as my boyfriend? That was, like, out of a Nicholas Sparks movie!"

I rolled my eyes. "Exactly what I was going for. Ryan Gosling will play me in the movie about our life."

She swatted at me with a pillow. "I'm serious, Charlie! Sometimes the best moments in life are unscripted. In fact, I'd be willing to bet that all the best moments in life are unscripted."

"The script in this case was pretty perfect. Did I tell you about the mariachi band?"

Mira sighed and laid her head in my lap. "You did. But tell me again. I want to hear about the rose petals on the bed and the champagne on the balcony."

So I described for her, in as vivid detail as I was able, the planned proposal. I told her about the hotel with the magenta bougainvillea dripping down the walls and the balcony overlooking the crystal-blue ocean. I told her about the chilled champagne and strawberries that would be delivered to us upon arrival. I described the thirty-three-foot beauty of a sailboat I had chartered for us for the evening, fittingly named *Sol Mate*, and the pink-streaked western sky, and how the sun would slip below the horizon line just as I was dropping to my knee with the ring. It was all so perfect that I got swept away in it myself, and suddenly I was angry again—angry for being robbed of what could have been.

"I'm so sorry," I said again, feeling defeated. "It should have been different."

Mira didn't respond. I looked down and realized she was fast asleep.

We arrived in Mexico two days later, grateful to be alive and engaged and no longer sleeping on twin beds at an airport hotel. As she slumped back in a hammock on the beach, a margarita in one hand and a book in the other, Mira sighed and said, "This is heaven."

"The beach?" I asked.

"The beach. You. Everything." She pushed her giant turquoise-framed sunglasses down onto her nose, and let her arm loll out of the hammock, her fingers brushing the sand.

"Do you want to get married on a beach?" I asked, trying to sound casual about it. We'd been engaged less than forty-eight hours, but I was already itching to get the planning under way. If left to her own devices, it was possible Mira would allow us to live in a state of perpetual engagement, and that was something I knew I couldn't tolerate.

"Actually, yes," she said. "And I know just the place. I can't wait to pick out the flowers and the cake. Oh, and my dress! I know exactly what I want it to look like." She paused, catching herself, and gave me a small, sheepish smile. "Don't laugh at me, but I've had the whole thing planned out in my head since I was ten. I'm such a cliché, right?"

"You *have*? That's so not you."

"Mortifying, but true." She paused, studying my face. "You look relieved," she said.

"I am! You never mentioned getting married before. To be honest, I wasn't sure you'd be that into the idea."

"The idea of marrying you? Or just marrying, generally?" Her lips twitched in amusement.

"Both. Either."

"Why? Because I'm some crazy hippied-out yoga teacher? You thought I'd be all, like"—and here she switched into her best stoner voice—" 'Man, we don't need a piece of paper. All we need is the love in our hearts.' " She threw her head back and laughed.

I shrugged, a little embarrassed. "Well, yeah. That was a distinct possibility. Also, you're not exactly the best at advanced planning."

"Ahhh," she said, nodding in agreement. "I see. So you were worried I'd never get around to it, right? Like the way I say every year that I'm going to have a Christmas party, but then December rolls around and I just can't get it together, so then it becomes a Valentine's Day party and then it's like a spring equinox party and then the idea just dies out all together until the next year when I do it all over again?"

"You do that? Wow, I never noticed."

"Shut up, Charlie. I bet you've been sweating a little, thinking I'd drop the ball and we'd end up just being engaged forever." She grinned at me, knowing she was right.

"Of course not," I said, busying myself with the sunscreen. "You'll do an amazing job with our wedding."

"Oh, please. You're going to micromanage this thing, I can see it already. Your tolerance for ambiguity is, like, zero."

"That is absolutely not true. I'm just organized. Really organized. Really really organized."

"You're going to be a groomzilla!" Mira cackled. "We could be on that reality show on WE tv! It would be hilarious. They'll show you running around with seven Excel spreadsheets two years before the wedding, and I'll barely make it to the rehearsal dinner on time. The lawyer and the yogi get married. The ultimate Odd Couple."

"Hey, opposites attract. Our differences are why we're great together. We balance each other out. And we're not waiting two years to get married, FYI."

"But finding the perfect monogrammed cocktail napkin takes time, Charlie. You can't rush these things."

"I ordered those *once*. For *your* Christmas party. Which, by the way, never happened."

"See, I knew that was bothering you! Admit it, you're going to freak out if I plan this, aren't you? You're going to take all the fun away from me and then you're going to whine to all your colleagues about how your wife burdened you with the minutiae of wedding planning."

I raised my palms in surrender. "You know what? I can't win here. *You* plan it. This one's all yours. You just tell me where and when to show up and I'm there."

"Wow!" Mira lowered her sunglasses and raised one eyebrow. "You sure? That's a lot of trust right there."

"If I can't trust you to plan a party, we're going to have a pretty rough go at this whole shared-life thing."

Mira clapped her hands together with glee. "Oh, yay! I'm super-excited. It's going to be amazing, Charlie, I promise you. Everything you would have dreamed of and more." She tapped her temple. "I told you, I have the whole thing planned out in my head."

"Do I get to know the details? Or do I have to wait for the invitation like everybody else?"

"Depends on how nice you are to me."

I reached over and ran my finger up her calf, then pushed her pareu up, exposing her gorgeous legs. "I can be very nice," I said, and kissed her just inside the knee.

"Oh, my," she said, fanning herself. "Why, yes, you can."

"So, where's our wedding, love?" My words came out muffled as I pressed my nose to the inside of her thigh and worked my way up, kissing as I went.

"I was thinking we could do it at my dad's house in Sag Harbor," she said dreamily, stroking my hair. "I haven't been there in ages, but it was my favorite place in the world when I was a kid. I always thought I'd get married there, right on the beach, and then have dinner on the lawn beneath the stars. What do you think?"

I looked up. "I love the idea."

"Just family, close friends. Nothing fancy."

"It sounds perfect," I said, because it did.

"It will be," Mira said. "But it will be perfect no matter where we do it. I just would like it to be somewhere personal. You know, somewhere that means something, not just a cookie-cutter venue where someone gets married every other Saturday."

"How about the La Quinta Inn at the Houston Airport? That's personal. We practically got engaged there. And I bet no one's ever gotten married there before."

Mira flicked me on the shoulder. "I was saving that for our honeymoon," she said, and we laughed. Then she leaned over and pulled me into the hammock with her. We stayed there until sunset.

Family Emergency

Forty-eight hours later, Caleb, Norman, and I are cruising east on the Long Island Expressway, bound for East Hampton. I should be thrilled: the sun is out, the traffic isn't terrible, and Caleb is dying to be reunited with Zadie. Zadie claims the house she's staying at is incredible, with room enough for everyone. Just a stone's throw from the beach, too. But what I'm most looking forward to is all of us being under one roof again. I hadn't realized how lonely the apartment would feel without her.

Still, it's hard to ignore the gnawing sensation in my gut that tells me this trip isn't going to be all sunshine and rainbows. Maybe it's the shotgun timing of this wedding that feels wrong. Maybe it's my stress level about work. Or maybe it's just being in the Hamptons: I haven't been there in years, not since my own wedding. Mira and I kept saying we'd go visit her father in Sag Harbor after we were married, but there was never a good time. On our first anniversary, a work crisis kept me trapped in the office all weekend. For our second anniversary, we were dealing with the reflux situation, and the idea of spending three hours in the car with a wailing infant was more than either of us could bear. On our third anniversary, there was another work crisis. We never had a fourth anniversary.

Since Mira died, I've gotten plenty of invitations, mostly from couples who were friends of Mira's and mine who didn't quite know what to do with me. Should they invite me to Saturday brunch, but as a third wheel? Do they seat me next to a single girlfriend at a dinner party? Worse still, do they wedge me between couples, the ninth chair at a table clearly meant for eight? Meals come with seating arrangements, and seating arrangements for the recently widowed are complicated. So, instead of shoehorning me into a table where I don't belong, they all invite me to the Hamptons.

It's an easy invitation, too, because I always decline. I'm sure they breathe a sigh of relief when I do, because, really, who wants a mopey widower and his kid rattling around their beach house for more than an hour or two? We are, when it comes right down to it, kind of a buzzkill.

One of the many unfortunate side effects of losing someone you love is that the places you once most enjoyed together suddenly become the most painful. That little Italian joint around the corner that you used to go to every week? Yeah, you never want to eat there again. The spot in Central Park where you picnicked on your second date? Definitely to be avoided. Even something as ridiculous as a fruit stand where Mira used to buy her strawberries can set me off, transforming what could have been a perfectly pleasant Saturday afternoon into a dark and miserable one. Our neighborhood is filled with these emotional land mines. For a while I thought it would be better if we moved somewhere new entirely, but Dr. Frank, Caleb's pediatrician, convinced me that it was better for us to keep Caleb's world as intact as possible. I understood that, and so I've learned to cope. But I'm not going to willingly wander into land mine territory unless absolutely necessary, which is why I'll probably never again see Mexico and I had very much hoped to permanently avoid the Hamptons.

And yet, here I am, stuck in the cheapest rental car I could find on short notice, an ancient white Corolla with Florida plates and an interior that smells strongly of nursing home. Not exactly the sweet ride I pictured myself in for my first weekend getaway with Caleb, but then, nothing about this trip is as I pictured it. A suit-case packed with turquoise Jeggings and ballet flats rattles around in the trunk. Norman, who is still emotionally recovering from a recent fray with Monica's cat, is riding shotgun. He keeps arrang-ing and rearranging himself on the seat, unable to get comfort-able. Norman is not built for car trips. His limbs are unusually long, and he's prone to both motion sickness and incontinence. I flirted with the idea of putting a diaper on him for the drive but decided against it. Given that the cat peed in his dog bed right before we left, I figured Norman had been humiliated enough for one day.

Norman finally settles in the most awkward position possible: sitting on the seat like a human, with his chin resting on the dash. Now that we've hit traffic, he lifts his head and looks at me, then out the windshield, then back at me again as if to say, *Are we really doing this?* Norman's never been a big fan of change.

"I know this is tough. Just remember, we're doing it for Zadie," I say aloud, more to myself than to the dog.

"Where's Aunt Zadie?" Caleb yawns from the backseat. He seemed especially groggy this morning when we left, so I had hoped he'd sleep for most of the ride, but no such luck.

"She's in East Hampton, bud. We're almost there."

"You said that before."

"I know. There's some traffic up ahead."

"Why?"

"Because the beaches out here are really nice. We're going to have so much fun, you'll see."

"Where will I sleep?"

"I don't know, but Zadie said the house is great."

"I want to sleep with Aunt Zadie."

"Well, I'm not sure that's going to fly with Uncle Buck."

"Uncle Buck has his own room."

I stifle a laugh. "You know, Uncle Buck and Aunt Zadie are getting married soon. So they might be sharing a room."

Caleb pauses, considering this. "So Uncle Buck is coming to live with us?"

Shit.

Zadie and I had agreed to talk through the logistics of her inevitable move out this weekend. Then, once we had come up with a plan, we would sit Caleb down together and talk it through. But the kid is smart. Damn smart. I stumbled right into this one without even meaning to. One comment about sleeping arrangements and now I'm going to end up explaining marriage, cohabitation, and where babies come from all by myself in one conversation.

Damn it, Zadie. Where are you when I need you?

"Not sure, bud. Why don't we talk about all that when we see them?"

"Is Aunt Zadie going to have a baby?"

Reflexively, my foot hits the brake and the car lurches to a halt. Norman yelps as he slides off the passenger seat. The Range Rover behind us honks angrily, stopping about an inch shy of our rear bumper.

Norman slinks back onto the seat. He looks fine, if slightly betrayed.

"Yikes! Sorry, Norman!" I reach over and pat him on the head. "You okay? Caleb, you okay back there?"

"You didn't answer my question," Caleb insists from the back-seat.

"Uh, what question was that?"

"Is Aunt Zadie having a baby?"

"Not that I know of. Why?"

"Because that's why people get married. To have babies." He narrows his eyes at me. If there's one thing Caleb hates, it's not being given the full story. That, and being told he can't wear purple.

"Well . . ." I hesitate, trying to choose my words as carefully as possible. "People get married because they love each other. And sometimes, when you love someone else, you also want to have a baby with them."

"Like you and Mommy?"

"Yes, like me and your mommy."

I watch Caleb closely in the rearview mirror, trying to gauge how he's feeling. If he's upset, he doesn't show it. His face remains placid. He looks out the window, watches the cars roll by. His white-blond hair stands up from static, like dandelion fuzz. His lips are stained blue from a lollipop that he found in the backseat pocket of the car and popped in his mouth before I had a chance to intervene. I wish I knew what he was thinking.

"Tell me again what Mommy looked like."

My heart tightens like a fist. "She was beautiful," I manage to say. "She looked just like you. She had the prettiest blond hair. One of her eyes was green and the other was blue. She had a pic-ture of a little bird inside her wrist, and her skin glowed, and she was always smiling."

"I used to be able to see her but now I can't anymore." He says this matter-of-factly, like we're talking about the weather.

"She was the most incredible woman in the world," I tell him.

"I see her all the time in my dreams. I tell her about how you're doing. She's very proud of you."

"Does she see us from where she is?"

"Yes, I think so."

"Does she see that we're going to Long Island right now?"

My heart aches. *He's too young to think about these things,* a voice inside me cries. *He should be thinking about kickball and recess and Dora the Explorer.*

"I think she sees everything, Caleb."

He nods, chewing his lip, considering this idea. Then: "There's hurricanes on Long Island. Every year."

And just like clockwork, we're back to natural disasters.

"Well, probably not every year."

"Every year. August until November is hurricane season."

"I don't think we've had one in a while."

"Hurricane Alex in 2010. *June,* 2010." How he knows this is beyond me. He wiggles his eyebrows when he says "June," as if to say, *See? Disaster can strike at any time.*

"Well, good thing it's not June, then."

It seems to be the right response, because Caleb is quiet for a full minute. Until he says, "I don't feel so good."

"What's wrong?"

"My tummy hurts."

Frankly, my tummy hurts a little, too, from the stop-and-go traffic. I say a quick prayer that nothing else is wrong. Sometimes Caleb's tummy hurts when he gets upset about Mira.

"I'm sorry, bud. My tummy hurts, too. But look!" I point to our right. "There's the turnoff for East Hampton. We'll be there really soon."

Caleb clutches his stomach. "Let's stop. I have to poop." He groans dramatically.

"Caleb, we'll be there soon. Five minutes, okay?"

"I HAVE TO POOP."

"Caleb, there's nowhere to poop on the side of the road. Five minutes."

"You said that before."

"I know, but I mean it this time."

Caleb begins to thrash in his car seat, and then, when he realizes he's trapped, dissolves into a fit of fake tears. I clench my molars and try my best to ignore him. I check the time on the dashboard: 3:32 p.m. We've been in the car for just over three hours, so we're more or less on schedule for an epic meltdown.

"I have runny poop now," Caleb whines from the backseat.

Silence.

Then: "I hate you!"

More silence.

New tack: "I want my iPad!"

"The iPad's out of juice, Caleb. I'm sorry."

"Stop the car!"

"I'm not stopping, Caleb! We're literally five minutes from the house!"

"I have runny poop! And Fiona does, too!" A fresh wave of hysteria rocks the backseat. Even Norman lifts his head and peers back there. Then he lets out an exhausted sigh and returns his chin to the dashboard, like all this drama is just too much to bear.

"Caleb, look!" I say, channeling my inner Mary Poppins. "Look right there! A big pink house!"

Indeed, to our left is an Italianate mansion painted in a jaunty Easter-egg pink. This stops Caleb dead in his tracks. He's been begging for a pink room, but a whole house? He hadn't dreamed such a thing was possible.

"*Daddy,*" he says, gobsmacked.

"*I know,*" I respond, and slow the car. We inch past, staring at the house in reverential silence.

"Who lives there?"

"I don't know. Maybe a prince or a princess."

"I think so."

"And look at that one!" I point to another multimillion-dollar monstrosity: a gigantic castle, replete with turrets that seem to glitter in the summer sunlight.

"It's beautiful here," Caleb says solemnly, his bathroom needs seemingly forgotten.

"That it is."

"Have you been here before?"

"Once, bud. A long time ago."

The farther we drive, the larger the houses become. In fact, we're in full-on mansion territory. More than once I slow the car to a crawl so that I can glance at the directions I hastily jotted down on an index card. According to them, we're on the right street. My gut, however, tells me there's been a mistake. There's no way Buck and Zadie could afford to rent a house in this neighborhood. Of course, this car is way too old to have GPS. The decision not to spring for the NeverLost at the rental agency now seems like an epic error in judgment.

I pull to a stop outside a metal gate. Just past it, sprinklers whir in the sunlight, watering a manicured lawn the size of a football field. Gardeners are everywhere. A man with a broom is sweeping the clay on the tennis court. There's even a maid buffing what appears to be a giant bronze apostrophe on the lawn. In the distance a white elephant of a house sits atop a slight hill. It's quite possibly the grandest house I've ever seen, the kind of thing one expects to see in *Architectural Digest* or on the *E! True Hollywood Story* about Martha Stewart.

I squint at the gatepost. A small sign, which I can barely make out, reads 39 Further Lane. Our alleged destination. I must have switched the numbers, I think. Maybe it was supposed to be 93 Further? Three thirty-nine Further? Maybe it was Farther Lane? I wrote down the instructions with one hand while trying to wrestle a loafer out of Norman's mouth, so it's possible I got them wrong. I pick up my cell phone and dial Zadie's number. When it goes to voicemail, I hang up without leaving a message. *Fuck.*

"Who lives here, Daddy?"

"I don't know, buddy."

"Is Aunt Zadie here?"

"I doubt it. I think there's been a mistake."

Caleb leans forward, as far as the straps of his car seat will allow, and shields his eyes with one hand, like an explorer pondering uncharted territory.

"They have a tennis court!" Caleb crows. "Let's go see."

"Caleb, stay in the car. I'll go see what's up." I switch off the engine and, with a sigh, hop out onto the side of the road.

Next to the gatepost, just as Zadie indicated there would be, is a keypad. Maybe she's renting a guest cottage on the property? With a sigh, I enter the code that she gave me: 1-9-8-0.

Nothing.

A family on bikes pulls up beside our car. The kids are in tennis whites, their hair combed back into perfect blond braids. Their mom wears a visor, a short tennis skirt, and a worried expression. She eyes our ancient Corolla, clearly wondering if we are gypsies setting up camp on the side of the road. She shoots her husband a look.

"Can we help you?" he calls out.

"Uh, no, thank you," I say as pleasantly as I'm able.

"Daddy!" Caleb bangs on the window. "I really have to poop again!"

"One minute, Caleb!"

"Are you lost?" the man persists.

"Nope, just can't read my own handwriting." I wave the index card with the gate code.

"Daddy, I'm pooping! I'm pooping right now!"

The two girls giggle in unison.

"We're really fine," I say.

"Okay," the dad says, unsure. He backs his bike slowly into the road. "Come on, guys," he says to his family. As they ride away, the mom turns to check us out over her shoulder. She narrows her eyes at me, like maybe she's contemplating a citizen's arrest.

"Jesus," I mutter under my breath. "People."

I punch the code in again. Still nothing.

"DAAAADDDDYYY!" Caleb howls.

"I'm coming, Caleb!"

I try again, adding "#" after "1-9-8-0."

Suddenly a figure emerges from the house. He stands on the front porch, gesturing frantically in our direction. He's yelling something, too, but I can't quite make out what.

"I'm sorry!" I shout. "I was just trying to open the gate!"

The figure trots down the driveway with what looks like a remote control in his hand. He appears to be pointing it at me, as though I'm a channel that he can simply turn off with a click of a button.

"It's okay, I'm leaving!" I raise my hands over my head, palms up.

"Stop! Stay right there!" the man shouts. I freeze in place. His face has turned shiny and red from exertion, and with each step his gut bounces up, then down, then up again. It's probably been a while since he had to chase someone off his property.

When he reaches the gate, he bends over, hands on knees, panting. After a second he straightens up. "Sorry," he says. "I'm a little out of breath."

"You okay, man?" I ask, not sure what to do. The guy looks like he might have a heart attack. "I have water in my car if you need it."

"Oh, I'm fine. So sorry about the gate. We've been having trouble with it all week." He holds up the remote control. "This is supposed to open it in a pinch, but it doesn't seem to be working, either."

"Ah. Well, I'm really sorry to have troubled you." I glance back at the car and wonder how this guy would feel about us using his bathroom.

"Nonsense. No trouble at all."

"Daddy!" Caleb screams from the car. "I wanna get out right now! I *POOPED!*"

"Oh, goodness," the man says. "Let's get you all inside." He disappears into a hydrangea bush, out of view. Suddenly, the gate springs to life.

"There you are!" he calls from the shrubbery.

"Oh, thank you, but—"

"I need a bathroom NOW!"

The leaves rustle as the man emerges. "The name's Sam Ives. Just call me Ives; everyone else does," he says. He sounds disheartened by this admission, as though he's been waiting his whole life for someone to call him by his proper name but has long since given up hope. "Just follow the drive up to the house. You can park right by the front door. I'll meet you up there. That little boy needs a bathroom!"

"Okay," I say, nodding gratefully. Caleb's screaming has reached a crescendo and I'm in no position to argue. We'll just use their facilities and leave. "Thank you so much. We'll be right up!"

"You'd better hurry! Looks like this is a bit of a family emergency." And with that, Ives takes off again, lumbering towards the house.

The Stranger's House

"Caleb, you're really going to have to just chill out."

This dictum comes out harsher than intended. Caleb falls into a guilt-inducing silence.

"I'm sorry, bud," I say, looking at him in the rearview mirror. "I didn't mean to snap at you."

"I feel bad," Caleb whimpers. "Really bad." I take a longer look, then try not to freak out. Caleb does, in fact, look bad. The color has drained from his face. His hair, once filled with static, now sticks damply to his forehead. It occurs to me for the first time that Caleb isn't whining. He's sick.

"Do you feel hot?" I say, my foot pressing down on the gas.

"No," he whispers. "Yes. I feel cold and hot."

I accelerate more than I should, given that I'm on a stranger's property. I catch a reproachful stare from a gardener pruning a gigantic poodle-shaped topiary.

"Daddy, slow down!"

"I'm sorry, bud, I'm just trying to get you to a bath—"

"HUWHUP." The car fills with a noxious smell, and the sound of Caleb hurling his guts out.

"Oh, shit. Caleb, you okay?"

Caleb doesn't answer. He's doubled over in his car seat.

I gun the engine and pull up in front of the house. As I step out onto the gravel drive, the front door of the house swings open. Ives strides through it, pushing an elderly man in a wheelchair.

"Hello again!" he calls out to me.

"My son just threw up," I announce as I race to open the passenger-side door. Norman hops out behind me, his tail wagging in the fresh air.

Caleb squawks and flails as I attempt to release him from his car seat. To my horror, not only is vomit everywhere, but poop is smeared across his thighs and, inexplicably, across his left cheek. A small streak has made it as far as the door handle. It looks as though he's been quietly finger-painting in the stuff for the last three hours.

"Daddy!" Caleb says gratefully. As I unsnap the car seat buckle, he reaches for me.

My heart melts a little.

It's not until I lift him up that I see the full extent of the problem. How a thirty-eight-pound child could produce that much poop defies imagination.

Trying not to breathe through my nose, I scoop Caleb out of the seat. He wraps his body around me like a baby koala. He smells horrible and his skin is clammy and hot. I can feel the squelch of bodily fluid on my neck as he nuzzles his face against it. If the kid is sick, there's no way I won't catch whatever's ailing him. I don't care. All I can think about right now is getting him washed, dried, and tucked into a warm, fluffy bed.

"Thank you, Daddy," he murmurs, then rests his head on my shoulder.

An almost superhuman burst of energy courses through my body as I run towards the house. *I've got this,* I think. *I am going to fix this problem.*

Then Zadie and Buck walk through the front door of the house and time grinds to a screeching halt.

"Zadie?" I say, stupefied. Caleb lifts his head off my shoulder. "What are you doing here?"

Zadie's hand falls onto the shoulder of the man in the wheelchair. *Oh my God,* I think, everything clicking into place. *It's finally happened. Zadie's gone back to her job as an in-home health aide for the elderly, and she's going to leave Caleb and me in the lurch.* Inviting us to her new client's multimillion-dollar Hamptons house is certainly one way to tell me.

Zadie is employed and getting married. I know I should be happy for her, but instead I'm consumed with rage. In fact, if Caleb wasn't potentially dying in my arms, I'd get back into my car and just drive home. How could she not give me some advanced warning? The engagement itself is bad enough, but now this? How am I going to explain this to Caleb? And how can she just stand there behind that man—her new charge—instead of rushing to help us?

"Hey, Chuck," Buck says, as he descends the steps to the driveway. "Let me help you."

He reaches out for Caleb, but I pull away. *I don't need help with my son,* I feel like shouting at him.

The elderly man in the wheelchair lifts his arm awkwardly, like a broken bird wing.

"Hello, Charlie," he says. "Welcome."

And that's when I realize. The man is not my sister's new client.

He's our father.

You Can't Go Home Again

I stop dead in my tracks. My father's voice is hoarse and soft, but I'd recognize it anywhere.

No.

"No way this is happening," I say, looking down into his hollowed eyes. He's lost weight. So much that his skin has shriveled around his skull like shrink wrap. It makes his jaw look sharper, his lips appear thinner. For a moment the two of us just stare at each other, speechless.

Caleb lets out a soft moan.

"Zadie!" I bark. "I need your help. *Now.*" Without waiting for permission, I stride into the house, Zadie trailing in my wake.

"We'll be right back," she says to the group, before the front door snaps closed behind us.

"What were you thinking?" I snarl at her as she ushers me into the nearest bathroom. "How did you even find him?"

Zadie ignores me. She opens the cabinet beneath the sink and pulls out a box of garbage bags. "This is the biggest mess I've ever seen!" she coos at Caleb, as though this were the seminal achievement of Caleb's five-year career as a human being. She strips Caleb's pants off and stuffs them in a garbage bag. "You poor sweetheart."

"I don't feel good, Aunt Zadie."

"I know, my love. But Aunt Zadie's here and everything is going to be just fine."

"*Zadie.*"

Zadie looks up at me, but not before rolling her eyes. "Charlie, why don't you try to be helpful? Draw a bath for him. Do you have a change of clothes handy?"

With a clenched jaw, I turn to the bathtub and start running the water.

"Make sure it's not too hot. Or too deep."

"Believe it or not, Zadie, I do have some experience bathing my own child."

"Could have fooled me."

"What the hell does that mean?" I snap. I know I shouldn't curse in front of Caleb, but I'm too pissed off to care.

"Just calm down, Charlie. You don't need to make everything into such a big deal." She pulls a thermometer out of the medicine cabinet, pauses to read the box, and then unwraps it from the package.

"Let me tell you what's a big deal. A big deal is bringing me out to *his* house without any warning whatsoever. *That* is a big deal, Zadie."

"If I had warned you, would you have come?"

"Of course not!"

Zadie shrugs. "So that's why I didn't tell you."

"This is not okay, Zadie. I have nothing to say to him. We are getting in the car and we are leaving the minute we get Caleb cleaned and dressed."

The thermometer beeps. Zadie examines it and then holds it out for me.

I bite my lip when I see the number on the screen: 105.1.

"You're not going anywhere," she says, "until Caleb sees a doctor. There's a bed upstairs. Let's get him bathed and comfortable and then we can talk."

A crowd has gathered in the foyer. It's a motley crew consisting of my father; Ives; Norman, who has made himself at home in what I'm sure is a priceless rococo chair; two blondes, one of whom looks vaguely familiar; a man who could easily pass for a Swedish model; and a silver-haired fellow holding what I hope is a doctor's bag.

"How is he?" Ives asks as Zadie and I descend the stairs.

"He's sleeping for now," Zadie replies. "He's got a fever. Could Charlie use the phone to call his pediatrician?"

"I'd really appreciate it," I say, grimacing. The last thing I want to do is ask my father for a favor, but right now my kid's got a fever of 105.1, my cell phone is dead, and I'm carrying a trash bag filled with his poop-stained clothes. If ever there was a time to swallow my pride, now might be it.

"No need," my father says, shaking his head. He gestures to the man with silver hair. "This is Dr. Simms. He's my personal physician. He'd be happy to take a look at Caleb."

I stop in my tracks, a few stairs up from the ground floor.

"That's great. Thanks, Dad." Zadie glares at me and I glare back. *Dad?*

"Maybe we should just go to the ER," I say. "His fever's over 105."

"The nearest hospital is in Southampton," Dr. Simms says. "On a beautiful weekend like this, the traffic will be murder. Why don't I have a look at the boy before you pack him up and put him back in a car? Perhaps we can avoid a hospital visit altogether."

I open my mouth to decline but quickly snap it shut. The last thing Caleb needs right now is another forty-five minutes in an un-air-conditioned car.

"Okay, fine," I say with a curt nod of assent. "Let's do that."

"I think what Charlie meant to say is: Thank you so much for your help," Zadie says to Dr. Simms. "We are so grateful that you'd drop everything to come over here, and so quickly."

Dr. Simms laughs. "Well," he says good-naturedly, "that's what your father pays me for."

Caleb's head looks tiny against the giant floral headboard, a lone dandelion in a bed of wildflowers. Because he was feeling the chills, Zadie tucked him beneath a fluffy duvet, better suited for January in Moscow than July in East Hampton. He's sleeping now with the duvet pulled all the way up to his chin. I kick myself for leaving Buddy, his pink fleece blanket, back at home.

As I watch Zadie hover at Caleb's bedside, I think back to those final days with Mom. The sight of my sick mother—with her gaunt face and gray skin—paralyzed me with fear. I never knew what to do when I was with her: Did I keeping talking to her even after her eyes slid shut? Did I pester her to drink the water and eat the food that most often she refused? Did I sit? Stand? Were jokes inappropriate or a welcome relief?

I didn't know what to do, so I did nothing at all. I hung back and let Zadie do the work. *She's more competent than me, anyway,* I told myself. *She's trained in this. She's a professional caregiver, for God's sake.*

The sicker Mom got, the more useless I felt. There were medicines to be measured, sponge baths to be given. My visits slowed from twice a week to once a month. I had excuses, some valid, some not. Zadie and I both knew the truth: I didn't come because I was scared of doing it wrong.

Don't do that this time, I think to myself as I stare at Caleb. *Be there for him. He's the only thing that matters now, and he needs you more than ever.*

I glance at Zadie. She puts her hand on my shoulder, pushing me gently towards my son.

I take a seat on the edge of the bed.

"Daddy?" Caleb's eyes blink open. His face floods with relief when he sees me, which is all the encouragement I need.

"I'm right here."

Caleb smiles. Then he crawls over, hangs his head over my lap, and upchucks into a wastebasket.

When he's done, he pulls himself up with some effort and slouches back against the pillows. "I don't feel good," he says, stating the obvious.

"I know, bud. But Dr. Simms is here. Maybe he can help you out."

Dr. Simms approaches the bed from the doorway. "Hi, Caleb," he says with a kindly smile. "I'm Dr. Simms. I understand you're not feeling too well. Do you want to tell me what's going on?"

Caleb furrows his brow. "You're not my doctor," he says flatly, as though it's obvious this guy's trying to sell him something. "My doctor's name is Frank."

Dr. Simms looks to me for guidance.

"That's right, Caleb, we see Dr. Frank in the city. But Dr. Simms is here now, and he came just to see you, so why don't you tell him a little bit about how you're feeling?"

"I'm your grandpa's doctor," Dr. Simms says, clearly hoping to instill confidence. Out of the corner of my eye, I see Zadie bite her lip.

"My grandparents are dead." Caleb practically yells this and then promptly hurls onto Dr. Simms's shoes.

"Oh!" Dr. Simms looks at me, then down at his shoes, then back at me.

"I'll get a towel!" I say, and flee down the hall to the nearest bathroom.

In the bathroom—which, incidentally, is roughly the size of my apartment—I have to splash a little water on my face to keep myself from freaking out. I never told Caleb that my father was dead, but it doesn't surprise me that he thinks that. After Mira died, we had one very detailed discussion of heaven. It went something like this:

Caleb: "Where is heaven?"

Me: "Well, I'm not sure. Some people say it's in the stars."

Caleb, looking confused: "Like Uranus and Pluto?"

Me, surprised: "Sure, okay. Like Uranus and Pluto."

Caleb: "And Mommy lives there?"

Me: "Well, yes."

Caleb: "Is there an elevator?"

Me: "Hmm. Yes. I think there might be an elevator."

Caleb: "And a doorman?"

Me: "And a doorman."

Caleb: "But we can't visit."

Me, reaching for him: "No, buddy. I really wish we could."

Caleb, dodging my hug: "Is she lonely?"

Me: "I'm sure she misses you. But she's not lonely. There are lots of other people in heaven to keep her company."

Caleb: "Like, who else?"

Me: "Well, your grandparents."

Caleb: "And?"

Me, searching for the name of another person Caleb knows who has passed away: "And Mrs. Hill from down the hall."

Caleb: "Mrs. Hill's cat, too."

Me: "That's right, and Mrs. Hill's cat."

Caleb: "I'm glad cats can go to heaven."

His grandparents—the three who matter, anyway—are dead. Mira's mother passed away shortly after we were married; her father died the same month as my mom. So it wasn't a lie, I tell myself, but rather, an honest mix-up. Still, the fact remains that Caleb thought my father was dead, and now, it turns out, he's not. Caleb has every right to feel angry, betrayed, lied to, and at the very least confused. He's not alone. That just about sums up how I'm feeling right now, so at least we're in it together.

"Everything okay?"

I spin around. The younger of the two blondes is leaning against the bathroom door, her arms crossed in a way that intensifies her cleavage. I know I've met her before, I just can't remember where. A friend of Zadie's, maybe? A law school acquaintance? *Though it's hard*, I think, as the pink lacy edge of her bra peeks out of her tank top, *to picture this girl at law school*.

"Oh, yeah, I was just looking for towels. I'm sorry, is this your bathroom?"

She tilts her head to one side and gives me a sly smile. Suddenly it clicks.

"Bungalow Eight," she says, reading my mind. "You were there for a bachelor party."

"Right, yes," I say, feeling my cheeks flush with embarrassment. "That was a long time ago."

"Was that nine years ago? I haven't talked to Justin in ages."

"Almost ten, I think." I know exactly when it was. It was four days after my first date with Mira. Because Mira hadn't returned my phone call, I convinced myself that she wasn't interested in me and that it was probably best to just move on. So I did what any normal guy would do: I got wasted and made out with a random girl in the middle of a nightclub.

That entire vodka-soaked weekend feels like it happened a lifetime ago, but as this woman walks towards me, it all comes flooding back. Nothing X-rated happened between us—in fact, our public make-out session was PG-13 at best. Still, it always made me feel dirty, because it happened around the same time I met the woman who I'd one day call my wife.

"My name's Madison, by the way."

"I remember."

"Probably didn't think you'd see me ever again, huh?" she says with a tight smile. My stomach twists uncomfortably as I recall the flirty post–make-out texts she sent me, none of which I returned.

"What are you doing here?" I blurt out, unable to help myself. "How do you know my father?"

She smiles again, ignoring my question. She walks over to a cabinet, bends far enough over for me to get an exceptional view of her exceptional ass, and removes a stack of towels from the bottom drawer.

"I'm Shelley's daughter," she says, holding them out to me.

"Who's Shelley?"

She chuckles, shaking her head. "You really don't keep in touch with your dad, do you?"

"Charlie!" Zadie shrieks from down the hall. "We need you!"

Madison steps aside. "I think you're being paged, Charlie."

"Good to see you again, Madison." I rush past, desperate to get away from her. "Thanks for the towels."

• • •

"What took you so long?" Zadie, now covered in vomit, glares at me from Caleb's bedside.

"I'm sorry," I say, feeling guilty, though I'm not quite sure what about. "I couldn't find the bathroom."

Zadie rolls her eyes and snatches a towel out of my hands. "Here, sweetie," she coos at Caleb, and gently pats the perspiration off his forehead. "Do you want to take a nice, cool bath?"

Caleb moans a little and slouches back against the pillow. "No bath," he says.

"He needs fluids," Dr. Simms says to me. "He's not holding down very much right now, but we have to try. How does he feel about Pedialyte?"

That stumps me. I have a vague recollection of doing a midnight run for Pedialyte when Caleb was a year or so old, but Mira was the one who administered it, so I'm not sure how it was received.

"He likes the freezer pops," Zadie pipes up.

"Great." Dr. Simms nods. "Someone should run out to the pharmacy and pick some up."

"I'll go!" Zadie and I both say at the same time.

Zadie shoots me a look. "Charlie, you really should stay with Caleb."

"Do you even have your license?" I snip.

"Buck will drive me," Zadie snips back.

"I'll go." Madison appears in the doorway. "I need to run to town anyway. What else do you need, Charlie?"

"We're fine."

"Oh, thank you, Madison," Zadie says, ignoring me. "Could you pick up a little extra Purina for Norman? And more Children's Tylenol?"

"Sure thing." Madison nods and turns towards the stairs. When I look back at Caleb, his eyes are shut. He's fallen back asleep.

"Probably best to let him rest," Dr. Simms whispers, and pulls down the shade.

I feel better after a shower, though not much. Norman and I hole up in a dark guest room across the hall from Caleb. I've made a point of leaving my suitcase in my car, so I dress again in the same rumpled shirt and shorts that I wore on the drive here. I don't need a change of clothes, I tell Zadie when she offers to fetch me one. There's just no way we're staying. She doesn't bother responding.

Part of me, the rational part, knows this isn't true. Caleb clearly has the stomach flu. He can barely make it to the bathroom; putting him on the Long Island Expressway would be tantamount to child abuse. If experience is any guide, we're not going anywhere for at least forty-eight hours, maybe more.

Caleb aside, my sister wants me to stay. At least, she wants me here enough to have willfully deceived me into coming. Zadie is many things, but she isn't deceptive. If anything, she's honest to a flaw, owning up to things she could easily get away with, like drinking the last ginger ale or forgetting to replace the toilet paper in the spare bathroom. As angry as I am with her right now, I know she has a reason for bringing me here. A misguided, poorly thought-out reason, I imagine, but a reason nonetheless.

When I hear a timid knock, I know it's her coming to apologize.

"Yes?" I say. My voice sounds stiff, possibly even hostile. Zadie might have good intentions, but that still doesn't mean I'm going to let her off easy.

"Hi," she says, poking her head around the door. "It's me."

"I know."

"Can I come in?"

"Sure."

Zadie takes a seat on the edge of the bed. She stares at me, waiting for me to say something, and when I don't, she drums her fingers anxiously on her knees. For the first time I notice the sapphire stone that glitters on her left hand.

"Nice rock," I say, nodding at the ring.

"Thanks. Look, I know you're mad that I dragged you out here."

"And?"

"And nothing. I thought maybe we could talk about it."

"How about you start with 'I'm sorry, Charlie, what I did was unconscionable and wrong and you have every right to be angry'?"

Zadie closes her eyes and lets out a long, noisy exhale. "I am sorry," she says, "that you are so angry."

"You don't think I have the right to be angry?"

Zadie's eyes flick open. "I think you have the right to be angry about a lot of things, Charlie. You have the right to be angry that your father wasn't around for you growing up. You have the right to be angry that your mom was so stubborn that she chose not to undergo the chemotherapy that could have saved her life. And you certainly have the right to be angry that a drunk pilot killed your wife."

I shake my head. "I wasn't talking about Mira, Zadie."

"I know. But I am. I'm talking about just a few of the many things that you could, in theory, choose to be angry about. But that's the thing, Charlie. It's a choice. What's anger done for you lately? It hasn't made you happier, that's for sure. And it's definitely not going to bring Mira back."

"What exactly is your point?" I narrow my eyes at her. "If you're going to get all 'Kumbaya' on me, please, don't waste your breath."

"My point is that you've been angry for years. And, fine, maybe you've had your reasons. But so what? Everyone has their reasons, Charlie. People who have had it a whole lot worse than you have found ways of moving on. It's time you did, too. If not for your sake, then for Caleb's."

"That's really easy for you to say. You have no idea what it's like to lose your spouse."

"You're right. I don't. But that doesn't mean I have to sit idly by and watch you waste the rest of your life. I'm tired, Charlie. I want my brother back. It's really that simple."

She turns towards the window.

"Ever since Mira died, you've acted like work is the most important thing in the world. And you know why I think you do that? I think you're scared. You're scared that if you were to take care of Caleb, you wouldn't do it exactly right. That was always your problem, Charlie. You were scared of not doing things perfectly. But you know what? I've been watching you for the past couple weeks. You're great with him. He loves being with you. You have nothing to be afraid of, except for losing more time with your family."

She lets out a long, resonant sniff, and I realize she is weeping. I shift uncomfortably, eyeing the door. Much as I hate getting into a whole thing with Zadie right now, it's not like I have anywhere to go. Caleb is sleeping in the next room. My father is downstairs, likely waiting for a father-son chat that's been thirty-five years in the making. I'm boxed in, unhappy Goldwyns on every side.

"How long have you two been in touch?" I say, sighing. I sit down beside her, letting my shoulder bump against hers.

"Since Mom got sick."

"Wow. So it's been a while."

"Yeah."

"Did he reach out to you? Or did you go looking for him?"

Zadie pauses. "It just sort of happened," she says. "Dad started visiting Mom after she got diagnosed. At first I was pretty cold to him. It bothered me, seeing him in her house. But she enjoyed being with him, I could tell. He always knew how to make her laugh. When she got really sick, towards the very end, she was out of it a lot. She was on so many drugs, some days she wouldn't even respond; she'd just slip in and out of sleep. And when she stared at you, her eyes were blank. I couldn't even tell if she knew who I was, you know? It was hard. But Dad took it in stride. He'd sit there for hours holding her hand or reading to her. To be honest, I was grateful for it. It wasn't easy, taking care of her alone."

"You weren't alone," I say, my stomach twisting with guilt.

"I know," Zadie says, far too generously. She pats my knee, the way our mother used to when she was trying to cheer me up. "I'm sorry, I didn't mean it that way. I just meant it was hard being alone in the house with her sometimes."

"I know what you meant. Please don't apologize. You bore the brunt of it."

Zadie nods, says nothing. For a minute we sit side by side in silence. Mom's death, I realize, is still a fresh wound for Zadie. Though they occasionally fought like feral cats, the two of them were inseparable. As a child, I resented their closeness. I hated the way Mom laughed harder at Zadie's jokes than she did mine. I hated that Mom praised Zadie for B pluses when I was getting As; I hated the way they rolled their eyes at one another whenever I acted nervous or uptight. Most of all, I hated coming upon them huddled over our dining room table, their heads bowed together in caucus, and how they would break apart when they heard me approach, their eyes wide and their faces flush with secrets.

While I couldn't get out of our little Long Island town fast enough, Zadie never really stopping calling it home. She'd move out for a time—she'd get a job or enroll in classes or shack up with a boyfriend—but after a few months she'd always return, suitcase in hand, to Mom's front door. For a while it irritated me. She was wasting her life, I thought, living at Mom's. The town itself was nice enough, a tidy bedroom community just east of the city, but for a young, single girl like Zadie it was a suburban purgatory. She never met anyone new. She hated the train and has always been a terrible driver, so she ended up working in town, at places that didn't require a commute. The jobs weren't exactly résumé boosters: waitress, bakery cashier, barista. The longer she stayed, the slimmer her prospects of ever leaving became.

And then Mom got sick.

She went in to see a doctor about what she thought was an ulcer but was, in fact, stomach cancer. They ran tests, then more tests. Zadie took the day off from work so that they could hear the results together. Zadie held Mom's hand as the doctor read off a bunch of numbers and statistics. When she called to update me afterward, Zadie told me she remembered only the number four. Stage four cancer. Four percent chance of survival. Four months left to live.

Mom opted out of chemo. "I'd rather have four pleasant months than ten miserable ones" was how she put it. Zadie was crushed but stoic. She surged into action. It wasn't long until Mom needed a professional nurse, too, but Zadie did everything else. She changed Mom's sheets, she took her for walks, she bought her *Us Weekly* and *Vanity Fair* the minute they appeared on the newsstand. She brought her Frappuccinos in the morning and made her favorite butternut squash soup from scratch. She bathed her, she changed her, she blow-dried her hair. If company came, Zadie applied foundation with a giant sponge, then varnished Mom's fingernails in the same slightly dated frosted pink that Mom had been wearing since the mid-1980s. Mom was always a little vain about company.

And where was I? I was at my desk at Hardwick, Mays & Kellerman. "Someone has to pay for the nurse," I'd say, though it was a preemptive defense, because Mom and Zadie had long ago stopped relying on me for anything more than financial support. I called too infrequently, visited even less. Mostly to assuage my own guilt, I sent a lot of checks.

"Getting to know Dad softened the blow, I guess." Zadie stares at her hands. She looks embarrassed, like she's just told me that she's picked up smoking or cheated on Buck. "He's not a replacement for Mom, obviously. But it was nice having him come into my life at a time when I was losing the person I was closest to."

"Why didn't you tell me? I mean, when he first came around? You never said a thing."

"I wanted to. But Mom told me not to tell you. She didn't want you to get upset. She knew how you felt about him."

"I thought we all felt the same way."

"We did. Or at least you and I did. Look, I wasn't thrilled to see him when he first showed up. But she was an adult, Charlie. And she was dying. I figured she should be able to see whoever she wanted to see without us passing judgment."

"But she hated him," I say stubbornly. And why wouldn't she? The creep had knocked her up and then left her to raise twins—his twins—without a thought. He never visited. He never sent so much as a birthday card.

She never said she hated him because she didn't have to. There would never be a custody battle over us. Mom didn't need to prove her case against Dad; we would never take his side or lobby in his favor. She was our mom. He was a stranger.

Until now.

"She didn't hate him, Charlie," Zadie says softly. "And I don't, either."

I flinch; her words feel like a cold, hard slap across the face.

"I know this is hard to hear," she persists, "but he wanted to be with her. He really did. He loved her. It was Mom who didn't want to be with *him*."

I shake my head dumbly. "No. He was *married*, Zadie. He was her *boss*. He took advantage of her."

"He didn't, Charlie. Mom wasn't exactly a wallflower. Think about it. *Mom*? She was as tough and opinionated as they come. You think she'd let some guy take advantage of her?"

I clench my jaw and refuse to answer. She has a point. Mom was no doormat. In fact, she was exactly like Zadie: strong-willed, defiant, always doing things her way. Still, this is a narrative I've subscribed to for years. After a short and ill-advised affair, Dad got Mom pregnant. He was married and unwilling to leave his wife for her. She was thirty-six and unwilling to terminate the pregnancy. So she raised us alone. End of story. It's going to take a lot to convince me that this story isn't true.

"She wouldn't have," Zadie continues, answering her own question. "Mom was independent. You know that. She was inde-

pendent to a flaw. She didn't *want* him to leave his wife for her. He
offered and she turned him down. She didn't *want* to marry Dad
and quit her job and move into his Park Avenue apartment and
live happily ever after like some kind of rescued princess in some
ridiculous Disney movie. That wasn't *her*. She wanted to do things
in her own way. And she did."

"By working and scraping and saving and never taking a day
off and never spending a goddamn dime on herself?" I snap.
"Yeah, she lived a really charmed life, being a single mom of twins.
Our father is obviously the victim here. How silly of me to have
thought otherwise." I stand up and walk towards the door. "I'm
going to check on Caleb."

"Please don't go, Charlie. I understand why you're angry. It's
a lot to take in. All I ask is that you talk to him so you can hear his
side of the story. Then you can decide for yourself."

"Listen to me, Zadie. Nothing can make up for the fact that
he wasn't there for us when we were growing up. Nothing. I'm a
father now, too, and I can tell you with no hesitation whatsoever
that I would never walk out on my kid. So whatever did or did not
happen between our father and our mother, at the end of the day,
doesn't mean shit to me. All I know is what happened between
him and us. He wasn't there *for us*. And that is what I can't forgive
him for."

We lock eyes. After a second, Zadie looks away, defeated.
"Okay," she says, almost in a whisper. "I understand. Maybe this
was a mistake."

"You're damn right it was."

"I'm sorry, Charlie. I really am. I just thought—" She's trying
her best not to cry, but she can't help it. Tears stream down her
face, and her shoulders shake with grief.

I feel the tiniest pang of guilt in my gut.

"You just thought what, Zadie?" I say, exasperated. "That we could spend a weekend together and somehow we'd magically become one big, happy family?"

"No," she says. "But I thought maybe we could start to try. What do we have to lose by trying?"

Never Too Late

Our first family dinner.

It can't be avoided. Caleb and Norman are both asleep, and I'm starving.

"You can't just stay up here all night," Zadie whispers, coaxing me away from Caleb's bed. "Let him rest. He's fine. You need to eat something eventually."

"There's a granola bar in Caleb's backpack."

"Don't be ridiculous."

I sigh. "All right. I'll come down for dinner."

"Good. I'm going to shower. I'll meet you downstairs in twenty minutes."

"If our father tries to have some kind of heart-to-heart, I'm leaving."

Even in the dark I can see Zadie rolling her eyes. "Twenty minutes," she says, before slipping back out to her room.

I return to the guest room where I've stashed my stuff and attempt to freshen up. Before I head downstairs, I call Fred to check in. I'm expecting it to go to voicemail, so when he picks up after half a ring, it throws me.

"Hey, Charlie," he says, sounding surprisingly relaxed and amiable. "I'm glad you called."

"I'm glad you picked up!" I reply, with an embarrassing amount of enthusiasm. "How are you?"

"I'm well, I'm well. I have good news for you."

"I like good news."

"You sitting down?"

I'm actually pacing back and forth like a madman, but I grind to a halt. "Sure, yeah."

"Today was my last day at Hardwick."

"You quit?" I say, stunned.

"I guess I did, yes."

How is that good news? I want to shout into the phone. *How are you going to help me get my job back if you don't even work there yourself?*

"Congrats," I mumble. "Terrific."

"I'm starting my own firm, Charlie. And I want you to come work for me."

Now I do sit down. I heard what he said, but it hasn't quite registered yet: I'm still processing the fact that Fred Kellerman is no longer at Hardwick, Mays & Kellerman. What is that firm without him? Fred helped build that firm. Fred *is* that firm. Hardwick without Fred is like the Patriots without Tom Brady. It just doesn't make sense.

Who cares about Hardwick? a voice in my head screams. *Fred is offering you a job! Take it! Take it now!*

"This *is* good news," I say, and realize that it is, in fact, great news. I jump to my feet, charged with excitement. "Wait, Fred, this is *great* news!"

He laughs. "Yes, I think so, too."

"I had no idea you were thinking of doing something like that."

"Well, I didn't want to mention it to anyone until I'd worked out an arrangement with Steve and Welles. They've been very gracious about the whole thing. They're allowing me to take my clients with me. It's going to be a boutique firm, all white-collar litigation work. I'm hoping to bring on maybe two or three others at your level, a few junior associates, and one or two paralegals, to start. I won't be able to pay you what you got paid at Hardwick, but I'll make you a partner."

My heart skips a beat. A partner. Fred's partner. More than money, more than anything, this is what I've always wanted. I've been working towards this moment for ten years, I realize. No, longer than ten years. I've been working towards this moment for my whole adult life.

"How does that sound to you? Can you be flexible about the money?"

"Yes," I say, without a second of hesitation.

"Terrific. We'll have to get started right away. The hours will be tough, especially in the beginning."

"Of course."

"You were never afraid to work hard, were you, Charlie?"

"No, sir."

"You're my guy."

"Thank you, Fred. I'm so excited about this opportunity."

"I'm out in East Hampton right now, but as soon as I'm back in the city, we should get together and talk."

"I'm actually out here, too, if you'd like to meet sooner."

"Are you? That's great. How about this coming Friday? That will get me a few days to get organized."

"Friday is perfect," I say without thinking. "Anyone else from Hardwick joining the firm?"

Fred pauses. "Well, no. That was part of the agreement with

Steve and Welles. I can take my clients, but I wasn't allowed to poach any of their talent."

I bite my lip. "But because I was fired . . ."

"Right. Because you were let go, you're fair game. So see, it was all for the best. Funny how life works out, isn't it?"

"Yes," I say with a jittery chuckle. "It sure can be."

Twenty-five minutes later I descend the stairs, feeling triumphant. I glance around, taking in the luxe surroundings. The house, I grudgingly acknowledge, is tastefully appointed. I was hoping for something garish, crass, hateable: gold gilt and zebra-skin rugs, maybe. Instead the floors are covered in soft sisal. The walls are painted in soothing earth tones—beiges and taupes and khakis—while the furniture is mostly white and pale blue, the colors of sea and sky. Most of the rooms open to the outside via French doors that, for the evening, have been left ajar. I can hear chatter from the veranda. When I hear my father's raspy voice, I feel my heart sink into my stomach. I momentarily consider breaking into the kitchen, pouring myself a celebratory glass of champagne, and sneaking back upstairs. Zadie would hunt me down and drag me to dinner by my ear. Better to walk in with some dignity intact.

That shouldn't be too hard to do, now that I'm officially a partner at the hottest new law firm in the city, I tell myself. *Take that, Dad. Take that, Todd Ellison.*

I throw my shoulders back and stride through the French doors. Zadie is nowhere to be seen. My father stands at the edge of the veranda, flanked by the two blondes.

The older one bounds towards me like a puppy.

"I'm Shelley," she says, wrapping me up in an unexpected hug. "I'm just so thrilled you're finally here."

She gestures at Madison. "This is my daughter, Madison."

"We've met," Madison and I both say in unison. She crosses her arms, looking about as uncomfortable as I feel.

"You want a drink, Charlie?" My father points me in the direction of a well-stocked bar at the far end of the veranda. "We've got everything. There's a nice bottle of Dom open. I'm a Scotch man, myself, so there's plenty of that. And Ives makes a mean martini."

And Christ, how I would love a drink right now. But I can't. I shouldn't. What if Caleb needs me? What if I have to drive him to the hospital in the middle of the night? He's asleep for now, but it's a feverish, restless sleep, one that could last twelve hours or twelve minutes, I can't be sure. Best not to drink.

Anyway, I don't want to give my father the satisfaction. He's trying to please me, I can tell; maybe "impress" is a better word for it.

"I'm fine," I say with a tight smile.

"Maybe just some water?"

"All right. A water would be fine, thanks."

"Pellegrino?" he asks hopefully. "Lemon? Lime?"

"Tap works for me."

"Just water, then." My father deflates a little. He nods to Ives, sending him scurrying back into the house.

"Beautiful evening." Zadie finally appears looking fresh in a yellow sundress and espadrilles. A shawl covers the giant butterfly tattoo on her left shoulder. She pushes back a strand of hair, flashing the new engagement ring. She's tan, I notice. Her hair has streaks of gold in it, either from the sun or a fancy Hamptons salon, I can't be sure. Apparently this life of leisure agrees with her.

"You look beautiful, my dear," my father says, beaming.

"Thanks, Dad. Buck's showering. He'll be down in a few."

"He did such a wonderful job with the hydrangeas."

Zadie grins. "He's got a green thumb for sure."

"He has a gift."

I turn away from them, resisting the urge to gag.

Ives reenters, looking at his watch. "Dinner is ready, sir," he says to my father. "Shall we?"

"Let's. I'm starved."

Ives wheels my father into the house, Shelley and Madison in tow. Zadie practically shoves me through the French doors behind them.

"Whoa, Tiger," I growl at her. "What happened to 'ladies first'?"

"Nope." She puts a firm hand on my shoulder. "You're staying where I can see you. No sneaking off until you've at least sat through dinner. It's only polite."

"I haven't eaten since breakfast. Trust me, I'm not going anywhere."

"Good. Because Dad made sure to serve all your favorites."

The dining room table seats sixteen, but there's only six of us tonight. Ives wheels my father up to the head of the table. Shelley tucks a napkin into the collar of his shirt and takes a seat to his left. Zadie and Buck sit next to her, leaving Madison to sit next to me.

"Please start," Shelley says, with the authoritarian air of a hostess.

I do a quick scan of her left hand: several expensive-looking rings, but none on the all-important finger. I wonder how long they've been together. My father was married when he had the affair with my mother, but that was thirty-five years ago. He could have been married five times over since then and I wouldn't know the difference.

It occurs to me how little I know about him. I always followed his career in the press, but I couldn't tell you the first thing about his personal life. The way Mom told it, my father didn't have a personal life. He was interested in one thing and one thing only, and that was making money. "He didn't know how to have fun," she told me once, after too much wine. "He didn't know how to live." Looking around this place, though, I can't help but wonder: Did Mom have it wrong? There's a swimming pool, a tennis court, a Ping-Pong table, a billiards room. There's a well-appointed library, the shelves of which are stuffed with books. And of course there's the ocean, a mere hundred yards from the front door. It's possible it's all for show. Or maybe, just maybe, the guy's changed.

Shelley's staring at me, I can feel it. I look up. She gives me a tender-eyed smile, the kind generally reserved for three-legged basset hounds and thirty-five-year-old widowers. I smile back, embarrassed. She obviously knows my life story; I don't even know her last name.

"I've heard so much about you, Charlie," she says. If she was close enough to take my hand, she would.

"Thank you for dinner," I mumble, unable to think of anything else to say.

"Zadie told me you love oysters. And I have all sorts of things for Caleb, too, whenever he's feeling up to it. I didn't know what he likes to eat, so I just got lots of everything." She laughs nervously.

"That's kind of you, but I'm not sure how long we'll be staying."

"Shelley used to be a nurse," Zadie says, as though this explains everything. "She takes such good care of Dad. He's really lucky to have her around."

Shelley blushes. She fingers a diamond heart pendant that has nestled itself between her generous breasts. A gift, I have to assume, from my father. Her nails are painted in the same orangey pink as her lips. "I'm the lucky one," she says, and beams at my father.

You certainly are, I think, glancing around the gigantic dining room. I knew my father did well for himself, but this spectacular oceanfront property tells me just how well. I don't know where Shelley came from, but I'm going to hazard a guess it's not nearly as luxurious as this.

"Any man would die happy after just one night with Shelley," my father declares. "And what's it been now, Toots? Eleven months we've been together?"

"A year next week."

"A year! We need to celebrate. I'm one lucky man." He raises his champagne glass, and everyone else follows suit.

"To family," my father says, and nods solemnly.

"Here, here." Buck stands up, and the two men clink glasses. Buck, I notice, has cleaned up rather nicely. His button-down shirt is tucked neatly into his jeans. His long hair is tied back in a ponytail and for once, he's actually bothered to shave. He's slimmer, too, and tanner. At six foot two, he dwarfs my sister, but they fit together nicely. As he sits back down, her head slips easily onto his shoulder. His arm falls around the back of her chair. They're a handsome couple, I have to admit. Handsome and happy.

Buck seems at ease around my father, which surprises me. As the dinner progresses, he listens intently to my father's stories about Wall Street in the eighties. He asks reasonably articulate questions about mergers and acquisitions. For his part, my father, who was once referred to as "the ultimate ball buster in the boardroom" by the *New York Post*, laughs easily at Buck's jokes and even appears engaged when Buck launches into a ten-minute-long seminar on how to properly prune a hedge. If he's disappointed by his daughter's choice of spouse, he doesn't show it. Likewise, if Buck's repulsed by my father's decadent lifestyle, his Dolly Parton-esque girlfriend, or his deep-seated commitment to the Libertarian Party, he's smart enough not to let on. From one outsider's perspective, Buck, my father, Zadie, and Shelley are one big happy family.

"They're cute together," Madison says to me, nodding at Buck as he steals a kiss from Zadie. "He worships the ground she walks on."

"He better."

"He does. I can tell." Madison takes a sip of her wine. "What about you?" she says after a second. "You dating anyone?"

I cough a little. No one's dared ask me that—at least, not in such blunt a fashion. Usually they dance around the topic, asking instead if I've been "getting out" or "meeting new people." No one wants to be the guy who tramples on the memory of my dead wife.

"That's kind of a personal question."

"Just making conversation."

"What about you? That guy you were playing tennis with—is he your boyfriend?"

She frowns, confused. "Oh, Sven? Tall, blond guy? Amazing body?"

"His name is actually Sven?"

"He's Swedish. He's, like, a really big-deal model over there."

"Of course he is."

She shakes her head. "He's just a friend. He's giving me free tennis lessons. He mostly teaches bored housewives who pay him a gazillion dollars a lesson because he looks so great with his shirt off. One of them lets him live in her pool house. It's a pretty sweet gig, if you can handle getting hit on forty times a day. Which Sven definitely can."

"Nice work if you can get it."

"If you're interested, I can introduce you. He's always telling me he needs another instructor to help out. July and August are his busy months. Maybe it would be fun for you while you're in between jobs."

"What makes you think I'm between jobs?"

"I hear you were captain of your high school tennis team," she says, ignoring my question.

"Where did you hear that?"

"From your dad." I can tell she's enjoyed catching me off guard. "He's very proud of that, you know."

"That was a long time ago. About eighteen years and twenty-five pounds, to be exact."

Madison looks me up and down. "I bet you can still play. I hear it's like riding a bike. I wish I'd learned earlier. I'm not sure I'll ever get the hang of topspin."

"You're just learning now?"

She chuckles. "Yes, I'm just learning now. I didn't exactly grow up in a place where people have tennis courts in their backyards."

"Neither did I," I say, annoyed. "I learned to play on a crappy court at the local community college."

"Hey, it's not a competition," she says. A bemused smile flits across her lips. "Listen, you want a competition, let's play tomorrow. You'll have to give me a spread, though. I'm a girl, after all."

"Sorry," I said, shaking my head. "I don't play anymore."

"Ever?"

"Ever." I look away from her, but I can feel her staring intently at the back of my neck. Zadie, who seems to have sensed the mounting tension between Madison and me, glares at me from across the table.

"Jeff will be disappointed to hear that," Madison says, sounding wistful. "He talks about how good you were all the time. He's really into tennis, you know. Still goes to the US Open, even in his condition."

"Impressing my father is not exactly a life goal of mine."

"Ah. So it's a coincidence, then?"

"What is?"

"That you went to the same law school he did?" She says this like it's nothing, like she's asking how I take my coffee.

"What's that supposed to mean?" I snap at her. "Look, you don't know me. You don't know the first thing about me."

"Charlie!" Zadie barks from across the table. "What's gotten into you?"

I glance up. Everyone is staring at me. Buck looks embarrassed. Zadie looks pissed. Shelley looks perplexed, like she can't begin to fathom where such anger is coming from. My father, well, he just looks sad.

"What?" I bark back at Zadie, crossing my arms defensively against my chest. "You didn't hear what she said to me."

"I just suggested he could teach tennis with Sven," Madison appeals to the table. "I was only trying to help."

"I don't need your help. And I don't need a job, either, FYI. I accepted a new position an hour ago."

"You did?" Zadie stares at me incredulously. "Already?"

"That's great, Charlie." Shelley gives me an indulgent smile, like I've just announced that I'm becoming a Boy Scout. "Good job."

"With who?" my father says. "You're not going back to Hardwick, are you?"

"No, I'm not," I say, surprised to hear him admit that he knows where I work.

"Good. Fred Kellerman is a dickhead if I ever saw one."

"Actually," I say frostily, "Fred is starting a new firm, and he asked me to work for him. I'm going to be his partner."

"Ah," he says, and tucks into his lobster.

I sit for a minute in stunned silence, expecting him to apologize or at least back-pedal a little. Instead, he chews. His bottom lip hangs open as he does it, like a door that doesn't quite hang right on the frame.

"For the record, Fred is not a dickhead. He's been a mentor to me."

My father shoves a giant piece of lobster claw in his mouth. "He's a great lawyer, I'll give him that," he says after a loud swallow. "If I was going to learn how to litigate from anyone, it'd be him. But he's a dickhead. I went up against him once, back when I was still practicing. He didn't think twice about re-trading us at the last minute. He's an Indian giver."

"Oh my God." I glare at Zadie, who refuses to make eye contact, "I can't decide what's more offensive: you insulting a man I just told you was my mentor, or the fact that you actually just used the phrase 'Indian giver.'"

"He offered us a settlement and then took it back."

"I know what it means."

"I just call it like I see it. That's all. I'm too old to pussyfoot around. If I don't like someone, I say so. And I don't like Fred Kellerman."

"Can't we drop this?" Zadie pleads. "Can't we talk about something else?"

"What, and pretend we're having a normal family dinner?" I say. "That's ridiculous."

"We don't have to pretend anything," Madison says crisply. "But we can try to behave like civilized adults."

"No one asked for your opinion," I hiss at her. "This isn't your family, so why don't you just butt out?"

"Actually, this *is* my family. Jeff—*your dad*—is about to propose to Shelley—*my mom*. We're going to be stepsiblings, you idiot."

My mouth drops open. Before I can speak, Shelley lets out a pig-like shriek. "You're going to propose to me, baby?" She leaps up and throws her body onto my father, covering his face in kisses. "Oh my God, are you really?"

"That's great," Buck says, raising his champagne glass. "Mazel tov."

"When was this supposed to happen?" Zadie says, looking slightly crestfallen. Clearly she's not loving the idea of her father stealing her engagement thunder. "You never said anything, Dad."

My father shrugs from beneath Shelley. His mouth flops open and closed, fishlike, but no words come out.

"Jeff?" Shelley says, pulling herself up. "It's true, right? You're proposing, right?" She searches his face, desperate for answers.

"I helped him pick out the ring," Madison insists. "Tell them, Jeff."

"You let her help you pick out the ring?" Zadie asks, pointing a finger at Madison. "What about *me*? Why wouldn't you ask *me*? And when exactly are you getting married? I thought you were okay with us getting married here at your house. But if you have your own wedding to plan—"

"Wait—what?" I push my chair back from the table. "You're getting married *here*? No way. That's so not cool, Zadie."

"It's hard for Dad to get around and I want him to be there," Zadie declares. "Anyway, why do you care where I get married? It's *my* wedding."

"Well, for starters, I never want to set foot in this house again. Not to mention the fact that Mira and I got married in the Hamptons, so it doesn't exactly bring back the best memories for me. You seriously couldn't find a more neutral venue?"

"Your wedding was in Sag Harbor!" Zadie shouts. "That's a totally difference place!"

"It's still the Hamptons!" I shout back.

"SHUT UP, YOU TWO," my father booms. "SHUT UP AND SIT DOWN."

Stunned, Zadie and I both fall back into our seats. Madison, Buck, and Shelley all stare at their hands, as though embarrassed to be caught in the middle of our family drama. The dining room is so quiet that I can hear the banging of pots in the kitchen and the far-off sound of the waves crashing against the shore.

"That's better," my father says in a normal tone of voice. "Now, look. I'm going to talk for a few minutes and you're going to listen. And after I'm done, you can scream at each other all you like, or you can scream at me, or you can get up and walk out and that will be that. All I'm asking for is two minutes of your time. Fair?"

Like petulant teenagers, we nod our heads.

"Good," he says. "All right. So first of all, Charlie, I want you to know that I understand how hard this must be for you. I have a ways to go in proving myself to you, and I know that we may never get to the point where you are comfortable visiting my house. When I offered to host Zadie's wedding, I worried how you would respond to it. The last thing I want to do is have you feel like I'm just strolling into your life after thirty-five years and trying to pretend that I'm the father that we both know I wasn't. I can't make up for the time I wasn't there for you. Trust me, if there's one thing I know, that's it. And I'm not trying to. I'm simply trying, as best I can, to be the best possible father I can be with the years I still have left."

He looks at me, hoping, I suppose, for some kind of reaction.

Keep your mouth shut, I tell myself. I stare straight ahead, refusing to make eye contact. *Pretend you're in court, listening to opposing arguments. Don't let him see you react. It's better to let him sweat.*

After an uncomfortable second, my father clears his throat and keeps talking. "Over the past five years, Zadie and I have managed to build a relationship. I'm grateful every day that she's allowed me to be a part of her life. It's meant more to me than you could ever imagine. When she and Buck told me they were going to get married at City Hall because they couldn't afford anything more than that, I told them I'd pay for them to get married in any fashion they wanted. It's what any father would do for his daughter. But Buck and Zadie said no. They just weren't comfortable having me foot the bill.

"Now, as you can see, the past few years have not been kind to me. I have Parkinson's disease, Charlie. It's hard for me to get around. So I suggested an entirely self-serving solution: Get married here, and soon. That way I don't have to get in a car, and Zadie and Buck get a free venue. And, given Buck's green thumb, I've gotten a whole new garden out of the deal. That's what, in my business, we call a win-win.

"Now, it's true, I would also like to marry Shelley. I don't have much time left, and what time I do have, I'd like to spend with her. I asked Madison to help pick out a ring because I figured she'd know her mom's taste better than anyone. I wasn't going to pop the question until after Zadie and Buck's wedding, because I wanted this to be their special time. They were kind enough to have a short engagement at my request, so I figured the least I could do was let them enjoy the few weeks of engagement they do get to have."

Here my father stops and gestures for Shelley to hand him a glass of water. He sputters a little when he takes a sip, and for the first time, I realize how weak he truly is. Despite everything, I feel a sudden urge to reach out and hug him.

"So that's it," he says. He sniffs a little; his eyes, I notice, are watering. Shelley and Zadie, too, are fighting back tears. Even Buck has his hand over his heart, like he's been touched deeply by my father's words. "That's all I've got. I may not have gone about any of this in the right way, Charlie, but I'm trying. I really am."

"You want to marry me," Shelley whispers. She shakes her head in disbelief. "I hoped, of course, but—"

"Shelley, you're the best goddamn thing that ever happened to me. Before you, I was just a sad sack in a suit. I worked twenty-four hours a day, three hundred and sixty-five days a year. All I did was work. I breathed, slept, and ate work. And why? I had all the money in the world, but it couldn't buy me the one thing I wanted. Happiness."

"Baby!" Shelley cries, and flings herself back into my father's arms.

"Aw, hell, this isn't the way I wanted to do it, but life's short, right? Can't do everything according to plan. And I have my whole family together for once, and who knows if that will ever happen again?" My father sighs. Then he lurches forward so abruptly that, without thinking, I leap out of my seat.

"Jesus, are you okay?"

I feel a hand grip my forearm.

"Sit down, you idiot," Madison whispers into my ear. "He's proposing."

My head swivels around. My father has, not without effort, found his way onto one knee.

"Shelley Ann Peters," he says, his voice shaking, "will you marry me?"

"Oh my God!" Shelley's cries of delight are muffled by the frantic bovine sounds of their kissing.

Madison makes a snorting sound. I turn, hopeful that at least one other person is finding this display as absurd as I do. But Madison, to my surprise, is wiping away a tear.

"That's beautiful," she says, biting her lip and nodding. "Really, really beautiful."

"It is," Buck chimes in. "Wow. It's never too late, is it, Jeff?"

"Never too late," my father agrees.

"I'm so happy for you guys," Zadie adds weepily. "You're great together."

"Thank you, honey." Shelley puts her hands over her heart. "I feel so blessed to have you and Buck in my life." She gestures at Madison. "In *our* lives."

"Jeff, I'm sorry I ruined the surprise," Madison says, pouting.

He waves her off. "Forget it, sweetheart. Listen, you probably did me a favor. Look at me. Who knows how long I've got? I'm too old for secrets."

"Stop it, baby," Shelley coos. "You're going to make it to a hundred. I need you to. I need you." She rests her head against my father's shoulder.

"Anything for you, Shel."

"I'm glad the cat's out of the bag," Zadie says. "Maybe we should have a joint wedding!"

"No," my father, Shelley, and Buck say in unison.

"I was kidding." Zadie rolls her eyes. "Don't you worry, Shelley, I'm going to make sure he throws you the best party in town."

Shelley laughs. "Oh, girl, you're too much. Listen, when you're on your third wedding like I am, you're not exactly expecting a big to-do."

"All the more reason."

"Hey, you two," my father barks. "Enough. I may be old and I may be immobile, but I still have a trick or two up my sleeve. Shelley, babe, I'm going to give you the wedding of your dreams. So don't you worry about *that*. In the meantime, though, we got ourselves another big Hamptons wedding to plan."

He looks over at me, and for the first time all night we lock eyes. "Whaddaya say, Charlie? This all right with you?"

"Please, Charlie," Zadie says, her eyes pleading. "Please say yes."

I bite my lip. If he had asked me thirty minutes ago, I would have responded with a resounding *No!* Maybe it's the wine I had with dinner. Maybe it's just fatigue. But somehow I just don't have the strength to argue anymore.

I shrug. "Fine with me," I hear myself say.

"Yes!" Zadie squeals. "Thank you, Charlie! This means the world to me!"

"Hey, thanks, bro," Buck says, pounding his fist against his chest. "That gets me right there."

"You'll be the best man, won't you, Charlie?" Zadie says, bounding over to give me a hug.

"Don't push your luck."

"We can talk about the details in the morning," my father says briskly. "I think we've made enough decisions for one night."

"You can say that again," I say, nodding at him.

"Look at you two," Zadie sighs happily. "Getting along and everything."

"It's been a long day," I say, shooting her a look. "I'm going to go check on Caleb and then I'm hitting the hay."

"That's a great idea," my father says. "Let's all get some sleep. We're going to need it. It's going to be a big month here at Casa Goldwyn."

The Fallen Leaf

I wake up feeling dirty.

For starters, I hooked up with my stepsister-to-be. Any psychiatrist would have a field day with that one. Then there's the fact that I agreed to let my father host Zadie's wedding. Not that Zadie needs my blessing, but I'm pretty sure I gave it anyway. My father really worked me over with that speech of his. Somewhere between the Parkinson's and the admission of deep, all-consuming loneliness, I actually started to feel sorry for the guy. Thirty-five years of neglect, undone in twenty minutes. At least now I can say I understand why he's been as successful as he has. The guy is a helluva negotiator.

Finally, I sold myself to Fred without a second of hesitation. It's not like I have a bunch of other offers to consider, but I could have at least told him I'd sleep on it. I definitely didn't need to accept his offer on the phone, without even discussing things like salary or health care or a 401(k). Where's my self-respect? Where's my pride? Where are my negotiating skills? I have a child to think about. I should've at least pushed him a little bit on the money. God knows he can afford it.

I glance over at Caleb, who's asleep beside me. He's curled up on his side, one hand draped over Norman's belly. While his nausea seems to have passed, the smell of it still lingers in the air. All the seagrass-scented candles in the world couldn't keep the infirmary smell out of this room. The trash can—the decorative kind not meant for actual trash—probably should be thrown out. A light crust of vomit can be seen on the carpet beside it. An unidentified stain, too, mars the headboard. My heart breaks a little when I see a wet washcloth on the nightstand. Whatever happened, I'm almost certain Caleb tried to fix it while I slept.

The thousand-count sheets—pristine and fresh when we arrived—are rumpled and sweaty. Caleb's fever spiked again in the middle of the night. I only noticed because his head lolled against mine on a shared pillow. I woke him, ladled Children's Tylenol into his mouth, watched his body go slack and his eyes roll closed the minute he washed it down. He fell asleep against me, my arm tucked around him like a wing.

My heart lurches when I think about going back to work so soon. We'll need to find a nanny, I guess, now that Zadie's out of the picture. I wonder how long that will take. It would be nice to have a few more weeks off. Not just for Caleb's sake, but for mine.

We'll just have to make the most of the next few days, I tell myself. *We'll try to pack as much fun as we can into the time we have.*

I feel strangely and suddenly compelled to wake him up just so I can talk to him. What does he want to do today? Go to the beach? Go into town and buy ballet slippers? Learn how to fly a kite? I don't care, as long as we're together. If I've learned anything in the past few weeks, it's that my kid is *fun.* He's funny. And he is wise as hell. He knows who he is and he just owns it. He could teach me a thing or two about a thing or two. If only we had more time.

A strand of hair sticks to his forehead. I resist the urge to reach out and push it off his face. It's seven thirty; I can't believe he's still asleep. Usually Caleb is an early riser. The rooster, Zadie calls him, up at the crack of dawn. I'm getting hungry, but I don't dare leave him. I don't want him to wake up alone in a strange house.

I pick up my phone, busying myself. I smile when I see a text from Elise:

Early morning at the 76th playground. :-) You boys around?

I wish! I type back. *Sorry to miss the fun. We're away for the weekend. Would love to see you soon.*

I linger over this last sentence before hitting Send. "Love" sounds too strong, I decide. Delete, delete, delete.

"Would like to see you"? No, that sounds vaguely ominous; like something a boss says to an underling when they've made a mistake at work.

"Would be nice to see you"? Too tepid.

"Would be great to see you." That works. I type that instead. Should there be a question mark at the end? The period seems so final. Like I'm not begging for a response, which of course I am.

Before I hit Send, she pings me again:

Ahh, total meltdown in progress. Have to jet. We're out in East Hampton through the end of August but let's plan a catch-up for when we return.

We're here! I type excitedly.

The playground?

No, East Hampton!

No way! That's awesome. Where are you staying?

I pause before typing: *At my father's house on Further Lane.*

Fancy, she says.

You have no idea.

Sounds like you need a rescue.

You have no idea.

I'll call you tonight. Planning to drive out early tomorrow morning. Hoping Lucas naps in car. *fingers crossed*

"Mmm-hmmm." Caleb clears his throat. I look up from my phone. He's staring off into space, blinking his blue-gray eyes. He looks pale but less sweaty.

"Hey, bud! How're you feeling?" I put my phone down on the nightstand, reach for his forehead. "Oh, good. No fever."

"I'm thirsty. And *hungry*."

"That's great news. Let's get you some breakfast." I walk over to the window, roll up the shade. The sky is gray; a fog has rolled in overnight, blanketing the ocean. Though this beach must certainly be beautiful beneath a cloudless sky, there's something majestic about the fog. Past the wooden deck, dune grass sways, giving way to a wide stretch of sand. The wind whips the water into frothy whitecaps; two surfers bobbing on boards break the horizon line. On the shore, a little boy sprints to the dunes and back, an alligator-shaped kite bouncing along the sand. His father trails him, then raises his hands in victory when the kite finally takes flight.

"What an incredible view," I say, more to myself than to Caleb.

Caleb swings his legs over the side of the bed. Like an old man, he presses one hand to his lower back, stretches, ambles over.

His eyes light up when he sees the beach.

"Wow," he says, nodding in approval. "Can we go?"

"Sure. After you eat something, though, okay? Maybe some toast?"

Caleb ignores this. "I want to swim in the ocean," he says, staring out the window. "And I want a kite. And I want to hang out with Aunt Zadie."

"I'm sure she'd love that."

He turns, cocks his head, squints his eyes. "Are you mad?"

"Am I mad?"

"Are you mad at Aunt Zadie?" He crosses his arms, as if to say, *Don't bullshit me, Dad*. "You yelled at her yesterday. A lot."

I sigh and sit down on the bed. I pat the duvet next to me. After a moment of hesitation, he joins me. "Listen, Caleb, I'm really sorry about yelling at Aunt Zadie, okay? I shouldn't have done that in front of you."

"You shouldn't have done that *at all*," Caleb corrects.

"That's true, you're right. Yelling's never okay. It won't happen again."

"Why were you so mad?"

"Hmm, that's a good question," I say, hoping that nonanswer will suffice.

Apparently not. "Is it because of your daddy?" Caleb persists.

"My daddy?"

"Because you thought he was dead and now he's not?"

"Wow. Okay. So here's the thing, Caleb. My daddy went away when I was really little. So he wasn't part of our family growing up. It was just me, Zadie, and Grandma Kay."

"So you thought he was dead?"

"No. I didn't think he was dead. He just wasn't part of our family."

Caleb frowns. "But that doesn't make sense," he says. "If he's your daddy, then he's part of our family. For sure. Like on the trees."

"The trees?" Sometimes talking to Caleb feels like talking to a small drunk person. The individual words make sense, but when strung together in a sentence, not so much.

"Yeah. The trees we made. For the hallway in the Green Room."

"Oh, the family trees." I blanch a little inside, remembering the family tree incident at Madison Avenue Preschool. Each child in Caleb's class was given trunks and leaves made from construction paper. With the help of their teacher, the well-meaning Ms. Wilson, family members' names were inscribed on the leaves and subsequently glue-sticked onto the trunks, then displayed in the hallway under a sign that read: "Green Room Family Forest."

A straightforward, seemingly innocuous assignment, or so Ms. Wilson thought.

Shortly after the project commenced, the Green Room descended into chaos.

One girl, Eloise Van Driesen, helped herself to three trunks—her daddy had been married that many times, she allegedly said—and, in so doing, incited a near-riotous run on the supply closet during which mousy Travis Barnstock was nearly trampled.

Dash Klein, unable to remember if his siblings were half or step-, had such an epic meltdown that a blood vessel burst in his eye.

Pierce Cortlandt stabbed his twin brother, Hunter, with a Popsicle stick (lifted from the supply closet) for "copying" his tree, potentially causing permanent hearing loss in his left ear.

And Barnes Shepson, the lone heir to the Shepson Pharmaceutical fortune, so thoroughly covered his trunk with the names of nannies, chefs, drivers, and assorted other caregivers that there was, according to him, "no room left for Mommy and Daddy."

"Only in Manhattan, right?" Ms. Wilson asked me, and attempted a weak smile. We had both been called into the program director's office to discuss, once again, what should be done about Caleb.

Jeannine French gazed at us from across her desk, her eyebrows knitted together in studied concern. Ms. Wilson smoothed the front of her dress over and over, declining to look up. I could tell that at that very moment she was considering packing it in and moving herself back to whatever Midwestern town she once called home.

"Just show me Caleb's tree," I said, cutting to the chase. It was, after all, the reason I'd left work early.

With some hemming and hawing, the tree was produced.

It took me a moment to realize what I was looking at. But once it clicked, I felt my heart drop out of my chest.

"You see, he glued you and your sister up here at the top—" Jeannine began.

"Yes, I see," I said, interrupting her.

"And your wife is here at the bottom . . ." Her voice trailed off. Indeed, Caleb has glued his "Mommy" leaf to the base of the tree instead of up in the branches as instructed.

I traced my finger over it.

"Any chance he just made a mistake?" I asked, knowing the answer. Not even five, but Caleb was smart enough to know where leaves grow.

"It's possible," said Ms. Wilson, though her eyes told me she didn't believe it.

"On one hand, I find this very impressive," Jeannine said, with forced enthusiasm. "The concept of a fallen leaf—well, it's very . . . *sophisticated* for a child of Caleb's age."

"Sophisticated, but morbid," I suggested.

She looked away. "Well, that's not a word I would use. But it does, I think, raise"—pause again—"*questions*."

"Questions."

"Yes, questions. About how Caleb is grappling with the loss of your wife. About his abilities to name his grief, to define it in such a way that allows him to make sense of it, process it, and eventually make peace with it."

"Is that what we're supposed to be doing?" I said, with a dry laugh. "Because if Caleb can figure out how to do that, I really hope he'll show me the way."

"Your daddy's a leaf," Caleb says, insistent. "The daddy always gets a leaf *no matter what*."

"Okay, that's right. He's a leaf on our family tree."

"Right next to Grandma Kay."

"Uh, okay. Sure. Right next to Grandma Kay." My stomach sinks as I say it, but I'm willing to concede my father a spot on my mother's branch if that's what it's going to take to get this conversation behind us.

Caleb nods, satisfied. "So, are you mad at him?"

"Who? My dad?"

"Yeah." He stares out at the ocean. The fog, I notice, is beginning to lift.

"Well, I was. For a long time. Maybe I still am, a little."

"Why?"

"Because he wasn't around very much when I was your age."

Caleb shrugs. Not such a big deal, in his estimation. "Maybe he had stuff to do," he says.

"I'm sure he did."

"We're all busy." He says this with such adult candor that I crack up. He looks up at me, confused and delighted. He hadn't meant to make me laugh.

"We're definitely all busy," I say, putting my arm around him.

"Especially you. You're always busy."

Not lately, I think to myself. "Especially me."

"Even Buck. Even when he's lying on the couch sometimes he still says he's busy."

I roll my eyes. "Even Buck."

"I think maybe you shouldn't be mad at him."

"I'll try my best."

"You wanna know why?"

"I do."

"A lot of reasons. But one is that he has a really nice house and he invites you over."

I laugh again. "That he does."

"I want to go outside. I think the sun is coming out."

"I do, too, bud."

"I want to stay here."

I bite my lip. "I do, too. I really do." To my own surprise, I mean it.

This Was Not the Plan

A year or so after Mira and I got married, everything changed. Suddenly everyone around us was either pregnant or trying to become so. Mira spent every other weekend, or so it felt, attending a baby shower or visiting a newly minted mom in the hospital. At parties, our friends discussed in vitro fertilization with the same enthusiasm that was once reserved for the playoffs or front row seats at a Jay-Z concert. And then there were the e-mails. My in-box overflowed with news of impending arrivals and photos of the recently born. "Our Little Angel!!!" the subject line would read, or "Welcome to the World, Baby Hazel!" Ecstatic declarations of weight and length would accompany a close-up of a squished little alien face, or, worse, a shot of a tiny human form draped across the exhausted mother's naked, blue-veined bosom.

"Doesn't this feel like TMI?" I handed over my phone to Mira, the screen open to a shot of a colleague's wife breastfeeding in a hospital bed. "I mean, how am I supposed to talk business with this guy now? We both know that I've seen his wife's nipples."

"I think it's beautiful," Mira said, handing back the phone. "That's what nipples are for."

"Among other things."

Mira let out a disapproving cluck. "I find it really sad that our culture doesn't celebrate breastfeeding. Look at her. She's giving life to her child. That's incredible. Why should she cover it up, like it's something to be ashamed of?"

"I'm not saying she should cover up all the time. Just maybe for the photo her husband is planning to send out to ten thousand of his closest friends and colleagues."

We talked about having children of our own, of course. What couple doesn't? But the whole concept of parenthood always felt—to me, anyway—theoretical and remote instead of logistical and immediate. Something we'd get to eventually but hadn't completely thought through. Not unlike Spanish lessons or a trip to Southeast Asia. A fun project for another day. In truth, it was hard for me to wrap my head around the idea of adding such a huge commitment to my already demanding schedule. Not to mention the expense, which was staggering. I was making decent money at Hardwick, but was it enough to support a child in Manhattan? I wasn't entirely sure.

Any pangs of paternal longing were effectively snuffed out every time I saw Dan, my closest friend from law school. Dan had three kids under three. Twins Sofia and Hannah, who everyone agreed were adorable, if a little high-maintenance; and then Max, who was a monster. Once Max arrived, Dan's house was thrown into a perpetual state of chaos. Cheerios crunched underfoot. Sprinkle, the dachshund, became so irritable that he was sent off to live with cousins in Teaneck. Dan started smoking again. Agnes, his wife, not only kept the baby weight but gained a few pounds on top of it. They could never find a sitter. If we wanted to have dinner with them, we had to trek out to their house in Park Slope. Inevitably, the entire dinner was spent talking about breast pumps and potty training. Occasionally, Dan would just zone out in mid-conversation. He'd slump back in his chair and just stare into his drink, as though he couldn't quite believe that his life had come to this.

On one such Saturday evening, we arrived at their house at the agreed-upon time bearing a Tupperware container filled with Mira's homemade tabbouleh. It was dark and raining. Not a pleasant, light rain but a wet, bone-numbing downpour. We rang the bell and waited. Nothing. We shivered, stamped our feet like horses. The sound of a child wailing could be heard from the upper reaches of the house. I grumbled something about Max that Mira pretended not to hear. Instead she flipped up the hood of her coat and rang the bell again.

"Are we sure it's tonight?" I said, staring impatiently at my watch. "If we leave right now we could still make a nine p.m. movie in Union Square."

Before Mira could answer, there was a rustling on the other side of the door and an unclicking of locks.

"Oh, hi," Agnes said when she saw that it was us. She looked harried and vaguely surprised, as though she hadn't been expecting to find us on her doorstep. "You're here."

"We're here!" Mira said with a big, cheerful smile. "Seven thirty, right?"

"Right, sure. Seven thirty. Come in." She gestured vaguely at the entryway floor, which was littered with sneakers and munchkin-sized Crocs. "You don't mind taking off your shoes, right?"

"Not at all," Mira said, and shot me a look that squelched all protest. As if on cue, a series of loud, bloodcurdling screams emanated from the second floor.

"That's Max," Agnes said wearily. "Just ignore him. We're doing 'cry it out.'"

"What's 'cry it out'?" Mira asked, alarmed.

"It's where you just let them scream. Until they fall asleep. It sounds inhumane, but it's better for everyone in the end. Truly."

Mira nodded and said something that was drowned out by an even louder wave of hysterics.

Dan emerged from the kitchen, beer in hand. "Sorry, guys. I feel like we should hand out earplugs at the door." Instead he proffered a thick stack of takeout menus. "I know we said we were going to cook, but we're sleep training Max for, like, the fifth time and we're totally zonked. Do you mind ordering in?" I couldn't help but notice a slight slur in his voice, though whether it was from drinking or exhaustion, I couldn't quite be sure.

"How many of those have you had?" Agnes said, nodding at the beer. "Don't you think you should slow down?"

"I will slow down once Max slows down," Dan replied through a tight smile.

"So you're planning to drink for the next eighteen years?"

"If that's what it takes."

"Are we scaring you yet?" Agnes asked Mira.

"Not at all. We totally understand," Mira said.

"Speak for yourself," I said. Everyone laughed, though I really hadn't been kidding.

Three bottles of wine later, nerves had settled, and Max had finally stopped screaming.

"I'm sorry if I seemed stressed-out when you guys arrived," Agnes said apologetically. "Bedtime is kind of the witching hour over here."

Dan nodded. "You guys should come for brunch some weekend. During daylight hours the screaming is only occasional."

"We'd love it," Mira said.

"Mira is terrific with kids," I said, already coming up with excuses in my head. "She is potentially the only grown-up I know who enjoys toddlers' birthday parties."

Dan and Agnes exchanged glances.

"So, what about you guys?" he said, emptying the last of the wine into his glass. "What's your plan?"

"What's our plan for what?" I asked. I glanced over at Mira, who was busying herself with a forkful of tabbouleh.

Dan laughed. "For having kids. You ready yet? What's it been, a year since you guys got married?"

"A year and three months," Mira said.

"A year and three months," Dan repeated. He shot me a knowing grin. "So, how about it, Charlie?"

"Kids aren't part of the immediate plan," I said, annoyed at Dan for putting me on the spot.

Agnes raised her eyebrows but said nothing.

"I mean, I'm up for Senior Associate in two years," I added quickly. "I was just thinking it made sense to wait until then, at least."

Silence. Seconds ticked by. Agnes coughed a little. Dan winced, as though embarrassed for me. "Right," he said. "That makes sense."

"So, how about ice cream?" Agnes offered.

"Ice cream sounds great." Mira hopped to her feet. She reached for my plate.

"I've got it," I said, but she snatched it away before I had a chance to stand up.

"It's fine," she said, her voice sharp. "You sit, Charlie. I've got this."

Suddenly we were all on our feet, bussing plates and glasses back to the kitchen, chattering quickly, as though if we just talked faster we could speed past the awkwardness of the last two minutes. Dan made a joke—something about teething—and though Mira laughed, she seemed distant. When I reached for her hand, she pulled away, following Agnes back to the table instead.

In the cab on the way home, Mira was quiet. She sat as far away from me as possible, her face turned to the window.

"That was weird about the beer, huh?" I said, sliding across the seat to be closer to her. "I mean, Dan's not really a big drinker. Agnes seemed so on edge."

"They're just tired."

"They're always tired."

"No one said parenting was easy."

"Hey," I said, dropping my hand onto her knee. "Are you mad at me or something?"

"Did you mean what you said about not wanting kids for two more years?" she said, the hurt in her voice apparent.

I bit my lip. The truth was, I did mean it.

It's just two more years, I opened my mouth to say. *I'll be thirty-one or thirty-two. That's not old, especially in New York City.*

But there was something about the look on Mira's face that stopped me.

"I'm sorry I said that," I said instead. "Dan just caught me off guard."

"You didn't answer my question."

"I do want kids."

"When?"

"I don't know, Mira," I said, frustrated. "To be honest, I'm pretty overwhelmed at work right now."

"You're always going to be overwhelmed at work. That's not going to change."

"I know," I said, nodding guiltily. "You're right."

"So when, then?"

"Can I have some time to think about it?"

She clenched her jaw and let out an exasperated sigh. "How's seven months?" she said, so quietly that I almost didn't hear her.

"Seven months?" I said, before realizing what she meant. Then: "Oh my God." I slumped back against the seat, stunned. Inside, my heart was doing backflips. Everything I had just said—everything I truly thought I believed—about waiting to have kids suddenly felt utterly, completely idiotic.

"Yep." She nodded slowly. "Apparently the pill is not one hundred percent effective."

"Oh my God!" I shouted, and nearly levitated off the seat. "Oh my God, that's amazing! That's the best news I've ever heard!" And as I said the words, I knew they were true.

Suddenly she was in my arms, both of us laughing and crying at the same time.

"I've never seen you this happy before," she said, her face flooded with relief.

"Except when I proposed to you," I corrected her.

"When you proposed, we both thought we were about to die."

"Okay, maybe when the plane landed safely. Shortly after the proposal."

She laughed and wiped away a tear. "You sure you're ready for this?"

"No," I said, and squeezed her tighter. "But I'm really, really happy about it. And don't you worry. Seven months is plenty of time. I'll quit smoking, of course. And we need a bigger apartment, won't we? Damn it, I knew we should have jumped on that two-bedroom when we had the chance."

Mira sighed and laid her face against my chest. "You know what, Charlie?" she said. "There are things in life you just can't plan."

What Kind of Father Are You?

Twenty-four hours later, Caleb is back to his old self.

"Let's push Grandpa around in his stroller," Caleb suggests over eggs and toast, as though he's proposing we squeeze in a round of golf at the club.

"Caleb. That's not something we say." This is a line I picked up from Zadie, though I'm not sure it applies here. I can already anticipate the questions: *What's not something we say? That Grandpa's in a stroller? Oh, a wheelchair, you say? What's the difference?*

"What's not something we say?" Dad's gravelly voice turns both our heads. He looks frail in his light cotton pajamas and moccasin slippers. Zadie told me he's at his worst in the morning; sleep no longer comes easily to him. Still, he smiles. A surprisingly easy smile that says, *You can tell me anything. I'm your grandpa.*

"Daddy says I'm not allowed to push your stroller."

"*Caleb.*"

"Why on earth not? What's the point of being in a stroller if my own grandson can't push me around? You might need Ives to help you, though. I'm heavier than I look."

"I can do it myself." Caleb slides out of his chair. He flashes me a jubilant smile as he wriggles past.

I glare at the two of them. I'm not sure who is annoying me more: Caleb for ignoring me or my father for encouraging him to.

Ives stands back, allowing Caleb to take his post. Caleb's skinny frame disappears behind the back of the wheelchair. It's an old-school number, not one of these electric jobs that weighs a thousand pounds. Still, this is going to be a Sisyphean effort for a kid who tips the scales at a mere thirty-eight pounds. Great. Now, in addition to teaching him that it's okay to be rude to disabled people, we're also setting Caleb up to fail.

"This is probably a bad idea," I interject, but no one blinks.

"Give it your best shot, now," Dad calls out. "Get your whole body into it."

For a moment nothing happens. Suddenly the wheelchair lurches forward one inch, then another.

"Thattaboy! We're cruising now!" They pick up speed. The wheelchair bounces slightly as it rolls across the tiled floor. Ives inhales when my father shifts his knees, narrowly avoiding the kitchen table. I can't help but notice that they are on a collision course with the dishwasher.

"Stop it," I say, sharply enough to halt Caleb in his tracks. "Someone's going to get hurt."

"Aw, you're no fun." My father waves me off. "Anyway, look at me. This body can't get more broken than it already is."

"Perhaps we might practice on the driveway," Ives says diplomatically. "It's a beautiful day."

"No driveway. Let's go to town. I want rocky road ice cream. Caleb, do you like ice cream?"

"I love ice cream!" Caleb cries, delighted.

"He hasn't eaten his breakfast, Dad." *Dad.* It slipped out, just like that. My hand flies to my mouth as though to stop the words from passing my lips, but it's too late.

"Don't be a spoilsport, Charlie. This may come as a surprise to you, but I'm not exactly Speedy Gonzales these days. By the time we get there, it will be lunch."

As if that makes it better, I think with an internal sigh. Clearly my father has never seen a five-year-old come down off a sugar high.

"There's a toy store in town," he continues. "And a bookstore. Some clothing shops. We can make a nice little day of it."

"I want a kite!" Caleb claps his hands. "And a dress!"

"Yes, we should all dress first." Dad nods, misunderstanding. "We can't go out in our pajamas. Ives, let's get me into some real pants. You, too, Caleb. We have to look our best. You never know who you'll run into. There may be some babes strolling around; it's a beautiful day, after all. Charlie, I'll meet you in the foyer in thirty minutes, all right? Don't give me that face. The Goldwyn boys are going to town."

The ice cream store is closed. This should come as a surprise to no one, given that it's nine thirty in the morning.

"Oh, shit," Dad mutters when we pull up in front of it. He looks to his left, then his right, then his left again, as though assessing whether or not he can escape before there's a scene.

Too late. Caleb stops, stares, and then hurls his body at the dark storefront, practically licking the glass.

"You promised!" he wails. His eyes are shut, as though he can't bear to look at me. "You said ice cream!"

A pin-thin mother with two perfect toddlers walks past, her face scrunching up when she sees Caleb. I glance up, and for a brief second we make eye contact. *Ice cream at nine thirty in the morning?* is etched across her face. Her children are snacking away on apples, no doubt handpicked from a local organic orchard. I look away, mortified. *What kind of father are you?*

A bad one, I want to call out as she herds her girls away from us. *But trust me, the old guy's worse.*

Caleb turns to me. "I hate you," he says, as though this is all my fault. "I really, really hate you."

I open my mouth, springing to my own defense.

"Charlie?" I hear a familiar voice call from behind me.

All four of us turn; there, in a haze of morning sun, is Elise. She looks immaculate in all white. White jeans, white button-down shirt, sleeves tucked up against her thin, tan forearms. Instinctively, I lower my sunglasses onto my nose to hide the bags beneath my eyes. With her trim body and radiant skin, Elise is a veritable insult to other parents. No matter what time of day, the woman looks gorgeous. She's fresh off the Long Island Expressway, where she no doubt battled bumper-to-bumper traffic with a toddler in tow, and still she's fresh as a daisy. If I didn't know better, I'd write her off as one of those high-maintenance moms who obviously outsourced her kid to a nanny in favor of the salon and the gym. In fact, I'm not sure Elise has a nanny—or any help at all, for that matter. She and Lucas are joined squarely at the hip.

Thank God she's going gray, I think, not for the first time. For one thing, it's sexy. More importantly, it's the only indication I've had so far that she's human.

Lucas stands beside Elise, one foot on a Razor scooter. He has Elise's hair—a full crown of thick, black curls—and her olive-skinned complexion. Though he's a few months younger than Caleb, he's taller and sturdier looking, the kind of kid that moms proudly refer to as "solid." The kind of kid who ends up captaining the football team. Potentially the kind of kid who, in a few years' time, I worry might beat the crap out of my son. Right now, though, Lucas is the new kid in town. He waves at Caleb, grateful for a familiar face.

"Caleb, say hi to your buddy," I say, pushing him in Lucas's direction. For once, Caleb needs no prodding.

"Hey, Lucas!" he shouts, enthused, the dearth of ice cream momentarily forgotten.

"Hi," Elise says, coming over for a hug. "Fancy seeing you here."

"I was going to call you later," I say, realizing I never responded to her last text the previous morning. "Glad you guys made it out okay."

Elise rolls her eyes in the direction of Lucas. "It was, shall we say, a challenging drive," she says dryly. "The iPad died just as we hit Exit 60."

"Ouch. Been there."

"Ouch is right." She turns to my father and Ives and extends a hand. "Hi, I'm Elise Gould. Forgive me for looking this way. My son and I had quite the epic drive out here."

My father laughs, just a little too hard and with an aggressive snort towards the end, and I have a sudden flash of what he must have been like in his younger, single years. Not nearly the smooth operator I imagined him to be.

"The gas station was a war zone. We had to wait for twenty minutes, and then, just as I was pulling up to the pump, a guy in a Land Rover swoops in and cuts us off. And then he has the nerve to just stand there, pretending I don't exist, taking his sweet time at the pump while he munches on Cheetos. I couldn't believe that."

"I can't believe that!" Dad exclaims loudly. "Charlie, can you believe that?"

What I can't believe is how awkward you're being around Elise, I want to say.

"Incredible," I mutter instead, feeling my neck flush with embarrassment. Elise shoots me a conspiratorial wink, one that says, *Don't worry about it. I get this all the time.*

"So, where are you all staying?" Dad asks. "We're right over there"—he gestures towards the beach with a clawlike hand—"on Further Lane."

"Dad," I murmur. Just when I thought it couldn't get any more awkward, now he sounds like he's bragging.

"Charlie mentioned that," Elise says kindly.

"Big white house right next to the Maidstone Club."

"That sounds so lovely. We've got a little place in the woods. North of the highway. Nothing fancy. We bought it so that Lucas could spend time with his grandparents during the summer."

"Who are Lucas's grandparents? I probably know them. Been in East Hampton for twenty-five years."

Elise looks down at the sidewalk. "Uh, the MacAndrewses," she says quietly.

"Nathan and Amelia? Well, of course, *everyone* knows them," Dad says, obviously impressed. "I mean, they're in the paper all the time now, what with—what's his name? the son? J. P., is it?—running for Congress. Wow, Charlie. You didn't tell me you had such fancy friends."

"Which is odd, because we talk so often about my personal life," I reply. To Elise I mouth: *I'm sorry.*

She shakes her head, waving me off.

"Yes," she says with a forced smile. "J. P. is Lucas's father."

"Now, isn't that a small world!"

"Charlie and I were classmates at NYU Law School." Elise smiles, tactfully transitioning the conversation away from her exhusband.

"You don't say? You know, that was my alma mater, too."

"I didn't know that. How lovely that you and Charlie went to the same school."

"Only for law school," I interject. "Dad went to Harvard undergrad. I went to SUNY Albany."

"It's great to meet a young woman who is not only beautiful but is also so academically minded," Dad says, ignoring me. He grins at Elise. "You sure don't see *that* every day."

"Jesus, Dad. It's not 1936. Women do attend law school with some regularity these days, you know."

"Oh, you've made my day." Elise laughs lightly. "Just being called young these days is enough, but beautiful! Well."

"Beautiful, brilliant, and absolutely charming. The trifecta." Dad raises his palms innocently. "And, of course, spoken for. No big surprise there. All the good ones are taken. J. P. MacAndrews is a lucky man."

"Dad. Elise is in the middle of a—" My eyes fall to the boys. "Never mind."

Elise nods. "A D-I-V-O-R-C-E," she explains.

Dad smacks his cheek indelicately. "Well, shit," he says, eyes wide. "Don't I feel like the asshole."

"Yeah, you've got a real way around the ladies. And children. Could you watch the language a little bit, please?"

"No need to apologize," Elise says, shaking her head.

"He didn't actually apologize," I point out. "Though obviously he ought to."

"I'm no good at apologies," Dad announces. "How about I invite you over for dinner instead? How's tonight? You got plans? We're supposed to be having a clambake at the house. Charlie here's got a new job, and his sister, Zadie, is about to be married. I just got engaged myself. So we have a lot to celebrate. Ives is going to drive to Montauk to pick us up some fresh lobsters." Dad nods at Ives, and Ives nods back in confirmation, though I imagine this is news to him. "Nothing says 'I'm sorry' like a good lobster. Right, Charlie?"

"My father, master of the apology."

"Charlie, you didn't tell me about the job! That's great news!" Elise says.

"It just happened," I mumble. "It's no big deal."

"It's a huge deal. I'm so happy for—"

"So how about it, then?" Dad interrupts. "Lobster and champagne?"

"Lobster and champagne sounds terrific. But please, you must allow me to bring something. Perhaps dessert?"

Dad shakes his head. "Absolutely not. This is supposed to be an apology lobster. If you bring pie, it cancels out the whole thing. Around six sound good to you?"

"Six it is."

"Daddy, look!" Caleb shrieks with joy. "The ice cream store is opening!"

Indeed, a woman in an apron is standing on the front steps of South End Creamery, rolling out its red-and-white-striped awning.

"Ice cream, Mama," Lucas says, tugging on Elise's hand. "Please?"

Elise ruffles his hair. "Not right now, sweetheart. No sugar before lunch, okay? But how about we go get some veggie burgers for the grill?"

"Okay," Lucas says quietly, nodding in resignation.

"I'm going to have rocky road and chocolate chip!" Caleb screams, already halfway inside the store. "Okay, Daddy?"

I look to Elise, wondering if she'll think less of me as a parent if I let my kid eat ice cream before noon. For a brief moment our eyes meet. Elise winks at me. I feel the hairs on my arms stand at attention.

"Live a little," she says. "Rocky road for lunch never hurt anyone."

"I knew I liked you," Dad says.

"All right," I say, nodding affirmatively to Caleb. "Go ahead. I'll be inside in a minute."

"Yeah!" Caleb cheers, and like a flash, he's gone.

"I guess I'll see you tonight, then," I say to Elise. I shove my hands deep into my pockets, the way I used to in grade school when I was talking to a girl I happened to like.

She steps closer to me, her hand finding its way to my elbow. I feel a shiver of excitement when she leans in, allowing me a whiff of her perfume.

"Charlie!" We both turn.

There, sitting in the driver's seat of a Mercedes convertible, is Alison. Like a panther, she's managed to approach us without a sound.

"Babe!" she cries, and waves frantically. She's wearing only a bikini top, Daisy Dukes, and sunglasses pushed up on her head.

Dad lets out a low whistle under his breath. I shoot him a look. Elise's hand, I notice, has fallen away from my arm. When I look up at her, she gives me a small, unreadable smile.

"Hey, Alison," I call out with a short wave. Never in my life have I been less pleased to see someone. It occurs to me that I haven't really thought about Alison—or, more to the point, about my plan to destroy Todd's life—since I got out to the Hamptons. Maybe it's because I have a new job. Or maybe it's because I've been too distracted by Caleb to care. Either way, seeking revenge on Todd no longer feels all that important.

"Babe, you have to call me!" Alison shouts across Main Street.

"I have great news! I spoke to Marissa! She wants to talk to you. She's *so over* Todd."

"Oh, thanks," I say, willing her to move on, to drive out of my life forever. "I'll call you."

"Totally." She blows me a kiss. The light has changed. The car behind her honks. "Gotta run! Love you!"

"Bye," I say lamely, feeling my cheeks flush with embarrassment.

"Wanna invite her over tonight, too?" Dad says as Alison pulls away.

"Absolutely not." To Elise, I say, "Long story."

"I'm sure."

"So we'll see you tonight, then?" I lean in to hug her, but she turns away from me.

"I guess you will," she says, and leans down to give my father a kiss on the cheek.

The Shark

"*You're welcome,*" Dad says, grinning at me like the cat that ate the canary.

"I told you I would have paid," I grumble into my mint chip cone. I didn't want ice cream myself, but Dad insisted. The first few licks weren't bad, but it's already beginning to melt in the July heat, dripping onto my fingers like sludge.

"Not for the ice cream, nimrod. For the girl!" Dad waves his empty cup at Ives, who quickly steps in, snatches it, and tosses it in the nearest trash can. "I told you there'd be babes in town. You going to finish that?"

I hand him my cone. "Elise? Yeah, about that. Are you always that awkward around women?"

Dad furrows his brow, considering. "Only the really pretty ones," he says. "Look, Caleb. Here's the toy store!"

Caleb, now jacked up on sugar, propels himself into the store like the Road Runner. I wince as he narrowly misses colliding with a stroller.

"Great kid," Dad says. "Really, he's got such spirit."

"That he does," I say, sighing.

"He's been through a lot."

"He has."

"You both have."

I shrug, blinking back tears.

"I wish I could have been there for you guys."

"It's fine," I say, my voice short. Of course, we both know it's not.

"Daddy, come look at this!" Caleb calls from the bowels of the toy store. "It's a princess jewel box!"

"Ives, could you go find him?" Dad says. "Buy him whatever he wants. I just want a few minutes with Charlie here. Charlie, that's okay, right?"

I bite my lip, then nod in assent.

"I did call, you know," Dad says once Ives is gone.

"I know."

"I understand why you didn't call back. I just wanted you to know I was thinking of you."

"Mm-hmm."

"I begged Zadie to put in a good word for me. But she kept saying you weren't ready. I respected her opinion. I didn't want to force myself on you, especially during a difficult time."

"Well, I'm glad you two were able to reconnect," I say, feeling terribly diplomatic. "It was really hard on her when Mom died."

Dad nods. "It was hard on us both," he says, his voice wavering. The emotion in his voice throws me a little. I've been preparing myself for this conversation for years, the way I would for an oral argument in the courtroom. I've anticipated his arguments. I've studied the facts, memorized the statistics, and carefully crafted my rebuttal. The case against him, I know, is airtight. And yet, here I am, feeling a strange rush of compassion overcome me. I ache with it. I want, I realize now, nothing more than to have my father convince me that I'm wrong about him.

For a minute we're silent. All around us, the store is filled with the sounds of children and parents crying, laughing, whining, begging, negotiating with one another.

"I was in love with her," Dad says. He doesn't look at me but instead stares straight ahead, into a shelf stuffed with bats and balls and Frisbees and kites. The words stick a little in his throat.

"With who?" I say, staring at the Frisbees.

"Your mother."

"Ah."

"I wanted to be with her, you know. Desperately."

"You were married, though. To someone else."

Dad bows his head. "I know," he says glumly, staring at his hands. "It was complicated. Helene and I were heading for a divorce no matter what. She hated how much I worked; I resented her for spending all our hard-earned money. We were living apart most of the time. Anyway, the timing was poor, I agree with that. I should have just waited until Helene and I had officially separated. When I started things with your mom, see, I told her I was divorced. That was wrong. I lied to her. She could never get past that."

"And then she got pregnant. With Zadie and me."

"Yes."

"And?"

"And I wanted to marry her!" Dad blurts out, frustrated. "You can ask Zadie: your mother told her that before she died. I asked her nearly every goddamn day. But she was stubborn, your mom. And fiercely independent. She said she could handle things on her own, and my God, did she ever. That was what I loved about her so much. She did everything in her own way."

"Why didn't you help her? Send her money? Anything." I narrow my eyes at him. I can't let him off the hook with just a couple of easy words and an ice cream cone. "Do you have any idea how hard things were for us, growing up? Mom worked all the time. Her sister had to move in with us to help out. Raising twins on her own—you just have no idea what you put her through."

Dad looks up at me, mouth open. His eyes shine with hurt. Then he looks away and shakes his head. "Zadie didn't tell you, did she," he says quietly.

"Tell me what?"

"I did give you money. I tried, anyway. She wouldn't touch it. She kept sending back the checks."

"I don't believe you." I fold my arms across my chest. I can feel my heart rattling in my rib cage. *Don't let him get away with it,* a stern voice inside my head whispers. *Don't be stupid. He's got nothing to support his case. It's all just words.* "I don't believe that. Mom wasn't that stubborn. Did you know that I got into Harvard?"

"I know."

"And you know why I didn't go? Because we didn't have the money. I got a full ride to a state school. That's how I made *my* college decision."

"And you graduated number one in your class."

"Fuck you," I snarl, loud enough to draw stares from several parents. I lower my voice. "Is that how you sleep at night? By telling yourself that it all worked out okay in the end? That maybe it was good for me to have to scrimp and scrape and save all my life instead of having things handed to me on a silver platter?"

"I don't sleep at night. And I don't tell myself anything of the sort."

"What did you spend that money on, anyway? A private plane? A tennis court? A vacation? I hope it was worth it."

"It's sitting in a trust with Caleb's name on it."

This stops me in my tracks. "What?" I say, flustered. I had so many more choice expletives that I wanted to throw at him first.

"It'll be his when he turns twenty-one. Before that, it can be used to fund his education. I was going to tell you about it"—he hesitates, as though choosing his words carefully—"when the time was right."

"I don't need your money," I say, though my voice has lost some of its venom. I feel like my head's spinning. Everything I thought I knew about my family is unraveling like a giant ball of twine rolling down a hill. Is it possible that I've had this whole thing wrong all along? That it was Mom who walked away from Dad and not the other way around? Was it by design that she raised us as she did, and not necessity?

"I know you don't, Charlie. That's why I put it in trust for Caleb. You've worked hard for what you have. I hope this doesn't sound condescending, but I'm so proud of you."

"Even though I work for a dickhead like Fred Kellerman?"

Dad sighs. "I shouldn't have said that. Look, he's a first-rate lawyer. He's just a shark, that's all. That guy would eat his young."

"That's an interesting characterization, coming from you."

"I'm not saying I was any better. I was a shark, too, in my day. You have to be to survive in that kind of environment."

I shake my head. "No, I don't agree with that. You don't need to be a bad person to be a good lawyer."

Dad shrugs. He disagrees, I can tell, but he's not going to fight me on it. "So, when do you start the new job?" he says, trying to get the conversation back on track.

"I don't know. Soon. Fred's taking all his clients with him, so there's definitely work to be done."

"They let him take his clients? That's generous of them. That certainly wasn't the case when I went out on my own."

Maybe that's because you were more of a dickhead than Fred, I think to myself.

"Is he taking other Hardwick associates with him? Or just you?"

"No, he agreed not to. I'm fair game, though, because they let me go."

Dad raises his eyebrows. "What convenient timing," he says.

"What's that supposed to mean?"

"Just that Fred got lucky. His best guy gets fired just as he's starting his own firm? He couldn't have planned it better himself."

"Well, he didn't. I got fired because I screwed up."

"Whatever you say, Charlie."

"He's not a shark. And even if he is, I can take care of myself. I have always taken care of myself." I've been waiting to say that to my father for my entire adult life. But somehow it comes out wrong, making me sound vulnerable and sad instead of confident and strong.

"I know you can. I know you have."

Dad looks away, swiping at his eyes with his shirtsleeve. Then he gestures at me, and I realize he asking me to get him a tissue from the bag Ives has slung over the handle of the wheelchair. I take one for myself before handing it to him.

"Thank you," he says, and blows his nose. "Look, Charlie, you have every right to be angry at me. Hell, I'm angry at myself. It hurts me every day that you kids wanted for things—things I could have so easily provided. But your mother had some pretty strong opinions. As you probably know."

I snort a little, recognizing the truth in his words. Still, I don't want to give my father the satisfaction of sharing this little moment with me. So I turn my chuckle into a cough and frown at him, reminding him that I'm not quite ready for jokes.

"She didn't want you guys to be spoiled," he continues. "She thought I'd screw you up. And, to be frank, she was probably right. At the time we met, I had just been made partner at my firm. My hard work was finally paying off; the money started to roll in. And I let it go to my head. I started buying nice clothes, a sports car . . . silly things, really, but they made me feel good about myself.

"Your mother, she was salt of the earth. I loved that about her. She was the opposite of me—just a no-bullshit, tell-it-like-it-is kind of gal. I tried to impress her with my big Park Avenue apartment and my fancy friends, and it all backfired. She didn't want any part of it. She said she'd rather die than raise her kids with silver spoons in their mouths. It was this constant push and pull between us. The more I tried to shoehorn her into this life I was creating for myself, the more she pulled back. I had a big chip on my shoulder, you see. I was angry a lot. I tried to bully her into seeing things my way. But the whole time I think deep down I knew she was right. Does that make any sense?"

I nod dumbly.

It does. It makes perfect sense.

I know this story.

It is, I realize with bone-chilling clarity, the story of Mira and me, just with a different ending.

Guilt rises up in my throat like bile. I pushed Mira, too. I pushed her to get on that plane, and now she's gone, and I can't ever get her back.

"Maybe I should have tried harder. Worked to see you kids more. Maybe even fought her in court. But I loved her. I knew if I got too aggressive, I'd lose her altogether. At least, when I let her do things her way, she was willing to stay in my life. That's why she worked for me for all those years. She'd show me pictures, tell me stories about you guys. I lived for that. It was her way, I think, of throwing me a line. Anyway, I didn't think I'd be much of a father. I know that's probably something you can't relate to, seeing how good you are with Caleb. But in those early days, when you and Zadie were just babies, to be honest, I didn't really know what to do with you."

My phone buzzes. I slide it out of my pocket and take a sharp breath when I see who is calling.

"Who is it?" Dad asks.

"Fred Kellerman."

"You should take his call."

"I know," I say, but I don't.

"Do me a favor, Charlie. Forget what I said about Fred. What do I know? I'm just an old guy in a wheelchair. Listen to your gut. You gotta do what's right for you."

I answer the phone. "Hey, Fred," I say, my heart racing.

"Hey, Charlie. Is now a good time to talk?"

I hesitate. It's hard to hear him from inside the store. His voice sounds far away, drowned out by the sound of Ernie singing "Rubber Duckie" over the store's loudspeakers and the screams of jubilant children playing with a dozen different musical devices all at the same time.

A month ago I would've said, "Of course," and walked out of the store.

Instead, I say: "I'm in a store with my father and son. Can I call you back this evening?"

"Sure, sure," he replies, sounding mildly surprised.

"Okay, thanks." I hang up. To my father, I say: "So how about you show us that bookstore you mentioned?"

He smiles, delighted. "I'd love to."

"Daddy!" Caleb comes careening around the corner, his arms laden with toys. On his head, perched slightly off-center, is a glittering tiara. "Look what Ives bought me!"

"Wow, buddy," I say. "That's a lot of stuff!"

"I know!"

"You shouldn't have," I say to Ives.

He shrugs and looks at my father as if to say, *I don't make the rules.*

"Really, it's too much."

"I'm sorry," Dad says, sounding genuinely apologetic. "If Ives went a little overboard this time, it won't happen again."

"No, it's fine," I say, nodding at Caleb. "Thank you."

"Thank you!" Caleb sings. "Thank you, Grandpa and Ives!"

"It was our pleasure," Dad says. "Now, let's go put this stuff in the car. Caleb, you're going to need both hands to push me around town. There's a lot to see."

"There's more?" Caleb looks up at me incredulously.

"There's more," I reply, and drop my arm around him.

"How much time do we have, Daddy?"

"All the time in the world, bud. All the time in the world."

Just Like You

We return home several hours later, flush with presents and sugar. Caleb, still wearing his tiara, streaks into the house, whooping with joy. The sun has brought out a light dusting of freckles across his cheeks, just like the ones Mira used to get every summer. I catch a glimpse of myself in the hall mirror. I also got some color. My hair's too long and I'm in need of a shave, but the tan has improved my appearance dramatically. The bags I'm used to seeing beneath my eyes have receded, and I don't look so damn old and stressed. I look better than I have in a long time.

My phone rings again. I hesitate, hoping it's not Fred or Alison. I don't want to talk about work, and I definitely don't want to talk about Todd. Alison's already texted me since seeing me in town; I deleted the text as quickly as I read it. My anger towards Todd now feels embarrassing and childish; trying to get him fired from Hardwick is clearly an epic waste of my time. Anyway, I've decided that slaving away at Hardwick for the next four decades is probably punishment enough for anyone.

When I see that it's Moose, I pick it up right away. I owe Moose more than a call: I owe him an apology. He's called me so many times over the last few weeks that I've lost track.

"Hey, man." I say, half expecting him to chew me out.

"Chuck!" he shouts, sounding joyful instead of angry. "Holy shit! You're alive!"

I laugh, letting out a sigh of relief. "I'm alive."

"Alive and answering your phone! This is good! This is great! This is progress!"

"I'm sorry, dude. I know I've been MIA. I've just—"

"You don't need to explain, Chuck. Unless of course, you've been in witness protection, and then I obviously want to hear every detail."

"I'm not sure they do witness protection for idiots. But it's a good suggestion. I'll look into it."

"Happy to help."

"You've always got my back, Moose."

"You are correct, sir. I do always have your back. Which is actually why I am calling you today. I mean, I've been calling you every day, I realize. I wouldn't call it stalking, necessarily, but definitely harassing. In a loving way. I like to think of it as a fun little game we play with one another. I try to come up with things that are so hilarious or touching or heartwarming that you can't help but respond. You ignore me, and then I try the next day. Sweet, right? What can I say? It's just part of my charm."

"With moves like that, you must have ladies just lined up at your door."

"Yeah, I do. With restraining orders. Which is weird, right? Is it too much? Am I coming on too strong?"

I wipe a tear from my eye. "Holy shit, man, you make me laugh."

"This is not funny, Chuck. This is serious. We're talking about my love life and your career. Which brings me back to the original point of this phone call. I have incredible fucking news."

"Hit me."

"So check this out: Fred Kellerman is leaving Hardwick. To start his own firm." Moose pauses for dramatic effect.

"Yeah, I know."

"You know about this already? Damn. News travels fast, I guess. Anyway. *Chuck!* Get excited! This is a huge development. You need to call him up. He'd hire you in a second."

"He actually already did. He called me yesterday."

"Yesterday! Well, shit. Way to bury the lede, Chuck!"

"Thanks, man," I say with a laugh. As always, Moose's enthusiasm is completely infectious.

"So, do you feel good about the job?"

"Yeah," I say, trying to ignore the gnawing sensation that's been growing in my gut since the chat with my dad at the toy store. "We still have to work out some of the details. But yeah, I'm pumped. Of course."

"That's terrific. Man, I'm so happy for you. I'm glad it's all working out."

"Yeah, looks like it's going to."

"Do you get to take some time off before you start? You definitely deserve a vacation."

"I think so. A few days at least. I'm actually out in East Hampton with Caleb and Zadie. We're staying at our father's house, believe it or not."

"Yeah, I heard. How's that going?"

My eyebrows shoot up. "You heard? From who?"

"From Zadie," Moose says, sounding sheepish. "I was worried about you, man. So I reached out to her, just to make sure you were okay. You've got one cool sister."

"That I do."

"She invited me to the wedding. I can't believe it's next weekend."

I laugh. "She did?"

"Yeah. She said it was no big thing, more like a party than a wedding. She said they were too lazy to do proper invites."

I roll my eyes. "They're too lazy to do a lot of things."

"Should I come?"

"You should absolutely come. It would be great to see you. And it means a lot to me that you've been reaching out, Moose. Really."

"You'd do the same for me."

"Yeah." I bite hard on my lip to keep myself from tearing up. "I would."

"Okay," he says abruptly, "I gotta jam. Hafta pick out my outfit for the big Hamptons wedding next weekend. Never know what kind of honeys are going to turn up, am I right?"

"You're hilarious."

"You should go work on your speech, dude. It better be epic."

"My what?"

"Your speech! You're best man, right?"

"I . . ." I pause for a second. "Yeah, I guess I am."

"Well, then, you're going to have to give a speech."

"Oh, shit," I say, wincing. "You think?"

"For sure! Don't sweat it, though. You're going to bring down the house."

Good God, I think as I hang up the phone. *The last time I did that, I got fired.*

I'm nervously pondering the possibility of a toast, when a text from Elise pops up. As I read it, my heart sinks:

bad news on tonight. sitter just canceled on me.

Before I can respond, she pings me again:

AND the A/C in our house is broken. FML.

Bring Lucas! I respond, trying to sound casual. *Will be fun!*

I would love to, but he goes to bed super early. Like 7 pm early. I'd have to walk out in the middle of dinner to go put him down!

I dash off another text before I have time to overthink it:

Do you guys want to stay over? We've got A/C and plenty of rooms. That way you can have a glass of wine at dinner and not worry about driving home.

When she doesn't instantly respond, I add:

PS: I hope you know I mean this in the most platonic way possible.

PPS: I saw your apology lobster in the kitchen. It is HUGE.

Seven minutes pass. I'm starting to panic, when:

You sure? I really don't want to impose, but . . . I'm not going to lie, A/C and wine make for a pretty tempting offer.

I smile, even give myself a little fist pump.

No imposition whatsoever. Just bring change of clothes, etc—we have everything you need here. Looking forward.

Likewise! Thank you SO much—you're a lifesaver! xE.

I sigh with relief. Crisis averted. Now I just have to clear this with my family in a way that makes it seem like no big thing, which, of course, it is.

"Elise and Lucas are coming to dinner, but their A/C is broken so I said they could just stay over," I blurt out when I bump into Zadie in the hallway.

She stares at me quizzically. "Okay. Who are Elise and Lucas?"

"Elise is an old friend from law school. Lucas is her son. He's buddies with Caleb. Anyway, we ran into them in town, and Dad invited them to dinner."

Zadie shrugs. "Cool," she says, and starts down the hall again.

"Do you think Dad will be mad?" I ask, trotting after her. "I probably should have asked him if that was okay first, right?"

"Do I think Dad will be mad? How old are you right now, twelve?"

I laugh, letting out an embarrassing snort. "Yeah, stupid question, I guess. I just figured, we have so many bedrooms here, what difference does it make? And Lucas—you know, he goes to bed early, so this way Elise can not worry about having to leave in the middle of dinner to take him home."

"Charlie, are you drunk?" she says. She leans into me, frowning. "You're being weird."

"No." I pull my face away from hers. "Don't be ridiculous."

"Oh my God!" She snaps her fingers and beams up at me with an irritating grin. "I know what's going on."

"What? Nothing's going on."

"Charlie!" Zadie punches my shoulder. "You *like* her!"

"What? What are you talking about? I like who?"

"Charlie, look at you! You're turning purple as we speak! Oh my God, I'm so right!" Zadie claps her hands with glee.

"Shut up," I mutter. "You are not."

"Oh my God, oh my God, oh my God!" Zadie's squealing now like a sixth-grade girl at a sleepover. "*Charlie and Elise, sitting in a tree—*"

"Seriously, Zadie, shut the fuck up." I push her into one of the guest rooms and shut the door behind us. When I turn around, Zadie is cowering, eyes wide, and I feel instantly guilty.

"I'm sorry," she says, chastened. "I was just joking around—"

"No, *I'm* sorry," I say, draping my arm over her shoulder. "I didn't mean to snap at you. I just didn't want Caleb to hear you."

"Caleb's helping Buck with the lobsters," Zadie says quietly. I can tell she feels bad, which makes me feel even worse. "I promise, I'd never say something like that in front of him."

"No, I know. I just—I'm not there yet, Z. I'm not."

"Hey," she says, and gives me a squeeze. "It's totally okay."

"Is it? Sometimes I feel like there's something wrong with me. Rationally, I know I should move on. It's been almost two and a half years. But it's like I don't even *see* women. That doesn't make any sense, does it?"

"Charlie, you *lost your wife*. There's nothing about this situation that makes sense."

"But don't you think most people would say it was time for me to move on?"

"Who gives a fuck what other people would say?" Zadie says fiercely. "There's no manual to being a widower. You have to do everything in your own time, in your own way."

"Yeah, I know. I just—I worry sometimes that I'm doing it wrong."

"Doing what wrong?"

"Everything."

Zadie sighs. "Honestly, Charlie, that's been your problem since you were, like, four years old."

"Thanks a lot. You always know just what to say."

"I'm serious, you big dork. You were always so obsessed with doing everything *right*. Straight As in school. Captain of the tennis team. Order of the Coif in law school."

I smile. "It's pronounced koi-ef."

"What?"

"Coif. It's pronounced koi-ef, not kwa-off."

Zadie scowls. "See? You are such a perfectionist, it's disgusting. That's why that job thing fucked you up so much! You've never failed at anything, Charlie. It's not healthy to go thirty-five years without failing. You know, sometimes Mom used to say, 'I just wish he'd fail at something once in a while.' But you never did."

I roll my eyes. "So glad you and Mom were in my corner."

"She *was* in your corner. She wanted you to fail so that you'd see that life goes on."

"Jury's still out on that."

Zadie shoots me a look. "It will. It always does. Take it from me. I have a PhD in failure."

I shake my head. "Don't say that."

"What? It's true. I've failed so many times, I've stopped counting. Most schizophrenics have résumés that make more sense than mine. I'm certified in both Reiki therapy and pastry baking, for fuck's sake. But you know what? I'm okay with that. My path is a winding one and I'm going to enjoy the ride. Life's a journey, Charlie, not a destination. If you never fail, it means you're not taking enough chances."

"You sound like Mira. Or a bumper sticker."

Zadie purses her lips and nods. "Yeah, Mira was cool like that. She really knew how to live in the moment."

"Well, she was a yoga instructor, after all."

"She was so fucking good for you, Charlie."

"I know."

"She hated that job of yours."

"I know."

"She would have wanted you to just loosen up. Embrace this time with Caleb." Zadie pauses, crossing her arms nervously against her chest. "Look, I know you're going to freak out at what I'm about to say, but I'm your sister and I love you and, really, what are siblings for if not for the occasional piece of unsolicited feedback? So I'm just going to say this one thing and then you can tell me to shut the fuck up and we can all move on. Okay?"

"Okay," I say, folding my arms across my chest.

"I know Fred's been like a father to you and everything, but I'm worried that you're rushing into this job without even thinking about it. You haven't taken any time off since Mira died. Hell, you haven't taken time off *ever*. I don't want to get all metaphorical on you and say that you got fired for a reason, but maybe you did, in fact, get fired for a reason. Maybe this is the universe's way of letting you take a step back. So that you can reassess and figure out how you actually want to live your life. Don't look at me like that, Charlie. Say something."

"That wasn't a metaphor."

"What?"

"You said you didn't want to get all metaphorical on me."

She frowns at me. "What are you talking about?"

"Forget it. Are you done? Have you said what you wanted to say?"

"Yes," she says, nodding her head solemnly.

"Okay. Thanks, Zadie. I appreciate it. I'll take it under advisement."

"You will?" she says, surprised.

"Yes." I nod firmly. Zadie's words, however jumbled and grammatically incorrect, resonate with me. Something about this job feels wrong. Maybe it's just the speed at which I accepted the position. Maybe it's the fact that I have to start so soon. Or maybe it's the fact that, deep down, I know I'm rushing back into a life that I'm not entirely sure I want anymore. Whatever it is, I need to figure it out, and fast.

"Oh, Charlie, that's great. I'm so relieved. It's just something I've been thinking, you know, since you told us you took the job and I didn't know if I should say anything or just bite my tongue, but you know me and—"

"Can we change the subject now, please?"

"First, can I say just one more thing?"

"Sure," I say with a sigh. "Why not."

She pauses before continuing, her voice low. "It's not your fault that she got on that plane, Charlie. You know that, right? You didn't do anything wrong. You didn't do anything to cause it."

"Yeah," I say, staring at the carpet. "I know."

Zadie puts a hand to my cheek. "Say it like you mean it," she says, her voice soft.

"I know," I repeat. "But thanks for saying it."

Zadie nods, her eyes welling with tears. She glances away, composing herself.

When she looks up at me, she gives me a watery smile.

"So," she says, sniffing a little, "tell me about this Elise."

I shrug. "She's nice. Going through a divorce. Her boy, Lucas, is sweet. Shy but sweet."

"Is she pretty?"

"Zadie."

"Well, is she?"

"I don't know. Maybe. I haven't really noticed."

She giggles. "I'm just joking around, Charlie. Seriously, I think it's great they're staying over. It will be terrific for Caleb. His first sleepover!"

"His first sleepover," I say, feeling suddenly teary myself. If someone had told me six months ago that Caleb would be having a sleepover with a friend—an actual friend, not Fiona or Mr. Beep—I wouldn't have believed it. "First sleepover" is not, I realize, the kind of milestone they talk about in parenting books. But to me it feels like something. "He's growing up."

"Maybe we all are," Zadie says. "Or at least, we're trying our best."

• • •

"Welcome!" Zadie cries upon opening the front door, and wraps Elise up in a hug that normal people reserve for old friends and close cousins. "I'm so happy you guys are here! I'm Zadie, by the way. Charlie's sister."

Elise smiles gratefully. "Hi," she says. "It's so nice to meet you. I'm Elise. Sweetheart, say hello to Ms. Goldwyn."

Zadie waves her off. "Call me Zadie. Don't let the house fool you. We're as casual as they come."

"Hi, Zadie," Lucas says shyly, leaning against his mother's leg.

"Thank you so much for having us over." Elise steps into the house and closes her eyes. "Ahhhh," she says. "Oh, air-conditioning. Delicious."

Zadie turns back to me. *She's gorgeous,* she mouths. I can't help but smile. Elise does look particularly beautiful this evening. She's wearing tight white jeans and a sleeveless top that showcases her toned, tan arms. Her hair cascades down her back in gentle waves, the overhead light picking up the threads of silver that run through it. Her legs are a mile long in heels. For once, she's wearing jewelry—bold turquoise earrings that draw out the blue in her eyes—and her full lips and high cheekbones seem flush with color.

She dressed up, I think to myself, giddy. I feel slightly less ridiculous for having tried on three different button-down shirts in the fifteen minutes before she arrived.

"Hi, there." I turn; standing behind me is Madison. I take a deep, calming breath. It hadn't occurred to me that she'd be at dinner tonight. And what is she wearing? Her dress is so short, it looks like she forgot to put on pants. I spin back around, nervously assessing Elise's reaction.

"This is, uh—" I stutter, wondering exactly how to introduce her. My dad's girlfriend's daughter? My former ex-fling?

"Madison." Madison smiles smoothly and extends a hand to Elise. "Charlie's dad, Jeff, is engaged to my mom, Shelley."

"Oh!" Elise says, visibly relieved. "That's so sweet!"

"Isn't it?" I mutter through gritted teeth.

"Hi, 'Lise," Caleb rounds the corner, looking spiffy. He's sporting a lilac-colored polo shirt, khaki pants, and his favorite pair of teal-and-lilac-striped socks with no shoes. "There's cocktails on the porch."

Elise bursts out laughing. "Well, thank you, sir."

"I'll take your bags upstairs." I reach for the duffel in Elise's hand just as she's bending over to help Lucas with his backpack. For a second our noses are so close that I can almost feel the flutter of her eyelashes. She smiles at me, her lips parting, her tongue darting inside her mouth. We're close enough to kiss.

"Let me," Zadie says, breaking the moment. She snatches the bags. "You guys go grab a drink. I'll see you in a few."

"Hi there, honey," Dad calls, waving to Elise through the porch doors. "Come out here and meet my gal, Shelley."

"Thank you for having us, Jeff."

"The more the merrier. Can I interest you in an oyster? The lobsters are almost ready."

"Welcome to the Goldwyn house," I say, ushering her over to the bar. "Where there is a shellfish for every occasion."

Elise knocks her shoulder into mine. "Even first dates?"

Even though I know she's joking, my stomach fills with butterflies. In the past two and half years, women have flirted with me. A few have asked me out; one or two even threw themselves at me. It always felt awkward, wrong, or just plain uncomfortable. Elise isn't throwing herself at me, of course. I actually don't think she's even flirting. But there's a suggestion of something, a question mark, in the arch of her eyebrow and the way her arm brushes against mine, and to my surprise it's not in the least bit unpleasant. In fact, it feels pretty nice. Suddenly I've forgotten about all my work stress. I've forgotten about Todd. I've even forgotten how awkward it is that Elise is standing next to Madison. I'm grinning from ear to ear, and in that moment, the world feels flush with possibility.

"Daddy, no more pie," Caleb moans, rubbing his hands against his distended belly. He slumps back against me, letting his head loll onto my shoulder, like a little drunkard. *"Tooooo much pie."*

Lucas, too, looks wasted. He's still upright, but just barely. His eyes are glazed over. Very slowly, he raises his pie-laden fork to his mouth, then lets it fall back on the plate, untouched.

"I think these guys are toast," Elise says, smiling at me. "Bed?"

"Yup."

"Need help?" Zadie offers.

"No, no." I shake my head. "Thanks, but I got it."

"Okay. Good night, you guys."

"We'll be back in a few," I say quickly, and Elise nods in agreement.

Wordlessly, the two of us trudge up to the second floor, our boys in our arms. I move slowly, deliberately, feeling out each stair with my foot in the semi-dark. I can sense Elise behind me. I want to turn and look at her, but I know I shouldn't. Both boys are asleep. It's best not to wake them.

At the end of the hall, I gesture her inside the room the boys have chosen to sleep in. It has two twin beds and a window seat overlooking the ocean. We tuck them in without waking them up to brush their teeth. Zadie suggested they don their pajamas before dinner; in retrospect, a great idea. Tonight there will be no reading of books, no bath, no ritualistic turning on of the night-lights and pulling down of the shades. Tonight Caleb will not beg me to check his closet for monsters or attempt to discuss the possibility of a tornado hitting at midnight. Tonight there was only fun.

"Mmm-buh." Caleb sighs when I place a kiss on his forehead. His breathing is labored, his limbs limp.

"Buddy, do you want me to put out the animals?" I whisper.

"No," he whispers back, still half-asleep. "Iz okay. I have Lucas." With that, he curls up into the fetal position and starts to snore.

Elise and I sign at one another from the shadows, confirming that both boys are asleep. Together we tiptoe to the door. Out in the hall, we high-five.

"That was weirdly easy," she says, her voice low. "I was worried he'd have trouble falling asleep in a strange house."

"How about you?" I ask, moving closer to her. Without meaning to, I reach up and stroke her cheek. Amazingly, she doesn't stop me. In fact, she steps closer, turning her face up to mine. "How will you sleep in this strange house?"

"I don't know." Her voice falls to a whisper. "This is all new to me."

"Me too," I start to say, but then she is kissing me, and my words get lost in her mouth. The wetness of her lips is so startling that I flinch a little, pulling away in the process.

"I'm sorry," she says, stunned. Her eyelids flicker, registering the hurt. "I didn't mean to—"

"No, don't say sorry, I—" I lean into her again, trying to restart, but the moment has slipped out of my fingers. She turns away, and my kiss lands squarely on her cheek.

"Oh my God," I say, feeling desperate, "I want to kiss you so badly. You just caught me a little off guard is all. I just wasn't expecting it. But that doesn't mean I don't want to kiss you. Because I do. Very badly."

"Yes, you said that," she says with a small laugh. "Charlie, I'm sorry. I don't know what came over me. Too much wine, I think. Can we just forget this whole thing happened?"

"No, Elise, please. I don't want to forget it."

She looks up at me then, her blue eyes locking with mine. Her hand cups my face. "I like you very much," she says, her voice filled with earnestness. "But I don't think either of us is quite ready for anything to happen. Romantically, I mean. I know I'm not." She laughs again, embarrassed. "I'm not even properly divorced. The way things are going with J. P., I may never be. Anyway, I made a mistake. Can you just forgive me so we can be friends? I really want us to be friends, Charlie. It's so important to me."

"Of course we can be friends," I say, because it seems like the only thing I can say. I have to squeeze my eyes shut for a second in order to drown out the chorus of voices in my head shouting, *NO! Kiss her, you idiot! Kiss her right now!*

"Good," she says, and nods. Her hand drops away from my face. "Thank you. You really are a terrific guy."

"Can I see you again?" I blurt out. I reach for her forearm. "I mean, like, not on the playground. Can we do something just the two of us?"

She bites her lip. "Like a date?"

"It doesn't have to be a date. It can be just like two friends grabbing dinner together. Or lunch. Whatever makes you feel most comfortable. I just want to spend time with you."

"I want to spend time with you, too," she says softly.

"When?"

"Well, for one thing, I'll see you tomorrow morning. Since we're sleeping over and all."

"Terrific. We can take the boys to the beach in the morning."

She smiles then, but it's a faraway smile, not the intimate, eyes-locked kind of smile she was giving me just moments ago. *I'm losing her*, I think. *I've lost her.*

"That sounds nice," she says.

"You can stay here as long as you like."

"I wish I could. I think we probably have to head back into the city. Anyway, I don't want to impose on your family any more than I already have."

"Don't be ridiculous. We love having you here. You just saw my dad making out with his fiancée, for God's sake. You're part of the family."

She throws her head back and laughs. It's a genuine laugh, giving me a flicker of hope that we can move past tonight and at least go back to where we were before. "Your family is awesome," she says.

"That's one word for them."

She gives me a playful swat. "They're the best! Your dad and Shelley are so sweet together. Ugh, it just melted my heart. And Zadie is wonderful. After ten minutes I felt like we were old friends." She pauses, like she's debating whether or not to tell me something.

"What?" I say, narrowing my eyebrows at her. "Uh-oh, what did Zadie say?"

"She invited me to her wedding." Elise grimaces. "I sound like a stalker now, right? Like a stalker who tries to kiss someone and then weirdly crashes their sister's wedding?"

"No!" I say, a little too loudly. Reflexively we both turn towards the boys' bedroom door. "No," I say, lowering my voice. "Not at all. I would love for you to be there."

"You sure?" she says, hesitant. "You don't think it would be weird if I came? Because I totally don't have to. I don't even know why I brought it up. I'm sorry. I just told her yes because it was so sweet of her to invite me. And I don't have friends in New York. I mean, I've got you and Tom but, like, no girlfriends. And your sister—"

I clamp my hand firmly across her mouth. Then I lean in, my forehead pressed firmly to hers. Her eyes go wide with surprise, but she doesn't move away. In fact, she takes my free hand in hers, interlacing our fingers together in one swift move.

"Elise," I say firmly. "Will you please come to my sister's wedding? I would love it if you would say yes."

"Yes," she says, her voice muffled. "I would love to."

I release her. We smile at one another. I try not to think about the fact that she's still holding my hand. Like sixth graders, we turn and walk hand in hand down the hallway, saying nothing. The door to my room—the room I was sharing with Caleb until tonight—is at the other end of the hall. A mere fifteen yards away.

Just get her there, a voice in my head insists. *Just get her to your bedroom. Then you can kiss her and everything will be okay.*

She stops short in front of the room that contains her overnight bag.

"I think this is me," she says, sounding unsure.

"Okay," I say, unwilling to let go of her hand.

"Hey, Charlie? Thank you."

"For what?"

"For everything."

She stands up on the tips of her toes and places a kiss on my cheek.

"Good night," she whispers in my ear.

"Good night, Elise. See you in the morning."

She smiles at me, and then closes the door behind her.

Morning After

"Good morning, sunshine," Zadie sings out when I stumble into the kitchen. "I thought you were never going to wake up."

I run a hand through my sleep-ruffled hair and grunt in response. Truth is, I've been awake for hours. I've just been staring at the ceiling, trying and failing to summon the courage to go downstairs and face Elise.

"Coffee?" Zadie holds up the pot. "You look like you could use some."

"Coffee would be great. Where is everybody?"

"Dad and Shelley went to town to get her ring sized. Buck's out back doing something to the hydrangea. And your girlfriend took the boys to the beach."

I shoot her a look.

"What?" Zadie says.

"She's not my girlfriend."

"Your friend that's a girl."

"She's thirty-five years old."

"Whatever, Charlie." Zadie scowls. "*Elise.* She's awesome, by the way. Did you know she volunteers with Amnesty International? I had such a great time with her last night."

At least one of us did, I think darkly.

"I hope you don't mind, I invited her to the wedding."

"Yeah, she mentioned that. Is there anyone you haven't invited to your wedding?"

"What's that supposed to mean?"

"Moose said you invited him. You guys doing a spread in *Town & Country*, too?"

Zadie's face clouds over. "For your information," she says, "the wedding is just going to be a big cocktail party. No dinner or anything. We did it that way to save money, and we figured as long as we're not feeding people, the more the merrier. Buck's doing all the flowers. I'm baking the cake. I'm wearing a dress that I own already. We didn't even send out invitations—just called people or e-mailed them. So, no, definitely no magazine spread."

I bury my nose in my coffee mug, embarrassed. Zadie and Buck are many things, but pretentious is not one of them. In fact, it's pretty sweet that she thought to include my friends. I shouldn't be giving Zadie a hard time just because I'm upset about Elise.

"I thought you'd appreciate the fact that I included your friends," she says, reading my mind. "I mean, you know I love Moose. And Elise is terrific. But I invited them for you, Charlie. We want you to feel comfortable."

I nod. "I know. That's nice of you."

"Anyway, I figured you'd probably screw things up with Elise somehow, so at least this way you're guaranteed to see her again."

"Thanks for the vote of confidence."

"What are sisters for?"

Unlike yesterday, which was perfect, today is unpleasantly hot and humid. The sand is littered with beachgoers in various states of undress. Some lie like stuck pigs on towels, while others hide beneath umbrellas. The energetic few are dipping their toes in the ocean. I step over a set of Kadima paddles, an abandoned sand castle, a volleyball net. Already I can feel my shirt sticking damply to my back. By noon, I think grouchily, these idiots will have fled the beach in favor of air-conditioning.

"Daddy!" I turn around to see Caleb and Lucas sprinting towards me, Elise bringing up the rear. Bouncing along the sand behind them, like a can tied to the back of a car, is a purple kite.

"Daddy, look, it's flying!" Caleb screams. For a second the kite flutters in air before crashing back to earth.

"Good job, buddy!" I call out, clapping my hands.

"We got some good air time back there," Elise says. She's slightly out of breath, and her cheeks are flushed from exertion. "It's not easy with no breeze."

"Did you see the kite that Grandpa and Ives bought me?"

"I did. Wow, that's cool." To Elise, I say, "Thanks for hanging with them this morning. I don't know why I slept so late."

She shrugs; no big thing. "We had a blast, right, guys? Anyway, Lucas and I have to head back to the city pretty soon, so we were psyched to get some beach time in first."

"No, Mommy," Lucas pouts. "I don't wanna go to the city. I want to stay here with Caleb."

The boys lock arms, a unified front. My heart wells up with pride. *Caleb has a friend,* I think. *He has a real friend.*

Elise ruffles Lucas's hair. "I know, sweetheart. I don't, either. But I've got some things I need to take care of. Just for a few days."

"Bummer you guys have to go," I say, kicking the sand with my toes. "You sure you don't want to hang for the afternoon at least?"

Elise pauses. For a second it looks like she's considering it.

"Nah," she says. "It's better if we get back. I think it's supposed to start pouring later, anyway."

I look out at the ocean. She's probably right—thick, angry clouds have gathered on the horizon—but I can't shake the feeling that the real reason she's leaving is me.

"That's really too bad. We love hanging with you guys."

"We should be back next weekend."

"You're coming to Zadie's wedding, right?"

She glances away. My heart lurches a little. I feel like this is the end of something—something we haven't even started.

"I'm going to try my best," she says, and I can tell she feels the same way. "There's some stuff going on with Lucas's dad and—"

I wave her off. I don't want to hear about Lucas's dad. "You don't need to explain."

Elise looks hurt. "I want to be there. I really want to hear your toast."

I wince. "Why does everyone keep saying I need to give a toast?"

"Well, you *are* the best man, aren't you?"

"Yeah, I guess I am."

"Isn't that tradition? For the best man to give a toast?"

"I don't think tradition is invited to this wedding."

Elise laughs, a full, genuine, all-is-forgiven sort of laugh. "I love your sister's style," she says. "She really marches to her own drum."

"That she does. I think everyone in my family does. Except me. I'm kind of the lame duck around here."

"I don't know about that."

"You really think she's going to want me to give a toast?"

"Of course. You'll be great. Just speak from the heart."

"We all know what happens when I do that." I let out a nervous laugh.

Elise smiles sympathetically. "Not to brag," she says, "but I'm actually pretty good at wedding toasts. I've been a maid of honor seven times."

"Seven times? Wow."

"Anyway, if you want help . . ." She trails off, like she's not sure if she really wants to finish that sentence.

"I'd love it. So, does that mean you'll come to the wedding?"

Elise sighs. "Yes," she says after a pause. "I'll be there. You Goldwyn boys are awfully persuasive, you know that?"

"It's part of our charm."

Natural Disaster

It's been raining for three days. It started about an hour after Elise and Lucas pulled out of the driveway, and it hasn't let up since. I've spent most of the time pacing around the house, trying my best to pen an elegant, heartfelt, non–YouTube-worthy toast for my sister, and it's going very badly. I've even stooped so low as to google "best man speeches" and "poems about family." The wastebasket by my bed is filled with all my failed attempts and half starts. As of now, all I have is: "My name is Charlie, and I'm Zadie's brother." After that, I draw a blank.

I haven't heard from Elise once, which is doing nothing to improve my mood. By now I would have expected a "Thanks for the lovely weekend" call or at least a "Hey, how are you?" text. Instead, nothing. Nothing but rain, rain, and more rain.

"Maybe it'll rain itself out by the weekend," Shelley suggests, her voice full of hope. She and Zadie have also spent the last three days pacing around the house, staring anxiously out of different windows. Like if they could just get the angle right, maybe they'll see the sun.

For the umpteenth time, Zadie pulls out her phone. "Nope. Still showing rain for the next seven days. Not just rain: angry-looking clouds, lightning, gale-force winds." Zadie stuffs her phone back in her pocket, annoyed.

"My mother used to say that rain on your wedding day was good luck," Shelley says.

"Well, if that's true, we're going to be the luckiest couple on earth."

"The weathermen are assholes," Buck declares. He looks over at Caleb. "Sorry, bud. I shouldn't have said that. The weathermen are *bad people*. They totally screwed me. I never would have planted all those peonies if I had known they were going to cause this." He gestures helplessly at the rain.

"Well, to be fair to the weather people, I'm not sure they *caused* this," I say.

"Oh, they caused this all right. If they had their facts right last week, I wouldn't have spent hours and hours on my knees in the dirt. All that work for nothing. Those assholes promised me sunshine."

"It'll be okay." Shelley gives him a squeeze around the arm. "Don't you kids worry. We'll just have to get a tent in here somehow."

"We don't have the budget for a tent!" my sister wails. "I knew we shouldn't have gotten those mason jars on Etsy. We blew all our money on those stupid mason jars." She stops, changes gears. "What if we did the whole thing in the basement? That's, like, a big open space. And that way none of the furniture needs to be moved—"

"No daughter of mine is getting married in a basement!" Dad booms. We all turn to stare at him. "Now, I've held my tongue for long enough. No invitations, fine. Bake your own cake? All right. No wedding planner? Wouldn't have been my choice but, okay, I can live with that. But the basement? *No way. No how.*"

Shelley darts over and begins to massage his shoulders. "What do you suggest, honey?" she asks nervously. "I mean, it's Wednesday. The rehearsal dinner is in forty-eight hours."

"Rehearsal drinks," Zadie corrects.

"Rehearsal drinks."

"I have people," Dad says mysteriously, "who take care of this sort of thing."

"Who are you, the Godfather?" I scoff.

"No," Dad says huffily. "I'm *your* father. And more importantly I am the father of the bride. Just give me a day. There's going to be a tent and it's going to be the best goddamn tent you've ever seen in your life."

On Friday morning I wake up to the sound of buzz saws and hammers, and for a moment I think I'm back in the city.

"Daddy, look!" Caleb scampers over to the window, pressing his forehead to the glass. "There's going to be a circus!"

There is, in fact, a circus on the lawn, just not the kind Caleb is hoping for. Buck, wearing an orange rain slicker, is directing a team of workmen who appear to be erecting a tent.

"*¡Cuidado!*" Buck shouts. "*¡Ten cuidado con las peonías!*"

"What's Uncle Buck doing?" Caleb says, awed.

"I think he's getting a tent set up for the wedding."

"Why?"

"Because the rain is so bad." A clap of thunder sends Norman cowering beneath the bed.

"Is it a hurricane?" Caleb whispers, backing slowly away from the window.

"No, bud. I don't think so."

"Because if it's a hurricane, a tent won't be enough to protect us."

"It's not a hurricane, Caleb, I promise. Let's get some breakfast, okay?"

"There's a hurricane coming," Dad announces as soon as we enter the kitchen. He flips off the television. "It's over Cuba right now and it's heading our way."

Caleb digs his fingernails hard into my palm. "I told you, Daddy." He glares at me, betrayed.

"Terrific," I say, and shoot my father a look. "Thanks so much."

"What do you want from me?" Dad shrugs. "I don't make the weather."

"It's not supposed to hit until *Monday*," Shelley chirps. "Plenty of time for a beautiful wedding. And look! Look at that magnificent tent!"

We all turn to the window. The tent—white with turrets—is indeed magnificent. I glance over at Dad. He gives me a small smile.

"It's looking okay, isn't it?" he says hopefully. Beside him, Zadie is staring out the window, mesmerized. The relieved expression on her face is enough to make me want to bear-hug him. I have no idea how much this is costing him, and I don't want to know. All I care about right now is how happy it makes my sister.

"It's looking great," I say. My stomach flutters nervously. *Dad pulled this off with twenty-four hours' notice*, I think, *and all I've come up with for my toast is "Hi, I'm Zadie's brother"?*

"Like for Cinderella," Caleb breathes, momentarily forgetting the impending natural disaster.

"It is spectacular, Dad," Zadie says, and kisses my father on the cheek. "We don't know how to thank you."

A howling gust of wind batters the windows.

"¡Cuidado, cuidado!" a workman screams as a giant tree branch sails overhead and comes crashing down on the tent.

Panic ensues. The wind howls again, scattering the potted plants around the perimeter of the tent like matchsticks. A porta-potty tips over, nearly crushing Ives. Workmen dash every which way, desperately attempting to batten down anything not firmly rooted in the ground.

"No!" Zadie screams.

"It's okay!" Shelley sings out. "Come on, you guys. We have nine hours. We'll all pitch in." She opens a window and calls out, "Buck! Come over here for a minute. Tell us what needs to be done."

Buck nods and jogs back towards the house. He leans in the window, rain running in rivulets off his jacket onto the kitchen floor. "All the floral arrangements are in the living room," he says. "We're going to have to wrap each one individually to protect them from the rain."

"Done," Shelley says. "Madison and I are on that. What else?"

"Those porta-potties are never going to make it in this wind."

"I'll call," Dad says. "I'll get them removed. People will just have to use the bathrooms in the house."

"I'll need help carrying the chuppah into the tent. Charlie and I can do that together."

I glance at my watch and grimace. "Actually," I announce, "I have a meeting with Fred."

No one says a word. The rain is coming down in sheets. The sky is charcoal black, the color of midnight.

"It will be quick," I add. "I'll be back in plenty of time for the rehearsal. I just don't know if I can help out with the prep work."

Silence.

Shelley nervously chews on her thumbnail. Dad stares at the blank television. Outside, Buck shifts nervously from one foot to the other.

I've made a mistake. That much is clear. Admittedly, trying to squeeze in a meeting with Fred this afternoon was probably not the best plan. That being said, it didn't occur to me that I'd be asked to do anything today. I just assumed that showing up in a tux would be enough.

Zadie looks up at me, her eyes brimming with tears. "Are you for real? Are you seriously having a business meeting the day of my wedding?"

"It's not the day of your wedding," I say, crossing my arms defensively against my chest. "The wedding's tomorrow. Anyway, it's just for a couple of hours. You won't even know I'm gone."

Zadie shakes her head. "I can't believe you're doing this to me," she says, disgusted. "Today of all days."

"Doing what?" I snap. "Trying to get my job back? I know this is really hard for you to understand, Zadie, but some of us actually have to work for a living. And yes, sometimes that entails doing things that are not convenient for us. But here's a newsflash: I need this job. Caleb needs this job. You need this job. It's really easy to sit there and criticize me and constantly point out all the manifold ways in which I'm failing as a father and a brother and a son, but at the end of the day, my career supports our family. And we're all going to have to make sacrifices in order for me to keep it."

Zadie's nostrils flare. "Are you actually trying to tell me that this meeting is so important that it can't wait until Monday? What

are you and Fred discussing? Peace in the Middle East? The cure
for cancer? Seriously, Charlie, tell me. I want to know what it is
you're doing that is so much more important to you than being
with your family."

I don't immediately respond. Instead I glance over at Caleb,
who is staring at us. I swear he looks embarrassed to be associated
with me.

"What is the meeting about, Charlie?" Zadie goads, her voice
rising. "What is it about *this time*?"

"*This time*?" I explode. "You make it sound like I'm always ruin-
ing everything!"

"Well, it's true, isn't it? Because of your job, everything always
turns into a friggin' disaster!"

"Maybe *my entire life* is a disaster!" I shout. "My job has obviously been a disaster! My love life is clearly a disaster! Hell, I'm
probably a disaster of a parent, too. You think I like that? You think
I'm happy with the way everything's turned out?"

"Enough!" my father snaps, exasperated. "Just . . . just go to
your rooms."

"What did you just say?" I turn to him, venom dripping from
my jaws. "Did you just have the audacity to ground us?"

Dad's eyes widen. "I didn't mean it that way," he says. "I just
meant, why don't you both just go cool off? We have guests arriv-
ing in nine hours. There's an actual hurricane blowing our way.
We really don't have the time or the energy to fight right now."

"I couldn't agree more," Zadie sniffs.

"Our rooms," I repeat, infuriated.

"It's raining out, you asshole!" Dad shouts at me. "There's nowhere else to go! You don't want to go to your room, *fine*. You're
a big boy. You have car keys. Go to Fred's. Do whatever you want.
But I, for one, am going to try and get this house ready for a god-

damn wedding." And with that, he swivels his wheelchair around and heads for the door.

"I'm on flowers," Shelley says, snapping into place behind him.

"Me, too," Zadie declares. She shoots me a final, searing look. "I'm going to do my best to enjoy tonight. With or without you."

"Hey, Caleb, you want to come out to the garage and help me with the chuppah?" Buck says. "We need to finish glazing the base."

Caleb looks up at me. The disappointment in his eyes causes my heart to shrivel up inside my chest like a salted slug. "You okay, Daddy?" he says.

I nod, unable to speak. I've never felt more wretched in my life. "I'm okay, bud," I manage to say. My voice comes out hoarse, like I have to force the words out of my throat. "Go help Buck with the chuppah. There's something I need to take care of right now. I'll be back soon."

Caleb nods and turns away. He seems unsurprised. He's heard that line before, I realize. He's heard it one too many times.

You're My Guy

I don't need directions to Fred's house; I've been there once before. During my first summer at Hardwick, Fred hosted the firm's annual summer retreat. We all awoke at the crack of dawn, boarded a bus, and headed out to Fred's for a long day of inter-firm bonding. The partners acted like camp counselors, organizing games of croquet and capture the flag, while the associates quietly grumbled about all the work that was inevitably accumulating on our desks while we were supposedly out having fun. At the end of the day, Fred's wife, Ann, invited us onto the back patio for a barbecue, at which point toasts were made and everyone got pleasantly sauced. Then we boarded the bus again and returned to the city while the partners scurried off to join their families at their own Hamptons houses for the rest of the weekend.

Though I complained along with everyone else, I loved spending the day at Fred's. For one thing, it gave me a chance to spend time with him out of the office. He shepherded me around his property, showing me its various updates and improvements. The new tiling around the pool. The stair climber in the basement. The roses he was training to grow around the garden arbor. He didn't do this with anyone else, just me. As stupid as it sounds, it made me feel special.

I pull up beside the house. There are a few new trees, I notice, but otherwise it looks exactly the same as it did ten years ago. As I switch off the car, my heart pounds uncomfortably in my chest.

You have to do this, I tell myself sternly. *You need to do this. It's the right thing to do, for everyone involved.*

Fred is standing on the front step, waiting for me. "Thank you for coming," he says. "I know you're busy today."

"Of course," I say, and extend my hand.

He hugs me instead. The move catches me off guard. I've never known Fred to be a hugger. In fact, he, like me, usually eschews any kind of intimacy. We've always spoken in a language of head nods and handshakes, all those small, subtle ways that men tell one another, *You're my guy.*

"What can I get you to drink? Scotch? Glass of wine?"

"I'm okay."

"Oh, come on." He checks his watch. "It's five o'clock somewhere in the world, right? Anyway, we have to celebrate. Welles dropped off this bottle of Johnnie Walker—it's Blue Label, fancy stuff. Ann won't touch it and I'd feel too badly opening it on my own."

"All right, sounds good."

Fred ushers me into his library, an imposing room that smells like leather and antique books. I take a seat in an armchair while Fred pours us drinks at the bar. The walls are studded with framed newspaper articles about Fred. I remember sitting in this same seat during my last visit. I'd just been staffed on my first case with him; he asked me inside for a drink so that we could "get to know each other." We talked about nothing—NYU Law School, the Mets. My hands shook so much that the ice in my drink rattled; I drained it quickly so that I could set it down.

There were articles on the wall then, too, but not nearly so many. It strikes me how much Fred has accomplished since then, thanks, in large part, to me.

"Cheers," Fred says. He sits down and clinks his glass to mine. "We have a bright future ahead of us, my friend."

"I sure hope so."

He takes a long, slow sip of his Scotch. "Perfection," he says. "You like?"

I nod into my glass, trying to summon the right words.

"We achieved so much together, didn't we, Charlie? A nearly perfect winning record."

I nod dumbly.

"I felt horribly about the way things ended at Hardwick," he continues. "It all happened so fast and it really should have been handled differently. I wanted to intervene, but you see, I'd already cut this deal to leave. So it didn't seem appropriate for me to force Welles and Steve to keep you on when we all knew I wouldn't be staying myself."

"It didn't seem *appropriate*?" I repeat. "I was the best guy you had, but you didn't think it was appropriate for me to keep my job?"

"No, that's not what I said," he says, frowning. The buoyancy in his voice is gone. "I said it wasn't appropriate for me to tell Welles and Steve what to do about you. It's their firm now, not mine. Anyway, anyway." He waves his hand as though I'm missing the point. "It's all for the best, you see. You are free to come work for me now. To be frank, it's the best thing that could have happened."

"Perhaps it was for the best," I say, and take a deep breath, steeling my nerves. "It allowed me to take a step back and really think about what I want going forward."

"That's good, Charlie."

"I'm not going to work for you, Fred."

He doesn't respond. He just takes another slow sip of his Scotch.

"Is this about money?" he says after a second.

"No." I shake my head. "Not at all. It's about quality of life."

He closes his eyes like he can't quite believe what he's hearing.

"I have a son, Fred. I'm his only parent. He needs me. And, to be honest, I need him. I can't work a hundred hours a week anymore. It doesn't make sense for us as a family."

"So you're going to be a stay-at-home dad now?" he says, his voice dripping with condescension. "Or find yourself some nine-to-five gig where you're just punching a clock? Come on, Charlie. Be realistic. That's not you. I know you. You'd be bored stiff in two weeks."

"Maybe so. But I owe it to myself to find out."

"You're making a mistake. If it's about the money, I'm willing to be flexible."

"It's not about the money."

"Is this about Todd? He talked to you, didn't he?" Fred shakes his head. "That little bastard. I knew I couldn't trust him."

"What?" I say, confused.

Suddenly it clicks.

My father's words come flooding back. *What convenient timing . . . Fred got lucky. His best guy gets fired just as he's starting his own firm? He couldn't have planned it better himself.*

"Oh my God," I say quietly. "*You* did this to me. You got me fired. Didn't you?"

Fred doesn't answer. His eyes, shining with guilt, say it all. He looks away from me, staring instead into the bottom of his crystal-cut tumbler.

"It was *your* idea to leak the video online. Todd was game because that meant he'd make partner. Am I right?"

Fred looks up, a deer caught in headlights. "No, no," he says, "you've got this all wrong."

"No." I shake my head. "I think I have this exactly right."

"Charlie, don't be ridiculous. You got fired because you acted like an asshole. You know that."

"I acted like an asshole, that's true. But you know what I think happened then, Fred? I think you saw an opportunity. An opportunity to get me fired. Once that happened, I'd be a free agent. A free agent who, I might add, could be picked up for pennies on the dollar because no other firm in their right mind would touch me."

Fred bites his lip. I've got his number. I know it, and he knows I know it. He'll never admit to it, though. He's too smart. Too smart and too proud to admit to stooping so low.

"I'm prepared to be very generous, Charlie," he says instead. "Hell, I *want* to be very generous. I want you to be my partner in this thing, damn it. I need you."

"Aren't you worried about my reputation?" I say, my voice shaking with anger. "Because *I* am. Everyone who saw that video—and the last time I checked, that means hundreds of thousands of people—thinks I'm a moron."

Fred waves me off. "Oh, please. You'll come work for me. Everyone will move on. In a few weeks, no one will remember how it all happened."

I place my Scotch on the table and stand up.

"Maybe I *will* move on, Fred," I say. "I can promise you this, though: I will *never* forget how it all happened."

"You're making a mistake, Charlie. I'm giving you a second chance here."

I look him straight in the eye. He seems so pathetic, sitting there alone on his giant leather couch, his walls studded with articles about himself. For one fleeting second I almost pity the guy.

"You're right," I say, and he looks relieved. "This is my second chance. So I'm doing what I should have done a long time ago. I'm out, Fred."

And with that, I walk out of the door, out of the house, and out of Fred Kellerman's life forever.

Just the Two of Us

I pull away from Fred's house and just drive. I have no destination in mind. After turning slowly down a series of small, winding country roads, I pull onto the highway. As I rev the engine, my shoulders begin to descend from around my ears.

I haven't done this since high school. Whenever I was sad or angry or upset, I'd hop in my car and just go. It didn't matter where I went or how far. Just thirty minutes in the car was enough to soothe my nerves.

I turn the radio on and up, blasting some hip-hop song that I neither like nor recognize. The thumping bass echoes the wildly accelerated pace of my heart. The traffic heading in the opposite direction is heavy; throngs of city dwellers have decided to brave the rain in order to spend the weekend in the Hamptons. I, however, am headed west, back towards the city. The highway opens up before me, allowing me to just drive. While I'm mostly jittery and terrified, a small part of me feels indescribably liberated.

I turn the radio up. The familiar sound of Will Smith's voice floods the car. He's changed Bill Withers's classic ballad, "Just the Two of Us," into an ode to his son. My heart seizes up as I think about Caleb. I crank the radio to full blast and hit the accelerator. As I try and fail to sing along, I can't help but laugh. I sound like an idiot, but I don't care. It's not like there's anyone around to hear me. When the song finishes, I pull off at the nearest exit and turn the car back around towards the town of East Hampton. I have just one thing left to do before I head home.

When I pull up, Caleb is outside, wearing an oversized pink raincoat that I suspect belongs to Zadie. His shins are covered in mud. When he sees me, his face breaks into a smile.

"Hi, Daddy!" he screams when I hop out of the car. He waves me over. "Come see what we did!"

Huge puddles have formed on the lawn. The rain is coming down so hard that it's difficult to see more than a few feet ahead. I hunch down and sprint over to him. Caleb takes my hand and ushers me into the tent.

"Oh, wow." I look up, wiping the rain from my brow. A thousand tiny tea lights have been strung overhead, shimmering like fireflies. Buck stands atop a ladder, adjusting one of the bulbs. He holds a screwdriver in his mouth and his face is red from exertion.

"This looks amazing," I call up to him. "Seriously, I can't believe you did all this."

At the back of the tent, two guys are setting up a bar. Workmen are placing large white floral arrangements on each of the small cocktail tables. All around, candles glow. The effect is magical, the setting for a fairy-tale wedding.

"You're back so soon," Buck says, descending from the ladder. "Meeting go okay?"

Caleb looks up expectantly at me.

"Yeah," I say. "It went great, actually."

"Cool," Buck says. "I'm happy for you. You really think this looks good?"

"I think you've outdone yourself."

Buck grins. "Well, it's definitely been a team effort. And there's a lot left to do before the guests arrive."

"Don't I know it. I still have a toast to write."

"Daddy, you can help me put out the candles on the tables," Caleb declares. "I'm almost done."

"You ready to help out?" Buck asks, raising one eyebrow.

"Ready and willing," I say, pushing up my sleeves. "But first I gotta show Caleb something. Picked these bad boys up in town this afternoon. Thought we could wear them to the wedding."

From a wet plastic bag, I pull out two pairs of bright purple Converse sneakers: one in his size, one in mine.

"What do you think?"

Caleb looks at the shoes, then up at me, then back at the shoes. His eyes widen in disbelief. "For real?" he says, like this might be a trick.

"For real," I say. "I heard somewhere that Converses look cool with everything."

The Deal with Me and Weddings

I have always hated weddings.

I blame this entirely on Cheryl Shipman, my mother's best friend. When Zadie and I were six, Cheryl moved in next door. Cheryl and my mother had almost nothing in common except for the fact that they were two single women in a town of young families. Cheryl's entire mission in life was to find herself a man. She was forever retouching her makeup, because, as she put it, "you never know who you're going to run into." She exercised like a fiend. Every Saturday morning Cheryl forced Mom into a tracksuit and off they went, weights in hand, for a power walk around the neighborhood. Cheryl, I imagine, talked the entire time. She was usually dating multiple men simultaneously, resulting in complex strategizing about which Mom offered counsel. Being friends with Cheryl, Mom always said, was the reason she didn't watch daytime television.

Cheryl was divorced when she moved in next door, and would marry twice more before Zadie and I went off to college. The first time was to Hector Marquez, the owner of Hector's, the local Mexican joint in town. Hector was handsome from fifteen feet away; if you got too close, you couldn't help but notice his dramatically sculpted eyebrows and the orangey undertone of his sprayed-on tan. He spoke with an accent that Cheryl would later claim was fake, an affectation that he thought lent authenticity to his restaurant. He was, according to Cheryl, from Long Island City and not even fully Mexican, but rather half Mexican, half Polish. Whatever the back story, Hector fully embraced his Latin roots. He and Cheryl were married on the back patio of Hector's on a sweltering day in August, a day so smoggy and hot that it did, in fact, feel vaguely like Mexico City. The wedding was fully Mexico themed. Don Julio was served in abundance. Cheryl considered renting a burro for the occasion, but settled instead for Hector's dog, Pancho, sauntering around in a tiny sombrero. And then, of course, there was Zadie and me. Zadie, the flower girl, got off relatively easily in a folksy embroidered number and sandals. When she walked down the aisle, tossing petals from her wooden basket, whispers of "How adorable!" and "What a little doll!" could be heard all around.

And then it was my turn. Even at seven, I knew I looked ridiculous in a three-piece charro suit replete with matching hat and red bow tie. I looked like the Fourth Amigo. The snickers started when I appeared at the end of the aisle; by the time I'd made it up to the front, the crowd had dissolved into full-blown laughter. "¡Olé!" someone called out as I tossed the ring at Hector and fled. It was the first and last time I would ever willingly participate in a wedding that wasn't my own.

Cheryl's second wedding was less humiliating, but only because she didn't ask me to be in it. I was fifteen at the time, far too old to be a ring bearer and still too young to be a groomsman. This time I hung out at a back table with Zadie, sneaking sips from glasses of wine that other guests had abandoned in favor of the dance floor. To my chagrin, Cheryl insisted that I dance with her. Being too drunk to argue, I ended up twirling and swaying to

"Tainted Love," the glittering disco ball overhead mesmerizing me with its ever-changing colors.

I was, as it turned out, also too drunk to dance. Two minutes in, I felt nausea rolling up through my body like a tidal wave. I don't really remember throwing up on Cheryl, just the look on her face seconds after I did so. It wasn't pretty. Years later, Cheryl Shipman-Marquez-Heines's screams remain the soundtrack to my nightmares.

"What's the deal with you and weddings?" Mira asked me, three years after our own. For weeks she had been campaigning for us to attend the union of Heidi and Jacob, two people I'd never met and who Mira hadn't seen since college. Despite the fact that we had already had one very public fight about this wedding on the corner of Seventy-Third and Lexington Avenue, Mira refused to let the issue drop. "You always act like they're this huge inconvenience."

"They *are* a huge inconvenience. You have to fly somewhere, pay for a hotel, pay for a present, get all dressed up, find a sitter . . ."

"Some people might argue that all of that is fun."

"Some people might. Those people are obviously not lawyers."

"So lawyers are fundamentally incapable of having fun?"

"That's not what I said. I meant that people who think weddings are fun typically do not have really stressful jobs that make it incredibly difficult to get away for a full weekend. Especially to Big Sur, which requires about twelve hours of travel time on either side."

"So the problem is your job. Not the wedding itself."

I sighed. "We've been through this. I really, really don't want to go, Mira."

"I really, really do."

"Why don't you, then?" I said, feeling aggressive. It was an easy thing to say because I thought there was no way that Mira would ever consider going to a wedding without me. For one thing, traveling solo with a toddler was enough to deter any sane person. And Mira was barely comfortable leaving me alone with Caleb for two hours, much less two days. "There's no rule that says couples have to attend weddings together."

"What about Caleb?"

"What about him?"

"It's a long trip for a kid his age, especially for so short a time."

"So leave him with me. We'll be fine."

"You sure? Because, to be honest, Charlie, I could really use a weekend away right now."

I looked up, startled. Mira was staring at the rug, her lips pursed in a thin, straight line.

"You could?"

"Yeah, I could." Her voice was flat. "You've not exactly been fun to be around lately. I understand how stressed-out you are at work. Really, I do. But you're barely home, and when you are, you're snappish and sometimes just downright rude. You never ask me about my day. And Caleb, well, you hardly even look at him."

Her words tumbled out, one after another, as though she'd been holding them in for quite some time. When I reached for her, she pulled back, crossing her arms across her chest.

"I had no idea you felt that way," I said, feeling blindsided. "Why didn't you say anything before?"

"I've tried. But you're always too tired or too busy or too distracted to hear me."

"I'm literally in the middle of the biggest case of my career."

"I understand that."

"Do you? Because it sort of feels like you're giving me a hard time about something I can't control. Yes, I work all the time. Yes, I'm occasionally irritable. But anyone would be in my position. I barely have time to shower. Flying to Big Sur is not what I need right now."

"What if it's what *I* need right now?" Mira said, fighting back tears. "Did that ever cross your mind? After being trapped inside all winter, two days of new scenery sound amazing to me. This may come as a surprise to you, Charlie, but you're not the only one in this house who has a tough job. I love being a mom, I really do. But it is exhausting. It's stressful. It's lonely. There are days when I drag out my order at Starbucks just so I can have an extra thirty seconds of adult interaction. I never see my friends. I never sleep in. I have never once spent a night away from Caleb. Hell, I bring him into the bathroom with me when I pee! So, yes, when I get an invitation to go to Big Sur for the weekend, where I can breathe fresh air and hike outdoors and catch up with old friends, *of course* I'm dying to go. I don't ask for much, Charlie. I really don't. But this . . . this is something I'd like you to give me."

"So would you rather go without me?" I asked slowly, still trying to absorb what she'd just said.

She sighed. "Honestly, Charlie, the last time we went to a wedding, you made the whole thing pretty stressful. You worked the entire weekend. You practically missed the ceremony because you were stuck on a conference call. I ended up wandering around the hotel all afternoon with Caleb so that he wouldn't bother you while you were working."

"I think I've apologized for that approximately four hundred and eighty-six times. We can go for four hundred and eighty-seven right now, though, if you think it would make a difference."

"I just want to relax. Really relax. I'm not sure you appreciate how much stress you bring into our household."

"What do you want from me, Mira? To quit my job? Last time I checked, we weren't exactly a dual-income household." The second the words left my mouth, I regretted them. "I'm sorry," I added quickly. "I shouldn't have said that."

Mira looked like I'd punched her in the gut. "It's fine," she whispered. "It's true."

"No, it's not fine. I'm really sorry." I felt horrible. It had been, after all, my idea for her to stay home with Caleb. My salary belonged to both of us, I truly believed that. And yet, here I was, wielding it like a weapon.

"It's okay, Charlie. I just need a break."

"From me?" I frowned.

"From life."

"So go to the wedding. Enjoy yourself. Sleep in. Go hiking. Caleb and I will be fine."

"But—"

"I want you to go," I heard myself saying, though of course I didn't mean it.

"What about your work?"

"Zadie will help me."

Mira nodded. "Thank you," she said. "I think I really need this right now."

She went. I booked her the ticket, using my own miles. I even upgraded her to business class, just to make the point that I really did want her to go and have fun. Zadie watched Caleb. I spent most of the weekend at the office, pretending to work, but really wondering what Mira was doing, and if she was having a better time than she would have if I had been there.

Mira didn't answer her phone on Saturday. Instead, she sent

me an e-mail saying that her cell had poor reception at the hotel and that she'd call me the following morning, when she was en route to the airport. When she finally did call, it felt as though a week had passed instead of merely forty-eight hours. I wondered if this was how she felt when I traveled for work, which was often.

"How was it?" I said, trying to sound enthused.

"Amazing," she said, and her voice was filled with light. "This is one of the most beautiful places I've ever seen."

"You must be sad to leave so soon."

"Not really," she said. "I'm so happy to be coming back to my boys."

She never did. It was the last time we spoke, just an hour before she boarded Flight 1173, bound for home.

Rehearsal Drinks

The minute I set foot in the tent, I panic.

For one thing, I'm completely surrounded by couples. Touching, hugging, laughing, kissing couples. Even at the bar—which, in my opinion, should be a safe haven for singles—I'm wedged between newly engaged Gemma and Hugh and newly pregnant Charlotte and Mark. Both couples hug me hello and, for a few minutes, we all make a good-faith effort at small talk. Given that I'm an unemployed widower, this is no easy feat. At thirty-five years old, what else is there to talk about besides family and work? I share a few anecdotes about Caleb, then ask polite questions: "When are you getting married?" and "Oh, you just got tenured at Columbia? How exciting!" Good news is relayed to me with guilty eyes, self-deprecating jokes. No one likes to brag, especially not to me. And when conversation necessarily stalls, both couples slip away with assurances that they'll catch up with me later.

More importantly, I still have no idea what I'm going to say in my toast. I'm carrying around a blank index card, which I've sworn to myself will be filled by the time I walk into the wedding tomorrow night. I reach into my pocket, running my thumb nervously along its edges. I have to start drinking, and fast.

I hang at the bar, swilling a vodka-soda and pretending to be busy. Every few minutes I check my BlackBerry. What I need, I've decided, is Elise. She'll know exactly what I should say in my toast. I've called her twice today and sent her a text. Radio silence. I watch the door like a hawk, hoping she'll miraculously appear, all smiles and hugs and funny stories about how she lost her phone and is *so very sorry* she hasn't gotten back to me this week. As the steady stream of arrivals slows to a trickle, this becomes less and less likely. I turn back to the bar, feeling deflated.

"You okay, man?" the bartender asks. He looks vaguely familiar, but through my slightly drunken haze I'm having trouble placing him. He's one of Zadie's friends from somewhere. Almost everyone at this wedding is, from the caterer to the waitresses to the guy officiating the ceremony. From the end of the bar, Madison tosses me a wave. It's basically one large tent filled with people out of context.

"Yeah," I say, shrugging. I nudge my glass across the table. "One more, please."

He eyes me. "You sure? Zadie's going to be mad at me if I get you too wasted."

I look up at him. "I quit my job today."

"Cheers."

"I don't know. It seemed like the right idea at the time. But it's entirely possible that it's just another one of my massive miscalculations in judgment."

The bartender gives me a polite nod, which I choose to interpret as an invitation to keep talking.

"I had a date. She's supposed to be here by now. I'm starting to think she's not coming."

He glances up, shoots me a sympathetic glance. "I'm sorry, man," he says. "That blows."

"Yeah."

"Maybe she got stuck in traffic. It's not easy to drive in rain like this."

"Maybe."

"Or maybe she's somewhere in the crowd, and you just haven't seen her yet. This place is jammed."

"It's possible," I say, feeling a small surge of hope. "But everyone ends up at the bar at some point, right? So I figure if I just hang here . . ."

"Sooner or later she'll turn up." He nods. "That sounds like a good plan." He reaches behind the bar, pulls out two shot glasses, fills them to the brim, and hands me one. "Don't worry. She'll be here. And don't stress about the job. Life's too short to waste it in a cubicle. You know?"

"I do," I say, and cough a little from the sharp taste of tequila.

"Charlie!" I feel a big hand descend on my shoulder.

I turn and find myself face-to-face with Moose. He's sporting a seersucker suit and a bow tie that's the same bright yellow shade as his knee-high rain boots. A dopey grin spreads across his face.

"Aw, man, it's good to see you," he says, pulling me in for a hug.

"Sweet boots, dude."

"Hey, if us Mainers know anything, it's how to dress for inclement weather."

"Well, you look great." He does, in fact, look great. He's dropped a few pounds and, for once, his thick red hair is neatly groomed. He's even got a light tan, a sign that he's managed to escape the office recently, for a few hours at least. "You look well rested."

"I took the week off." Moose shrugs, a little embarrassed. "I've been staying out in Montauk. Your sister's wedding gave me a nice excuse to hit the Hamptons."

"Wow, you're on vacation? That's new for you."

"Yeah, first one since I started at Hardwick. It was Julie's idea, actually." Moose's arm falls over the shoulder of a smiling brunette whom I've just noticed standing beside him.

"Hey," she says, and, to my surprise, embraces me. "It's so nice to meet you, Charlie. Moose talks about you all the time."

I nod, too dumbstruck to respond. This girl is beautiful. She's got big, almond-shaped eyes, full lips, a decidedly cute nose. She slips an arm around Moose's waist.

Holy crap, she's his girlfriend, I think. *Moose has a girlfriend.*

"This is my girlfriend, Julie," Moose says, grinning like an idiot. He turns to Julie. "I can call you that, right? That's cool to say in public?"

Julie giggles. "Of course it is, goofy," she says, and stands on her tiptoes to kiss him.

"Wow," I say, shaking my head in disbelief.

They both turn to stare at me.

"You okay, dude?" Moose asks, looking concerned.

"I turned down the job," I blurt out.

Moose's mouth drops open. "For real?"

I shrug, feeling uncomfortable at his surprise. "For real. It just didn't feel right, man. I didn't want to go back to that life. Maybe it's a mistake. I don't know. I just think I need to cool my jets for a while. Maybe try yoga or something. Just learn how to *be*. You know?"

Moose eyes me suspiciously. "Chuck, you been drinkin'?"

"Maybe a little." I hold up my thumb and pointer finger an inch apart. "A squinch. A scootch."

"Uh-oh. How many drinks have you had?"

I look lazily at my watch. "A few. A few too many. I was just waiting on Elise, see—"

"Jesus, Charlie." Moose shakes his head. "We've been to this rodeo before."

"Izz not a rodeo. Izz a circus," I say, laughing at my own joke.

Moose and Julie exchange looks.

"Okay," he says, taking me by the elbow. "You and I are going to take a little walk."

"Bye, Charlie," Julie says with a sympathetic wave. "See you boys later."

"She seemed nice," I say as soon as Julie is out of earshot. "Why didn't you tell me you had a girlfriend?"

"Well, you've kind of had your plate full."

"I'm so happy for you, man. Seriously. Are you happy for you? 'Cause you don't look so happy right this second."

"I'm happy about Julie," Moose says through gritted teeth. "I'm not happy that you're wasted right now."

"I'm not wasted."

"Yes, Chuck, you are. You're wasted."

I hold up my hands. "Okay. Maybe I am. Guilty as charged, Counselor."

"You need to sober up, and fast. We're not going to have a repeat of the Hardwick summer associate welcome party. Not on my watch." He pauses at the door of the tent, looks up at the angry gray sky. "You ready to make a run for it?"

Fifteen minutes later I'm feeling more clear-headed, thanks to a quick run in the rain and the pot of black coffee that Moose brewed for me in the kitchen.

"Okay," I say, setting my mug down on the counter. "I feel good. I'm ready."

Moose crosses his arms, enforcer-style. "Finish it," he says, nodding at the mug. "And then we shower."

"I don't have time to shower, Moose."

"You're right, you don't. But you're going to do it anyway, so make it snappy."

"Sheesh," I mutter, taking a swig. "Tough crowd."

When the mug is empty, Moose marches me up the stairs.

"Damn," he says, pausing at the top. "This place is huge."

"Yep."

"Which room is yours?"

I shrug. "None of them are mine. It's not my house. But that one"—I point to the nearest door—"is where I've been sleeping."

"Swell," Moose says, and pushes it open. "Oh, shit!" He turns back to me, his face suddenly a deep shade of crimson.

I peer inside. Sitting on the bed are Zadie and Buck.

"Whoa," I say, covering my eyes.

"We're clothed, you idiots," Zadie says.

"Charlie just needs to—uh—freshen up. Sorry."

"You can come in. Just shut the door behind you, please."

"We'll just grab a shirt and be on our way."

The door clicks closed. I blink, adjusting to the dark room. As promised, Zadie and Buck are fully clothed. In fact, they're now sitting apart, Zadie on the bed, Buck on an armchair across from her.

Zadie's bright pink lipstick practically glows in the dark. Her mascara has run down her cheeks in angry black streaks. It takes me half a second to realize that she's crying. She tries to wipe her eyes quickly with the back of her hand, but it only exacerbates the mascara situation.

"You okay, Z.?" I say, sitting down beside her.

"I've been better," she says, staring at the floor.

"What's going on?"

When Zadie doesn't respond, I look up at Buck. He shrugs, wide-eyed.

"I think we're just having some pre-wedding jitters," he says in a soothing voice. "Right, sweetie?"

"This is not pre-wedding, Buck." My sister shoots him an icy look. "This *is* our wedding. This is it. It's happening right now. And it's all a big disaster." With a sob, she buries her face in her hands.

"Hey, now." I attempt to rest a comforting hand on her shoulder, but she pulls away. "It's not a disaster! What are you talking about? We just came from the party and everyone's having a great time!"

"No, they're not." Zadie's voice comes out muffled. "It's pouring rain. There's not enough food. The music is coming from an iPod. We didn't even have invitations!"

"But that's fun, right? Wasn't that what you wanted? A fun, spontaneous wedding?"

Zadie looks up and glares at me. With her rumpled reddish hair and crazy eyes, she looks about as sane as Chuckie.

"I wanted it to *feel* spontaneous," she says, "not actually *be* spontaneous."

"What?" Buck and Moose both cock their heads in unison.

"Forget it!" she wails. "You're *guys*. You don't understand."

"But we want to!" Buck says, dropping to his knees in front of her. He takes her hand and kisses it. "Please, princess. Tell me what's wrong and we'll fix it."

"I'm not a princess!" Zadie roars. Buck jumps back into his seat. "And I don't want you to fix anything! Jesus Christ! What century do you people live in? Have you heard of feminism? I'm not looking for some knight in white shining armor to sweep in and save me! What is it with you men? Why does there always

need to be a solution to everything? Can't you just shut up and listen to me vent for once?" She covers her face with her hands and
dissolves into a fresh wave of tears.

No sudden movements, Moose mouths to me, and I have to bite
down hard on my bottom lip to keep from laughing.

"I just feel like it's all happening so fast!" she cries. "I wish I'd
had more time to plan. I'm no good at this, Charlie. I'm no good.
Look at that!" She gestures in the direction of the window. "Look
at that tent! It's gorgeous! Have you been inside? It's incredible!"

"Isn't that a good thing?"

"No! I didn't do any of it! If it wasn't for Buck, there'd be no
flowers. If it weren't for Dad, there'd be no tent, no food, nothing.
I didn't do anything. I'm useless! How am I going to be a mom if I
can't even plan a wedding?"

Out of the corner of my eye, I see Moose's mouth drop open.

"I'm sorry," I say slowly. "Did you just say you're going to be a
mom?"

Zadie clamps her hand over her mouth. Her eyes go wide.

"Ah, jeez," Buck says quietly.

"Zadie, are you pregnant?"

Zadie looks at Buck, who gives her a slight nod.

"Mm-hmm," she whispers. "You're not mad, are you, Charlie?"

"Mad!" I say, sweeping her into my arms. "Are you insane?
This is the best news ever! Oh my God! Buck, get in here!" I wave
him into our hug. "I'm so happy for you guys!"

I'm grinning so wide my cheeks are hurting. It feels like fireworks are going off inside my heart. Zadie begins to laugh and then
nestles her head tight against my shoulder. I can feel Buck's tears,
wet and hot, drip against my neck. Ordinarily I'd roll my eyes at
Buck's tears, but right now, I've got nothing but love for the guy.

"This is so cool of you, man," Buck says, openly weeping. "See,

Z.? I told you he'd be cool with it. We were going to wait to tell people, you know, until after the wedding. But I'm so glad we told you now."

"Why wouldn't I be cool with it?" I say, withdrawing from the hug.

"I just thought . . ." Zadie trails off.

"You thought what?"

"I thought you'd think I was going to be a bad mom." Her eyes well up again with a fresh set of tears. "I mean, *I* think I'm going to be a bad mom. I've never done anything right in my entire life. The longest I ever kept a job was being a barmaid at Medieval Times, and that lasted eleven months!"

"Well, pregnancy's only nine, so . . ."

"Charlie, I'm being serious! I'm a screwup. I'm not like you. I'm not ready for this."

"Zadie." I put my finger beneath her chin and tilt it up so that she's looking me in the eye. "Listen to me. You're going to be an incredible mom."

"Really?" she whispers.

"Yes. You're warm and loving and openhearted and kind. You wake up happy every single day. You always look on the bright side and you choose to see the good in everyone. You're endlessly creative and can have fun anywhere, with anyone, at any time. You truly believe that family should always have your back, and that no matter what, everyone deserves a second, a third, and maybe a fourth chance. You know that time is precious and that you can't waste a single minute of it trying to be someone you're not. You actually have 'Love is the answer' tattooed over your heart—and guess what? You're right. It is."

My voice is wavering, but I forge on. "This is why you're going to make such an incredible mom, Zadie. These are the lessons that most of us will struggle our whole lives to learn. Hell, I'm still struggling with all of them. But I have a leg up because I have you as a teacher. And whoever's in there"—I point to her stomach— "he or she will, too. And, damn, we're lucky. I am so very lucky and proud and grateful to have you as my sister."

"Oh, Charlie," Zadie sighs, and throws her arms around my neck. "You really feel that way?"

"Of course I do. You're already a mom, Zadie. You're raising my son for me. He's the most precious thing I have. You think I'd let just anybody do that?"

"*With* you." She smiles. "We're raising Caleb together."

"That was beautiful, man," Buck says, pounding his heart. "Aw, screw it." He opens his arms for another hug. "Let's hug this out again."

"I'm really happy for you guys," Moose says. He lets out a loud sniff. "Really, really happy."

"Come here, you big goofball," Zadie says. She wraps her arms around Moose's waist. "You're the best, Moose. Thanks for taking such good care of my brother."

"We all need a little help sometimes," Moose says, blushing.

"We better get down there," I say, checking my watch. "You ready?"

Zadie walks over to the mirror, looks at herself, and yelps, "Oh, good God. Just give me two minutes in the bathroom."

"Okay," I nod. "Let's all freshen up real fast. And then we'll meet out in the hall in five, all right?"

"Sounds good," Zadie says, already wiping at her face with a tissue.

"Good. Because I, for one, am ready to celebrate."

•   •   •

"You think I'm good to go?" I say to Moose, straightening my shirt and jacket after the door is closed behind us. "I don't want to make a fool of myself again."

"You're fine, bro. Just lay off the booze."

"I can't believe she's pregnant."

"I know. It's great."

"It really is." I pause. "Moose, what am I going to do about this toast?"

"You'll do just fine."

"Unsurprisingly, I have a mild-to-moderate fear of public speaking."

Moose breaks into a wide grin. "Shit, dude. If you give a toast that's one-tenth as moving as the speech you just gave in there, you're going to win a fucking Oscar. Just do your thing. No one wants to see you reading some canned speech off an index card, anyway."

I let out a long breath. He's probably right. Maybe, for once in my life, it would be better to just wing it.

"Thanks, Moose," I say. I reach into my pocket and crush the index card into a ball. "I mean it. You saved me from myself back there."

"Ain't no thang, jellybean," he says, and punches me lightly on the shoulder.

"You boys ready for this?" Zadie emerges from behind the door. She smiles, her eyes bright again. In a flowing white dress and heels, her hair swept elegantly off her face, Zadie looks beautiful. I feel a surge of brotherly pride.

"Ready as I'll ever be," I say, and offer her my elbow.

The Toast

The rain clears by noon, leaving the trees sparkling in the afternoon sunlight. After a round of "Should we, should we not?" Zadie decides she wants to move the ceremony back outside. It takes Buck, Moose, Ives, and me nearly two hours to reposition the chuppah and all the chairs, but the end result is worth it. Buck and Zadie are married on the dunes overlooking the ocean, the sun fading behind the horizon line as they say their "I dos."

As the guests filter into the tent for another round of celebratory cocktails, Moose snags me by the arm.

"You guys need a family photo," he insists. "Now—while the sky still looks like that."

We turn and look out over the water. The sunset is incredible, a tapestry of pinks and golds and burnt orange. Down the beach, someone is shooting off fireworks one by one.

"Good idea." I nod. "We didn't hire a photographer, but I'll go get some shots of her and Buck."

"No. You need to be in it. Julie's a photographer. Well, a photographer's assistant, but whatever. Let me get her. You go round up your family."

"Thanks, man. This is great."

"I got you covered, bro." Moose winks and then lopes off, looking for Julie.

"Goldwyns!" I call out. "We're doing a family photo in two minutes!"

Zadie and Buck, who haven't come up for air since their first kiss as husband and wife, finally surface.

"I need a mirror!" Zadie laughs. "Buck smeared my lipstick!"

"I need a hairbrush," Madison says, patting her perfect blond waves.

"Here you go, ladies," Shelley sings, and opens her purse. "I always come prepared." Zadie and Madison both peer inside, snatching up compacts and lipsticks and mascara.

"You women." Dad clucks at their preening, but I can tell he is thrilled to be surrounded by so much beauty.

Caleb tugs on my sleeve. "Daddy, I want to look pretty for the photo."

"You look great, bud." He does, in fact, look great. He's sporting a tiny suit—his first—with the purple Converses that match mine.

Caleb nods, unsure.

"Hey, how about this," I say, and pluck my boutonniere off my lapel. "Want to wear my flower?"

Caleb beams. "Yes," he says, "I do."

"Cool." I kneel down beside him and take my time affixing the small spray of lilac to his jacket. It's hilariously large on him, and there's no way to make it stand up the way it's supposed to.

"It's beautiful, Daddy," Caleb says, staring lovingly down at it. "It matches our shoes."

"Well, it's not on right. It's crooked somehow."

"No. It's perfect," he says.

"Hey, buddy?" I say, clasping his shoulder. "You know how proud I am of you, right?"

"Sure," Caleb replies.

"You've taught me a lot of stuff over the past few weeks. About how important it is to just be myself."

Caleb flashes me a confused smile.

"Like these shoes, for example," I say, pointing to my Converses. "They look really cool. And I never would have bought them if it weren't for you."

"They do look pretty cool."

"Remember how in the car we talked a little about your mom?"

Caleb bites his lip and looks away.

"Well, you remind me so much of her. You have all of her best qualities. Your mom was confident and independent and kind. She was funny and smart. She had a totally unique and awesome sense of style. So whenever you feel like you're forgetting what she looked like, just look in the mirror, bud. Because you will see her looking right back at you."

I take a deep breath and blink back tears. Caleb is staring off at the ocean. His face is still. A light breeze ruffles his hair. I wonder for a minute if he's listening to me, if he understands what I'm saying. Maybe he's too young.

Then he turns his face to mine and a shiver runs through my body. He smiles that crooked, knowing, dimpled smile that reminds me so much of Mira.

"Okay, Dad," he says, and reaches for my hand. As I take it, he squeezes it three times, just the way she used to do.

"I love you," I say, and squeeze it back.

"Picture time!" Julie calls out, and we all snap to attention. "Hurry, hurry, before we lose the light!"

"Where do we stand?"

"Zadie in the middle?"

"Someone grab Norman. Norman! Over here! Good boy."

"Are we standing in one row or two?"

"Do you guys want me in this?" Madison steps back. "Or should it be just Goldwyns?"

"Oh, yes, should we sit out?" Shelley says, joining Madison.

"Or do you guys want to do one together, and then Charlie and me in another one?" Zadie asks.

"Shut the hell up, everybody!" Dad bellows. "Now get in one goddamn row like one goddamn family or we're going to lose the light!"

"Beautiful picture." I hear her voice before I feel her fingers graze my arm.

I turn; there she is, her silvery-black hair glistening in the twilight.

"Hi," she says.

"Hi."

"I'm here."

"I can see that," I say, not sure whether or not I'm angry or relieved that Elise has finally turned up without much of an explanation. Maybe a bit of both. Between the excitement of Zadie's pregnancy and the ceremony itself, I had managed to push her out of my thoughts. Now, just as I'm starting to enjoy myself, she has to turn up looking more beautiful than ever. "I'm glad you made it."

"Hey, Elise. Charlie, we'll meet you down at the party, okay?" Zadie strides by, grabbing Caleb's hand as she goes. At first it annoys me that she doesn't stop to greet Elise properly, but then I realize that she's just giving us our space.

Elise and I watch as Zadie, Buck, Caleb, Dad, Shelley, and Madison make their way into the tent. Someone inside shouts, "Announcing the bride and groom!" and wild cheering and clapping ensues.

"You ready for the toast?"

"Right, the toast. Still not sure what to say. Thought you were supposed to help me out, given all your maid of honor experience."

"I'm sorry, Charlie."

"No, it's fine. Everyone seems tipsy already, so I have that going for me, at least."

Elise nods. We stand for a second in awkward silence, not quite looking at one another. The last of the guests have found their way to the tent; it's just us now, alone beneath the electric blue sky.

Elise shivers in the breeze. She pulls a wrap around her shoulders.

"Look, I know I owe you a call," she says, not quite looking at me. "I'm sorry I went radio silent last week."

"It's really no big thing." I shrug, trying to sound far more nonchalant than I am.

"J. P.—my ex—well, you probably heard what happened."

I cock my head, confused.

"No," I say, because I haven't. "What happened?"

"Oh." Her eyebrows shoot up. "He was arrested. For taking bribes from lobbyists. It was kind of all over the press."

"Oh my God," I say, stunned. "I haven't picked up a paper all week."

"That's why I had to go into the city. To meet with our lawyers. We've known about this for a while, but it's hard to prepare yourself for when it actually happens."

"I'm so sorry, Elise. Are you okay? How's Lucas?"

"He's okay," she says, but her bottom lip quivers as she says it. "It's been hard to explain it all to him."

"Come here." She presses her head against my chest, and I fold her up in my arms. My chin fits neatly on the top of her head. I close my eyes, feeling her body shudder with tears. *All I want,* I suddenly think, *is to protect this woman.* "I had no idea you were going through all this," I whisper to her, my lips grazing her skin.

"It's okay," she whispers back. "Or it will be, anyway."

"It will be," I say, and kiss her on the top of her head.

"I know this must all seem trivial to you. You've been through so much."

"Yeah, when it comes to suffering, don't try to compete. I got you beat, girl."

It takes her a second to realize I'm kidding, but when she does, she bursts into laughter. It's a messy laugh, all tears and snot, the kind that happens between friends.

"I'm so sorry I kissed you that night, Charlie," she says.

"Please don't apologize for that."

"But I am sorry. I really don't want things to get weird between us. They aren't weird, right? Please say they're not, because I don't want to lose you as a friend."

I pull back from her and hold her firmly at arm's length.

"Elise," I say, looking her straight in the eye, "there's nothing you could do that would ever make me not want to be friends with you. Okay?"

"Well, there's probably *something*," she says, looking relieved.

"How do you feel about dancing?"

"I feel good about dancing."

"How do you feel about dancing with me, right now, to whatever song comes on next?"

I tilt my head towards the tent, which is currently quiet. Then a strumming guitar begins to reverberate, and the sound of the White Stripes singing "We're Going to Be Friends" fills the air.

"Works for me," Elise says. Her eyebrow is cocked, a single question mark. "If it's okay with you?"

"It's perfect," I say, and offer her my hand.

An hour later, we're still on the dance floor, swaying to Van Morrison's "Into the Mystic." While I originally eschewed my sister's decision not to hire a band, I have to admit now that the music has been pretty stellar. We've been dancing so hard for so long that I've lost my tie and Elise has ditched her shoes. All around us, couples are swaying and laughing, even carrying plates of cake onto the dance floor so that they won't miss a minute of the action.

"I love this song," Elise sighs, and nestles her head against my shoulder. "We used to listen to this album over and over when I was in prep school. We'd all be in pajamas and fuzzy slippers and we'd drape our arms around each other and stand in a big circle in our common room and just sway." She laughs. "God, it's been a long time since I thought about that."

"It's been a long time since I danced with someone like this," I say, pulling her close. I can feel her breasts pressed against my chest and her fingers laced firm in between mine. As I rest my cheek against the top of her head, her familiar smell fills my nostrils. I take a deep breath and close my eyes, feeling content.

"Charlie." My eyes pop open. There beside me is Shelley.

"Hey, Shelley," I say, trying not to sound irritated. Elise stops and our bodies pull apart. "What's up? Are you cutting in?"

"I need you for a minute."

"Um, can it wait?"

"I don't think so."

"It's okay," Elise says, though there's a hint of disappointment in her voice. "I've been monopolizing you all night."

I check my watch. "Oh, right. I'm supposed to give the toast right now." As I say this, my stomach lurches uncomfortably. *Here goes nothing,* I think to myself.

"The toast has to wait. Your dad needs you," Shelley says, her eyes wide with concern.

"Go, Charlie," Elise says, nodding.

"I'll be right back, okay?" I say to her. "Just give me a minute."

As Elise slips off into the crowd, I spin around, looking for Caleb. When I see him doing the twist with Zadie on the dance floor, I nod to Shelley. She takes me by the hand and leads me off in the opposite direction.

"Where are we going?" I say as we exit the tent, but she doesn't answer.

The moment we set foot in the living room, I know something is really wrong. Dad is in an armchair flanked by Ives and Dr. Simms. All three turn when we walk in, their eyes wide, as though they've been caught doing something they shouldn't be.

Dad shakes his head, annoyed. "Shel, I told you not to bug him," he says. His voice is strained, as though he's having trouble breathing.

I step closer. Dad's skin is a strange bluish color and his face looks drawn and pinched.

"What's going on?" I say, frowning. "Dad, you okay?"

"I'm fine. Go back to the party," he says, and his throat sounds like it's filled with gravel.

"You're not fine," I say, looking to Dr. Simms for confirmation. From the look on his face, I can tell that I'm right.

"He needs to go to the hospital," Dr. Simms says in a low voice. "I'm worried it could be aspiration pneumonia."

"What's aspiration pneumonia?" I ask, my pulse quickening. "That doesn't sound good."

"It's a swelling or infection in the lungs. It happens sometimes in Parkinson's patients who have trouble swallowing."

"I'm not leaving in the middle of my own daughter's wedding," Dad growls. "Anyway, it's too late. We can go in the morning, if it comes to that. Just get me antibiotics."

Dr. Simms bites his lip. "That may not be good enough. God forbid the infection spreads. We need to get a chest X-ray and a CT scan and a blood culture at a minimum. And I'd like you to be somewhere that has a ventilator on hand."

"We're going right now," I say, forcefully enough that it leaves no room for negotiation. "Ives, you're driving. Dr. Simms and I will come with you."

"What about me?" Shelley asks. She looks visibly terrified.

"Shel, you stay here, okay?" Dad says, in between coughs. "I don't want you sleeping in the waiting room in that pretty dress of yours. Just make sure Zadie is happy. Tell her not to worry. In fact, make something up. Tell her I've gone to bed. I don't want her thinking twice about me on her wedding night."

"Are you sure?" Shelley looks to me. "Charlie, I can go if you want to stay. You have your toast to give and everything."

I shake my head. "Please watch Caleb for me. I've got this one."

Not wanting to attract attention from wandering wedding guests, Ives brings the car around back, and Dr. Simms, Dad, and I slip out the kitchen door. Getting Dad into the car is no minor task. Shelley hovers on the steps, anxious to watch us go.

"I'll have him back in no time," I say to her, with as much authority as I can muster. Inside, my stomach is churning so fast

I worry that I'm going to vomit. "Everything's going to be fine."

Once in the car, Dad slumps back and lets out a groan. He's in a lot of pain, I realize; he'd just been putting up a good front for Shelley. His breathing is sharp and labored, and his skin is a ghostly white. His eyelids flicker at half-mast, as though it takes effort just to stay awake.

Even though it's late, there's still traffic on the highway. Ives is driving. I'm riding shotgun, while Dr. Simms sits beside Dad in the back. Every few minutes I glance back at him, scanning his face.

"Dad?" I call out. "You okay back there?"

When he doesn't answer, I panic.

"Pull over," I say to Ives. "I'll drive."

"There's nothing to be done about this," Ives says, annoyed. He gestures at the traffic. "It'll just slow us down to switch."

"Fine," I say, knowing he's right. "But I know a back road we can take, at least."

Ives shoots me a dubious look but doesn't say anything.

"I'm serious," I insist. "My wife showed me once. The week before we got married, one of her little cousins jumped off the porch and broke his ankle. Mira and I drove him to the hospital and we took this route to avoid the traffic."

"Are you sure you remember it?"

I nod, praying that I'm right. "Yes," I say firmly. "You're just going to have to trust me. Now, take the first road on your left."

We pull off onto a small winding road. Though the speed limit reads thirty-five miles per hour, Ives guns the engine; there's no one around but us. As we fly past darkened houses, my heart starts to race. What if we're going in the wrong direction? It's been years since I've been out here. *If I lead us astray and something happens to Dad,* I think, *I'll never forgive myself.*

We come up to a fork that feels vaguely familiar.

"Left," I say after a moment's hesitation.

"You sure?"

"I think so."

Ives doesn't move the car but stays idling at the stop sign instead. "I need you to be sure," he says. "We don't have time to waste."

"Listen to him," Dad grunts from the backseat. Ives and I both spin around. He lets out a hacking cough. "He knows," he says, gesturing at the road ahead. His voice is feeble and wheezy. "He knows."

I nod to Ives, and Ives nods back. Then we're off again, speeding through the quiet night air.

"Jeff," Dr. Simms says from the backseat. "Jeff, can you keep your eyes open for me? I need you to keep your eyes open, okay?"

"How's he doing?" I say, trying to keep my voice even. "Dad, how are you doing back there?"

"We need to keep him conscious," Dr. Simms says.

"How do we do that?"

"Talk to him."

I crane my neck around.

"Dad?" I say. "Dad, are you listening to me?"

"Charlie, he may not be able to respond," Dr. Simms says. "But he's listening, so keep talking."

I bite my lip. For the first time in my life, words fail me.

Say something, I think. *Anything.*

All of a sudden I hear Moose's voice in my head.

Just wing it, dude, he says. *If it's half as good as what you said to Zadie, you'll win an Oscar.*

"So, Dad," I say, my voice cracking, "I've been pretty nervous about my toast tonight. Frankly, I had no idea what I was going to say. How does a guy with no wife and no real relationship with his own father stand up at a wedding and say something inspiring about marriage and family? I've had pretty mixed feelings about both those things since I was a kid.

"But you know what? Zadie never has. When Zadie and I were seven or eight, Mom took us to this costume shop so we could pick out outfits for Halloween. And of everything there, Zadie wanted to be a bride. It was the creepiest little getup you've ever seen. Like something out of a horror film, actually. This tiny little veil and these long white gloves and a plastic pearl choker. Mom told us years later that she thought it was the worst costume she ever saw, but she let her get it anyway. Zadie was so happy. For weeks after Halloween, she'd get all dressed up in it and stage her own wedding in the backyard. She'd line her stuffed animals up and she'd make me be the rabbi. And after, she'd go around saying to everyone, 'It was perfect. Just perfect.' It was hilarious, actually, in retrospect. She really couldn't wait to be a bride.

"I remember one day I asked her what was so great about getting married, and she said, 'Well, if you get married, it means you have a family.' And that made me sad. Because, you know, I thought that meant we weren't really a family. So I asked Mom about it. And she just laughed and said, 'There's all kinds of families, Charlie. There are married families and unmarried families. There are people whose friends are their families. What binds a family together isn't a piece of paper. It's love.'

"It's been a while since I thought about that. It's funny, because I realize now that Mom was right. This family is the furthest thing from normal. We are one dysfunctional bunch. But I love all of you, I really do, and I know you love me. And that's enough. It's really all we need."

Dad doesn't respond. The only sound from the back is the rasp of his breath, which has slowed to an almost inhuman cadence.

"Anyway," I say, swallowing hard. "That's it. I don't know if that was exactly the right way to say it, but there it is."

But there's more I want to say. *I forgive you,* I think, my heart racing. *I forgive you for everything, you bastard. Just wake up and be okay. Shelley needs you. Caleb loves you. Zadie wants you to meet her baby. And me, well, I want to get to know you. We've lost thirty-five years to do that, Dad. We don't have a minute more to lose.*

"We're here," Ives announces, interrupting my thoughts. We turn down a long driveway, and I see the sign for Southampton Hospital. "Nice, work, Charlie. I think you saved us a good hour back there."

"There they are," Dr. Simms says. He taps on the window, pointing out a pair of nurses who stand by the hospital doors. "Good job, everybody. We made it."

Caleb's Birthday

Twenty-One Months Later

"So, buddy, whaddaya think?"

I squat down beside Caleb, and together we survey the space. The purple balloons and streamers pop against the sunshine yellow walls. The newly varnished hardwood floors gleam; I imagine they'll never again look as clean as they do today. The windows are open, letting in a gentle spring breeze. Origami paper birds, handmade by Buck, flutter and twirl, suspended from the ceiling by multicolored strings.

"It's great," Caleb says, staring up at the birds. "Uncle Buck did good."

"Hey!" I punch him lightly in the shoulder. "What about me?"

Caleb turns and flashes me a goofy, gap-toothed grin. He's lost three teeth so far, two on the bottom, one on the top, the last of which he proudly pulled out himself.

"You did *really* good," he says, and gives me a high-five. "This is the best place ever."

"I'm glad you like it. I gotta say, it turned out pretty great."

As I look around at the Nest, the play space that Tom and I have been working on for the last eighteen months, my chest swells with pride. I've literally built this place with my own hands. Unlike anything I've ever done before, this place is real. It's tangible. I can run my hand along the windows that I installed, and the walls that I painted, and the table I spent two frustrating hours assembling. I've sunk as many man-hours into this place as I did the Harrison Brothers settlement, but it's been a hundred times more rewarding. And I can honestly say it almost never feels like work.

Starting next week, the Nest will be offering a full schedule of music, gym, and art classes for kids, as well as parenting classes, support groups, and CPR training. We'll be doing birthday parties, too, and hopefully lots of them. Today's will be our first.

"And no one has ever had a birthday party here ever," Caleb says, still awed by this fact. "I'm the first one."

"That's right. So it's gonna be really good, I promise."

Caleb hesitates, his face clouding over.

"What's up, bud?"

"Nothing," he says, looking pensive.

"No, tell me." I put my arm around him, pull him in close.

"What if no one comes?"

I give him a squeeze. "Everybody's going to come. It's going to be so packed in here you're not even going to believe it."

"But no one's here yet." He points to the cuckoo clock in the corner. "It's almost four."

"Bud! No one comes to a party *early*. That's so not cool."

"What's not cool?" Tom calls out from the doorway. In his hands, he holds a gigantic purple cake. Beside him is Delaney, her arms wrapped around a present.

Tom nudges Delaney. "Ugh, Delaney, looks like we're the big dorks who arrived first. Guess we'll just have to eat this cake ourselves."

"Cut the cake!" Delaney cries with glee. "Daddy, cut the cake!"

The sight of the cake stops Caleb dead in his tracks. "That's the best cake I ever saw."

"Well, it's definitely the heaviest cake I ever carried," Tom says, heaving it onto the table with a groan. "That's, like, four hundred pounds of sugar right there. You guys are going to be high for days."

Tom holds out his hand to me, pulling me into one of his signature complicated handshakes. "Dude," he says, "this place looks amazing."

"It better," I say. "I was up literally all night hanging the birds."

"They're perfect. I mean, I loved the idea of them, but seeing them in the space . . ." He shakes his head in disbelief. "We did it."

"Lucas!" Caleb suddenly shouts, and sprints to the window. I walk over to join him. Outside on the curb, I see Elise and Lucas hopping out of a cab. Lucas is in the middle of telling a story; Elise is laughing. I wonder what they are saying; I wonder how she is doing, even though I spoke to her only yesterday. I take a deep breath, calming myself. After all this time, Elise still makes my heart race a little. I let the breath go when I see Jared, Elise's boyfriend, scramble out of the cab behind her.

"Hey, birthday boy!" Zadie calls from the doorway. Caleb turns and runs to her, wrapping himself around her leg. She bends down and gives him a hug. "Ugh, my big kid. You're huge. I swear, you've grown since last week."

"Hey, man," Buck says from behind Zadie. In his arms he holds their daughter, Wren. "Gimme five. Or should I say, gimme seven."

Caleb slaps his hand, then leans in to give Wren a kiss.

"Hi, Baby Wren," he says shyly. "I love you."

"Aw, buddy, that's so sweet," Zadie says. She covers her heart with her hand. "Cousin love," she sighs.

"Wow, the place looks amazing." Buck glances around, admiring our handiwork.

"Dad would have loved this," Zadie says. She stands, hands on hips, staring up at the ceiling. For the first time, I can see just a shade of a bump rising beneath her dress. She's five months along, another little girl on the way. I shiver with excitement, remembering the way it felt to hold my niece in my arms for the first time. Next to Caleb's birth, it was one of the happiest days of my life. Dad made it to the hospital for the birth—no easy feat, given his health. He died just a few weeks later, a day shy of Wren's one-month birthday. "He would have been so proud of you, Charlie. Shelley sends her love, by the way. Spoke to her this morning."

"How's she doing?"

Zadie shrugs. "You know. She's okay. Settling into the new house. I think she's happy in Florida. Madison's with her, for the time being."

She gives me a bittersweet smile. Zadie took it hard when Dad passed away, though she didn't fall entirely apart as I feared she might. Wren, I think, kept her together. She was so new at the time, just a helpless little thing, still nursing at all hours of the night. My sister, as expected, has thrown herself wholeheartedly into motherhood, and it suits her well. Just as she did with Mom, Dad, and Caleb, she nurtures Wren with every fiber of her being. She seems calmer now, more at peace. With Buck and Wren, Zadie finally seems at home.

A few weeks after Dad passed, Caleb and I moved to Fort Greene, a two-minute walk from Zadie and Buck's place. At the time, I told myself we were doing it to support my sister, but the truth is, I love having her nearby. Though I finally hired a part-time nanny to watch Caleb while I'm working, Zadie still does a lot of the heavy lifting when it comes to him. We're over at her place on weekends almost as much as we're home. She and Wren pick Caleb up from school nearly every day and sometimes stop by in the morning, too, bearing coffee and bagels. Zadie's offered to sit anytime I have a date. Maybe one day I'll take her up on it.

A fresh wave of people arrives, all smiles and gifts and hugs. Tom switches on the music, and suddenly it feels like a party.

"Daddy, they came," Caleb says excitedly. "Everybody came. Hannah and Delaney and Lucas. And Alexi and March and Christopher and . . ." He's still ticking friends off his fingers when he wanders off into the crowd. He's adjusted remarkably well to his new school in Brooklyn. While he still has the occasional nightmare about impending natural disasters, for the most part, it feels like the clouds above his head have parted and the sun's come out. He has friends, too. Just a few, but they're very real and, I notice with satisfaction, they're all here to celebrate his birthday.

"See, bud. Told ya," I say, but he's already gone.

"Helluva party." Elise appears by my side. She opens her arms and pulls me in.

"Hi," I say, and hold her a little longer than usual. "Thank you for hanging around this weekend. I know you could have been in the Hamptons. It means a lot to Caleb and me that you guys came."

She gives me a look. "The Hamptons? Please. And miss the hottest party in town? Anyway, I wanted to check out this cool new play space. I hear it's tough to get a reservation, but I happen to know the owner."

"And what do you think?"

"Honestly?" She glances around appraisingly.

"Honestly."

"I think it's amazing." Elise looks up at me, and for a moment we lock eyes. She looks away first, as always. "Seriously, Charlie, you did an incredible job."

"Thanks. That means a lot."

"This place is hopping! Is Moose here?"

"Nah, he's still on his honeymoon."

"Still? Didn't he and Julie get married, like, a month ago?"

"They're hiking the Appalachian Trail."

Elise chuckles. "Julie is a good sport. I guess there's a pot for every lid."

"Right?"

We both fall quiet for a minute.

"Look at what you built. I hope you are proud of yourself." Though she's smiling, there's a touch of something else in her voice: wistfulness, or maybe just nostalgia.

"I am. I mean, I don't know how it compares to those fancy play spaces you guys have going on the Upper East Side, but here in Fort Greene we think this is pretty cool."

"Ugh, shut up." Elise slaps me on the arm. "Less than a year in Brooklyn and you're going all hipster on me. Nice glasses, by the way. Very Buddy Holly."

"Listen," I say, raising my palms, "I'm not the one dating a hot young photographer. Speaking of—"

Elise cranes her neck around until we both spot Jared.

"There he is," she says. "Over by the piñata, with the kids."

"Glad to see he's found his peers," I say, unable to resist. The truth is that Jared is a nice guy who treats Elise with the reverence she deserves. While a part of me will always be a little jealous of whomever she's with, if it's going to be anyone, I'd like it to be someone like Jared. Still, I can't help but poke fun at the fact that he's still in his twenties. What else are friends for?

"Charlie." Elise shoots me a look, but she can't keep the twinkle out of her eye.

"What? I meant that sincerely. You know, you can drop him off here anytime. We have some great art classes he might enjoy."

"You're mean. You're making me feel like cradle robber."

"Actually, you're my inspiration. Age is just a number, right?"

Elise raises her eyebrows. "Did you ask out that pretty young thing from your therapist's office? The one who was making eyes at you in the reception room? I told you something good would come from seeing that doctor."

"Yeah, what's sexier than a guy coming out of a grief counselor's office?"

"Well, did you? Ask her out, I mean."

"I did. We met for coffee on Saturday."

"And?"

"And she's a little younger than I thought."

"How young is young?"

"She's a senior at NYU."

Elise buries her face in her hands. "Oh, Charlie!" she groans. "Too young."

"Trust me, I know. She was sweet and all, but . . ."

"I mean, what could you possibly have in common with a girl that age?"

"Well, more than you'd think. We both like foosball. We both consider Lucky Charms to be a primary food group. And I'm bragging here, but I think she would be pretty impressed with my Grand Theft Auto skills. So what else is there? You have the same connection with Jared, right?"

"Look, Jared's great," she says, moving closer. "He's fun and sweet and he makes me laugh."

"I think I just threw up a little in my mouth."

"Don't interrupt. What I was trying to say was that he's great for right now, but neither Jared nor I have any delusions about where our relationship is going. He's too young for me, we both know that. He wants kids of his own."

"You wouldn't have another?"

She shrugs. "Maybe one more. If the right guy came along."

"What if the right guy had a kid of his own?"

"That, I think, would be perfect."

We look at one another for a nice, long while.

"Daddy!" Caleb shouts from across the room. "I need you!"

I look at Elise.

"Go," she says softly, nodding her head in his direction.

"To be continued?"

"To be continued," she says with a wink.

Acknowledgments

Writing, like parenthood, takes a village. I am so grateful to all the people who make up mine. This book is for:

Jonathan, without whom I could not do what I do and still be a half-decent mom. You make everything possible.

My mother, who has been listening patiently to my stories for thirty-five years and counting.

Emma, who is already funnier and more entertaining than I could ever hope to be.

Mary and Paul, who make me feel as though I've won some sort of in-law lottery.

Pilar Queen, who has supported me since the beginning.

Sally Kim and the wonderful folks at Touchstone, who nurtured this book into being. I am so grateful to work with all of you.

Michelle Kroes and everyone at CAA, who embraced this book even in its very early stages.

Elizabeth Shreve and Ilsa Brink, whose expertise and creativity bettered this project.

My friends, who make me feel loved, supported and accepted, even when I haven't slept in three days and have Cheerios crushed in my hair.

The readers who have sent me encouraging notes and emails over the years. Your support means more than you know.

About the Author

Cristina Alger is a lifelong New Yorker. A graduate of Harvard College and NYU Law School, she worked as a financial analyst and a corporate attorney before becoming an author. Her first novel, *The Darlings*, was published in 2012. She lives with her husband and daughter and is currently working on her third novel.